HARDLY ABLE TO BREATHE, TESS LOOKED DOWN AT THE NOTE.

John Hawkins knows where most outlaws go in Texas. Let him come find his son and daughter— just him and you, Tess, you pretty little thing. Your daughter is a pretty little thing, too. Both of you better come alone, or your children will die. Don't try to fool us and bring help, because where we're going, we'll be able to see you coming. Your brats are with me—and Sam Higgins.

Billy

P.S. My real name is Lonnie Briggs. My brother was Darrell Briggs. Hawkins knows the name.

Tess struggled with an urge to turn into a screaming, weeping, useless woman. Honor! Tex! Her babies! "John knew," she answered. *"John* knew, and we all thought he was being too cautious." Tears began trickling down her cheeks.

She told herself not to panic. Her children had been kidnapped, and someone needed to get on their trail as soon as possible. That someone would be John Hawkins, and if he ever managed to rescue Tex and Honor, there would be no sorrier men on earth than Sam Higgins and Lonnie Briggs.

BOOK YOUR PLACE ON OUR WEBSITE AND MAKE THE READING CONNECTION!

We've created a customized website just for our very special readers, where you can get the inside scoop on everything that's going on with Zebra, Pinnacle and Kensington books.

When you come online, you'll have the exciting opportunity to:

- View covers of upcoming books
- Read sample chapters
- Learn about our future publishing schedule (listed by publication month *and author*)
- Find out when your favorite authors will be visiting a city near you
- Search for and order backlist books from our online catalog
- Check out author bios and background information
- Send e-mail to your favorite authors
- Meet the Kensington staff online
- Join us in weekly chats with authors, readers and other guests
- Get writing guidelines
- AND MUCH MORE!

**Visit our website at
http://www.zebrabooks.com**

TEXAS PASSIONS

Rosanne Bittner

Zebra Books
Kensington Publishing Corp.
http://www.zebrabooks.com

ZEBRA BOOKS are published by

Kensington Publishing Corp.
850 Third Avenue
New York, NY 10022

Zebra and the Z logo Reg. U.S. Pat. & TM Off.

First Printing: March, 1999
10 9 8 7 6 5 4 3 2 1

Printed in the United States of America

Dear Reader,

My Zebra book, *Texas Embrace,* spawned a passionate love between a man and a woman who were a most unlikely match . . . Tess, a woman of strength and honor, and John Hawkins, a half-breed Texas Ranger as rough and wild as the state of Texas. Now I continue their story, one that is a grand mixture of romance, action . . . and inspiration. *Texas Passions* will touch your heart. It is a story about passion's strongest forces of love . . . and of hate.

One

A wicked summer storm ripped across the open plains of Kansas, and vibrant bolts of lightning exploded in all directions, lighting up the endless horizon in blinding flashes. Coming out of the north, ferocious winds brought a sudden drop in temperature that felt cold compared to the hot, humid air that went before it. Rain poured down in torrents, blowing through the bars of the prison wagon and pelting its occupants.

In spite of the dangerous turbulence, the wagon drivers continued over the treeless land with nothing to protect them from the elements.

"Hey! Find us some shelter, you sons-a-bitches!" Sam Higgins shouted the words with a growl, addressing the drivers. He got no reply. He hunched forward and shivered as he turned to the two men who sat across from him. "Bastards!"

"You ought to know by now, Sam, that prisoners don't get no special attention. If you die from pneumonia, who the hell cares? It's just one less man for them to worry about feedin'."

Sam studied the bags under Truby Bates's eyes. He often wondered if Bates had had those bags all his life. The man had been his cellmate for years. Along with a face that was never clean-shaven, the bags made him look much older than his thirty-eight years, and the man's flabby belly jiggled as the wagon bounced over prairie-dog holes.

"You give up too easy, Truby," Sam yelled above the storm. Truby shook his head, wiping at his nose with the back of his hand. "Well, we ain't got much choice, partner. We rotted in that cell back in Yuma for eight years. Now they're takin' us to Leavenworth for another ten. We'll probably die there."

A gust of wind blew more rain into Sam's face, and he squinted and bent his head for a moment. "I'm not dying until I have a chance to get my hands on John Hawkins. I don't care what I have to put up with until then."

Truby chuckled. "By the time you get out, you'll be too old and decrepit for revenge."

"Yeah? Well, I might be free sooner than you think."

"What the hell does that mean?"

The clattering wheels of the wagon splashed through a deep puddle, throwing splatters of mud onto the prisoners, interrupting their trains of thought.

"Shit!" Sam kicked at the thin steel barrier at the front of the wagon that separated the prisoners from the drivers. "Get us someplace dry!" he shouted.

"There *is* no place dry for miles around," one of the drivers yelled back. "Shut your damn mouth in there! At least you have a roof over your heads."

"Is that what you call this useless piece of tin?" Sam pounded at the iron above them, which was rusting and pitted. Rain made its way through cracks and dripped on them from above. "At least you have slickers on! We don't have anything to keep us dry!" Sam shouted.

". . . what you get . . . burning a woman . . . baby alive," he heard in reply, catching only some of the words.

"They deserved it," Sam grumbled, more to himself than anyone else. He glanced at Truby. "Tess Hawkins screwed up the best cattle-rustling ring in Texas. I would have been a rich man."

"I've heard your story a hundred times." Truby sat huddled forward, his back to the wind. "Too bad for you the woman was married to John Hawkins," he reminded Sam. "Hell, *anybody* on the wrong side of the law knows you don't mess with him, at least that's what I'm told by every prisoner who's had a run-in with him and lived to tell about it."

The wagon hit a hole, and Truby grunted. Sam's head banged against the wagon's bars.

"Damn!" Sam raised his cuffed wrists and rubbed a hand over his forehead. "Just *thinking* about that half-Indian bastard makes this trip even more miserable," he shouted. "I'm putting up with this shit, and he's having a good time in bed with a woman a man like him never should have been allowed to marry in the first place. Tess Hawkins is a whore, far as I'm concerned. Hell, Hawkins was half-outlaw himself—hardly ever brought in a man alive. Almost got himself kicked out of the Rangers more than once. He ought to be *hanged,* same as the men he chased down!"

"Sounds to me like you're lucky to be alive yourself then." The comment came from Ronald Calhoun, the third prisoner. "I've never met the man, but I'll bet I could take care of this Hawkins fella."

"I'll do it myself," Sam yelled back.

A bolt of lightning struck nearby, and the wagon lurched when one of the draft horses pulling it whinnied and reared. Sam fell to the floor, and outside the driver shouted curses at the horse. Sam scrambled back to his bench, and the wagon rocked and bumped its way over the narrow road. Another rush of rain swept through the bars.

"Rider up ahead!" one of the drivers shouted. "Might need help."

Sam's heart raced with anticipation. Had Lonnie Briggs finally shown up to free him? He'd promised to do just that. This rain could be the perfect method of confusing the drivers and catching them off guard.

"Hold up there!" one of the men up front shouted. "Help you, mister?"

"Well, now, I'd sure be obliged," came the shouted reply. "I got a little confused in this storm, and I'm not sure which way is east."

"Just follow us! We're headed east, to Leavenworth."

"Appreciate it."

The prisoners could not see the rider because of the steel roof and the barrier at the front of the wagon, but suddenly they heard gunshots, and at almost the same time, lightning struck again, hitting so close that it hurt their ears when it exploded in a huge pop that made the horses bolt. The prisoners grabbed the bars and hung on as the horses took off at a gallop. The wagon rocked and lurched wildly, the horses out of control. The vehicle careened and finally spilled over.

Sam felt himself tumbling over and over. Every part of his body banged fiercely against iron bars and other bodies. He blacked out for a moment, only to wake up to find himself lying in a sea of mud, rain pelting him, nothing but the sound of the storm around him. It took him a moment to realize he was not surrounded by iron bars, that he lay in the open. He winced with pain in his left shoulder and arm as he got to his feet and looked around to see the wagon lying on its top nearby, the horses nowhere in sight.

"Higgins!" someone shouted. The rider who had approached earlier rode up to greet him. He dismounted. "Sorry about that. I didn't count on the storm. You all right?"

Sam nodded to Lonnie Briggs. "I think so. You shoot the guards?"

"I got one, but then the lightning struck. We'd better find the bodies and make sure they're both dead."

"And find the keys. Get these cuffs off me!"

The rain began to let up, and the sky brightened a little. Truby Bates got to his feet from where he'd landed several yards away. He stumbled toward Sam and Lonnie, his eyes showing bewilderment combined with joy at realizing he was free. Blood streamed from a cut on his forehead. "What's goin' on, Sam? You know this fella?"

"Let's find the other bodies," Sam told him, rather than giving him a straight answer. "I'll explain later."

The three men spread out. "Calhoun is over here!" Bates

shouted moments later, indicating he'd found the third prisoner. "Hurt his ankle, but I think he's okay."

Sam and Lonnie could see Calhoun getting to his knees. Sam walked up to the wagon to see one of the guards lying under the iron contraption, a bullet hole in his right cheek. He knelt and felt for a pulse at his throat. There was none. Sam grinned. "Over here!" he yelled. "Get the keys off him!"

Lonnie hurried over and fished through the man's pockets, finally finding the keys. "Got them!" He unlocked Sam's handcuffs, then unbuckled the guard's holster and handed it and the gun to Sam, who smiled with joy as he strapped the gun around his own waist.

"Over here!" Truby yelled. "I found the other guard! He's still alive!"

Lonnie and Sam rushed to where Truby stood, looking down at the second guard, a heavyset young man who stared up at them wide-eyed. "My . . . legs," he gasped. "I . . . think they're . . . both broken."

Sam looked at Lonnie, always amazed at the evil gleam that sometimes showed in his blue eyes. Lonnie was an extremely handsome young man, but the look in his eyes now gave even Sam a chill.

"I'll help him," Lonnie said. "I'll put him out of his misery." He pulled his gun and pointed it at the wounded man's head.

"Please—don't—" the man begged.

Lonnie fired, and the man died with his eyes still wide-open. Calhoun and Truby stared in disbelief at the cold-blooded killing.

"Get his gun," Lonnie told Truby.

"There's a rifle over here," Calhoun told them, pulling the weapon from under the wagon. He handed it to Sam with a shaking hand while Truby obeyed the order to remove the man's gun belt and gun.

Sam threw his head back and let out a war whoop. "We're free!" he yelled. "Free! Whooeee! John Hawkins, here I come, you half-breed sonofabitch! I don't know if you're still a Texas

Ranger, but whatever you are and wherever you are, you're gonna die!"

Truby shook his head and grinned. "You really planning on going after that bastard, Sam? Hell, why not just get yourself the hell to Mexico? We all have a chance for a good head start." He watched Sam and the stranger who had met up with them laugh and shake hands. "Sam, who the hell is this? How do you know this guy?"

Sam turned to Truby. "You sure are slow to catch on, Truby. This is Lonnie Briggs, and this whole thing was planned, except, of course, for the lightning and the accident."

"That only helps our plan," Lonnie offered. His blue eyes shone with evil glee. "Now they'll just think there was an accident and you three escaped. No one knows about me."

Truby frowned. "So what?"

"Yeah, what's this all about?" Ronald Calhoun asked. He limped closer, wincing at the pain in his ankle. "Hell, I never even met any of you till they picked me up in Indian Territory. I'm not sure I want anything to do with any of this. And who is John Hawkins?"

"He's a half-breed who once rode as a Texas Ranger," Lonnie answered. "He broke up a cattle-rustling ring that meant big money to Sam here, and before that, he blew my brother Darrell to smithereens with dynamite, blew up the cabin where Darrell was holed up. Never gave him a chance to give himself up. Hearing about his death killed my *mother,* too. She died of a broken heart, and I swore then that someday I would kill John Hawkins."

Truby looked at Sam. "How do you know Lonnie?"

"He read about Hawkins breaking up the cattle-rustling ring. Hell, it was in the papers all over Texas. The man at the head of the rustling was one of the richest ranchers in the state. Lonnie came to see me a couple of times in prison. I never told you about it. He was too young back when Hawkins killed his brother to do anything about it. But now he's ready, and he came to me to talk about it. We think we've figured out a way to bring Hawkins to his knees. I told Lonnie I was getting shipped to Leavenworth, and he agreed to spring me so we can go after Hawkins."

Calhoun scratched his head. "I don't think I want anything to do with this."

"We need all the help we can get," Sam told him. "Hawkins is a tough sonofabitch to fool, and almost impossible to get the better of. But his day is coming!" He looked from Calhoun to Truby. "There's money in it for both of you, if you help me and Lonnie in this. When I was involved in the cattle rustling, I stashed away plenty in a bank in Mexico. Helping us with this is worth two thousand dollars to each of you. You can live damn good in Mexico for that kind of money."

Truby turned to Calhoun, and they both shrugged. "As long as there's at least four of us," Truby told Sam. "I've heard you talk enough about Hawkins to know I don't want to face him alone."

Thunder rumbled in a dark line of clouds to the east, where the storm continued its rage.

"You in with us, too?" Sam asked Calhoun.

The dark-haired, slender young man, who Sam guessed to be about twenty-five, grinned. "Hell, sitting back in Mexico with two thousand bucks sounds a lot better than sitting in prison another five years."

"What were you in for?" Lonnie asked.

Calhoun scratched at a several-day-old growth of beard. "Me and a friend robbed a bank, shot a woman. He got hanged for it. And if you want the whole truth, I got away with a couple of rapes before that, and another bank robbery. Hell, easy money—easy women—what you're offering means both. I wouldn't mind taking up with a pretty little *señorita*."

Truby rubbed at the bags under his eyes. "Well, you and I have been cellmates for eight years now, Sam, and I've got no family, no place to go. What the hell? I'll help."

Sam shook his hand. "You won't regret it, Truby."

"Let's hope not."

They all looked at each other, allowing a moment for the unexpected freedom and quickly formed alliance to settle in their minds. Then Sam took a deep breath before speaking again.

"Well, we have to find some extra horses and some decent clothes," he said. "There ought to be a ranch somewhere out here, people with no one else around to help. We can steal whatever we want. Maybe there will even be a woman there. God, I'd like to feel myself inside a woman again."

Calhoun laughed. "I could use a poke myself."

Sam let out another war whoop. "John Hawkins, your ass is mine, and so is your woman!"

They rounded up two of the wagon horses that grazed nearby, now finally calm again. The other two horses had run off and were nowhere to be seen. Truby and Calhoun mounted one horse bareback, and Sam, a tall man too big to share a horse, mounted the second horse. Lonnie Briggs climbed onto his own mount, and all four men headed south. The sun had not shone long, but already flies began to gather on the bodies of the dead guards.

Two

Tess twisted her long, red hair into a thick bun on top of her head, securing it with combs. Then she dipped her toes into the warm bathwater she'd prepared, satisfied that it was neither too cold nor too hot. She closed her eyes and smiled as she slipped into the sudsy bath, fully immersing herself, loving her husband even more for buying the copper tub. Even though 1891 had brought a railroad and more civilization to El Paso, a hot bath in a real tub was still considered a luxury in southwest Texas, especially on a ranch far from town.

She relaxed in the knowledge that although outlaws and renegade Indians were still sometimes a threat, she had little to fear. After all, her husband was John Hawkins, once known as the most ruthless Texas Ranger who ever served the state. She'd seen him in action firsthand, and although the circumstances were still something she tried to block out of her mind, she had to be grateful the whole event led her into John's arms.

She moved deeper into the water, until the suds tickled her chin. Breathing in a deep sigh of relaxation, she luxuriated in the rare moment of quiet and freedom from chores. She'd worked extra hard yesterday baking bread and finishing her wash, and her still-red knuckles burned slightly in the hot water. Now her efforts at catching up on chores had paid off in a day of relaxation. Outside John and the hired hands kept her eight-year-old son, Texas, occupied with chores and riding, and her five-year-old daughter, Honor, slept soundly in her bedroom. Thank goodness the girl still took long afternoon naps.

The thought of John's reaction to his daughter's birth still made her laugh to herself. What a sight those two were! Tall, dark, strong John, with dark eyes and waist-length black hair . . . so Indian; and Honor, with her red hair and blue eyes, her tiny build, her light skin and freckles. John Hawkins worshiped his daughter, and Honor worshiped her father. Tess shook her head at the thought of what John would do to anyone who dared hurt either of his children.

Young Texas looked so much like his father, and Honor like her mother; and the two children were as different in preferences and personality as they were in looks. Honor was afraid of horses; Texas already rode nearly as well as his father. Honor loved books; Texas would rather help his father train a wild horse than learn to read. Honor liked to dress becomingly; Texas preferred leather boots, denim pants, and no shirt, whenever the weather permitted, and sometimes, even when it didn't.

Tess took pride in knowing both her children had been taught good manners and respect, even more proud of how John had adapted to a settled, family life. Certainly the farthest thing from a family man as anyone could be when she met him, she never dreamed then that she could actually fall in love with him.

She raised one leg, sponging it off and watching the suds run down toward her thigh. Through two full-term babies she had managed to keep her slender shape. A third child, born too soon, lay in his grave on a grassy hill behind the house. The loss of the child who would have been John's firstborn son by blood was the only dark spot in their nine years together.

She had mourned the lost baby for months, her heartache made worse by the fact that the doctor told her there would be no more children. But now her sadness had turned to joy. She was quite certain another child was again growing in her belly. At thirty-one, she thought she might be getting too old to have another child, and childbearing was always dangerous in this rugged country. After complications with Honor, and then losing a baby, she might not be able to hold onto this one either. That was why she still had not told John about the child. He would worry, and it was time for spring roundup. He had enough on his mind for now. She had not even told Doc Sanders about the pregnancy.

"I will think positively about this one," she told herself. "I will not lose it."

She could hear her son's wild cries somewhere outside. Tex was probably riding Shadow, the black mare John promised to let him ride today, a bigger horse than he had ever ridden. Tex was probably pretending to be a little wild Indian, maybe even jumping the horse. His riding made her nervous, and she often refused to look when he jumped fences. She could not imagine life without her son, but there had been a time when . . .

No. She must never think about that. It was wrong to remember not wanting him. More than eight years had passed since his conception, and Texas knew only one father, a man who truly *was* his father in every way . . . except one. Still, John loved Texas to his very soul. He would die for the boy.

Love. That was all anyone required to survive, to belong to someone. Even John Hawkins needed to be loved. She'd seen that in him after she got to know him better. That need, and her own, had led to sweeter love than she ever thought could exist.

She hummed to herself, wishing every day could be like this, wondering sometimes what it might be like to live the pampered, spoiled life of a rich woman, waited on hand and foot, always able to wear lovely dresses and fancy hats and have hands soft as silk. She studied her own hands, hands that scrubbed clothes and kneaded bread; hands that helped shovel out horse stalls and pitch hay; hands that wielded a hoe and pulled weeds.

"I *am* rich," she murmured. "Richer than the wealthiest woman around." She was rich in things that cost nothing at all. She did not doubt there were plenty of wealthy women who would give up all they had to have a husband like John Hawkins . . . if only they understood what kind of man he really was. His attractiveness went far deeper than just his rugged build and handsome face, and the fact that no man could match his skill and bravery when facing danger. He was honest, devoted, determined to be a good father and husband, and a good provider. She knew when she married him that settling would not be easy for a man who had been little more than a lonely drifter most of his life, an outcast to most because of his Indian blood.

She could not be happier now that she had been the woman who tamed his wildness. John could make a woman feel so beautiful and alive. At forty, he was as virile as any younger man, and his hair still showed no gray. He worked hard building the ranch, and now they enjoyed a good life, the kind of life she once thought might never be possible for her again.

She lathered her other leg, softly singing now, a song she had made up years ago to sing to Tex when he was a baby.

"There was a dark stranger who had not a home.
No father, no mother, he liked just to roam.
So lonely that one day he took him a wife,
And then came the little boy who changed his whole—"

Suddenly a big, strong hand clamped over her mouth from behind, quickly changing her moment of contentment and singing into one of terror.

Three

"You're *mine* now, woman, and there's no changing it!"

The hand came away from Tess's mouth, and she rolled her eyes as she breathed a sigh of relief. "John Hawkins! Are you trying to give me a heart attack?"

"Depends on what kind of heart attack you're talking about. Is your heart pounding a little too hard knowing I might get right in that tub with you?"

"Don't you dare! There isn't room." Tess turned to look at him, noticing his shirt was off. The April day was surprisingly hot for spring, and unless in public, John always left his shirt off on days like this one, more of the Indian in him. Sioux blood it was, not Apache or Comanche. Circumstances had led him to Texas, and his skill with tracking and weapons landed him a job with the Texas Rangers.

She reached out and traced her fingers over his muscled arm. "I will never understand how you can sneak up on someone like that," she told him. "It is truly amazing."

John grinned as he knelt beside the tub. "You know it's the Indian in me."

Tess studied the dashing smile she'd grown to love so. "Yes, well, I was just thinking how the Indian in you is rubbing off on Tex. You must help me instill in that boy a desire to learn something besides how to stand up on the back of a horse. Speaking of which, where is our son now? I don't want him walking in on me."

"Ken is keeping him occupied, per my orders." John scooped up some suds and set some on her nose. "Thought I would come in and see if you need your back washed."

Tess noticed the impish look in his dark eyes. "I intended to just sit here and enjoy the peace and quiet."

John reached into the water, running a hand along her leg. "Fine. I can think of ways to make the peace and quiet even more enjoyable."

"I'm sure you can," Tess answered wryly. "You never cease to embarrass me, John Hawkins. Every man outside knows exactly why you came in here."

He moved his hand to her belly. "And they're all jealous as hell." He leaned forward and kissed her eyes. "Where's the soap?" He felt around the bottom of the tub, touching her in places that made Tess lean back and close her eyes. "All right, you wash me. After a week of hard chores, I feel like being pampered."

"Hmmm." John found the soap. "Maybe I'm spoiling you, getting you this fancy tub and all."

"I certainly don't object to being spoiled." Tess watched the shine of desire in her husband's eyes as he gently moved the bar of soap over her warm, relaxed body. He pushed it between her legs, rubbing it against her in a way that stimulated the sweet desires he was always able to draw from her.

"You are such a devil," she told him, sucking in her breath when he let go of the soap and used his fingers to build the fire he'd started in her soul.

In moments the warmth of the water and her husband's expertly probing fingers sent waves of passion rippling through secret places, culminating in a sweet climax. Tess sat up straighter, wanting to taste his mouth. He met her lips in a hot, delicious kiss as he rubbed the soap over her breasts. He moved his lips to her ear.

"I'll finish washing you," he told her.

Tess kept her eyes closed and leaned forward so he could wash her back, and even after nine years, she still found his every touch enticing, beautiful, full of fire. He massaged her neck and back, then rinsed her, splashing water over her breasts. He picked up a towel then and held it out. "May I dry you off, madam?"

Tess looked up at him, only then realizing he was completely naked, and obviously ready to make love. She burst out laughing, and John grinned as she stood up and let him wrap the towel around her.

"What am I going to do with you?" Tess asked, as he pulled her into his arms.

"All I know is what *I* want to do with *you*," he answered. He leaned down and kissed her again, a long, hard, hungry kiss, before releasing her lips to rub her down gently. He kissed nearly every part of her body as he moved down, and Tess still found it amazing that this man, who was so tall and strong, this man, who could be chillingly ruthless against an enemy, could be so gentle and loving toward a woman. She still suffered moments of jealousy at thinking how he once slept only with loose women, some of whom she guessed didn't even ask for pay. Surely they were eager to have John Hawkins in their beds for free.

John picked her up in his arms, and she pulled the rawhide tie from his hair so that it hung loose as he carried her to their bed and laid her on it.

"Sorry to interrupt your quiet moment," he told her. "But I couldn't stop thinking about you in here taking a bath." He moved on top of her. "All naked and slippery and warm."

"I really don't mind the interruption," she answered, opening herself to him. She drew in her breath when he entered her, that part of him as virile and wild and hard as the rest of him. Tess felt the solid muscle of his arms, ran her hands over his shoulders, up to his handsomely chiseled face, and through his hair, which hung loose, tickling her breasts. She thought what a strangely lovely way this was to spend an afternoon, certainly far from the ordinary day full of chores and running after the children.

She arched up to him and he thrust himself deep in an exotic intercourse of perfect rhythm that made her cry out. For a fleeting moment she remembered that first time, when she was so frightened and still so full of horror from her abduction by *Comancheros*. But John reminded her how beautiful and painless this could be, how wonderful lovemaking was when the people who shared in it were truly, totally in love.

John leaned down and met her mouth, groaning as he moved faster, tasting every part of her mouth with his tongue until Tess wondered where her next breath would come from.

Finally she felt his life pulse into her, and he whispered her name, licking her cheek, her throat, before meeting her mouth again in one last kiss. He nestled down beside her then, still kissing her neck.

"We can't lie here too long. Honor will wake up soon," Tess reminded him.

"I know." John sighed and rolled to his back, stretching his arms over his head. "Want to go to a dance?"

Tess grinned, raising up on one elbow and tracing the fingers of her other hand over his chest. "Since when do you volunteer to go to a dance? You hate things like that. I'm usually the one begging *you* to go. I simply decided not to beg this year."

John laughed softly. "Well, *I* decided I didn't want to hear you nag about it this year, so I'll go willingly this time."

"John Hawkins, I don't nag!" Tess playfully hit at him, and he grabbed her wrist and rolled her onto her back.

"You nag me about everything," he teased. "You nagged me right into this bed."

Tess sucked in her breath, her eyes wide with mock indignity. "Who snuck up on whom? I will remind you that I was enjoying my time alone, Mr. Hawkins, relaxing in my new bathtub for the first time."

"And who bought you the tub?"

"You did, of course."

"And why?"

"Because I—" Tess broke into laughter. "Because I nagged you to get me one."

John nuzzled her neck. "There. You see? What did I tell you?" He moved his lips to hers, kissing her gently.

Tess studied his dark eyes, reached up and toyed with a piece of his hair. "Well, I didn't really nag. I just dropped hints."

"Mmmm-hmmm. You're very good at that."

Tess thought to tell him about the baby, but she decided it was still too soon. "There are all kinds of ways to get what you want without nagging, Mr. Hawkins."

He leaned down and kissed each of her nipples. "And women have a special gift for it."

Tess grasped his face and leaned up to kiss his eyes. "We do, do we?"

John met her mouth in one more deep kiss before moving off the bed. "You know damn well you do. I've got to get back outside now before Tex gets too curious about what we're doing in here. Ken can keep him occupied only so long."

"I do wish you would discourage him from jumping that black. He's not big enough for that, John. He's going to get hurt."

John stood up, pulling on his underwear. "That kid is a wonder. Not a bone of fear in his body. I do what I can, Tess, but he definitely has a mind of his own."

Tess shook her head. "What are we going to do with him when he gets bigger?"

John pulled on his denim pants. "He's being raised to know right from wrong, and he has a good heart—your heart. You don't have to worry about what he'll be like when he's bigger."

Tess could not help the sudden tears that came to her eyes, guilt consuming her, as it always did in those little moments when she could not help thinking about Tex's real father.

"Stop it, Tess. That's water long over the dam. And we all start out innocent. It's how we're raised that makes us what we are. There was a pretty thin line between the good and bad in me most of my life, but the good my mother taught me won out. Texas Randall Hawkins is a damn good kid who understands respect for his parents and knows right from wrong."

A tear slipped down her cheek. "And he has a good father to teach him those things."

"A father who loves him just the same as if he came from my blood. You know that, Tess."

She smiled through tears. "And you know how much I love you for that." She reached out and embraced him, and John returned the hug, in that strong, reassuring embrace that always soothed her fears . . . the way he first embraced her nine years ago . . . when he risked his life to save her from *Comancheros*.

Four

Sam took another swallow of whiskey. "Those folks back there had a nice stash of everything we needed." He handed the bottle to Lonnie. "Including a nice, soft woman, huh?"

Lonnie scowled slightly as he took the bottle. "You didn't have to hog her for so long."

Truby Bates laughed. "She was worth the wait."

Ronald Calhoun rubbed his swollen ankle. "She even made me forget the pain in this ankle."

They all chuckled, leaning back against stolen saddles, while stolen horses grazed nearby, tethered to stakes. They drank stolen whiskey, following a fine meal they'd cooked with stolen food.

"Too bad the husband didn't put down his rifle like we told him to," Truby said.

Sam shrugged. "He's not the first man I've killed. Besides, the woman had a couple kids old enough to help her out."

"They'll get by," Lonnie added.

"I almost wish we'd brought the woman with us," Calhoun said, taking his swallow of whiskey and handing the bottle back to Sam.

Sam sobered. "From here on we have more important things to think about, like finding a way to do the same thing to Tess Hawkins that we did to that farm woman. Better than that, I want to do it right under John Hawkins's nose. What a treat that would be." He stretched out his long legs, his broad shoulders easily filling the saddle sideways as he rested against it. "Glad the husband back there was big as me. His clothes fit pretty good."

"The pants are too long for me, but the shirt is okay," Truby said.

"Same here," Calhoun added. "We need to stop at some little town where nobody knows us and steal more money to get us by till we get to Mexico."

"Speakin' of money, how do we know you'll pay us what you promised for helping you get Hawkins?" Truby asked Sam.

"You've known me eight years now. You'll get paid."

"Yeah, and earn every penny the hard way, I expect."

"What's that mean?" Calhoun asked.

Truby shifted against his saddle. "It means from what Sam's told me over the years, this is gonna be a dangerous job."

"He's just one man," Calhoun reminded him.

Sam shared a look with Lonnie, who drank down more whiskey as Sam explained to Ron. "In Hawkins's case, you might as well be facing four or five men. He's a big man, wild and fierce as any Indian warrior, good with a gun *and* a knife. And he's got no conscience when it comes to getting his man, or defending himself. He looks and sometimes dresses like an Indian. That's how he could move on a camp of renegade Comanche or Apache; or a band of *Comancheros*. He fits right in. He's tough as nails and has no respect for rules. I still can't believe the Rangers themselves didn't hang him."

Calhoun turned his gaze to Lonnie. "So, John Hawkins blew up your brother and his gang in a cabin a few years back?"

Lonnie nodded and capped his whiskey bottle. He began rolling himself a cigarette. "He did. He should have given Darrell a chance for a fair trial. My brother fought in the Civil War. He was seventeen. I was just a baby then. My pa was killed in the war, and my ma was left alone with a baby to take care of. Darrell got in with some men who lost everything in the war and were pretty angry over it. They started robbing banks and trains in the North. Darrell, he always came home with money for Ma and me, took care of us. To me, he was a hero."

He lit and took a drag on the cigarette. "When Darrell was killed, Ma went into a kind of depression, quit eating. She died about a month later of pure starvation and a broken heart. When I found out how Darrell died, I looked up a couple men who once rode with Darrell, asked them to help me find a way to kill Hawkins for what he did."

He stared at the central fire as he continued.

"They wouldn't help, said they weren't about to go up against a man like Hawkins. Then I read about Sam, the cattle-rustling ring Hawkins broke up. It made the papers all over Texas because the head of the cattle-rustling ring was a man named Jim Caldwell, one of the wealthiest ranchers in Texas, from over by El Paso, a pillar of the community. I figured somebody like Sam might have it in for Hawkins like I do, so I found out where he was sent and I visited him in prison. When he told me he was being transferred to Leavenworth, I saw my chance."

Calhoun sat up and rubbed his ankle again. "So, what's this about *you* havin' it in for Hawkins's wife?" he asked Sam.

Sam sniffed and scratched at his balding head. "The bitch worked for Caldwell for a few weeks. She wasn't Tess Hawkins then, she was Tess Carey. She needed the work because her husband and father were killed by *Comancheros*. She'd been taken by them, too. Hawkins rescued her. She claimed she was never raped, but only a couple months later, she up and married Hawkins, the last man on earth any decent woman would want to call husband. A few months later she gave birth to a kid who looked all Indian, maybe Mexican. Hard for us white men to tell the difference."

They all laughed at the remark, and Sam shook his head. "At any rate, she tried to pass Hawkins off as the father, but nobody believes it. And while she worked for Caldwell, she must have heard or seen something, because Hawkins started sticking his nose into Caldwell's business. One of Caldwell's men shot him in the back, and we all thought that was the end of the bastard;

but he lived and ended up investigating Caldwell, hunted the rustling ring all the way down into Mexico, where our biggest buyer lived. The Rangers set a trap for Caldwell's men, who were herding some cattle into Mexico. They were caught, and when things went to trial, Tess Hawkins testified as to what she heard and saw while she was working for Caldwell, which included seeing me there in the middle of the night plotting to get rid of Hawkins. I was sheriff of El Paso then. When I first found out what she knew, I tried to burn her alive in her own house, but she escaped. It's like once you carry the name Hawkins, you're invincible. I never saw two people who could go through so much and survive. I plan to end their streak of luck."

He stopped to light a cigar, another item stolen from the farmhouse. He waited to let his story sink in before continuing. "I remember the incident when Hawkins blew up the cabin where Darrell Briggs and his bunch were holed up. Just one more vicious act that nearly got him kicked out of the Rangers. I never knew then that Darrell had a younger brother." He glanced at Lonnie. "It's time for John Hawkins to be the victim." He turned to Truby and Calhoun. "You two in this with us?"

Calhoun shrugged. "I guess. Makes me a little uneasy, though. What's your plan?"

"We think we have one that will work," Sam answered.

"How can you be so sure?" Truby asked. "Maybe Hawkins isn't even around El Paso anymore."

Lonnie sighed and stood up, pacing nervously. "He's there, all right. I've kept track without him knowing it. I've never met him because I never wanted him to see my face until the time was right, but I took the El Paso paper, under a fictitious name, so I could keep up on town gossip. John and Tess Hawkins own a ranch somewhere northeast of town, and the best part is . . ." He stopped pacing, looking at Truby and Ron. "They have *two* kids now. Whether the boy is John's by blood or not doesn't matter. He took the kid in and gave him his name, so he's sure to love him like any father. And he had a daughter by his wife. A little girl, about five years old now. You can bet your ass a man like Hawkins thinks the world of his daughter. She's his weak spot."

"So?" Ron asked.

"So . . . we get our hands on his kids, and John Hawkins will do whatever we ask, including letting himself be lured away from civilization, someplace so remote he'll have no help at all. My guess is he'd walk right up to the end of a gun barrel and let somebody shoot his guts out if it meant saving his kids. So would Tess Hawkins. But we have other plans for her, something more pleasant."

Truby shook his head. "Just how do you think you could get the man's kids away from him?"

Lonnie grinned, kneeling beside the fire. "I don't look anything like my brother. I'll just go to El Paso, find me a job, maybe as a ranch hand for John Hawkins."

They all sat quietly for a moment, and finally Calhoun grinned, then laughed. "You cocky sonofabitch! You'd walk right into the man's house?"

Lonnie shrugged. "Why not? I can be damn personable when I need to be. I guarantee I can make friends with the kids in no time, and with Hawkins himself."

Sam threw his cigar into the fire. "It will work. We can't go to Hawkins and take him out—certainly not on his own ranch, where he's bound to have plenty of men working for him. The key is to make *him* come to *us*. And the best way to do that is to use his kids for bait." He chuckled and rubbed his hands together. "I can't wait! Lonnie wants him to suffer. He'll *suffer!* And once I get *my* hands on him, he'll suffer even worse! Lonnie and I plan to make it long and slow."

Truby sighed. "I don't know. Maybe it will work like you say, but I can't imagine anything that would make a man like that angrier more than somebody taking his kids. If this guy was so good against men he didn't even know, and over *victims* he didn't even know, what's he gonna be like against somebody who dares to steal and maybe harm his kids?"

"It won't matter," Lonnie answered. "He'll be completely helpless. He can't come barging in firing his guns for fear of shooting his own. He'll have to come crawling to us on hands and knees, and that's exactly what I'm going to make him do. Hands and knees. John Hawkins is going to *beg* me to let his kids go and take him instead. I'll gladly oblige."

Calhoun sat up straighter and shook his head again. "Whew! This sounds exciting. I think I'll hang in with you just for the excitement, and just to see if you can really pull this off."

The look of pure hatred and revenge came back into Lonnie's blue eyes. Sam thought they actually seemed to get a darker blue when that look came.

"I'll pull it off, all right," Lonnie said. "John Hawkins is a doomed man."

Five

"Look, Pa!" Young Texas Hawkins jumped Shadow over a small wheelbarrow John had made for Honor. His little sister, who stood nearby, screamed and grabbed up the rag doll she'd put in the wheelbarrow, then ran to her father.

"Daddy, make him stop that!" She pouted. "He'll hurt my baby."

John picked her up and gave her a hug. "Worse than that. He could have hurt you. Your brother is going to get a good talking to." John patted Honor's bottom and set her back on her feet. "Put your doll back in the wheelbarrow and go inside the house, Honor."

Honor plunked the worn and faded doll into the wheelbarrow and rolled it away, looking up at her brother as he rode back in her direction. "You're in big *trouble,* Tex Hawkins," she announced with a haughty air.

John could not help an internal smile. Honor reminded him of Tess when she was angry, especially when she sported that chastising attitude. It brought back memories of how Tess behaved when he rescued her from the *Comancheros,* refusing to cry, accusing him at times of being no better than the men from whom he'd rescued her, putting on a brave, strong front, when inside she was falling apart. Even when they became closer, how often had she scolded him for taking the Lord's name in vain, or for living too wild and reckless a life?

That was all different now. It wasn't that he'd turned religious or didn't enjoy drinks and a card game once in awhile, but he'd come to like this family life more than he'd thought possible. Who would ever have thought, the way he was raised, that he could someday be married to a beautiful, respectable woman like Tess and take the role of father to boot?

He grabbed the bridle of the sleek, black mare when Tex rode closer.

"Did you see that, Pa? That was nothing. I can jump over things higher than that!"

"Get down, Tex." John's anger over the boy's carelessness momentarily overshadowed his more pleasant thoughts.

Tex's smile faded. "Why?"

"Why? Because you got careless. You could have hurt Honor, even killed her, if one of Shadow's hooves had hit her."

"Shadow wouldn't—"

"Use some common sense, Tex. It could *easily* have happened! If you're going to be this careless, I can't keep letting you ride."

Tex sighed and grudgingly dismounted, jumping down from the stirrup. He looked up at John, and the regret in his son's big, dark eyes made John want to crumble. He figured he must look like a giant to his eight-year-old son, and Tex was such a good boy at heart.

"I'm sorry, Pa. I just wanted to show you—"

"I know what you wanted to do. Just think first next time. I don't know how else to get that through your head except to forbid you to ride Shadow for the next couple of days."

"Pa!"

John detected a hint of tears in Tex's eyes, and again a little voice told him to give in, but a louder voice told him to stand his ground. "You're just lucky your mother didn't see what you did. If she had, you'd be ordered off this horse a lot longer than a couple of days. Would you rather I let *her* choose the punishment?"

Tex looked at the ground. "No," he mumbled. "But Honor will probably tell on me anyway."

"Don't worry. I'll explain to your mother that I have already talked to you."

Tex nodded. "I wouldn't never hurt Honor."

John sighed. He could hardly stand making either of his children feel bad about anything. He'd suffered so much hurt in his own life, but in far different ways. Many times in his own growing-up years he'd longed for a father to lean on, to guide him. But his Sioux mother had been raped, and the name bastard still angered and hurt him. He never had a father, and Tex could have grown up the same way. He bent down, grasping Tex's arms.

"Tex, I'm just trying to teach you to be responsible, and most of all to look out for your sister. If anything ever happened to me, I'd want you to always take care of her and your mother, to protect them, keep them safe. Just now you could have seriously hurt Honor. Do you understand that?"

Tex nodded, silent tears spilling down his cheeks, making tracks through the dust on his face. John thought how much the boy was growing, tall for eight years old, taking on the overall look of a young man in the making. He wore his straight, black hair tied at the back of his neck, just as John did. His features were strikingly handsome. John's ranch foreman and best friend, Ken Randall, always teased that Tex was a lady-killer in the making.

John squeezed the boy's arms reassuringly. "Take Shadow in the barn and brush her down, son."

"Okay." Tex took hold of Shadow's reins and led her to the barn, a barn townspeople had helped build, just as they'd helped build the house John and Tess now shared. The previous home on the property Tess had shared with her father and first husband had been burned down by the *Comancheros,* who killed her father and husband and hauled Tess away to rape and terror.

The new home was a sprawling stucco home, designed much like the many other Spanish homes and structures in the area. Many of John's hired help were Mexicans who had knowledge of building a stucco home. The house had a porch across the front with six arches. Roses Tess had planted at the base of each arch already showed large buds.

Tess liked flowers, liked things neat and feminine inside her home. Her taste belied the tough woman who dwelled inside that slender, velvety body. Few women had suffered what Tess Hawkins had suffered. She deserved the peaceful life she led now. In the past nine years her only heartache had been the loss of a son . . . his son . . . the first son of his own seed. The hurt still ran deep in both their hearts.

"Ain't always easy playin' the father, is it?"

The words interrupted John's thoughts. He turned to see Ken approaching.

"I was behind the smokehouse there, heard what you told Tex."

John smiled rather sadly, rubbing at his neck. "Do you think I did the right thing?"

Ken shrugged. "I'd say so. Personally, a whack on the butt wouldn't have hurt. That was a real dangerous thing he did."

"I know." John took off his deerskin jacket. This time of year a man could never tell from one day to the next if it was going to be warm or cold. Yesterday had been very warm, but today started out cold. Now the air was warming again. "I'll never lay a hand on my children. You know that."

Ken nodded, then chuckled. "You sure are a far cry from the man I used to ride with. Nine years, and I still can't get over it, you ranchin', supportin' a woman and two kids, stayin' in one place."

John leaned against a corral gate. "Well, Tess is the kind that gets in your blood and stays there. Which reminds me, my friend, when are *you* going to get married? Hell, you're ten years older than I am. Time is running out."

Ken shrugged. "I can make babies anytime, clear up to the day I die. I'll just have to be sure to pick a younger woman."

Both men laughed.

"What about Jenny? She's turned respectable now, selling her saloon and opening a boardinghouse and a dress shop. Besides, you've shared her bed long enough that you might as well make her your wife."

Ken climbed up the corral fence and sat on the top tie, chuckling. "You know I've tried. But Jenny seems to think she ain't good enough for any man. She's happy just the way things are, but I love her, and I expect she loves me. She actually thinks I'm too good for her. Can you imagine that? An old, used-up, ex-Ranger like me?"

"You're as strong and able as you were when we still rode together."

"Yeah, well, we both know where Jenny's heart *really* lies, and whose bed she'd love to share again."

John laughed lightly. "You're talking a long time ago . . . another life."

"I know." Ken, still well-built for his fifty years, looked down from his perch at the man he considered his best friend, the man who had saved his life more than once when they rode with the Texas Rangers. "You ever miss it, Hawk?" he asked, using the nickname he'd given John years ago.

"The Rangers?" John looked up at him. "Sometimes, but not in a longing way. The only thing I miss is the ability not to care about a living soul, the ability to live however I want without the risk of hurting someone. Hell, back then I didn't even care about *myself,* let alone anybody else." He put on a look of mock concern. "Except you, maybe."

"Bullshit!" Ken jumped down, then groaned slightly. "Jesus, these bones is gettin' old, Hawk."

"Yeah, I've been thinking maybe I'll hire a few extra men to help with roundup this year and let you stay here, watch over Tess and the kids. I usually leave someone else, but I know it's getting harder for you to sit in a saddle all day long and half the night, then sleep on the hard ground, rain or shine."

"You sayin' I can't handle a roundup anymore?"

John shrugged. "No. I'm just saying I think you put up with it for my sake, and that you've done enough for me over the years. I'm just giving you a little bit easier job, that's all."

Ken sighed, looking at the ground. "Well, normally I'd argue with you about that, but much as it hurts my pride, I have to say you're right. Sometimes my joints ache so bad I can't hardly get out of bed in the mornin'." He walked a few feet away, feeling angry and embarrassed. "But I can still damn well handle a gun good as ever. You know that." He turned to face John. "And I'd die for Tess and those kids. You know that, too."

John nodded. "So, you'll stay here this time and keep an eye out?"

Ken shrugged. "Sure."

John grinned. "What you need right now is a woman to give you a hot bath tonight and help you forget your aches and pains."

Ken brightened. "I expect I can get that much out of Jenny if I ride into town and spend the night with her."

"You'll get more out of her than a bath."

Both men laughed, and Ken shook his head. "Well, I ain't no John Hawkins, that's for sure, but much as she misses you, she's happy for you and Tess. You know that."

"Jenny's a good woman, in spite of her reputation. I think a lot of people in town are beginning to see that."

Both men walked quietly for a moment. "You going to the big shindig in town Saturday?" Ken asked then, changing the subject. "I think several of the cowhands from here are going. Might as well kick up your heels a little yourself before roundup."

"Oh, you know Tess. She wouldn't hear of *not* going, even though she knows how much I hate things like that." Just then John heard an eagle call. He stopped walking and looked up, seeing nothing. An eerie feeling moved through him. "You hear that?"

"What?"

"An eagle."

"In these parts? This time of day?"

John was sure he'd heard it. He looked around again.

"Somethin' wrong?" Ken asked.

"I don't know." John stood with his hands on his hips. "Just a funny feeling. I don't know how to explain it."

Ken rubbed at the day-old stubble on his face. "I don't like when you talk like that. When we rode with the Rangers you were usually right about your hunches. We always ended up in trouble."

"Well, we aren't Rangers now. Come on. Let's go see if Tess will rustle up something for us to eat."

Honor appeared at the screen door, then opened it and ran out to John.

"Pick me up, Daddy!"

John obliged her.

"My God, you spoil that girl rotten. You know that, don't you?" Ken teased.

"Sure do. And I love every minute of it."

"I told Mommy what Tex did," Honor told him.

"Well, now, you should have let me do that," John answered. He handed the girl over to Ken. "Go on inside. I'm going back to the barn and get Tex."

"Mommy said Tex can't ride Shadow for a whole month!"

John rolled his eyes. "Yeah, well, we'll see about that."

Ken laughed. "I want to see this one. You ain't never yet won an argument with that woman."

John waved him off and headed for the barn. Again he was sure he heard the cry of an eagle, but when he looked back at Ken, the man kept walking, behaving as though he never heard the call. John felt as though the cry was meant only for him.

Six

"So, what's the plan." Calhoun stood staring out at red-rock formations that jutted up against the otherwise endless horizon of northern Texas. There was nothing for miles around, and the vast plains sprawled green with spring grass.

Truby rubbed at the bags under his eyes. "Seems pretty simple to me. We head south, rob a few people on the way, maybe a bank or two, get ourselves down to El Paso, and let Lonnie steal the Hawkins kids."

Sam let out a long sigh. "No wonder you got yourself thrown in prison. We're wanted men now, not just for escaping, but for killing those two prison guards. They will probably also link us to the attack on that ranch. And just about everybody in west Texas knows my face. I don't dare go anywhere near El Paso. Lonnie and I have a better plan."

Lonnie stirred the beans he was warming over a fire. He wiped sweat from his brow. "It's getting hot for the sixth of April."

"How do you know it's the sixth of April?" Calhoun asked him.

Lonnie answered with a cigarette between his lips. "Saw a calendar in that clothing store we stopped at." He pushed back the brand-new hat he'd purchased in a tiny settlement the day before.

"I still feel funny about this," Calhoun spoke up. He unbuttoned his new shirt, sweat stains showing under the arms. "I don't have anything personal against Hawkins like you and Sam do. I'm not sure I want to go along and help with any of this. If this guy is as good as you say, I don't know if I want any part of trying to bring him down."

They all thought quietly for the next couple of minutes, while Lonnie dished up the beans. "Believe me, this will work. I don't look anything like my brother. I'm not sure Hawkins even knew Darrell *had* a brother. And Darrell was dark, shorter than me. I'll use a fake name when I go into El Paso. Hawkins will never realize who I am, until it's too late."

"You've never told me if you've ever been in prison," Sam told him. "You're not wanted, are you?"

Lonnie ate a bite of beans before answering. "I killed a woman who cheated on me, but I never got caught for it. I also robbed funds from a church, and I killed a couple of rich old ladies who took me in. Took the money they had hidden in their houses. Blamed it on intruders."

"How in hell did you get away with all that?" Truby asked.

Lonnie smiled. "Look at this face. Do I look like someone who could do such terrible things?"

Truby grinned. "I see what you mean. An ugly old cuss like me could never get away with them things, but by God, I believe you could at that."

"And that's how I plan to move in on Hawkins."

Ron shook his head. "Why did you kill the two old ladies?"

He shrugged. "I don't know. It just made me mad that my own ma died the way she did, poor and heartbroken, and those women were rich and always had a good life, the kind of life my ma should have had. Besides, it kind of gets my goat that they let me in just because of my looks and charm. I get a strange kind of pleasure out of fooling people that way. And after killing the first girl, it just got easier." The look of hatred came back into his eyes. "Imagine that. A pretty young girl saying no to me, Lonnie Briggs. I don't like being turned down." He grinned again. "Maybe Tess Hawkins will be so taken with me that I can charm her into bed instead of having to rape her. What do you think?"

They all laughed. "Maybe then John Hawkins would kill you *and* her!"

More laughter filled the night air.

"All I want to know is what are the rest of us supposed to do while you're charming the underwear off of Tess Hawkins," Truby asked. He shoveled another spoonful of beans into his mouth.

Sam set his plate aside. "Lonnie and I already talked about it. There's a place in the Guadalupe Mountains called Thieves' Hollow. The whole area is an outlaw hangout, similar to Indian territory in Oklahoma, except they've cleaned that up quite a bit, I hear. Hawkins had something to do with that, too. Anyway, Lonnie says Thieves' Hollow is still a pretty good place to hang our hats for a while. It's been raided by the Rangers many a time, but those who live around there are good at keeping their mouths shut. They'll hide us if we ask them. Most of the ones there now aren't wanted men anymore. They're just ex-cons, or just down-and-outers who don't have anyplace to go."

"I thought you were going to lure Hawkins out to where nobody else is around."

"We are," Lonnie continued for Sam. "All you'll do at Thieves' Hollow is stock up on supplies, maybe pick up a prostitute to take with you to where we'll actually take the Hawkins kids to wait for their father. Past Thieves' Hollow is a place called Eagle Pass. There's a cabin there, high on top of a cliff, and you can see someone coming from miles away. There's no way a man can sneak up on you. That's where Calhoun and Sam will go to wait for me and Truby."

"Me?" Truby asked. "What am I doing?"

"You're going to find a way to hang around El Paso and wait till I get word to you that I have the kids. I'll need help taking them all the way to Eagle Pass. It's a good hundred miles from El Paso. Hawkins's boy is old enough to give me trouble if he wants. I could just knock the shit out of him, but I want to keep both kids as healthy as possible so when Hawkins comes for them, they'll be in good shape—all the more reason for Hawkins to come to us unarmed. And there is only one way to get to Eagle Pass. You can't come up from behind because it's set in a whole string of cliffs. No way to come in from the side, and behind the cabin is just a small area big enough to graze a couple of horses. Beyond that are even higher cliffs. It's all but impossible to get to the cabin any way but from the road leading up to the cliffs. And from there is a narrow, winding path only wide enough for one horse at a time that leads up to the cabin."

"What if somebody in El Paso recognizes me?" Truby asked.

"I don't think they will," Lonnie told him. "Just don't attract any attention. Get a job or something, stay out of the saloons and stores and such, keep your head down and your mouth shut."

"Why don't you take me?" Calhoun asked.

Lonnie shook his head. "Truby has been friends with Sam for a long time now. He's more likely to see this thing through. I'm worried about you running out on me."

"Well, I won't. You'll see. I'll be there at the cabin with Sam when you get there."

Sam looked around at all three of them. "It's settled then. Calhoun and I head for the Guadalupes, and Lonnie and Truby go on from there to El Paso. I think it's best if Truby waits and goes in a few days after Lonnie." He centered his attention on Lonnie. "You shouldn't ride in together."

Lonnie nodded. "I agree."

"This Tess woman, is she pretty?" Calhoun asked.

Sam shrugged. "Last I saw her, she was the prettiest woman in Texas. But that was nine years ago, and she's been living with John Hawkins. Lord only knows what he's put her through. Then again, maybe he's been good to her. All I know is that she is apparently still his woman, and Hawkins has two kids. Knowing him, he'll go to the ends of the earth to save any of them. And the country around the Guadalupes is about as close as you can get to that."

"How can you be sure the woman will even *be* with Hawkins

when he comes after his kids?" Truby asked. "No man would bring his wife along when he's goin' after outlaws and kidnappers."

Sam swallowed some beans and licked the spoon. "You don't know Tess Hawkins. She's the kind of woman who would put up with any kind of hell to find her own. You can bet she's one tough woman to marry a man like John. If we can get our hands on those kids, Hawkins won't come after them alone."

Truby shrugged. "Maybe Hawkins won't *let* her come along."

Lonnie sighed. "I have to agree with that one, Sam. Can you really be sure the woman will come, too?"

Sam shook his head. "You just don't get it, do you? *Any* of you." He set his plate aside and rose. He rubbed the back of his neck as he walked past the other three men, then placed his hands on his hips and turned to face them. "I know she'll be with him because, however strong John Hawkins is, Tess Hawkins can match him in *inner* strength. I didn't know her in a personal sense, but I know *about* her. I know that she survived the murders of her husband and father and capture by *Comancheros*. I know after Hawkins rescued her she returned to El Paso holding her chin up like nothing had happened. Anybody who knows anything about *Comancheros* knows no good-looking woman gets taken by them without being raped. But Tess Hawkins never owned up to any abuse, never hung her head, never cried in front of anyone. She just went right on, then up and married John Hawkins and carried a baby everybody in town knew had to belong to one of the outlaws that took her, but she never would admit it."

Sam came back to sit down again, lighting a cigar before continuing. "The woman took a job for my ex-boss, the man who headed the cattle-rustling ring. I guess that's when she somehow discovered what was going on. She left there and opened her own seamstress business, then had her bastard baby, claiming it was John's kid. Later, when I realized she knew something about the cattle rustling and my connection, I tried to burn her house down around her. The bitch managed to escape the fire, baby and all, and I got caught. Whatever happens to that woman, she manages to survive and just keep going. Hawkins is the same—he even survived a bullet in the back."

Sam took a flask of whiskey from his vest pocket and drank some, licking his lips. "I just want all of you to understand what we're up against. We can't let anything go wrong, and by God, this time nothing *will* go wrong! If Lonnie finds a way to get close to Hawkins and gets his hands on those kids and gets them out of there, John and Tess Hawkins will follow them right into hell if they have to, and that's what we're going to make them do! They won't have any way out. The whole family will be *ours!* Bet on it! There's no surviving this one!"

The others looked at each other and nodded. Lonnie faced Sam, grinning. "I *am* betting on it, Sam. I'm betting my *life* on it. That should show you how confident I am that this will work." He looked at Truby and Calhoun. "You boys still with us?"

The other two looked at each other, obviously nervous but excited. "I'm still game," Calhoun answered.

"So am I," Truby agreed.

Sam held up the flask of whiskey. "Then let's drink on it."

Seven

Buggies and wagons lined Oregon Street, leading to the large barn where festivities involving the spring dance continued. The celebration had started two days earlier and would continue for another day, allowing time for people from areas several hours' ride from El Paso to get to town without missing some of the fun.

"Look at all the wagons," Tess commented, holding on to her white straw hat. "It looks like there are more here than ever before."

One buggy pulled away, and John took its spot, about one block from the huge barn owned by Harold Jeffers, owner of El Paso's largest feed supply store. He had been sponsoring the celebration for years, and since the arrival of the railroad brought a rapid growth of population to the area, the dance had become a crowded event and an opportunity for newcomers to meet established citizens.

"Sheriff Potter says El Paso's population is up to about eight thousand now," John said. He shook his head. "This sure is a far cry from the sleepy little settlement I knew when I first came here."

"Pa, can I get down?" Tex asked.

"Go ahead. Just stay in sight. And help Honor down."

Tex obeyed, and John lifted Tess down from the seat.

"My, aren't we the gentleman today?" she teased. "You know I can get down perfectly well by myself."

"Today is different." John's eyes raked over her in a way that made Tess feel things inappropriate for a public place. "I haven't seen you dressed up for a long time. And pink makes you look even more beautiful than you already are."

"Does it really?" Tess tugged at her white gloves. "Do I really look all right?"

John rolled his eyes. "You know damn well you're prettier than any woman here."

"Well, the ladies will be wearing their best." Tess took a deep breath, touching her stomach. "This is, however, a most uncomfortable corset. I may have to shop for a different one before we leave El Paso."

John laughed softly. "How many times have I told you not to bother with those things? Let it all hang loose and comfortable, like the Indian women do."

"John Hawkins! I can't come to a thing like this without being properly dressed."

"Properly cinched, you mean. If I'd pulled those corset strings any tighter, I'd have had to bring you here in two pieces."

"Oh, stop it! Help me with the pies. I'll take the doilies. You can leave the rest of our supplies in the wagon."

John lifted out a basket of pies. "You sure you don't want to stay over this time?"

Tess opened a small chest and took out a handful of hand-crocheted doilies. "I don't think so. We got a real early start, and we'll have the whole day here. We can at least start home tonight, maybe sleep in the wagon on the way and get home nice and early. I have so much to do, and so do you, with roundup time and all. The hotels are always full during the dance, and so is Jenny's boardinghouse. We always come for just one day."

"Doesn't matter to me. I just don't want you to get worn-out."

"Daddy, pick me up!" Honor asked.

Keeping the basket of pies in one hand, John leaned down and scooped his daughter up with his other arm. Tess led the way, stopping just outside the barn door, where tables spread with white tablecloths displayed pies, cakes, knitted wear, blankets, clothing, crocheted doilies and tablecloths, handmade quilts and other assorted products of the talents of El Paso's female population. The items would be raffled off, the money going to a fund for city improvements.

Tess stopped and handed her doilies to Bess Johndrow, wife of a boot and saddle maker. A longtime friend, Bess greeted her and John warmly.

"No clothing this year?" she asked Tess.

"Too busy making clothes for my own family," Tess told her.

"Oh, you're such a good seamstress, Tess," Bess answered. "The ladies in town so miss the lovely work you did for us when you had your business here."

"Well, thank you. I did bring pies. Two for the raffle and two for the food table inside."

"Oh, that's good. The food in there is going fast!" Bess commented on how the children were growing, as Tess gave her two pies to set out on the pie table. She took the basket with the remaining two pies from John, and they both went inside the crowded barn, where voices and laughter filled the air, as well as a fast-paced square-dance tune, played by a group of men and women who got together for this every year and offered their talents on fiddle, piano, and guitar. A man called out the dance steps, and some of the dancers laughed as they tried to keep up with the constantly changing calls.

Tess could not help noticing how some people stared at her and John, stares that for the most part were kind, not cruel—welcoming looks—combined with a fascination people still held for John Hawkins. Tess little doubted that she and John remained food for curious gossip. John, once a Texas Ranger, but considered hardly more than a heathen by some, carrying his pretty, fair, delicate little daughter who looked more like a captive than someone of his own blood. Tex, her dark-haired, dark-eyed son, standing next to his very fair, red-haired mother. Tess knew people still wondered if the boy really was John's.

She would never tell them any different. Let them believe what they wanted.

She smiled and greeted some of her closer lady friends, feeling pleased with the pink-cotton dress with its lace bib and leg-of-mutton sleeves she'd made for the occasion. Her wide-brimmed hat was decorated with pink-silk flowers she had made herself, and, as most women did, she wore gloves to cover hands that were browned and beginning to show some age because of the Texas sun.

"John, that son of yours looks more and more like his father every day." The comment came from Harold Jeffers as he shook John's hand.

Tess handed the basket with the remaining two pies in it to Louise Jeffers, who was being helped at the food table by Mary Sanders, wife of one of El Paso's first doctors. Tess listened to John accept Harold's remark as confidently as if Tex truly was his son, and in John's heart, he really was.

A few more people gathered around as Tess visited with Louise and Mary, and some laughed good-naturedly at the contrast between John and little Honor, who very willingly remained in her father's arms, clinging to him fiercely; since she was still shy around crowds of people.

Tex, on the other hand, quickly left his mother and father to visit the food table and see what goodies might be available. Tess was relieved to have managed to get the boy to wear clean, black-cotton pants and a white shirt, but he'd refused to wear good shoes. Instead, he'd donned his worn, dusty, leather boots. Tess had tried to get him to let her cut his hair, but again he refused, insisting he wear it long and pulled into a tail at the back of his neck, just like John's was, saying he would never cut his hair unless his father did.

"Oh, look at you," Louise was exclaiming over Honor. "What a pretty girl!"

Honor grinned bashfully, showing her dimples, then buried her face against John's shoulder.

"She's a daddy's girl, that's certain." The words came from

Wilber Booth, captain of the Texas Rangers since before John quit his work with them. In spite of his advanced age, Booth remained a tough, active man, whose short, wiry build belied his strength and skills. The man laughed and shook his head as he put out his hand to John. "What a pair you two make, John. Whoever would have thought."

John kept Honor in one arm and shook the captain's hand. "Captain, what the heck brings you to a spring dance? Shouldn't you be out chasing the bad guys?"

Booth shook his head. "Well, Hawk, things just aren't the same without you."

Tess felt a flash of dread at the thought of John ever wearing the badge of a Texas Ranger again.

"You mean you miss the public outcries over the way I handled my work?" John answered. "I was your biggest headache, don't forget."

"Oh, but things used to be so much more exciting with you involved."

John moved an arm around Tess's shoulders. "Life isn't quite so dangerous anymore, but it sure is satisfying."

Booth laughed and winked at Tess. "Just goes to show the power of a woman." He held out his hand, and Tess shook it, blushing. "How are you, Tess? Any regrets over marrying this wild half-breed?"

"Not one," Tess replied. "But I do work hard at making sure he prefers married life to chasing all over Texas and beyond after dangerous men. And most of his energy is used now in training wild horses. Little Tex is already wanting to help. I think our son is going to be more of a challenge than his father."

"I don't doubt that," Booth replied, squeezing her hand.

Tex ran over to where they stood and tugged Honor's dress. "Come get some lemonade with me, Honor. They have cake, too."

"Okay, but don't leave me alone," Honor told him.

John set Honor down. She took Tex's hand and walked off with him. Booth watched them a moment before commenting,

"Hard to believe they're brother and sister. I'll bet young Texas watches over his sister like a little man."

John nodded, watching the two children slowly walk around the food table, Tex helping Honor pick out a cookie. "They have their moments, but they are close. Honor worships her big brother." He sighed, turning to Booth again. "And I worship both of them."

Tess felt a hint of alarm at a strange look that came into Captain Booth's eyes. He sobered slightly, as though concerned about something. "I have no doubt about that." He brightened a little. "Say, how about a cold lemonade?"

"I'd rather have a beer, but the women insist on no alcohol at these events."

"I can't imagine why," Booth returned. "By the way, is your old friend Ken here?"

"He's around somewhere, rode in ahead of us with five other men."

"Well, let's find him—talk over some old times."

Tess could not help wondering if Booth wanted to talk about more than old times. "Just don't go trying to convince my husband to rejoin the Rangers," she called out as they walked away. "I like having him around full-time and not having to worry about what kind of trouble he's getting himself into."

"Oh, don't worry about that," Booth answered.

Tess turned to help Louise and Mary arrange the pies. Amid conversation, she watched John, noticing after a few minutes that they had found Ken. The three men were talking in a corner, and watching them together reminded Tess of another time, another Texas . . . another John.

Eight

"So, John, you still enjoy married life?"

John grinned. "What do you think?"

Captain Booth chuckled and shook his head. "Well, you look good, John, happy and healthy. That old back wound ever give you trouble?"

"Once in a while." John shrugged. "I've gotten used to it."

"Well, you're lucky to be walking." Booth rubbed at the back of his neck. "Ready for spring roundup?"

"We start in one week."

Booth nodded, putting his hands on his hips and looking around at the crowded barn. "Quite a turnout."

John glanced at Ken, read his eyes. He knew Ken agreed with what he was thinking. Booth was acting a little strange, as though he wanted to say more but was covering it up with small talk. John took a small leather pouch of tobacco from where it was tied to his belt, then took a cigarette paper from his pocket. "Cap', it's been eight years since I quit the Rangers, but I worked with you long enough to know when you've got something on your mind." He poured some tobacco onto the cigarette paper, then tucked the pouch strings back into his belt and licked the paper to seal the cigarette. "What's up?"

Booth said nothing at first. He waited while John prepared the smoke, then took a match from his own shirt pocket and flicked it with his thumbnail. He held it out and lit John's cigarette.

"Might be nothing," he finally said. "Maybe I've just been in this business too long. I see the worst side of things most of the time. Let's step outside. I believe I'll have a smoke, too."

John shared a look of concern with Ken, and the two men followed Booth outside, where Booth took a cigar from his shirt pocket and lit it.

"Want a cigar, Ken?"

"No, thanks. Maybe later."

Booth took a few puffs on his own cigar before speaking again. "Sam Higgins escaped."

John's eyes narrowed in alarm, and he took his cigarette from his mouth. "When?"

"Just a few days ago. They were shipping him up to Kansas . . . at Leavenworth. Somehow he and a couple other men got the better of the prison wagon guards and got away. Some kind of accident, I guess. One guard was shot through the cheek. The other was apparently pinned under the wagon, but he was found shot in the forehead. They must have shot him while he lay there injured." He puffed on the cigar again before continuing. "I figured you should know, since you're about to go out on spring roundup. You might want to keep an extra guard on the wife and kids."

John took a long drag on his cigarette, then put his head back and blew out the smoke in a long sigh. "Shit!" he muttered.

"There's no guarantee the man will be stupid enough to come down here and mess with you, John," Booth reminded him. "If he's smart, he'll take off for parts unknown. He shows his face around here, he'll be caught again."

"Or get his head blown off," John added.

"I can't believe he'd be that stupid," Ken said. "Hell, the man tried to kill Tess and little Texas, burned the house down around them. He knows damn well he was lucky you didn't kill him then, John, or that the townspeople didn't hang him."

"Yeah, well, see what happens when you try to be more civilized? My gut instinct was to slit him from his balls to his Adam's apple. I should have done it."

"The Rangers don't operate that way anymore, John. You know that," Booth reminded him. "The public expects us to abide by a code of ethics, to let the law take care—"

"Bullshit!" John spoke the word quietly but firmly. "Ethics? You think Sam Higgins has learned any ethics? Two guards are dead. The man tried to kill a woman and her baby, helped Jim Caldwell rustle cattle, and was perfectly aware of who shot me in the *back!* I have my own code of law, and that sonofabitch better not come within fifty miles of the Hawk's Nest. I'll by-God *smell* him!"

"Don't get your dander up, Hawk," Ken told him. "You know Tess. She can read you like a book, and she'll know somethin's up. You might be best not to even tell her about this."

John glanced inside the barn. He could see Tess and Honor, who were laying out cloth napkins at the food table. He still found it hard to believe someone as gentle and refined and educated as Tess had actually married him, regardless of the circumstances under which it had all happened. She didn't love him then, but he damn well loved her beyond any love he thought possible. He and Tess had been through plenty, and survived it all. Sam Higgins was not going to make their lives miserable again. He looked back at Booth. "Is there a marshal or someone looking for Higgins and the other two?"

"Oh, they're looking, all right, and so are the Rangers, but no luck yet. He, uh—" Booth rubbed nervously at his neck again. "He did head south, but that doesn't have to mean he's coming here. Like I said, he'd be crazy to do that. He's probably headed for Mexico."

"Sure he is," John said sarcastically.

Ken watched a look of revenge and hatred come into John's dark eyes as he took another drag on his cigarette. "Thanks for warning me, Cap."

Booth nodded. "You just be sure to let the Rangers know if you catch one glimpse of Higgins. Let us take care of it, John. You're too important to that wife and kids to go riskin' your neck again."

"Yeah, well, that depends on the circumstances. I'll do whatever I have to do to protect them."

"And God help the man who would dare to lay a finger on any of them," Ken added.

Honor came racing outside then to find her father, interrupting the conversation. "Tex won't let me have another cupcake," she complained.

"Well, maybe he's right to tell you no," John answered, picking her up again. "You have to save some of that food for other people, Honor. That's the polite thing to do."

"I helped Mommy fold napkins," she answered. "That's polite, isn't it?"

"Yes, that's very polite." John threw down his cigarette and ground it out, then glanced at Booth. "We'll talk again later. Keep me informed."

"I'll do that."

John left them, carrying Honor to where Tex took a dish of noodles from Louise Jeffers and set it on the food table. John managed a warm smile when Tess approached him.

"So, I suppose Captain Booth had all kinds of stories to share with you," Tess told him.

"Oh, that he did," John answered. "That he did." *Damn!* he thought. The last thing he wanted to do was tell Tess about the escape, or to even have to mention Sam Higgins's name again.

Nine

It was nearly dark when Jenny finished taking down sheets from the clothesline. She shoved the last one into a bushel basket and picked it up, turning to go inside. She noticed then that Ken Randall stood near the back fence watching her.

"Need some help?"

Jenny grinned. "Why aren't you over at the barn dance?"

"Because I'd rather be here with you. Got time for some company?"

Jenny looked him over. "Depends on what the company wants."

Ken shrugged, coming closer. "Just to talk. Got some coffee on?"

"You know I *always* have coffee on, you ole codger. I run a boardinghouse, remember? I cook breakfast and supper every day for guests, most of whom, I might add, are at the barn dance right now. We're alone, except for one old man on the second floor who hardly ever comes out of his room."

Ken followed Jenny up the back steps and into her kitchen, studying her robust figure as she walked ahead of him. Jenny Simms always had been a little plump, but pleasingly so. Over the past eight years she had taken on a few more pounds, but he didn't mind that. It just gave him more to hold . . . and fondle. She no longer wore plunging necklines and feathered hats, nor did she layer her naturally soft skin with powders and rouges. At thirty-six, she looked much older, but she'd lived a hard life. Now the former saloon owner ran this boardinghouse, and she was doing a damn good job of it. The place was nearly always full, and her talent for cooking good meals was well-known, at first a surprise to everyone. There was a time when most folks figured the only thing Jenny Simms could do well was serve drinks and take men to the upper room of her saloon. But then once John Hawkins became one of her customers, she'd quit seeing other men . . . until John married Tess.

"John and Tess over at the barn dance with the kids?" Jenny asked when they got inside. She set down the basket of laundry.

"Yup. Little Honor is helping at the food table. She likes to think she can do anything her ma can do."

Jenny smiled and shook her head. "That little girl is something, isn't she? God knows there isn't a person in this country who would believe she's John's daughter." She set two cups on the table, then turned and used her apron to wrap around the handle of a coffeepot sitting on her oil-burning stove.

Ken removed his hat and hung it over the post of another chair. He watched Jenny pour his coffee, then pour a cup for herself before sitting down. She shoved a sugar bowl toward Ken.

"Here. I probably should have just poured the coffee into the sugar bowl."

Ken spooned several teaspoonfuls into his coffee. "You know me too well. Which reminds me, when are we gettin' married?"

Jenny leaned back and cast him a look of chastisement. "I didn't know we *were* getting married."

"I thought it was an understood thing," Ken told her with a shrug.

"You devil." Jenny shook her head. "Is that why you came over here? To try again to get me to marry you? Hell, we're both getting too old for such things. How many times have you proposed now? Six? Seven?"

Ken stirred his coffee a little longer. "I can understand why you'd maybe hold out for a man a little bit younger and in better shape—"

"Ken Randall!" Jenny interrupted. "You know it's got nothing to do with your age, or your condition. Last time we shared a bed, I never noticed that either one seemed to affect the way you can please a woman." She took amusement in watching him redden a little as he grinned.

"You can find a lot better than me, and you know it. And *I* know where your heart lies, Jenny."

Jenny set her cup down. "That's long over." She sobered, thinking about John and the old days. "Ken, you know I'm not the type of woman *any* man marries, and I know John is probably the happiest man in Texas. I love him and Tess both, and those kids. I'm happy for them. And I *do* love *you,* Ken Randall. But you're the one who deserves better. You're the gentlest, most caring man I've ever known."

"And there ain't no woman who understands me like you do, Jenny. Oh, there's a couple of Mexican women at the ranch who give me the eye once in a while, but they ain't Jenny Simms." He looked her straight in the eyes. "I love you, Jenny, and I'll say it again. I want to marry you. Soon as you figure out that's the right thing for us to do, you come let me know and we'll get hitched."

Jenny laughed and leaned back in her chair. "Well, now, isn't that romantic?"

Ken grinned. "That's as mushy as I can get."

Jenny studied him a moment. At fifty, Ken still carried a hint of his once-handsome youth. He'd grown up parentless, wild and free, no schooling. He'd joined the Rangers at a young age, and that was all he'd known. When John Hawkins came along and was assigned as his partner, a great friendship developed between them, and now Ken was the top hand at John's ranch. Ken's face was lined from years of exposure to the Texas sun. He had a nice smile and gentle brown eyes. His dark brown hair was receding at the temples, and graying; but what was left was still thick. He was strong for his medium build, and she liked his arms, the way he hugged her. He was a good man, honest, devoted to his friends.

Jenny rose and stood in front of him, leaning down and kissing the rough skin of his cheek. "I can think of a way to be even more mushy."

Ken leaned up and met her lips, rising as he did so and pulling her into his arms. He released the kiss and leaned back a little, studying her pretty green eyes. "Does this mean you're acceptin' my proposal?"

"No it does not. It means I want to go down the hall with you."

Ken frowned. "What if I said I don't want to take to your bed again unless you agree to marry me?"

"I'd say you could never hold out that long."

Ken chuckled, kissing her again. "I couldn't hold out five minutes when I feel you against me." He turned, keeping his arm around her as they headed for the back stairs.

"Just a minute," Jenny said, pulling away. "You don't get off that easy, Ken Randall."

Ken frowned and faced her. "What do you mean?"

"I mean I noticed the troubled look in your eyes when I saw you standing at the fence. I saw how you put on a look of happiness and unconcern. You forget how well I know my men. You didn't come over here for this. You had something on your mind to tell me. Let's hear it."

Ken stared at her a moment longer, then sighed and shook his head. "You are a wonder, Jenny. I ain't never known a woman who could read minds like you can."

"So? What's on *your* mind?"

Ken sighed deeply. "Sam Higgins escaped from a prison wagon up in Kansas."

Jenny, too, lost her jovial countenance. "When?"

"About three weeks ago, according to Captain Booth. Two others escaped with him, and not long after that a ranch was raided south of there, the man killed, a woman raped, food, money, and horses stolen. Booth thinks they're still headed south."

"South?" Jenny turned away. "You think Higgins is headed this way to look up John and Tess?"

"Could be. I wouldn't put it past him."

Jenny turned and moved closer, putting her arms around his waist. "Then John will just have to keep an extra watch. Hell, he's got men all over that place—good, loyal men."

"And most of them have to head out on roundup, includin' John. He even needs to hire more. That ranch has really grown, Jenny."

"Still an' all, he'll just have to keep an extra guard on the place. He's already proven to Higgins he's no match for the likes of John Hawkins."

"I know. It's just a worry, that's all. A big worry."

Jenny leaned up and kissed him. "Why don't we go upstairs, and I'll see what I can do to help you forget *your* worries?"

Ken hugged her close. "Normally I wouldn't argue with that, but first you ought to come over to the barn dance, do a two-step with me. I've got nobody to dance with over there."

"Oh? And since when did you care about dancing?"

Ken studied her eyes. "Since I started carin' about you bein' over here all alone when everybody else is over there havin' a good time."

Jenny smiled. "I don't belong over there. Besides, I have this place to watch over."

"You said yourself all the guests was over at the dance except one old man who don't give a damn. And why do you think you don't belong over there?"

Jenny shrugged. "You know the answer to that. I can do everything in the world to show I'm a respectable woman now, but most of the proper women in this town have long memories. I feel their stares. I know what they're thinking."

Ken studied her full lips, the lines in her still-pretty face. "All the more reason to marry me. It looks better, a married woman running a boardinghouse instead of a single one."

Jenny sighed. "Just don't forget that if I ever marry you, you either have to come help run a boardinghouse, something a man like you would hate; or I have to go live on a ranch, something a woman like *me* would hate. How would we possibly work that out?"

Ken kissed her nose. "I'll think on it." He turned and led her out of the kitchen and down the hallway, to a bedroom that was now familiar to him. A picture of John, Tess, and both children sat on her dresser, and for one quick moment that little sinking feeling he got when he thought about Sam Higgins being "out there" somewhere returned. But Jenny surely was right. John Hawkins was enough of a handful himself, let alone the fact that he had a crew of fifteen men, all loyal and capable. What could possibly happen to Tess and the kids? Since John and Tess's marriage, John and the men had fended off attacks from renegade Indians, an attempt at cattle rustling, and two separate attacks by former enemies John had made. All had failed, and most involved in the incidents had died. In the last two years there had been no trouble at the Hawk's Nest. Apparently there was no one left who was willing to try giving John Hawkins any trouble.

Ten

"For someone who hates dances, you do dance well, John Hawkins." Tess followed his lead, proud of how handsome John looked in black pants and white shirt, with a black string tie and black jacket. She made the pants and jacket for him herself. John hated dressing "fancy" as he called it, so she did not often get to see him this way.

"Jenny taught me well." John looked down at her with a teasing grin, and Tess could not help the fleeting sting of jealousy that still plagued her at the thought of Jenny Simms and the fact that before she met John it was Jenny's bed he slept in whenever he was in El Paso. She raised her chin slightly.

"She taught you a *lot* of things well."

John laughed, and Tess could not help a continued attraction to her still-virile husband. She did not miss the way some women looked at him, and she knew that in spite of the outward assumption that white women did not befriend or marry Indians, what woman would not appreciate a handsome man like John? Her own marriage to him had been accepted, and few who had come to know John shunned him, appreciating his bravery while a member of the Texas Rangers . . . and the fact that he had broken one of the biggest cattle-rustling rings in southwest Texas.

"You should appreciate the things she taught me," John told her.

Tess felt her face reddening. "Oh, I do, Mr. Hawkins."

John kept a firm hand to her waist as they turned to a slow waltz. "At any rate, I will never really *like* dancing. More than anything, I hate having to wear these clothes. And these damn new boots are killing my feet."

"Well, it won't be much longer. We can leave soon. It's already dark, but we can make it several miles yet tonight."

"I think we'll go stay at Jenny's tonight, if she has a room for us. We'll head home after light."

Tess frowned. "We've never stayed in town, no matter how late it gets. Why do you want to stay this time? It's only a couple hours' ride home, and we have the buckboard. The children can sleep in the back on the way, and plenty of men came with us."

"I know, but I would rather stay the night this time."

"At *Jenny's?* Missing your old girlfriend?" Tess teased.

John shrugged. "Maybe."

The music ended, and Tess followed him off the temporary dance floor that had been constructed inside the barn. All evening she had sensed there was something bothering her husband, although he had remained jovial and supposedly relaxed. Still, he had not eaten nearly as much as he usually did at potluck banquets. It took a lot of food to keep a man John's size fueled, but he'd seemed uninterested tonight. She tugged at his arm, pulling him away from others. "Out with it, John Hawkins. What is the *real* reason you don't want to go back tonight?"

He rolled his eyes and stepped away.

"John?"

He turned and looked her over. "Have I told you how beautiful you look in that pink dress?"

"Yes. Quit trying to change the subject."

Their conversation was interrupted when Honor ran up to her father, asking to be picked up yet again. John obliged her, and the little girl put her head on his shoulder. "I'm tired, Daddy."

"I know." John patted her bottom. "How would you like to go stay with Aunt Jenny tonight?"

"Okay," Honor answered sleepily. "I like Jenny. She tells funny stories."

John turned to Tess, and she gave him a chastising look. He never broke a promise to Honor, which meant they *had* to stay at Jenny's tonight, no matter what. And she suspected he was grateful for the interruption to their conversation. "You might have got your way for the moment, Mr. Hawkins, but I still want an explanation."

"I'll explain when we get there and get the kids to sleep. Ken went over there, and he might as well be in on the conversation. Even Jenny should."

Tess felt alarm move into the pit of her stomach. "All right. Let's go right now then. I'll go and get Tex, and he can help me carry the baskets we brought."

"I'll get the buckboard."

John walked out with Honor still resting on his shoulder. Tess gathered their things and said her good-byes to friends, many of whom sincerely wished her and the family well.

"You tell John we hope he finds lots of new calves out on the range during roundup," Doc Sanders told Tess. Mary Sanders embraced her.

"I'm so happy to see *you* so happy, Tess. You have such beautiful children, and they are so mannerly. Whoever would have thought John Hawkins would turn out to be such a good family man and father?"

Tess smiled and squeezed her hand. She longed to tell the doctor about her new pregnancy, but the chance did not present itself, and John would be concerned if he knew she'd seen the doctor. "He certainly is different from the man I met nine years ago!" She kept her smile, even though the comment brought back flashes of horror over the way John had found her . . . and the ruthless way he'd killed the men who held her captive. She gave Tex a basket to carry and led him outside to the wagon, where Honor sat half-asleep in her father's lap.

"I'll drive," she told John. "That way you can keep holding Honor. Maybe we'll be able to lay her on a bed when we get to Jenny's, and she'll just sleep the rest of the night."

Tex set the pie basket in the wagon and climbed in, always

refusing help from his mother because he was "too big" for such things. Tess climbed up onto the seat and took up the reins.

"Why do I have a feeling Ken already knows what this is about, and by now Jenny probably does, too. I don't like being the last to know, John."

"I know that. It couldn't be helped. I didn't want to ruin a good time."

Tess snapped the reins to get the horses moving. "Well, *that* makes me feel better." She headed the wagon toward Jenny Simms's boardinghouse, a neat, white-frame structure north of town. Jenny had the house built with money she'd earned running a saloon for years. Tess had no doubt some of that money was earned by means even less reputable than running a saloon. Jenny worked hard now at running a "respectable" business, and she did well with the boardinghouse, which contained ten separate rooms for guests as well as Jenny's own room, a parlor, library, and quite a large kitchen, where Jenny served breakfast and supper to her guests, but not lunch.

Oil lamps on posts burned along the walkway from the hitching posts and along a fence to the front porch, which was swept clean and painted bright blue to match the trim and shutters of the house. John climbed down, holding Honor in one arm, using his other hand to help tie the horses.

"I'll come out and unhitch them later."

Tex jumped out of the back of the wagon, running up the steps and sitting in a porch swing while his parents knocked on the front door. After a few minutes' wait, Tess sighed impatiently.

"We shouldn't have done this, John. Ken is here, and you know what they're probably doing. I feel embarrassed bothering them."

The door opened then, and Jenny stood there holding a heavy cotton robe closed with one hand.

"Do you greet *all* your boarders this way?" John asked teasingly.

Jenny's eyes widened in surprise. "John! Tess! What on earth are you all doing here?"

"Got a room for the night?" John asked.

Jenny looked John over, her surprise turning to a teasing smile. "Well, I could answer that one in a lot of ways, but then your wife is with you." She opened the door wider, and John walked in, still carrying Honor. Tess knew Jenny too well to be offended by the remark she'd made to John. The woman liked to kid with both of them about her relationship with John in his wilder days. Tess knew that in her heart, Jenny Simms loved John Hawkins, and that would never change. But Jenny respected John's marriage, and there had been moments after John saved Tess from *Comancheros* when she was not sure what she would have done without Jenny Simms's help and understanding.

Tess ordered Tex off the swing, and the boy followed everyone inside. Jenny embraced Tess. "How are you doing, honey?"

Tess caught the whiff of a strong perfume only women like Jenny wore. "Fine, I think." She pulled away. "John refused to go home tonight. He wants to wait till morning, but he hasn't told me why yet. I'm sorry to interrupt your evening this way."

"Oh, it's no bother." Jenny released her hug and stood back, pulling her robe even closer around herself. "Lord, I must look a mess. I planned to fix up my hair and face and get dressed before most of my roomers returned from the dance. Ken came over and—well, you know."

She shrugged, and Tess felt a flush of embarrassment warm her cheeks.

"When are you going to marry the poor guy?" John asked.

"Oh, I'm not fit to marry a good man like that, and you know it." Jenny tucked a few strands of hair behind her ear. The rest hung in straggles from what was once a neat twist at the back of her head. A good deal of gray could be seen at the roots of her bleached blond tresses. "Listen, there's a little room behind the kitchen with a couple of cots in it. I only use it when I'm full up and I get a guest who doesn't care much about a fancy room. The kids can sleep in there. I'll go change the linens in my room and you two can sleep in there."

"Oh, Jenny, you don't have to go to all that work. If you're filled up, John and I can sleep on the floor in the parlor or something," Tess told her.

"I wouldn't think of it. Ken can bunk out in the horse barn. There's fresh hay out there. I'll give him some blankets. I'll just sleep on a couch in the parlor."

"Jenny, you really don't have to—"

"No arguing! You two put the kids to sleep and fix yourselves some tea or something. Ken and I will be in the kitchen soon. If my guests come back, they won't disturb us in there."

Jenny vanished down a hallway, and Tess looked up at John. "We're putting her out, John. And Ken shouldn't have to sleep in the barn! We should have just gone home or gotten a hotel room."

"You know Jenny. She doesn't mind a bit. Besides, she needs to be in on our conversation. And she's right about Ken. He can sleep anyplace. So can I, for that matter. Hell, the two of us slept in worse places than fresh hay in a barn when we rode together. Come on. Let's put the kids down."

With a sigh, Tess followed. "I didn't even bring clothes for staying over," she told him as she followed him through the kitchen into the back room.

"Lord knows Jenny probably has enough nightgowns for twenty women. I'm sure she has something you can sleep in."

Yes, Tess thought. There had been another time when Jenny helped her out with clothes. Until then, she had imagined Jenny Simms as an awful whore with whom no woman should associate. She'd discovered a very nice person under all the paint and feathers, a woman who truly cared, whose own background had been tragic and had led her to the kind of life most women abhorred.

John laid Honor on a cot and removed her shoes. She had slept through every movement and conversation, and now she curled into a little ball as John pulled the covers over her. Tex complained he would rather stay up with the "grown-ups," but John ordered the boy to stay put and go to sleep. Grudgingly, the boy crawled into the other cot, and Tess leaned down to kiss his cheek.

"Good night, Tex."

" 'Night, Mom."

"Good night, son." John reached down and smoothed back Tex's long, dark hair. With a sigh he looked over at Honor again, then looked down at Tess. "I love all of you so much," he told her.

Tess knew by the look in his dark eyes how troubled he really was. John Hawkins did not easily become so serious, expressing his love with such an urgent, desperate air. She put her arms about his waist and rested her face against his chest. "I know you do. Whatever is bothering you, John, you have to have faith that things will work out." She pulled away and looked up at him, and for a brief moment she saw the old John there, the ruthless Texas Ranger, the wild Indian, the man who could kill as easily as swatting a fly. Whatever was wrong, it was serious.

Eleven

Tess looked around Jenny's kitchen for cups and tea strainers. She found both, setting four cups out on the table, then measuring some tea out of a can into the strainers, putting one of the small strainers in each cup. John had said nothing since she sensed his anger and concern after putting the children to sleep. He sat at the table rolling a cigarette.

"You're awfully quiet," Tess told him. She took a kettle from the stove, left there by Jenny so there would be hot water available at all times for her guests.

"Just thinking," John answered.

Tess poured hot water into her cup and John's. "Well, I'll be glad when I learn what this is all about."

Ken came into the kitchen, smoothing his hair back with his hands and looking a little embarrassed. "You should have warned me, Hawk."

"Sorry to interrupt your, uh, pleasant evening," John answered, finally smiling a little.

"Yeah, well at least you gave me a *little* time alone with Jenny." Both men shared a grin, and John chuckled.

"You two," Tess grumbled, pouring water into Ken's cup. She could not help a little tinge of jealousy as she also filled Jenny's cup. Jenny came into the kitchen just then, still in a robe, but now her hair was retucked and her robe properly tied. She thanked Tess and sat down, and Tess took her own chair.

"All right," she told the other three. "It's time I knew what was going on. I'm not exactly the fainting flower here."

John sighed, keeping his cigarette between his lips as he ran a finger around the top of his cup. He stared at it a moment, then moved his gaze to Tess. "Sam Higgins escaped from a prison wagon up in Kansas, about three weeks ago. They think he's headed south with a couple other men who escaped with him."

Tess felt a tightness grip her stomach. She closed her eyes and leaned back in her chair. "Oh."

"If it was just me I had to worry about, I would have gone home tonight. But having you and the kids along . . . just in case Higgins is out there somewhere . . . I wouldn't want a bunch of shooting going on with Tex and Honor right in the middle of it. If we wait till morning, Ken can go with us. Captain Booth said he'd go along, too; and he's got a couple of extra men in town right now. They'll all go with us in the morning. Some of our own men will stay the night, so we'll have plenty of protection on the way home."

Tess nodded, staring at the checked tablecloth. "I see." She looked at John again. "He hates me worse than you, you know. If I hadn't survived that fire, I couldn't have told others who did it, and that he was in on the cattle-rustling ring. It's possible he could have gotten away with it, or at least escaped El Paso before others learned the truth."

"All water over the dam," Jenny offered. "The point is, what do you do after tonight?"

John and Tess still held each other's gaze. "What I'd *like* to do is go find the bastard myself and get it over with so I don't have to worry and wonder when he might show up behind my back," John said. He turned to Jenny. "But with spring roundup about to start, a ranch to run, a wife and children to look after, I can't do that."

"Not like the old days, huh?" Ken said.

John rose, walking over to peek in at the children. "No."

Tess studied him closely. She knew John Hawkins all too

well, felt his restlessness. She knew he could probably track down Sam Higgins just as easily as a coyote could smell out a rabbit. This situation left him torn between.

"We've both survived a lot of things, John. We'll survive this. Don't let Sam Higgins run your life now. Go out on roundup. Leave Ken and a few other men with me and the children. I will keep an eye on the children every second, and don't forget I'm pretty damn good myself with a rifle. Besides, I can't believe Higgins is crazy enough to try giving you trouble. If he's headed south, he's probably on his way to Mexico."

"That's my bet," Ken said.

John sighed, taking a long drag on his cigarette. "Not mine. I have no doubt where he's headed."

"Oh? How's that?" Ken asked.

John sat back down, taking one more drag, then smashing the cigarette out in an ashtray. He still had not touched his cup of tea. "Because of something I got a couple of years ago, something I never told anybody about because Sam Higgins was in prison and expected to stay there another ten or twelve years." He looked at Tess. "I never even told you."

Tess folded her arms. "Since when do you think you need to protect my poor, frail nerves?" she asked. "You know me better than that, John Hawkins!"

John rubbed his eyes and ran his hand through his hair and down to the piece of leather at the back that kept it tied. He pulled out the tie and let his hair fall over his shoulders. "I know. Life's been so good, I just didn't feel like bringing up Higgins's name, or anything else from the past." He leaned back in his chair, his long legs sprawling under the table. "I got a letter from Higgins, saying when he got out of prison, whether he escaped or served his full sentence, he was coming after me and you both. I won't go into all the dirty details. I burned the letter, but I felt like going to Yuma, Arizona, and murdering him right then and there. God knows I could give a shit about myself, or that Sam Higgins can threaten me and get away with it. But when he mentions the woman I love and my son . . ."

His hands moved into fists. "He doesn't even know about Honor. If he finds out we have a daughter, too . . ." He rose again, pacing.

"Lord God, heaven help the man who thinks to lay a hand on that little girl," Jenny said.

"I'd skin him alive, from his toes to the top of his head," John said in a dark, cold voice. "I know how to do it so that the man doesn't die until the last piece of skin is removed."

Tess shivered. She knew he meant every word.

"Remind me not to play with Honor anymore," Ken said. "If she ever gets hurt while I'm playin' with her, I'll be a sorry man."

The comment broke the mood enough that everyone chuckled, all except John, who finally sat down again. "So, what do *you* think I should do?" he asked Ken.

The man shook his head. "I agree with Tess. Let me and some of the other men keep watch while you go out on roundup. If Tess and the kids stay right close to the house at all times, I don't see what could happen."

"I'd have to hire some extra men to help with roundup."

"Then hire them. If you're talkin' money, I don't need my pay. You know that. All I need is Tess's good cookin'. I'll sleep right in the house every night. I can name two or three other men who work for you who would gladly forgo their pay to protect Tex and Honor while you're gone. We'll stock up on supplies so Tess won't have to make no trips into town, and Jenny can come out once in a while to see if she needs anything, and she can bring supplies out to her."

"Sure. I don't mind doing that," Jenny agreed. "Besides, I like coming to the ranch."

"You have a boardinghouse to run," John reminded her.

"I have good help. I have a Mexican woman, Julia Ruiz, who knows the routine here, helps with the wash, the cooking, all that. She can run the place whenever I'm not here. Besides, you know I'd sell my whole business in a minute, if I had to, if it means helping you and Tess."

"And Captain Booth will stay on top of things," Ken reminded John. "He'll let you know every detail of the progress they make. You know that. And he'll stop by once in a while to check on things. We can also let the officer know at Fort Bliss. They'll keep a check on things, too."

John glanced at Tess, then threw his head back with a deep sigh. "Yeah. Just like they kept watch on Tess and her father when *Comancheros* attacked their ranch all those years ago." He rose again. "We'll have to do most of the work ourselves. The trouble is, until we know for certain that Sam Higgins has been recaptured, we won't have a moment's rest. Even if he goes to Mexico, he could be going there just to find the kind of men he needs to do what he wants. He'll rob and kill his way south in an effort to collect the money he needs to pay such men. He's already robbed and rape—"

John glanced at Tess, and she realized he'd not meant to speak the words. "Yes? What else haven't you told me?"

John rolled his eyes in disgust with himself. He let out another long sigh. "Higgins and the men with him already attacked a ranch near where the wagon accident took place. They killed the owner, and they, uh, they raped the man's wife, then stole clothes, food, horses, saddles, money, anything of value they could find. They beat the woman and left two little kids alone there with a dead father and a wounded mother. The woman was found by neighbors. She described one of her attackers, and he fits Higgins's description. Before she described the others she slit her wrists."

"Dear God!" Tess gasped.

"She bled to death," John said. "Left two kids with no mother or father." He gripped the table, leaning closer to Tess. "Do you see now, the kind of men we're dealing with? They have no respect for women or for human life! And their likely leader, Sam Higgins, hates you *and* me! He already tried once to burn you and Tex alive! You saw the look in his eyes that day in court when you and I both testified against him. If we could have nailed him for murdering someone, he would have been hanged, with Dunlap and Caldwell; but since we couldn't prove anything like that, and since Higgins didn't take part directly in the cattle rustling, the sonofabitch got away with a prison sentence! I wanted nothing more than to see him hang with the other two, who I might add were in prison for various counts of rape and robbery, as well as assault." He straightened. "The other two men are named Truby Bates and Ronald Calhoun."

Tess stood up and faced John squarely. "Sam Higgins is a wanted man, John, and everybody in this area knows him by sight. He wouldn't dare come here. Captain Booth has probably already given you a good description of the two who are with him, *if* they are still with him, so we know what to watch for. And they might not even all be together still. Why should the other two care about Sam Higgins's grudge against us? They have clothes and money and horses. They will probably all go their separate ways, and Sam Higgins wouldn't dream of coming after you alone. What man in his right mind would do that?"

"She's right there, Hawk." Ken guzzled down his tea and rose. "You could be gettin' all worked up over nothin'."

John turned away and walked to the door between the kitchen and hallway. "Yeah. Could be." He headed out.

"John, where are you going?" Tess called to him.

"I need to go out and think."

The other three listened to his footsteps going down the hallway, listened to the door open and close. Tess closed her eyes and rubbed her forehead. "I haven't seen him like this in years. He's like a different person when something like this happens."

"Oh, I know that person real well," Ken told her. "So does Jenny."

"He'll get over it," Jenny told Tess. "This is so frustrating for him. He wants this over with, wants you and those kids out of danger. He'd like to go after those men himself, but he's got a family to support, a roundup to take care of. He doesn't know which way to go with this, and he's never had to worry about a family before. Give him some time, honey. He'll get his head straight on this thing and be back." She rose and put her hands on Tess's shoulders. "Why don't you go get some rest? I laid out a nightgown for you. Ken can go out and unhitch the horses and put them up, and I'll be sleeping close to the kitchen here, so I can look in on the kids. I love them both like my own, you know."

Tess nodded. "I know. Thanks, Jenny. I'll help with breakfast in the morning."

"Don't worry about it."

Tess looked at Ken. "He won't do anything stupid, will he? I mean, like heading out alone to try to find Higgins?"

Ken shook his head. "I don't think so, not till he knows a little more about this and has a firm idea what to do with you and the kids in the meantime."

Tess cast Jenny a sad smile. "He worries too much."

"Yeah, well, John Hawkins spent most of his life fighting to defend himself and his ma before she died," Jenny said. "Self-defense is all he knows, and getting rid of his opponent the quickest way he can is all he understands. He's been learning a different way to live, thanks to you." She squeezed Tess's shoulders. "Go on, now. Go to bed. He'll be back before the night's over."

Tess rose from her chair, facing Ken. "John Hawkins knows better than to baby me and my feelings. You tell him he'd better quit lying to me and hiding things from me from now on."

Ken chuckled. "I think you'll be sure to tell him that yourself. And you're right, Tess, when you said you'd get through this just fine. I believe you will."

Tess gave Jenny a quick hug. "Thanks for putting up with us tonight." She walked out and down the hallway to Jenny's bedroom, closing the door. The smell of Jenny's perfume reminded her of that "other" John her husband had been before he married her . . . just to give her son a legal name . . . to keep young Tex from being labeled a bastard.

Twelve

Tess felt hot, and restless. She threw back the bedcovers and got up to open a window, leaning out to see a few lights in town. Beyond that was only darkness.

Where was John?

The night seemed too quiet, in spite of the fact that she'd grown accustomed to the dead stillness of country life. Still, even in the country, she heard the distant sounds of coyotes, a horse whinny, an occasional bawling of a calf, the singing of night's insects. Here in town she heard none of those things, not even the tinkle of a piano in the distance, laughter, voices somewhere. But those sounds were from yesterday, a time when El Paso was small and less civilized. Now they had a good sheriff in Hank Potter, certainly more honest and sincere than the former Sheriff Sam Higgins!

"Damn him," she whispered, furious that the man had come back into her life as boldly as if he stood right in front of her. If not for this latest news, the pain of the past could be gone forever. All this talk of Higgins and his dealings with Jim Caldwell, the hanging of Caldwell and his foreman, Casey Dunlap . . . it all brought back other memories . . . memories of John lying near death with a bullet in his back . . . memories of her attack . . .

She shivered in spite of the heat and sat down on the bed, remembering how boldly John had walked into the *Comanchero* camp, as wild and sadistic-looking as the renegade Indians and

Mexican outlaws who held her there. How surprised she'd been to discover that the tall, wild-looking man with the straight, black hair and evil look in his dark eyes was a Texas Ranger, come to rescue her.

Then came the realization that the *Comanchero* named Chino had impregnated her. Her humiliation knew no bounds. And even though she should have still been mourning the loss of her first husband, she'd gone to John Hawkins, admitting she needed a husband, a man who could easily pass for the father of her child—a child who would most likely look Mexican or Indian. She never had been sure which race Chino was. Determined to make sure the baby she carried never suffered the same humiliation he'd suffered growing up a half-breed bastard, John married her, even though she could not promise she would ever love him or be a proper wife to him . . . and she truly thought she never could . . . until John Hawkins placed those big, strong arms around her and showed her a tender side of himself no one else would believe existed.

They became friends . . . and they became lovers. But before she married him she'd lived for a short while with the wealthiest rancher in the area, Jim Caldwell, who'd given her a temporary home. That was when she overheard a conversation one night, among Caldwell, his foreman, Casey Dunlap, and Sheriff Sam Higgins. That was when she learned Caldwell was at the head of a cattle-rustling scheme that only made him richer.

That was when she learned Sam Higgins was as crooked as a snake and was informing Caldwell of every move the Texas Rangers made. When John rode onto Caldwell land to investigate, he ended up shot in the back. Tess realized then that she truly loved him after all. Now the same thing could happen again, and she could not bear the thought of living without him.

Finally she heard the front door close, and she opened the door to Jenny's room and looked out into the hallway. She heard voices in the parlor. Jenny was talking to someone. Finally John appeared at the end of the hallway.

"John!" She ran down the hallway and was quickly swept into those familiar, strong arms. "Where did you go?"

He didn't answer at first. She wrapped her legs around his waist as he carried her back into the room and kicked shut the door. His lips met her own, and quickly she was lost in him. He needed her tonight. He needed to know she was alive and well and everything was all right. Tess needed the same from him. Neither of them had to say it aloud.

John laid her back on the bed without even removing his clothes. He pushed up the flannel gown Jenny had left for her, and Tess sat up slightly so he could pull it off over her head. He tossed it aside, his lips hardly leaving hers through all the other motions. He moved his own lips downward then, licking at her throat, moving down to savor her breasts, groaning with need as he raised up on one arm and unbuckled his belt, unbuttoned the dark cotton pants he'd worn to the dance.

"Don't say anything," he softly groaned. "Just don't say anything."

Without undressing any further, even still wearing his boots, he entered her depths with a swollen shaft that made Tess cry out with its hot hardness. She arched up to greet his thrusts, taking great joy in having him close and safe. He leaned down and explored her mouth, then rested his chin above her head and pounded into her almost desperately.

Tess pressed her fingers into the hard muscle of his upper arms, leaning up and kissing at his chest, tasting the salt of his perspiration, taking great joy in again discovering the pleasure of a man. John taught her things her first husband had never shown her, brought forth from her a desire her first husband never stirred. Each time this man mated with her, it was as glorious as the first time. After the horrors of the *Comancheros,* John Hawkins taught her the gentle side of a man again, taught her all the ways there were for a man to love a woman. And he'd called Tex his own from before the boy was even born. She loved him even more for that. He'd even helped *her* learn to love the baby she didn't think she wanted.

They moved in rhythmic passion for several minutes, and Tess relished the climax her husband always managed to bring to her deepest being. She gladly pulled him inside as deeply as possible, glorying in being able to please this man who before her had been pleased by wild prostitutes. Now he turned only to her for such pleasures.

He groaned her name then as his life pulsed into her. He held himself deep for several seconds before finally relaxing and moving to sit up. He removed his new boots and the black pants he still wore, then lay down beside her, saying nothing for the next few minutes. Tess waited, and finally, following a deep sigh, he spoke up.

"I love you, Tess. Let's not talk about the rest of it tonight."

Tess had no idea what decisions he'd made, what he planned to do next. She simply agreed that lying there in each other's arms was enough for now. She snuggled into his shoulder. "I love you, too," she whispered.

Thirteen

Lonnie dismounted in front of the sign reading JENNY'S ROOMING HOUSE. El Paso was much bigger than he'd expected, but that was good. The bigger the town, the easier for a man to go unnoticed.

He tied his horse and adjusted his hat, well aware of his good looks and wondering who "Jenny" was. He walked onto the porch, noticing lace curtains at the oval glass of the front door. He banged the brass knocker, and moments later an older woman, quite plump but showing traces of past beauty, opened the door. There was no mistake reading the quick look of appreciation in her eyes, and instantly he sensed that this woman liked men.

"Can I help you?" she asked with a smile.

Lonnie studied the painted lips. *Yessirree, this woman likes men.* "Yes, ma'am, I'm needing a room."

"Come on in." The woman stepped back to allow him inside. "How long do you intend to stay?"

"I'm not sure. I'm just kind of drifting around, looking for work. Know of any?" He followed the woman into a parlor, noticing an enticing sway to her hips, the walk of a woman accustomed to strutting for men.

"Oh, this time of year plenty of ranchers need help with roundup. I know one man in particular who's wanting to hire extra men for a while." She opened a ledger and handed it to him. "Sign your name. I have one room available till you find work. Three dollars a night, includes breakfast and supper and clean linens."

"Sounds fair." Lonnie took the book, signing Billy Williams. He handed it back to Jenny. "There you are, ma'am."

Jenny took a look. "Billy Williams." She met his eyes. "Where are you from, Billy?"

"Oh, men like me are from all over. No one special place."

Jenny closed the ledger and laid it aside. "Oh, everybody has *some*place to call home."

Lonnie leaned back in the satin brocade chair. "For me home is wherever I am at the time. For now it's El Paso. What about you? Have you always lived here, or did marriage bring you west from someplace else?"

Jenny chuckled. "Oh, circumstances brought me here, but it wasn't marriage. I've never been *any* man's wife."

Lonnie flashed her his most fetching smile. "And how could a pretty lady like yourself go all her life without a dozen different men asking for her hand in marriage?" He watched her sly smile.

"Well, Billy, I never said I hadn't been *asked*. I just said I've never married."

Lonnie shook his head. "Now why in the world not? Can't find a man to, uh, please you in all the right ways?" He looked her over with as much desire in his blue eyes as he could muster. He suspected this woman knew everybody in town and beyond. She could come in handy.

Jenny leaned forward, resting her elbows on her knees. "Don't try your sweet words on me, honey. You're young and handsome, and I know how you see me . . . as what I am. Getting old and fat, whatever beauty I once possessed fast fading. I'm no fool when it comes to men; so don't think that just because I run this place alone that I'm a lonely old woman who falls for pretty blue eyes and a devil of a smile." She rose and nodded toward the hallway. "Come on. I'll show you where your room is."

"Yes, ma'am." Lonnie removed his hat, telling himself he

had to begin thinking of himself as Billy Williams, had to respond to the name properly. Everything he did had to seem perfectly innocent and respectable. "I didn't mean to offend you, ma'am. You say you know men well, so that tells me something right there. And I've been a long time on the trail looking for work. You can't blame a lonely man for trying to spark the first decent-looking woman he's seen for a long time."

"Oh, I don't blame you. I just thought I'd set you straight. And there *was* a time when those eyes of yours would have melted me right down to a puddle." She opened a door. "Fact is, I've got a steady man now. I might even marry him. He's asked me enough times. His name is Ken Randall. Used to ride with the Texas Rangers."

Lonnie struggled not to show his delighted surprise. "That so? Now *there's* a famous bunch."

Jenny stood with one hand on the doorknob and the other on her hip. "They sure are. One of the best-known Rangers was John Hawkins, half-Indian, meaner than a hungry bear, wild as a wolf and merciless as Satan himself. Ever hear of him?"

"No, I don't think so, but then I've never been down in these parts, so that doesn't mean much. I sure wouldn't mind meeting him, though. Does he still live around here?" Lonnie walked into the room to look it over, hardly able to believe his luck.

"Sure does. Has a wife and two kids now. Runs a ranch east of El Paso. He's the one who's looking for help. My Ken used to ride with him. Works at John's ranch now. I can take you out there tomorrow if you want to see about a job. I know that over a week ago he was getting ready for roundup."

Lonnie faced her with a grin of sincere appreciation, more sincere than Jenny Simms could ever imagine. "I'd be obliged, ma'am. Much obliged." He looked around the room. "This is nice. I'll pay you your three dollars." He fished into his pocket. "By the way, where does a man go in this town for a cold beer and maybe a game of cards?" He handed out the money, and Jenny took it.

"Well, there was a time when he'd go to my saloon, but I

sold it to a gambler from Louisiana, name of Leonard Reed. It's called Reed's Oasis now, over on San Francisco Street. He put in a kitchen, so you can even eat steak there if you want."

"Well, I sure do thank you, ma'am." Lonnie made a point to stop in front of her, glancing down at her full bosom. "I sure do."

Jenny pushed at his chest. "Go find your saloon, Billy. And don't get so drunk that you can't get out of bed in the morning and go with me to the Hawkins ranch."

He gave her a wink. "I'll be ready. What time is breakfast?"

"Eight o'clock. And it's about a two-hour ride to the ranch. There's a horse barn out back where you can put up your horse for the night."

"Yes, ma'am. I'll bring in my things first, then go see about a steak and a beer." He turned and walked out, strolling down the hallway in big strides, suspecting Miss Jenny Simms was taking account of his fine build. He wondered how a woman like Jenny knew John and Tess Hawkins so well. Maybe in his single, wilder days John Hawkins was more than good friends with the woman. She exuded sexuality, a woman who obviously had been someone far from respectable at one time.

Fourteen

John noticed the approaching buggy as he rode in from the south pasture. Even though still at quite a distance, he thought he recognized Jenny's fancy rig, fringes around the canopy, a shiny black gelding strutting prettily as it pulled its mistress. He grinned at the sight of a bright green dress. In spite of now wearing dresses with more respectable necklines, Jenny still dressed colorfully whenever she went out. There was no mistaking now who was coming, but he frowned in curiosity that she would come out in the middle of the day like this . . . or that she would bother coming all this way at all when they had just seen and visited with her a week ago.

Two trusted men he had left to guard the house rode out to greet Jenny. John could see she had someone with her, and a horse was tied to the back of the buggy. He rolled and lit a cigarette, his distrust of any new face moving in to erase his recent joy at the birth of a new foal. He intended to come and tell Tex and Honor about the foal and take them out to see it, since he'd promised Tex that when Tulip delivered, the foal would belong to him . . . the first horse that would truly be all his own. Right now he intended to find out why in hell Jenny was bringing a stranger to Hawk's Nest. He took a deep drag on the cigarette and rode closer. Jenny was talking and laughing with the guards, and he heard her ask where Ken was.

"Ken's out in the north pasture mending a fence," Frank Fuller answered. Frank was another ex-Ranger who worked for John. He was getting old, but was still adept with gun and fist, and he'd turned out to be a dependable ranch hand. With him was Marv Tickner, a drifter who had ridden in two years ago looking for work. After checking all wanted notices and past arrest records with the sheriff in El Paso and with the Rangers, and finding nothing on Tickner, John hired him. He could never quite relax, knowing there were many men out there who still hated him. He did not worry so much for himself, but for Tess and the children.

"Hello, Jenny."

"John! Glad you happen to be here! I found you more help," Jenny answered in her usual robust voice. "This here is Billy Williams. He rode in yesterday and took a room, said he was looking for work. I didn't mind a chance to visit with Tess again, so I told him I'd bring him out myself so he could find the place easier. I know you need more men. This one's young and strong and eager." She laughed, slapping Billy on the shoulder.

John remained on his horse, his smile fading as he turned his gaze to Billy. There was something about the stranger's mouth, and the way he flashed that smile, that seemed familiar, but John could not quite place the man. Perhaps it was just coincidence, or maybe it was just his inability to trust anyone. He nodded to Billy, keeping his cigarette in his mouth. "Afternoon."

"Hello, Mr. Hawkins! Glad to meet you! Jenny has told me all about you once being a Texas Ranger and all. I'm proud to meet you."

"Is that so?" There was that smile again—too friendly. Young and handsome as he was, he was just the type Jenny would warm up to. "Where are you from?" John watched Billy's smile fade a little. He could tell by his eyes that he realized his line of bullshit did not impress John Hawkins.

"Well, sir, I'm kind of from all over. Been drifting since I was orphaned at twelve—odd jobs here and there."

"You know anything about cattle?"

"Sure I do. That's why I'm here. Jenny says you're ready for spring roundup."

"You ever been in trouble with the law?"

"No, sir. You can check me out if you want."

"John, don't be so rude," Jenny said with a laugh.

John dismounted, taking a last drag on his cigarette, throwing it down and stepping it out. "You know the problem, Jenny. You took a chance bringing him out here."

"Oh, don't be silly, John. He's just a kid."

"Jenny!" Tess came out of the house and hurried down the porch steps, followed by Tex and Honor. "How nice to see you again so soon! I hope you can stay a while and visit."

Honor climbed up on Jenny's lap and gave her a hug. She looked at Billy then and grinned. "Hi, mister."

"Honor get down from there!" John ordered. He turned to Billy. "Come with me to the bunkhouse. And I'll take that side-arm for now, that rifle on your horse, too."

Billy climbed down with a shrug. "Whatever you say, sir." He handed his gun over to John and walked around behind the buggy to untie his horse.

"John, who is this?" Tess asked him.

"Name's Billy Williams, ma'am," Lonnie answered before John could. He tipped his hat and nodded to Tess. "You must be Mrs. Hawkins. Jenny told me how pretty you are. She sure was right."

John walked over and jerked Billy's rifle from its boot on the man's horse. "Seems like Jenny told you an awful lot about us," he said, casting an angry glare at Jenny.

"John Hawkins! What is the matter with you?" Tess scolded.

"This man has come here looking for work." He kept his eyes on Billy. "He isn't here for an idle visit. In fact, Mr. Billy Williams, I think I'll have you ride right back to El Paso with Frank here. He can have the sheriff there check you out. If everything looks okay, come back with Frank tomorrow morning. I'll keep your firearms until you get back."

Billy scowled. "Heck, Mr. Hawkins—I mean, John—I just came here for a job, not to kill somebody."

"John, you are embarrassing me to death," Jenny protested.

"You know my reasons, Jenny. Go on inside with Tess and the kids."

Jenny climbed down, shaking her head. "Whatever you say." She lifted Honor into her arms. "Let's go in the house, little one."

"Mind if I ask what the heck is the problem?" Billy asked, folding his arms in front of him.

"Yes, I do mind," John answered.

Billy turned and mounted his horse with a deep sigh. Just then another ranch hand, Tom Decker, rode toward them at a hard gallop. He dismounted before his horse came to a full stop. "John! I think Tulip has another foal inside her! She's tryin' to give birth again, only this time the foal is turned. If we don't do somethin' quick, we're gonna' lose her *and* the foal!"

"Daddy, is Tulip having her baby?" Tex asked. "Can I go see?"

John feared the worst. "You'd better stay here, son. Tulip is having a little trouble, and we can help her better if you stay out of the way." He handed Billy's firearms to Frank and hurried over to mount his horse. "Go on to El Paso," he told Frank.

"Wait!" Billy protested. "If you're having trouble with a foal, let me help, John. I used to help my ma with things like that after my pa died. Give me a chance to show you what I can do."

John hesitated, glancing at Tom.

"I don't know who the hell he is, John, but if he can help, you might as well let him," Tom told him. "You know what Tulip means to Tex, and it's gonna take all three of us to help her."

John felt angry with all of them. He didn't like being put on the spot, but there was no time to waste. Against his better judgment he turned to Billy. "I've handled plenty of situations like this myself, but this horse is extra special to my son. Come on along. You can show me if you really know what the hell you're doing."

Billy again smiled in a way that made John uneasy.

"Sure thing!" he answered.

Tom rode off, and John waited for Billy to follow, deciding he was not ready to allow this newcomer to ride behind him. He followed both men, still angry with Jenny for bringing a stranger to Hawk's Nest.

Fifteen

Tulip whinnied and grunted in pain, her first foal stumbling about just a few feet away. Tom helped hold back the foal, which wanted to go to its mother to feed, and John held Tulip's head, trying to calm the mare while Lonnie reached inside the horse to try to turn the second foal in her uterus.

Lonnie glanced at John Hawkins every chance he could. He was indeed an intimidating man, damned well built for his age. No one needed to take the chance of testing him to know John Hawkins was tough. The years since leaving the Rangers had not dulled his edge. It was not going to be easy to bring such a man down, but already he understood some of John's soft spots. His wife and son were number one on the list, and, of course, his little girl.

Then there was this horse—more like a family pet than just one of the remuda. Helping deliver this foal was important toward his own goal of winning John Hawkins's confidence. He'd offered to do the delivering, suggesting John would be the better one to keep the horse calm, since Tulip knew him. He was just glad that he had done this once before, only not for his mother. It was for a rancher in Arizona who just happened to steal his stock rather than raise his own. Lonnie made good money keeping him supplied.

"I feel it turning," he told John. "I'm doing the best I can, John. Just don't let Tulip give me a swift kick."

Because of the hot sun, John quickly removed his shirt. "I'll try my best," he answered. He leaned over Tulip, speaking softly to the horse in Spanish.

Lonnie gritted his teeth, getting hold of the foal's head and beginning to pull hard. "I figured you to be part Indian," he told John, "not Mexican."

"I *am* part Indian—Sioux. But nobody lives in Texas without knowing Spanish. You'll have to learn some yourself if you're going to ride with my men. Half of them are Mexican, and just as a note of warning, I don't keep any man on who has something against them. My Mexicans are my best help."

Tulip reared slightly, and both men perspired in the Texas heat as they worked with her. Again the weather had turned unusually warm for the time of year.

"Here it comes!" Lonnie announced. He kept pulling, and finally the foal emerged in one kicking, slippery bundle. Lonnie fell back on his rear and threw out his arms. "Whew!" He rolled away slightly as Tulip suddenly got to her feet and zealously shook her mane before turning to begin licking membrane off her second foal. "Look at that! How in hell can she get up that easy after an ordeal like that!" Lonnie exclaimed. "Hell, it was harder on us than on her. A minute ago you would have thought she was dying." He felt a hint of relief when John actually smiled.

"That's an animal for you. Too bad it isn't that easy for a woman."

So, Lonnie thought, *little miss Tess had a hard time of it with one of your kids. Yes, sir, the woman and kids are his weak points, just like I figured.*

Tom let go of the first foal, and it immediately went to its mother to nurse, while the mother continued to lick the second foal clean.

"They actually both look healthy," Tom commented. "Who would have thought?"

John nodded. "Wait till Tex sees this. He'll be so excited. This is the start of his own herd. I told him Tulip and any foals she births belong to him."

"Hey, that's real nice," Lonnie told him. "He looks like a great kid." He saw John's smile fade slightly, saw the look of wariness return to his dark, discerning eyes.

"He is."

Lonnie felt a chill. John Hawkins was one bad sonofabitch. This situation was going to take all the charm and lies he could muster. Hawkins was not the kind of man who was easily fooled. God, how he'd like to shoot him on the spot, but that would be too quick and easy. He wiped sweat from his brow with the back of his arm. "Say, uh, earlier—what you said about any man working for you better not be against Mexicans or Indians. Does that mean I've got the job?"

John sat and watched the first foal feed. "Let's just wait till Frank gets back from El Paso. You can stay at the bunkhouse tonight. I will say you have a couple of things going for you. You helped save that foal, and you didn't argue about letting me take your firearms." He looked at Lonnie. "And keep your eyes off my wife."

So! Hawkins had a jealous streak. Maybe it was because his wife was white, and he was Indian. And Tess Hawkins looked much younger than her husband. "I didn't mean any offense. It was just a compliment." Lonnie reminded himself not to look away when John was addressing him. A man like John would take that to mean he had something to hide.

John got to his feet. "All right." He took a leather band from his hair and shook his hair loose, then retied it. "Sorry for the rudeness, Billy, but I'm being extra careful for a while. An old enemy of mine escaped from a prison wagon a few weeks ago, and I'm worried he'll try to harm my wife and kids in retaliation for me proving he helped in a cattle-rustling ring. He also set fire to my house years back—came close to burning up my wife and son."

Lonnie shook his head. "That's awful. I hope they catch him."

"Yeah, so do I."

John picked up his shirt and headed for his mount. Lonnie

watched him for the moment his back was turned, noticing a scar there, too, no doubt the result of being shot in the back. Too bad he didn't die then. It would have saved him a lot of heartache. He grinned and rose, turning to the ranch hand who'd helped with the foal. "We haven't officially met, what with all the commotion here. I'm Billy Williams, and I'm here to see about a job."

Tom grinned in return, putting out his hand. "Tom Decker. You like to play cards? Me and the boys have a game goin' tonight."

"Sure. I'm game. Long as the boss doesn't mind."

"John?" Tom laughed and shook his head. "The only thing he minds is dishonesty—and speakin' against Indians and Mexicans. 'Course he went after plenty of both when he was a Ranger, but them was the ones who broke the law—mostly horse thieves, rapists, bank robbers, and the like. I'll tell you, any man with John Hawkins on his ass knew he'd run out of luck and his days was numbered."

"That so?" Lonnie mounted up. "Well, then, I'll be sure to stay on his good side." He tipped his hat to Tom. "Thanks for the invite to play cards." He rode toward the ranch house, hoping to get another look at Tess Hawkins. A mighty fine-looking woman, that one.

Sixteen

"John is angry with me." Jenny took two pins from her wide-brimmed hat and set it on a chair, then quickly looked at herself in a mirror that hung next to coat hooks near the door.

"Oh, I imagine you are right about that," Tess answered. "I think he is even a little upset with me." She laughed lightly and walked to her iron cookstove to remove a teapot that still held warm water from the recent lunch she'd shared with John and the children. "He will get over it. Besides, Billy Williams seems harmless enough."

"Yeah, well, I'm still a softie when it comes to handsome young men like that one, and he's polite as hell."

Tess set two cups and saucers on the table. "Don't let Ken hear you say that. The poor man dearly wants to marry you, Jenny. When are you going to take the big step?"

Jenny's smile faded. "Ken is way too good for me. Let's talk about something else." She sat down and let Honor climb onto her lap. Tex sat down beside her. "So, kids, Tulip's having a baby, is she?"

"Something is bad wrong, I think," Tex answered Jenny despondently.

"Oh, you know your pa, Tex. He's good at fixing just about anything that goes wrong."

Tess set tea strainers on the table, thinking how right that comment was. John had "fixed" a terrible wrong in her own life. "Your father will know what to do, Tex. And he has plenty of help. How about a cookie or a piece of apple pie while we wait?"

"I'll have a cookie!" Honor spoke up with childish unconcern for Tulip. "My dolly wants one, too."

"Is that so?" Jenny laughed. "You wouldn't be trying to trick your mommy into giving you two cookies, would you?" She tickled the child's tummy, and Honor giggled.

"I'm gonna go sit on the steps and wait for Pa," Tex told them, getting up from the chair and heading for the door.

"Don't go out to where Tulip is until your father says it's all right," Tess ordered.

Tex left, and Jenny shook her head. "He's really attached to that horse, isn't he?"

Tess carried the teapot over and sat down at the large round pine table John had specially made for her by a carpenter in El Paso. "Shadow, too," she answered. "But Tulip is special because her foals will be Tex's horses, free and clear. It will be good for Tex, give him some responsibility. Besides, he's as natural and adept around horses as John is." She poured hot water into Jenny's cup and pushed a can of tea leaves over to her place setting. "I'll let you fix your own tea as strong as you like. I hope you intend to stay and eat supper with us. It's the least we can do for barging in on you and Ken the other night. I still feel bad about that."

"Don't be silly. You couldn't help it. When John makes up his mind to do something, he does it. I know that. There's no arguing with John Hawkins." She pinched some tea leaves into her strainer. "As far as staying to eat supper and maybe staying overnight, that all depends on how angry your husband is with me."

Tess smiled as she stirred her own tea. "I feel sorry for poor Billy Williams. John can be so intimidating at times, and Billy has no idea what he is angry about."

"I want my cookie, Mommy," Honor spoke up.

"All right. You may take two out of the cookie jar, but you

have to take them to your room and play with Dolly so your Aunt Jenny and I can talk."

"Okay!" Honor gave Jenny a kiss on the cheek and climbed off her lap, running to the pantry to take out the cookies.

"That child is such a treasure," Jenny said with a sigh.

Tess lovingly watched Honor to make sure she took only two cookies. "She is. And she has big, mean John Hawkins wrapped right around her little finger."

Jenny gave out a hearty laugh. She glanced around the room then, admiring the large stucco structure, one very big central room with a kitchen on one end and a sitting room on the other, decorated with stuffed chairs, a divan, and two rockers. Potted plants were placed decoratively, and braided rugs brightened the clay tile floor. Curtains made of Spanish lace graced the windows. Wooden shutters that folded back for light but could be closed for protection outlined the windows. Two bookshelves filled tightly with books were placed on either side of the stone fireplace at the sitting-room end of the great room, and another grand fireplace sprawled across the kitchen end of the room. Doors to four bedrooms at the back of the house opened into the great room. The house was grand and spacious, yet simple and lovely, fitting for both a big man who cared little for feminine decorating; yet tidy, and lovely enough for a woman like Tess.

"This place sure fits both of you," Jenny told Tess. "I sure never thought I'd see John living like this."

Tess sipped some tea. "I think he's still a little astounded at all of this himself." She sighed and met Jenny's gaze. "You know him as well as anyone, Jenny. Do you think he misses his old life?"

Jenny's eyebrows arched in surprise. "John? Oh, my dear, no!"

Tess stared at her cup. "Sometimes I fear it will return to steal *him* away from me—not from him going back to it, but through death. I'll never forget how it felt to think he would die from that bullet in the back."

"Hey, honey, that was a long time ago. This is now, and so far nobody has heard from Sam Higgins. Hell, he's in Mexico by now. Bet on it."

Tess studied Jenny's still-pretty blue eyes. "I'd like to."

"Well, just in case, I have an idea to help protect you and the children while John is gone bringing in cattle for the next week or two. Why not have Tex and Honor come into town and stay with me? Tex can help haul wood and tend the guests' horses, and Honor can help me with laundry and cooking and all. She loves doing that kind of stuff. I'll keep them busy and entertained, and they would be right in town, where there's a sheriff and lots of people. Sam Higgins wouldn't dare show his face within a hundred miles of here. I would enjoy being with the kids. I don't get to see them nearly often enough. What do you think?"

Tess pondered the offer. "I really don't know. I'll have to talk to John about it. But thank you so much for the offer. It would relieve John's mind greatly while he's gone to know the children are in a safe place."

"Well, then, your problem is solved. All we have to do is convince John."

"He's coming!" Tex interrupted, yelling from outside the screen door. "Pa's coming!"

Tess prayed John was bringing good news. She hurried out after Tex, relieved to see John dismount and pick the boy up in his arms with a smile on his face.

"Tulip not only had one baby, son, but two! Twins! A male and a female. How about that?"

"Two?" Tex let out a yell of happiness. "Can I see them?"

Billy rode up behind them, and John turned to greet Tom Decker, who also approached. "Tom, take Tex out to see his new foals," John said. He plunked Tex onto the man's horse, and Tex let out another cry of happiness as Tom rode off with him.

"I wanna go see, too, Mommy," Honor told Tess, who only then realized her daughter stood beside her.

"You will get your turn, Honor. This is a special time for your brother. Why don't you go to the henhouse and see if any of the chickens have laid more eggs? If you can find six more eggs, it will be the most you've ever collected in one day. You can help me fix some for your father in the morning like I promised."

Honor turned and ran into the house, and Tess heard John telling Billy Williams to go to the bunkhouse and wait for him there. He thanked the man and shook his hand.

"Looks like Billy was a help after all," Jenny said from behind the screened porch door.

"Looks like," Tess said contemplatively.

Honor ran outside then, shouting to her father that she would cook his eggs in the morning. John glanced at Tess as he walked closer, his shirt draped over his shoulder. "That should be interesting," he told her.

Tess smiled. "Well, however they taste, you be sure to tell her how good they are. Besides, all I'll do is let her scramble them and pour in a little milk. She is far too young to let her do any cooking by herself." She looked deeper into her husband's eyes when he stepped up onto the porch and stood in front of her. "So, it went well?"

John sighed, leaning against a support post. "The second foal needed turning. I kept Tulip calm while Tom kept the first foal out of the way. Billy managed to turn the second foal and pull it out."

"So he *did* know what to do."

John turned to watch Billy dismount in front of the bunkhouse. "Yeah." He faced her again. "He seems friendly enough, wants to work. I guess if I hire him, it will give me one more man to help out on roundup, which will free up one more to stay here with you and the kids."

"I can see by your eyes that you still have doubts."

John glanced out at the bunkhouse again. "I don't know why. It's just something about that smile of his. It reminds me of somebody, but I can't think who." He turned his attention to Tess again. "And he's too damned nice."

Tess smiled and shook her head. "Since when is it a crime to be nice?"

He grasped his shirt and handed it to her. "Since I decided I don't dare trust anyone for a while." He stepped off the porch and walked over to a hand pump. He vigorously pumped the handle, then held his hands under the spigot, rinsing his hands and arms, then filling his hands with water and splashing it over his face and neck. He held his head under the running water and let its coolness run through his hair.

He straightened then, shaking his wet hair behind his shoulders.

"Still a damn well-built man, isn't he?" Jenny said from behind the screen door.

Tess turned to her. "Jenny Simms, you just never change, do you?"

"Oh, I'm getting too old to change."

John tied his wet hair back into a tail with a rawhide cord. "I need a clean shirt," he told Tess, walking back onto the porch. He followed her inside, where he gave Jenny a scolding look. "I'm not through with *you* yet."

Jenny looked him over. "Oh, I hope not."

John only scowled. "Sit down."

The warm, dry afternoon air had already dried his skin. Tess walked into a bedroom to get him a clean shirt while Jenny took a chair, facing John when he sat down across the table from her.

"I'm sorry if I made you angry, John Hawkins, but I was only trying to help."

John leaned back in his chair, folding powerful arms across his chest. "I know that. But for one thing, you took a chance driving out here with a perfect stranger."

Jenny could not help breaking into robust laughter. "You know damn well, John Hawkins, that there isn't one thing a man can do to me that hasn't already been done."

Tess brought a shirt out to John, laying it over the back of a chair. John remained sober. "Oh? Well, one hasn't killed you yet."

Jenny's smile faded. "I am touched by your concern, my sweet man, but you don't really think that nice young man out there is capable of killing a *woman,* do you? And why on earth would he want to?"

John rubbed at tired eyes. "I don't know what to think of that *nice young man* as you keep calling him. I will probably hire him, but I am going to keep an eye on him for a while. I'm just warning you that if he had been using you to help him find me, and intended to bring me or my family harm, he might have killed you because you would have been the only one to know he came out here, the only one who could identify him."

Jenny frowned. "Once a Ranger, always a Ranger. Quit worrying, John. No man in his right mind is going to go up against you. Besides, I have a plan to help you stop worrying about Tess and the kids during roundup. How about sending them in to El Paso? They can stay with me, and Ken could come, too. There isn't a man alive you trust more than Ken. It would give him and me some time together, something we don't get enough of, and it would free up all your men for roundup instead of having to leave some here to guard your family. Send someone out to find Ken and have him come back here and accompany me and Tess and the kids back to town. They'd have the whole town to watch out for them, sheriff and all. Sam Higgins wouldn't think of coming anywhere *near* El Paso. They couldn't be in a safer place."

John studied her for several quiet seconds, then slowly nodded. "Not a bad idea. I just might forgive you for bringing Billy Williams out here." He directed his gaze at Tess. "You've already talked about this?"

"Yes. But I don't like the idea of letting my house go uncleaned for that long. And what about milking the cows and gathering the eggs and—"

"The Mexican women can do that. They already help you

with some of the chores. And with most of their men gone out on roundup, they will welcome the extra work to keep them busy."

"I suppose. I just don't like the idea of someone like Sam Higgins forcing me out of my own home."

"I don't either," John answered, "but I see no other option during roundup. It won't be all that long. Before you know it you'll be back home. I'll have someone ride out and find Ken and bring him back here. He can accompany you and Jenny back to town."

Tess always hated their time apart every spring. Having to leave the ranch would only make her miss him even more, but she understood that this time there was little choice. "You will have a time of it getting Tex to leave Tulip and her foals behind."

"I'll find a way to make him understand."

Tess felt pain stab her heart. "I'm more worried about you than about us," she told John. "It was one of the men who worked with Higgins who shot you in the back, don't forget."

"Oh, I'm not likely to *ever* forget that, or the fact that they came close to burning you and Tex alive!" John rose and put on his shirt. "You might as well start thinking about what you will need to take with you to El Paso."

He reached down and squeezed her shoulder reassuringly. Tess knew he hated to be apart as much as she did. But if going to El Paso would help relieve his mind during the hot strenuous work of roundup and branding, and especially if it meant the safety of their children, she had no choice but to go. Besides, there was no arguing the matter with John.

She could not stop the lump from forming in her throat. "All right," she answered quietly. "I'll start packing."

Seventeen

"I don't like this, John. Sam Higgins would think nothing of shooting you in the back if he got the chance. What if something happens to you? El Paso is over two hours away."

They walked together under a black sky alive with millions of brilliant stars. John squeezed Tess's hand. "The important thing is keeping the children safe. We should have the new calves rounded up and herded back here for branding within a couple of weeks, three at the most."

Tess leaned her head against his arm. "I haven't been away from this place for more than three *days* since we came here to start our life together. Nothing seems right about any of this."

"I don't know what else to do until I know if Higgins has been found. If I didn't have a family and this ranch to take care of, I'd sure as hell go find him myself and get this over with. I'd go clear to South America if I had to."

Tess stopped and leaned against a wooden fence. "I know you would."

John bent closer and kissed her eyes. "What I hate worst about roundup, whether you're here or in El Paso, is being away from you for so long."

He met her mouth, and Tess could feel the heat of his desire as his lips parted to savor her mouth. He had a way of kissing her that made her feel totally under his control. He moved his lips down over her neck.

"John, we have company in the house."

He wrapped her closer in his strong arms, lifting her slightly off the ground. "Why do you think I suggested we go for a walk?"

"John Hawkins, we can't just lie in the dirt and—"

"I know."

John whisked her up in strong arms, and Tess laughed. "Where are you taking me?"

"We can't tell each other good-bye for close to three weeks without making love."

"But where—"

"That new shed I just had built. I told you it was for tools, but it's really a surprise for Honor. Tex has horses now to call his own. Honor should have something, too, so I have two little lambs ordered for her from Jack Luden's sheep ranch. The shed is for the lambs."

"Oh, John that's *wonderful!* Why didn't you tell me?"

"I intended to surprise you both and just have the lambs brought over after roundup." He kissed her quickly when he reached the shed and kicked open the double doors that led inside. "At any rate, there's fresh hay in here, and I stole some blankets from one of the bunkhouses."

Tess gasped when he dropped her into the haystack. He closed the doors, and she could hear him latching them.

"Nobody will find us in here, and I told Jenny not to expect us back till morning."

"Jenny? John, you know how she will tease us in the morning, the suggestive remarks she will make!"

"I told her not to say a damn thing." By dim light that peeked through an open window at the back of the shed, Tess could see her husband removing his clothes.

"John, I've hardly had time to think about this."

He laughed lightly as he bent over to pull off his boots. "You've thought about nothing else since I said you had to go stay at Jenny's. You don't fool me, Tess Hawkins."

Off came his denim pants, his underwear. Tess drew in her breath. "I'll be a mess in the morning."

A naked John Hawkins went to his knees, straddling her. "You sure as hell will."

He met her mouth again in a demanding, heated kiss, and what little protest was left in Tess vanished. How did he always manage to do this to her? In this man's arms she became completely helpless. He made her burn clear down to her toes.

She'd grown up never knowing making love with a man could be like this. Sometimes the painful memory of her first husband revisited her, his lack of passion, his cowardliness the day the *Comancheros* attacked their ranch. John Hawkins sure as hell would never have hidden under a bed while his wife tried to defend herself against savage raiders! That memory had always made it difficult to mourn Abel Carey. Not one thing about the man could compare to the one who undressed her now. John's passion in taking his woman equaled his passion for justice; and he mated with the same power and wild determination as he wielded gun and knife.

John never left her doubting if he found her attractive, or if he desired her. At first she found his lovemaking almost startling in its energy and forthrightness. What other women might consider shameful, John Hawkins made beautiful. At women's meetings in town she had sometimes heard women whisper and giggle about making love in the dark, under the covers. Once a woman commented that she wondered what a man looked like naked. John Hawkins left no doubt. To him, nakedness when making love was as natural as breathing, and he had taught her never to be ashamed of her own nakedness. He took great pleasure in it, and the way he savored every part of her with lips and tongue, the way he explored every curve and valley, the way he tasted and cajoled and drove her near to madness with her own desire made her nearly burst with her own wicked passions.

Every inch of her skin came alive as he touched and explored, making her moan with a great need that only John Hawkins could fulfill. "John . . ."

Simply speaking his name was all he needed. He kissed his

way back up to her throat, her ear. "Tess . . ." he whispered in reply.

She gladly allowed his powerful body to move between her legs, and she drew in her breath when he filled her deep and full, moving rhythmically, teasing her senses, pulling every ounce of passion and need from her soul until she became lost in him, unaware of where they were, unaware of the dark night, their disagreement over Billy Williams, the embarrassment she would suffer in the morning.

None of those things mattered. John was going away. She and the children were also going away. She did not want to go so far. She did not want to tell him good-bye. But if it had to be, then she would make sure he knew how much she loved him. She arched up to him in naked splendor, whispering his name again, grasping his powerful arms and thinking what a grand specimen of man he was.

For several minutes he drew forth every ounce of pleasure she could enjoy, bringing her to a breathtaking climax that made her lean up and search for his lips, groan when his mouth found hers in a hot, desperate kiss. Finally his life surged into her, and briefly she wondered if now she should tell him about the baby.

No. The news could wait until after roundup.

John relaxed half on top of her with a deep sigh. "I'll miss you, but at least I won't have to worry about you," he said. "You understand, don't you?"

"I understand."

For the next few minutes they enjoyed the precious closeness, then John moved on top of her again.

"I won't be able to get enough of you tonight, Tess Hawkins."

She pushed some of his dark hair back from his face. "Then take all of me that you need."

Eighteen

Truby Bates kept his hat pulled low over his eyes as he rode into El Paso, determined to draw as little attention to himself as possible. Per Sam's instructions, he'd made a point to dress like a simple cowhand drifting through town. A saddle blanket hung just far enough over his horse's rump to hide the brand there, and the handgun he'd purchased in another town was packed in his gear.

Just as Lonnie told him to do, he headed for the telegraph station, which a passerby told him also served as a post office. He hoped a message from Lonnie would be waiting there for him.

He dismounted, nodding to two women who walked past. He tied his mount and walked up onto the boardwalk that led to the entrance to the telegraph office, greeting the telegrapher with a friendly smile. "Afternoon."

"Afternoon, mister. What can I do for you?"

"Well, sir, a friend of mine told me a while back that he wanted to head down this way—said he'd leave me a message at the telegraph office and let me know where he was. I don't even know if he decided to settle in here for a while, but I just finished up workin' for a farmer up in Oklahoma and thought I'd come this way and see if I can track Billy down—Billy Williams. That's his name. Did somebody by that name happen to come through here and leave something for me? My name is Jeb Hansen."

Joe frowned. "He a young man? Good-looking?"

Truby laughed lightly. "That's Billy, all right. You've seen him?"

"Yes, I have." Joe looked around under the counter for a moment. "A young man named Billy was in here just yesterday, in fact, in a big hurry, he was—said he had only one day to spend in town before going out on a roundup—new job he got here."

"Oh, yeah? Who's he workin' for? Maybe I can get a job there, too."

"Oh, apparently John Hawkins has all the help he needs. I think he and his men already headed out today to ride the back fences and see what they can find. John has several thousand acres now. Quite a story there, him marryin' Tess Carey after he rescued her from *Comancheros* and all. Nobody ever expected John Hawkins to marry and settle—ever—let alone to a pretty, educated woman like Tess, but then she was never quite the same after what happened to her."

Truby forced himself not to show his surprise and joy at the news—Billy was actually working for John Hawkins! Things could not be working out better.

"Comancheros?"

"Yes, sir." Joe, a gangly, homely man with a large Adam's apple, found the letter and handed it to Truby. "If you want to know the truth"—he leaned forward, resting his elbows on the counter—"some folks believe their son, Tex—he was born only about eight months after she was rescued—some folks believe he don't belong to John Hawkins. They think the kid was fathered by one of the *Comancheros,* and that was why Tess married John Hawkins—so's the kid would look like his father, on account of the *Comancheros* is mostly Indian and Mexican, and Hawkins is half-Indian himself."

Truby felt as though he had hit a gold mine. Joe was apparently one of the town gossips. He shook his head, pretending unconcern. "Well, I don't know any of them, and I don't much care why Hawkins married the woman. I'm just glad to know

Billy got himself a job there. I expect I'll look for work here in town. I'll leave a message for Billy on where to find me, so's next time he comes in, after roundup, we can find each other. Soon as I find me a room, I'll come back with a letter to leave here for him. When we parted we agreed to do this, to try to keep in touch. We're pretty good friends, you see."

"Sure enough." Joe handed over the letter, and Truby opened it.

Found him, it read. *Has a ranch northeast of town, two-hour ride by buggy. Am working there. Wait in El Paso. Stay low, but keep an eye on Jenny's Rooming House. The whore who runs it is good friends with Hawkins and his wife. Will contact you when ready to move. Great setup. He's all ours. So is the woman.*

Truby breathed a deep sigh, hoping he would not have to hang around El Paso too long. It made him nervous. Sam and Calhoun were waiting in a deserted cabin in the Guadalupes. They would get real itchy if this took too long.

Truby had been itchy from the beginning. After all, he didn't know John Hawkins or care that much about Sam's beef with Hawkins, or Lonnie's. But he didn't have anything else to do, no friends, no place to call home; and Sam seemed to know Texas like the back of his hand. If anyone could avoid the law, Sam could, and once this plan to do in John Hawkins was finished, they would all head to Mexico, and they would probably take Tess Hawkins along for a good time. It was easy to rob banks in Mexico. They could have a damn good life there. As for himself, he did not intend to spend another minute in any prison anywhere. If this was what it took to stay out and live free, he'd help. After all, he didn't really have anything else to do, and he'd come to think of Sam as a good friend. The man deserved his help.

"Well, mister, I thank you for keeping this letter. I'll just wait in town for Billy to get back. Once I settle, I'll leave a message here for Billy. He'll most likely stop in here next time he's in town to see if I've been here."

"Sure thing. By the way, my name's Joe—Joe Beal. It gets a little lonesome and boring sitting here all day. Anytime you want to know a little more about the folks in this town, come on over and sit a spell."

"Well, I'll just do that." Truby put the letter in his shirt pocket. "Thanks for your time and your help." He tipped his hat and left, feeling a nudge of apprehension. How in hell did this John Hawkins rescue his wife from a whole gang of *Comancheros?* He could only hope he was not getting himself into a fix helping Sam Higgins go up against the ex-Ranger.

Nineteen

John whistled at several strays, charging his horse into position behind them.

"Go easy, boy," he told the horse softly. Pepper was a damn good gelding, although it irked John to call the animal Pepper. Tex named the horse three years ago, insisting that all the animals have names. John wasn't much for assigning "cute" names to horses, and before becoming a father he usually never named his horses at all.

"Get up there, Pepper!" he urged, kicking the horse's sides as he maneuvered the animal back and forth to force the strays to head back toward the bigger herd. Night was falling and it was time to make camp. The black-and-white spotted horse was one of his best at the job of keeping strays in line. The horse could run at a full-out gallop and in a second or two come to a halt, turn on a dime, dodge back and forth at the merest touch of a rein to his neck. Besides that, the horse was good-natured.

He removed his hat and wiped sweat from his brow before putting the hat back on. May was visiting Texas with a heat rampage, and he wondered if this was an omen of one long, hot summer to come. Dust rolled as he urged Pepper into a gentle run, whistling again to move more cattle into closer grouping for the night. He noticed Billy riding down a ridge, herding several strays ahead of him. John slowed Pepper to a halt and took a cheroot from his vest pocket while he watched. He flicked a match and lit the smoke, keeping it between his lips, and leaned forward, resting his arms across his saddle horn.

Billy seemed to know his business, although John sensed the young man was a little out of practice their first few days on the trail. Something still nudged at him about Billy, but the damn kid was a good worker, helpful, friendly, created no problems. But that smile . . . that damn smile. Why couldn't he trust it? All the men seemed to like Billy, and the sheriff had found no record on him. But then a man could change his name anytime he wanted.

Billy rode up beside him, pushing his hat back, the ever-present smile on his face. "Not many more to go, John. Plenty of branding to do, though. You did real good on calves."

John nodded, puffing on the cheroot before taking it from his lips. "We had a productive winter."

Billy laughed. "Well, we know the bulls had a good time, anyway."

John grinned obligingly, feeling uneasy again. "Apparently," he answered.

"That reminds me, you must be anxious to get back to the missus. I bet you miss your family."

John did not appreciate the young man linking the mating of cows to how much he missed his wife. He wished to hell he could like this kid as much as everyone else did. "I do," he answered, turning Pepper. "Come in and get something to eat. I want you to take first watch with Jack tonight."

"Sure thing." Billy rode beside John. "Got my singing voice ready."

John simply nodded, resenting the young man for making him think about Tess and the kids. For over two weeks he had not seen them, but it felt good to know they were safe in El Paso with Jenny and Ken, although Ken had balked at missing roundup. His old Ranger partner was probably bored to death sitting around in town, and John could not help smiling inwardly at the thought of it. Considering all the wild times they had experienced together through the years, guard duty over a couple of kids in a boardinghouse was not exactly Ken's cup of tea. But then Tess and the children could not be in better hands, other than John's.

Back at the ranch, more men kept watch on the house and buildings. As far as John knew, there had been no problems so far, and he was beginning to believe maybe there wouldn't be after all. Still, he would feel better if he knew Sam Higgins was again behind bars . . . or better yet, dead. He wouldn't mind the pleasure of taking care of the situation his own way.

Billy handed his horse over to David Hill, a boy of only eighteen who landed in El Paso when both his parents died nearby as they traveled from Louisiana to California. The whole town felt sorry for David, who had no other relatives, and John gave him a job at the ranch cleaning stalls and helping care for the horses. David eagerly took the horse, and it was obvious the boy thought the world of Billy Williams, who seemed quite traveled and worldly for his age. Billy had taken to David like a big brother.

Still . . .

"Hey, Billy, come join us!" one man shouted from where he sat around the campfire.

Billy walked over to join the others, taking a tin plate full of beans and pork from the camp cook, Jim Tooms. "You keep feeding me beans, and I'll end up scaring the cattle tonight with all the noise I'll be making," Billy told him.

The rest of the men broke into uproarious laughter. John dismounted, leaving Pepper to graze until David would return from tending to Billy's mount. He took a long drag on his cheroot as he approached Frank Fuller.

"Jim saved you some extra pork, Boss," Frank told him.

"I'm not all that hungry," John answered.

"Big man like you? I remember in our Ranger days you could wolf down half a cow sometimes."

"Yeah, well, I don't get all that hungry when I'm this hot." John took another pull on his cheroot, then bent down and stamped it out on a log so he could put it back in his pocket and save it for later. "Jim does make damn good pork, though. Just throw one piece on a plate—no beans."

Frank nodded, walking over and fishing out a large piece of pork from the pot of beans that hung over the campfire. "Still worried about the wife and kids, aren't you?"

John took the plate. "Can't help it. If I knew Sam Higgins was caught or dead, I'd sure rest easier." He glanced at Billy to see if there was any reaction to his remark, but Billy was still joking with the men. John motioned Frank aside leading him behind the cook wagon. "You notice anything about Billy?"

Frank, a cagey old Ranger who was still tough as nails, shrugged. "Like what?"

John sighed, setting his plate aside on a barrel. "I don't know. There's something about his eyes, his smile, something that looks a little familiar, but I can't place it. I don't know why, but I just don't trust him."

"Billy? Hell, he's a great kid—right helpful, real respectful, don't make any trouble." Frank scratched at a stubble of a beard and shook his head. "You need to relax, John. Tess and the kids are safe in El Paso, the ranch is bein' watched, and there are plenty of men here to guard the herd. Everything's gonna be okay." He shook his head. "I swear, that old Ranger instinct is stuck fast to your gut. You just can't let go of it, can you?"

John picked up the pork with his fingers, deciding to dispense with the amenities. Out here a man didn't much care how the next man ate, or if he shaved or how much he sweated. "I can't let go when I know somebody like Sam Higgins is loose out there somewhere."

Frank snickered. "Are you forgettin' who you are?"

John grinned as he chewed on the meat, then swallowed. "I'm just a man like any other."

"Bullshit! Ain't a better man ever sat a saddle and wore the badge of a Texas Ranger. Sam Higgins would have to be flat out of his mind to come anywhere near you, and he damn well knows it. I shudder to think of what you'd do to any man who dared mess with your wife or kids."

"Yeah, well, don't forget I've been back-shot once already, something Sam Higgins helped plan. If something like that ever happens again, promise me you and Ken and some of the others will watch after Tess and the kids."

Frank waved him off. "You're talkin' crazy now."

"Promise me."

Frank frowned, looking up at John. "You know damned well every man on the ranch and in El Paso would help watch out for them. I just don't understand why you keep suspectin' every stranger who comes near you. Some time has passed, and there's nothin' wrong, so let's start herdin' this beef back to the ranch tomorrow and somebody can go get Tess and the kids."

"Sounds good to me. We've had a good year. Most of this beef should bring me top price at market." John grabbed his plate and started to walk away. He stopped and looked back at Frank. "If you do notice something familiar about Billy Williams, you tell me. Understand?"

"Oh, yes, I understand." Frank shook his head, and John headed back to the campfire.

". . . meanest sonofabitch who ever wore a Ranger badge," he heard Norm Bradshaw saying. He noticed Norm was talking to Billy, who glanced at him, then looked away when he stepped closer to the campfire.

"You telling stories about me again, Norm?" John asked the man.

Everyone quieted, and Billy stared down at his plate of food. So, Billy had been asking about him. "Norm, you talk too much," John said, sitting down on a barrel laid on its side. "Anybody ever tell you that?"

The others laughed. "Hell, Norm's like a woman when it comes to gossip and tellin' stories," Jim said. He spooned out more beans for Norm, whose face reddened a little.

"Shoot, John, you know damn well what your reputation is. Billy here has heard stories and was just askin' if they're true. Might as well fill the kid in, so's he knows the kind of man he's workin' for—one who deserves a lot of respect, I might add."

John shook his head. "You don't need to sweeten it, Norm. Lord knows my reputation is my own fault." He glanced at Billy again, who finally met his gaze. "Got any questions to ask me to my face, Billy?"

Billy grinned. "Just curious. I've heard the men talk a time or two." He shrugged. "Heck, you can't blame a kid for wondering."

John set down his plate and took his cheroot again. "I guess not." He sensed the nervousness of the others at being caught talking about him. He didn't like Billy asking, but neither did he want to spoil the joviality the others were feeling. A happy crew was a crew that worked hard for their boss. He smiled faintly as he glanced around at the rest of the men. "Everything you've heard probably *is* true, Billy. I guess maybe I *was* the meanest sonofabitch who ever walked."

The others looked at each other and smiled, as John relit the cheroot, then turned to Billy. Why couldn't he bring himself to trust the young man? "And you know what, Billy?"

Billy finished his plate of beans. "What's that?"

John breathed out the rest of the smoke he'd just inhaled. "Don't let the fact that I have a wife and kids fool you." He rose and stepped closer to Billy. "I still *am* the meanest sonofabitch who ever walked. I can be your best friend . . . or your worst enemy. Simple as that."

Billy looked up at him. "Well then I reckon' it'll be best friends, won't it?"

John put the cheroot between his lips. "I hope so, for your sake." John walked away to prepare his bedroll, aware the others probably wondered why he obviously didn't take to Billy like he did to the rest of his men; but if a man didn't follow his instincts, he could get himself into a lot of trouble.

Twenty

Truby rode casually behind the two-seater carriage driven by a man. Two women and two children rode in the vehicle, and he knew the heavier, talkative woman was Jenny Simms. It did not take long to find people willing to talk about Jenny's past, her present boardinghouse business, or her lover, a tough ex-Ranger named Ken Randall. He already knew that her two best friends were none other than John and Tess Hawkins. He'd gleaned so much information from his own boss, the local blacksmith, and from Joe Beal at the telegraph office, that he felt he already knew all of them well, even though he had still never met any of them.

He'd taken the job helping the blacksmith because he could work inside the shop, away from the public eye most of the time. He'd let his beard grow, kept his hat pulled close over his eyes most of the time, staying away from other people as much as possible. In his spare time, he spied on Jenny Simms, Tess, and the children, deciding it might help Lonnie if he kept an eye on their daily routines.

"Word is, an old enemy of John Hawkins is on the loose," Joe Beal told him two weeks ago. "John don't trust the man not to try to come after him. Figures Sam Higgins wouldn't dare come into El Paso. He used to be a sheriff here, you know, till Hawkins proved he was in cahoots with one of the richest ranchers in the area—cattle rustlin'."

Truby had to smile at how easy it was to get Joe and others

to talk. John Hawkins had indeed left his impression on just about everyone who ever knew him during his days as a Ranger. Truby figured roundup must be about over now. Hawkins should be coming soon for his wife and kids, and Truby was getting anxious. He still had not heard from Billy. All he could do was keep watching the movements of Jenny and the others, but he wondered what the hell he should do if Billy didn't show.

Jenny pulled her buggy in front of the local mercantile store, and all the occupants climbed down. After waiting a few minutes, Truby rode up to a barbershop two doors down and dismounted, tying his horse and walking up some steps to the boardwalk. He casually strolled to the same store where Jenny went. He walked inside, keeping his head down slightly as he pretended to be looking around. Jenny Simms was talking and laughing with the store clerk, and Tess Hawkins was scolding her son for trying to take a peppermint.

"Oh, let him have it, Mrs. Hawkins," the clerk told her. "It's okay. Say, John should be coming for you soon, shouldn't he? Roundup must be just about done."

"Yes, Parker, and none too soon. I do so miss the ranch. And the children miss their father."

"I'll bet. And what can I get for you and Jenny today?"

Truby moved just a little closer while they talked, glancing at the children, a handsome, dark-skinned boy of eight or nine, he guessed, and a little girl with pale skin and beautiful, curly red hair. The child clung shyly to her mother's skirt.

Truby made sure not to stare too long. He moved away again, walking to study a display of tobacco. The clerk was busy filling an order for Jenny and Tess, and he took a quick, careful look at Tess Hawkins again. He'd seen her from a distance several times, admired her fine shape. She was a damn pretty woman, and the thought of getting hold of her was pleasing indeed. He folded his arms and sighed, as though getting impatient, and he looked toward the doorway. Ken Randall stood there, a pretty good-looking man, rather short but with powerful-looking arms and shoulders. He kept a steady eye on Tess and the children, but suddenly he looked straight at Truby. Truby knew he would draw suspicion if he looked away too quickly, so he nodded a hello. Ken nodded in return, but he did not smile.

Slowly Truby turned away, and the clerk walked over to wait on him. "Something I can do for you while the ladies make up their minds on a few things?" he asked.

"Yes, sir. I'd like some of that there tobacco in the red can." He could not read. He only knew the kind in the red can was the kind he liked. "You got cigarette papers?"

"Sure thing. I see I've run out in my display. I'll get some from out back."

Truby leaned on the counter, looking at the floor wanting to grin at what John Hawkins would think if he knew one of the men planning to steal his children and rape his wife was standing right next to all of them right now. The biggest problem would be how to get rid of Ken Randall. He didn't like the idea of shooting people in the back, but it just might have to be done.

The clerk brought out more cigarette papers. "How many do you want?" he asked.

"Oh, about thirty, I expect."

The clerk counted out the papers and handed them over with a can of tobacco. "That'll be fifteen cents, mister, two for a penny. Say, I've seen you in here a couple other times. New in town, aren't you?"

Truby did not appreciate being asked in front of Ken Randall. "Yes, sir. Got me a job working over at the blacksmith. I kind of like it here."

"Well, El Paso is growing, that's sure. And Clarence is pretty busy this time of year. I'm not surprised he needed the help. When ranchers start bringing in their cattle, it will get busier yet."

"I expect so." Truby paid for his tobacco and took the can and papers, heading out the door.

"Say, mister, I didn't get your name," the clerk called out.

Truby turned. "Jeb. Jeb Hansen," he answered. He glanced

at Ken again as he headed out. "Mornin'," he said, giving him a friendly smile.

Ken nodded. "Morning."

Truby left, feeling Ken's eyes at his back. "Damned ole buzzard," Truby thought. Taking down a man like that meant taking him by surprise and getting it over with quick. He wondered if Lonnie realized how hard it might be to get Tess and those kids away from Ken Randall. And how was he going to get to town and get hold of them before John Hawkins got here?

He sat down on a bench and nervously began rolling a fresh cigarette.

Twenty-one

"Keep movin', there!" Lonnie shouted as he trotted his horse around the west side of the herd, choking on dust. He coughed, then shouted and whistled again, deciding he must make his move today or not at all. The men and herd were no more than another day's ride from the main ranch. He had to find a way to get to El Paso before John sent someone else or went there himself to get his wife and children. Hawkins was sure to do that as soon as he reached the ranch and got the men started with branding.

Lonnie felt just about crazy with the thought of how many chances he'd had to shoot John Hawkins; but if he'd done that here, every man who worked for Hawkins would be after his ass. Besides, making Hawkins suffer first would be worth the wait and self-control. Let the bastard's gut wrench with worry over *his* wife and kids. Let him hurt for them, the way Lonnie's own mother had hurt; the way *he* had hurt, at the news of his brother's death.

He had to make this work, and quick. Sam must be getting mighty anxious by now—Truby, too. He spotted John closer to the front of the herd, and he kicked his horse into a faster lope, riding close enough to be seen. Then he leaned over the side of his horse and shoved a finger down his throat until he gagged and vomited. A young whore who wanted to stay slim once told him this was how she made herself vomit after eating. It damn well did work, and he felt like hell.

Hanging his head, he rode closer to John, finally catching him. "Boss!" he spoke up, deliberately looking weak and haggard. "Hold up, would you?"

John reined Pepper in and waited for "Billy" to catch up. "What's wrong? You look sick."

"I *am* sick." Lonnie held his stomach. "I wondered . . . since we're so close and all . . . do you mind if I ride on to the ranch?" He grimaced and bent over. "I feel awful. Maybe . . . if I lie down for a day or so . . . I'll feel better . . . and can help with the branding."

Frank Fuller started riding back toward them, but John waved him on. "Keep 'em moving! Everything's okay." He looked back at Billy. "I hope you don't have something that all the men will come down with. There's a lot of branding to do. Maybe you *should* go back. It will keep you away from the rest of the men for a day or two."

Lonnie nodded. "Yes, sir. I'm . . . real sorry, John. For all I know, I'll feel better by the end of the day."

"It happens," John said. "Can't be helped." He studied the herd. "It's early. If you start out now, you can probably get there by night, or at least early morning. I'd send a man with you, but I can't spare any."

"I understand. That's . . . okay. I don't need . . . any babying. I just need to . . . get to my bunk."

"Get going then. Stop at the chuck wagon and get your bedroll and things. And when you get to the ranch, tell them we'll be arriving late tomorrow afternoon. They should send someone to El Paso tomorrow morning to get Tess and my son and daughter. I want them back at the ranch by tomorrow night or the next morning."

Billy nodded and started away.

"Billy," John called out to him.

Lonnie stopped and waited.

"You've done a good job."

Well, well, Lonnie thought. *He's actually beginning to trust me.* "Thank you, John. Means a lot hearing you say that." He gripped his stomach again. "I'd . . . like to stay on at the ranch . . . if you need the help."

"We'll see. It depends on how many of my men decide to leave. Some of them are drifters, like you. I never know when they'll decide to move on."

Lonnie nodded again and rode off at a soft trot. Inside he wanted to kick his horse into a full gallop. He'd found a way to get to El Paso in time to make off with John Hawkins's children, soon enough to keep from being easily tracked! By God, this just might work!

Twenty-two

Lonnie approached Jenny's boardinghouse, stopping at a distance to breathe deeply and go over in his mind again what he must do. Last night he arrived at the ranch, where he rested a while, then saddled his own horse and set out at dawn for town. He told Cal Decker, one of the men left behind to guard the house and livestock at the ranch, that John was sending him to El Paso to tell Tess and the children they could come home.

He grinned and shook his head at how easy it was to fool people by simply being pleasant and charming. Cal swallowed his story, even helped him saddle his horse and told him he hoped the doc in town could help him feel better. Once he arrived in El Paso about 10 A.M., Joe Beal at the telegraph office had gladly let him know where he could find Truby, or "Jeb Hansen," the name Truby was using.

Poor Truby had been greatly relieved to see him. The fool was getting itchy. Lonnie hoped Truby wouldn't do something to mess up their plans. He was not the brightest man he'd ever known. Truby was to make up an excuse to leave his job early and ride out to an abandoned home and barn east of town. Lonnie had searched for a good meeting place before coming here, and the abandoned farm seemed the best. It was out of sight of most other homes and buildings. From there a man could ride hard and get far from town before anyone knew he'd gone. If he could get John Hawkins's brats to the abandoned farm without being caught, Truby could help him from there, and they would be home free . . . and John Hawkins would be at his mercy. He only wished he could be present to see the look on John's face when he found out who "Billy Williams" really was.

This was it. It was now or never. Circumstances could not have presented a better opportunity. The only remaining obstacle was one Ken Randall. *You better catch him off guard, or you'll have a time of it,* Truby had warned. *Don't forget he rode with John Hawkins. I expect anybody who rode with him is just about as hard to bring down as Hawkins himself, but the man is getting old. Catch him by surprise, and I reckon you've got him.*

Lonnie knew he did not dare use a gun. The noise would draw too much attention. Besides, there might be boarders around. He had to be quiet about this.

He rode up to Jenny's house and dismounted, tying his horse to a hitching post. Jenny's horse and buggy were also tied there. Apparently she was going somewhere, or had just returned. Before he could reach the screen door on the front porch, he could hear Honor shouting to her mother.

"Mommy, Mommy! That Billy man is here!"

Lonnie knocked on the door, and quickly little Honor pushed it open. "Hi, Billy!"

"Well, hello there, Honor! Your mom here?"

"Honor! What have I told you about letting people in before checking with me and Jenny?"

Lonnie looked past the child to see Tess Hawkins approaching the entranceway. She looked crisp and clean, and her dress fit her slender waist and full breasts beautifully. No wonder John Hawkins was anxious to see her again, but this time their reunion would not be such a happy one. And if things went right, Lonnie himself would enjoy what was under those skirts.

"It's okay, Mrs. Hawkins," Lonnie said aloud. "It's just me, come to tell you your husband is on his way in to the main ranch this very day and will be there by nightfall, early tomorrow at the latest. Told me to come on ahead and let you know to start back tomorrow morning."

"Oh, what a relief!" Tess said, picking Honor up.

"Hi, Billy!" Texas ran up behind his mother and moved in front of her. "Is my pa coming?"

"No. He's not quite back yet, son, but he said for you and your ma to start back tomorrow morning, with your Uncle Ken, too, of course."

"Come in, Billy," Tess told him graciously. "You must be tired."

"Oh, that I am." Lonnie followed Tess and the children inside, where Ken greeted him with a nod.

"How you doing, Billy?"

"Just fine, Ken. I'll bet you're anxious to get back to the Hawk's Nest."

Ken smiled. "Sure am." He looked Lonnie over. "You and John apparently got to be decent friends, I see."

"Sure did."

"Oh, I'm glad," Tess told him. "I'm so sorry for the rude way John treated you when you first came, but he is so worried about this Sam Higgins thing."

"Well, ma'am, I can understand that. But it looks like there won't be any trouble. I checked at the sheriff's office before I came here, and he said there's been no sign of Higgins anywhere; and there's been no trouble at the ranch, either."

"Good. Maybe we can get back to a normal life," Tess answered, setting Honor down. "Run and play, Honor. Go tend to your dolly."

Honor smiled, dimples showing. She clapped her hands. "We're going home to see Daddy!" she said gleefully.

"Yes, we are," Tess answered with a smile.

Honor ran off, and Tess, still grinning, faced Lonnie. "She misses her father so much, Billy. They are very close. Both the children are close to John."

"Oh, anybody can see that."

"We just finished up from lunch, Billy. Would you like something? I'm sure we can find—"

"No, thank you, ma'am. I ate at Ruby Watson's eatery. I'll just sit here and rest a while."

"I'll have Tex go out and unload your horse," Ken told him. "He likes doin' them things. The kid can take care of a horse good as any man."

"I'm sure he can, Ken, but I might need my horse later. I haven't had a good drink and a good card game in quite a spell. I thought I'd go back into town after I rest a while."

Ken grinned. "I know the feelin'."

"How's Tulip?" Tex asked. "And how are her babies?"

"Oh, they're growing like nothing you ever saw," Lonnie answered. "Just wait till you see them."

"Thanks for helping save the second baby," Tex told him.

"Well, it was my privilege, boy." Lonnie turned his most handsome smile to Tess. "You're looking very pretty, Mrs. Hawkins." He watched her redden a little.

"Thank you. Jenny and I were just about to leave to go to see the milliner in town and see about new hats. Once a year I actually get John to go to church with me, and I want a new outfit this year. It's such a special occasion."

Lonnie could not help a light laugh. "Well, now, from what I've heard about John Hawkins, I expect it *is* a special occasion getting him into a church!"

They all laughed, and Jenny came into the parlor just then, wearing a snug-fitting blue-cotton dress that accented all the right places, and a dark-colored straw bonnet decorated with blue-silk flowers. "I heard that remark!" She joined in their laughter. "There was a time when I never thought I'd see that man in a house of God, but he does it every year, right after roundup—for Tess. I'm not all that sure she's really Christianized him, but she's trying, poor soul."

"Jenny Simms, I am not a poor soul. I am the luckiest woman on earth."

Jenny chuckled and grinned sarcastically. "Don't I know it?" She wiggled her eyebrows, and Tess scowled at her.

"Jenny!"

Ken and Lonnie laughed, and Lonnie couldn't have been happier than to realize these people totally believed the story that he'd come to deliver John's message.

"Come help me pin on my hat," Tess told Jenny. "You're so much better at placing it right than I am." She breathed a deep sigh. "Oh, Jenny, I'm so glad this is over."

"You don't like my company?"

"You know what I mean. I'll be so glad to get back to a normal family life. And I'm sure you must be tired of our company by now."

"Never. I always enjoy having you around." Jenny walked up to Ken and pinched his cheek. "And you, lover. I'll miss you when you go back. Why don't you stay here with me?"

"And why don't *you* come to the ranch with *me?*"

Jenny kissed his cheek. "You keep working on me that way and I just might do that someday. But I'm a city woman, Ken Randall." She gave him a wink and walked off with Tess.

Ken shook his head and sat down across from Lonnie. "Billy, someday I'll get that woman to marry me, no matter what," he said.

"Not the marrying type?"

"Well, that's what she thinks. But I'll change her mind."

Tex came over and sat down next to Ken. "Tell us about the roundup, Billy. Did Pa get a lot of calves?"

"Oh, he sure did. After tomorrow there will be a lot of branding to do."

Tex grinned, and Lonnie thought what a very handsome boy he was. "Pa said I could help with branding this year. I used to cry 'cause I thought he was hurting the cows, but he said it doesn't really hurt that much. They just burn the hair off. He said it's important so nobody can steal his cattle."

Lonnie nodded. "He's right, Tex."

Jenny and Tess returned, both carrying parasols. "We are on

Rosanne Bittner

our way, Ken," Tess told him. "Tex, you mind Ken, and watch out for your sister."

The two women left, and Lonnie realized his opportunity to make a move could not be better. "Do those two take all day to shop?"

Ken grinned. "Just about. Jenny figured she had plenty of time because there's no boarders around right now. Three left on the stage this mornin' for parts unknown, and the rest are off workin' or doin' whatever. There's usually not many around this time of day. I expect Jenny can give you a room for tonight, since three of them won't be comin' back."

"Well, that's good to know." Lonnie stretched. "I think I'll go get my horse and take him around back to graze a while."

"I can do it, Billy!" Tex spoke up.

"That's okay. There's a couple things I need to get out of my saddlebags, Tex."

"Are you coming right back? I want to know more about Pa and the roundup."

"Yes, son, I'll be right back." Lonnie rose and reached over to tousle Tex's hair. "You sure do look like your pa, Tex."

"Pa's part Sioux Indian, so I am, too," the boy answered. "I wear my hair long 'cause Pa does. Sometimes he lets me paint my cheeks and pretend I'm an Indian."

"Well, I'll bet someday you'll be big and strong like your pa. I bet you can't wait."

Tex giggled. "I can't. But I don't know if I'll ever be big as him."

"Sure you will." Lonnie gave him a wink. "I'll be right back." He walked outside and untied his horse, looking around. The town seemed quiet today, and the boardinghouse was in a quieter part of town, several hundred yards from the nearest business. He could ride off with the kids and no one would even know it, especially since the women were gone, and all the guests were, too. He walked around behind the house, where he breathed deeply for courage. He had to move fast now. He couldn't give Ken Randall one extra second to react, or the tough old buzzard might get the better of him.

He tied his horse behind the horse shed, then walked up to the back porch. "Hey! Ken!" he called.

Moments later Ken showed up in the kitchen. "What is it?"

"Come on out here a minute. Leave Tex inside to watch his sister. I've got something to show you that John had me bring with me." He lowered his voice. "It's a surprise for Tex and Honor."

Ken grinned, turning back and yelling to Tex to stay inside. "I'll be right back, son."

"Tell Billy to hurry up," Tex answered.

"You watch your sister," Ken ordered. "And lock the front door till I come back in." He walked outside, following "Billy" to the horse shed.

Twenty-three

"I see you're riding your own roan," Ken said as he approached Lonnie near the shed. He stopped to look the horse over, running his hands over her muscled shoulders. "Did you use her in the roundup?"

"No, Sara's no good for things like that. Oh, she's a fast horse," Lonnie answered, "good and solid, and only four years old. Has a lot of stamina, too, but she's a bit too rowdy sometimes to have around cattle at night. She spooks easy after dark. I never could figure out why, but I figured maybe I should leave her at the ranch during roundup."

Ken's back was turned, and Lonnie took his chance. Ken reached up to pat Sara's nose, and Lonnie whipped out his skinning knife. Without hesitation he plunged it between Ken's shoulder blades.

Ken grunted and gripped Sara's mane. When Sara whinnied and jerked away, he fell to the ground. Lonnie looked around to be sure no one saw. A smokehouse blocked them from view of the house, and bushes hid them from anyone who might be coming along the street from town.

Quickly he plunged the knife again, making sure Ken Randall would not be able to move. He stabbed his arms, his legs; deciding he would rather know this man was suffering than for him to die quickly. After all, he had heard enough stories by now to know that Ken Randall had ridden with John Hawkins on just about every killing or capture that took place while they were Texas Rangers. No doubt he was with John when he blew up the cabin that held Lonnie's brother.

Finally he wiped off the knife on Ken's shirt and shoved it back into its sheath at his waist. He pulled Ken's gun from the holster at his side, shoving it into his own gun belt, then hurriedly dragged Ken inside the horse shed.

"The time has come for you and your Indian friend to know the truth," he half growled, jerking a bleeding, grunting Ken into an empty horse stall filled with a storage of hay. He shoved him into the hay as best he could and used some of the hay to cover all but his face.

He leaned close then, enjoying Ken's wide eyes and the horror they showed. He then took from his own pocket the paper he'd written on earlier. "This, my friend, is a note for one John Hawkins," he sneered. He pushed some hay away and shoved the note between Ken's gun belt and pants. He piled more hay over him again. "The note gives John a hint where he'll be able to find his kids." He grinned at the pleading look in Ken's eyes.

"No," Ken said weakly. "Don't . . . do this."

"I *am* doing it, you bastard! You and Hawkins killed my brother, and now Hawkins will die. But he's going to *suffer* first, like *I* suffered! Like my *ma* suffered! That's why *Tess* Hawkins *also* has to suffer! And if they want to see their kids again, John and Tess Hawkins better come out to us alone."

". . . us . . . who . . . are you?"

Lonnie pulled out his knife again. "Name's Lonnie *Briggs*. Does that ring a bell?" Before Ken could answer, Lonnie shoved the tip of the knife up under Ken's chin and pushed up, cutting into the underside of his throat just enough to poke through the skin. He could tell by Ken's eyes that he'd recognized the name Briggs. "And by the way, I'm taking the kids to Sam Higgins. You recognize that name, too?" He watched tears well up in Ken's eyes, and he grinned.

Lonnie stood up. "You might live through this. If you do, I don't really care. I like Jenny, and she likes you, so maybe you two will be happy together. At least I know you're hurting, and you'll *be* hurting for a long time to come!" He grinned. "Didn't do your job so well after all, did you, Ken? I wonder what John will think of his best *friend* when he finds out how bad you failed him this time?"

He watched a tear slip down the side of Ken's face, then chuckled and turned away, hurriedly saddling a black-and-white mare he knew belonged to Jenny. She'd told him so when he helped her hitch one of her other horses to her buggy the day she brought him out to John's ranch.

He yanked the cinch tight and led the horse out of the shed, then threw a rope around the neck of Ken's horse and led it out and around the shed, where he tied it so that Tex would not see it. Then he headed for the house. "Hey, Tex!" he shouted as he reached the back door. He went inside. "How would you and Honor like to go for a ride?"

"A ride?" Tex came running down the hall from the parlor. "Where we going? Can I ride a horse by myself?"

"Well, I guess so. That way I can hold on to Honor easier. I saddled up that black-and-white mare that belongs to Jenny. I don't think she'll care."

"Honor won't ride by herself. She's scared to. But *I'm* not," Tex said proudly. "Pa says I ride as good as any man."

"Well, now, I bet you do. Now you can show me. Go get your sister."

"Where's Ken? Is he coming, too?"

"No. I gave him a special message he's supposed to take to the telegraph office for your pa, something about telegraphing someplace up in Kansas that wants to buy some of your pa's cattle. Ken left to ride to the telegraph office. He said you'd probably love to go for a ride, seeing as how you've been stuck here away from the ranch for so long."

"Yeah!" Tex ran to get his sister, telling her to hurry up.

"I don't want to ride," Honor protested.

"Come on! You know I'm supposed to look out for you, Honor. I can't leave you here alone. Pa said we have to be with one of his men all the time. And you like Billy, anyway. Come on, Honor! He's fun!"

Lonnie breathed a sigh of relief when Tex reappeared with Honor, who shyly carried a rag doll. He was glad she was coming willingly. It wouldn't be easy getting out of town with a screaming, crying little girl.

"Hey, Honor, we'll have fun!" he assured her. "We're going to ride to an old abandoned house a little ways from here. There's something secret there I want to show you." He gave her his most charming smile and knelt, putting out his arms. "Come on, honey. Your daddy said it's okay."

"I want to ride with my daddy." The girl pouted.

"And you will. By tomorrow afternoon you'll be home, and you'll see your daddy again."

The girl brightened a little. "Okay." She ran up to Billy, and he picked her up in his arms. "Let's go, Tex."

"I gotta get my hat." The boy ran into the kitchen and took a wide-brimmed hat from a hook. "Ma says if I don't wear a hat when it's sunny and hot, my brains will cook," he said with a laugh. He also took down a small slat bonnet. "Honor has to wear one, too, on account of her light skin. She gets burned easy."

"Oh, I see." Lonnie set Honor on the kitchen table and tied on the hat, his patience wearing thin. The sooner he got out of this place, the better.

"She's gotta wear this cotton shirt, too," Tex told him, handing him a little blue shirt. "She can't let her arms be in the sun."

Lonnie took the shirt with a smile, but he rolled his eyes with frustration when he turned around to slip it on Honor. The girl clung tightly to her rag doll, moving it from one hand to the other as he put on the shirt. "Is that all?" Lonnie asked.

"Yup," Tex answered. "She's got on long bloomers, so her legs won't get burned."

The boy ran out, and Lonnie grabbed Honor and hurried after

him, worried he might go into the horse shed and find Ken. "Just get on Jenny's black-and-white there," he shouted to Tex.

The boy obeyed, and Lonnie plopped Honor on his own horse and climbed up behind her, taking the reins into his right hand while he kept a firm hold on Honor with his left. "Let's go the back way," he suggested to Tex. "That way we can race if we want to without running into people in the street. You like to race, don't you? You a good enough rider for that?"

"Heck, yeah!" Tex answered. "Sometimes Pa even lets me race him."

Lonnie laughed. "Good. Follow me first to that oak tree way out there behind Jenny's house. We'll have a little race from there."

"I don't like to ride fast," Honor objected. "I'm scared."

"Oh, I've got a good hold on you, honey. You'll be just fine," Lonnie answered. "It will be fun."

"Will we be back before my mommy gets home?"

"Sure we will."

"She'll be real worried if I'm not here when she gets back."

"Don't you fret. I'll have you back in just a few minutes." Lonnie rode toward the oak tree . . . and Tex followed.

Twenty-four

Jenny guided her horse along a narrow drive that led around the side of the house to the horse shed. "John is going to love that gorgeous pink dress, Tess. Pink is so beautiful on you with that red hair, and I swear somebody made that dress just for you, the way it fits."

"I'm so excited about it," Tess replied, holding on to the small railing at the side of the buggy seat as Jenny turned a corner. "I usually make my own clothes, but there will be so much catching up to do when I get back—" She stopped talking and frowned, noticing Ken's shiny black horse tied at the back of the shed. "Why would Ken tie his horse back there like that instead of letting him graze or putting him in a stall?"

"I'll be damned," Jenny replied. "I have no idea. Ken treats that horse better than he treats me. Is that a rope around Devil's neck?"

Tess felt a little pang of apprehension, but she pushed it away. "It looks like it."

Jenny pulled the buggy closer, dropping the reins and climbing down. Tess followed, and both women walked over to Devil, who whinnied and yanked at the rope.

"You poor thing," Jenny soothed the horse. "What are you doing tied out here in the hot sun, and not even enough rope to bend your head down and graze?" She untied the rope and removed it from around the animal's neck. "I don't understand this. Ken would never do this."

"I know," Tess answered, the little hint of apprehension returning. *No,* she told herself. *Nothing is wrong.*

"Ken?" Jenny shouted. She walked into the horse shed and called his name again.

No reply.

"Well, he's not out here anyplace. Let's take our packages in and ask him what's going on." Jenny walked back to the buggy and loaded her arms with packages wrapped in brown paper. Tess did the same, and both women carried their things inside to the kitchen. Jenny plunked her things on the kitchen table. "I'll have to go unhitch Baxter from the buggy," she told Tess.

"Oh, let me do it," Tess answered. "You have things to do to get ready for supper. Most of your boarders will be returning by then."

Jenny took the pins from her hat. "Well, I'd sure appreciate it." She set the hat on the table. "Ken?" she shouted. "What's your horse doing tied out back?"

No reply.

Suddenly Tess's apprehension turned to fear. "Tex? Honor?" She looked at Jenny. "Something isn't right."

Both women hurried into the parlor and began calling for Ken and the children. Tess checked the room she shared with both her children, but it was empty. She glanced at the little cradle Honor used for her rag doll. It was empty. That meant Honor had gone somewhere, for wherever she went, the rag doll was always with her. She left the room and met Jenny in the hallway.

"Did Ken say anything to you about taking the children anywhere? Maybe for a walk?"

"Ken? Go for walks? That man doesn't walk any farther than it takes to get on a horse, unless he goes into town with us in the wagon. You know that."

Tess's heart began pounding harder. "I don't like this, Jenny. Honor's rag doll is gone. That means *she's* gone—somewhere. Let's look for a note. Maybe Ken left us a note." She rushed past Jenny to the parlor, glancing around at all the tables. Nothing. She hurried with Jenny into the kitchen. Nothing. It was then she noticed that Tex's and Honor's hats were gone from their hooks. "Jenny, their hats are gone, and even Honor's little sun jacket is gone."

"Let's check out back again."

Tess ran out the back door, and Jenny followed. Tess took a look around the backyard, ran behind the horse shed, and scanned the land in every direction.

"Tess!" Jenny shouted from the horse shed.

Tess hurried to meet her. "What is it?"

"Maggie is gone, my black-and-white mare!"

Tess put a hand to her chest. "Maybe for some reason Ken took your horse and is giving the children a ride."

"Like hell! Ken would never set his carcass on my horse, or even take her out with one of the kids on her. He hates Maggie, says she's stubborn and stupid. He's always teasing me about that horse because one of her front hooves is half again bigger than the other. He thinks that makes her deformed, but dammit, she's a good horse, strong and— Oh, hell, who gives a damn. What the hell is going on? Ken would never tie his own horse behind the shed like that!" She looked around the shed as she spoke, then met Tess's worried gaze, noticing she was beginning to shake.

"Jenny—"

"Hang on," Jenny told her, grasping her arms. "Let's not panic yet. There might be an explanation for all of this. Let's go back to the house and—"

Both women heard a groan. They turned in the direction of the sound and noticed some hay move slightly.

"Dear God," Jenny muttered. She rushed to lean down and dig through the hay. "Oh, my God!" she screamed. "It's Ken! Oh, God! Oh, God! He's all bloody!"

Tess knelt on the other side and helped Jenny brush away most of the hay. "There's blood everywhere!" she gasped. "His pants, his shirt—"

"Look at his throat!" Jenny screamed. "Ken! Oh, my God, Ken! Tess, get the doctor! Get the doctor!"

Tess froze, a horror washing through her with such force that it took her breath away. Jenny leaned over and grasped her shoulders, shaking her slightly. "Tess! Take the buggy and get a doctor!"

Tess met her eyes. "The children," she said in a near whisper. "Whoever . . . did this . . . must have taken my babies!"

Jenny closed her eyes and withered slightly. "No. No, this can't be true." It was then she noticed the note stuffed into Ken's gun belt. With a shaking hand she pulled it out. She glanced at Tess before opening it. She read it silently, then handed it to Tess and bent over weeping. "No. No. No."

Hardly able to breathe, Tess looked down at the note.

> *John Hawkins knows where most outlaws go in Texas. Let him come find his son and daughter— just him and you, Tess, you pretty little thing. Your daughter is a pretty little thing, too. Both of you better come alone, or your children die. Don't try to fool us and bring help, because where we're going, we'll be able to see you coming. Your brats are with me—and Sam Higgins.*
>
> *Billy*
>
> *P.S. My real name is Lonnie Briggs. My brother was Darrell Briggs. Hawkins knows the name.*

Tess gripped the note in her hand and slowly rose, looking down at Ken. "Is he still alive?"

A weeping Jenny nodded. "I think so." She looked down at her own now-bloody hands. "Oh, Tess, even if he lives he's going to die inside, knowing those men got hold of John's kids while he was in charge of them."

Tess closed her eyes. "And I was out shopping . . . such a frivolous, stupid thing!"

"We didn't know, Tess. How could we know? Billy is so young and sweet and friendly."

Tess struggled with an urge to turn into a screaming, weeping, useless woman. Honor! Tex! Her babies! "John knew," she answered. *"John* knew, and we all thought he was being too cautious." Tears began trickling down her cheeks. "I'll go get Doc Sanders . . . and the sheriff. And I'll send someone to get John."

She hurried out, telling herself she must not panic. Ken was likely dying and needed help. Her children had been kidnapped, and someone needed to get on their trail as soon as possible. That someone would be John Hawkins, and if he ever managed to rescue Tex and Honor, there would be no sorrier men on earth than Sam Higgins and Lonnie Briggs.

Twenty-five

John finished washing up, then put on clean clothes, smoothing back his wet hair and tying it at the back of his neck. It felt damn good to be clean. A good night's sleep in a real bed would feel wonderful, and he could hardly wait to share that bed with Tess when she got home. She could make it home yet tonight, although it was getting pretty dark already. She probably planned on coming tomorrow, wanting the children to get a good night's rest first.

He carefully shaved, thinking with a smile how much fun it would be to see Tex and Honor again. God, he'd missed them . . . missed Tess . . . missed the feel of her against him in the night . . . missed Honor's little arms around his neck . . . missed Tex's bright smile and the joy in his dark eyes.

It concerned him a little that Billy had gone on to town to let Tess know she could come home. When he arrived with the herd three hours ago, Cal Decker told him Billy felt better and had gone on to town early that morning so he would arrive by noon, that if Tess could leave within a couple of hours of his arrival, she could still make it home tonight. He supposed there was nothing wrong with that, but there was still something about Billy . . .

He sighed, disgusted with his feelings. Hell, Ken was with Tess and the kids, and they were right in town. What could go wrong? Billy had probably already landed in some whore's bed, and by now Tess was packed and ready to leave, bright and early

tomorrow. He decided he would head out early in the morning
with a few other men and meet her halfway.

He stepped outside and dumped his used water out of the
washbowl. He set it down and breathed deeply of the cool evening
air. It felt good after a long, hot day of pushing the herd so that
they could get here before dark. Now the huge herd grazed inside
wooden fences, and he felt proud of how much he had accom-
plished in building the ranch. Never in his wildest dreams did
he once think he could ever be this happy, this settled.

Bright stars and a full moon lit the sky. It was a pretty night.
He sat down in a porch chair and rolled himself a cigarette, glad
Maria Valdez had kept the house so spotless. Tess would not be
returning to a lot of work. Maria often helped Tess with chores
and was a godsend when Tess had Honor and was bedridden for
nearly a month afterward.

Maria's husband, Pedro, helped watch the herd tonight. Everything was peaceful . . . maybe too peaceful. He grinned and
shook his head, chastising himself for this constant worry in the
back of his mind. Billy had proved himself to be a hard worker,
dependable, respectful, well liked by all the men. Why in God's
name couldn't he let himself trust the boy?

He lit his cigarette and put a foot on the porch railing, tipping
back his chair and smoking, thinking how nice it would be if
Tess were already home. He could almost smell her, that pretty
perfume she sometimes wore after a hard day's work and a bath.
He could smell her hair, feel it in his fingers. He could taste her
lips . . .

"Shit!" he swore, getting back up. He began pacing. Something just didn't feel right. Maybe he should ride into town tonight. Still, he was so damn tired from the extra effort it had
taken to get the herd in by nightfall, he would probably fall asleep
in the saddle. He walked to the end of the porch and looked in
the direction of town. By wagon, El Paso was almost two hours
away, along a twisting road that crept through dry, open land,
through a couple of canyons and over a hill not quite big enough
to be called a mountain . . . a little much for a weary man after
dark. Still, one man on a good horse could make it in about an

hour, if he wanted to run his horse into a lather. It was tempting to try it tonight, but he didn't like abusing a horse that way.

No. He might as well wait till morning. They were as safe in Ken's hands as his own. He smoked quietly, then tossed the stub of his cigarette out into a patch of dirt. He started inside, and it was then his keen ears picked up the sound . . . a horse approaching from the southwest . . . at a gallop. Who the hell would be riding that hard at night? It sounded like the approaching rider was coming along the road from El Paso.

He listened closer. One rider. It couldn't be outlaws. No single man in his right mind would try to ride in on a ranch this size in the middle of the night. But just in case, he hurried inside and took his Winchester rifle from where it was propped in a corner. He hadn't had time to clean the thing yet, but this roundup had been uneventful. No Indians. No rustlers. He never even had to fire the thing.

He quickly struck a match and lit a porch lantern. He retracted the rifle's lever and waited, listened as one of his men farther out told the rider to halt. It sounded like Cal Decker. He heard two voices then, figured it was the rider talking with Cal, but he could not hear what they said.

"Marv! Bill!" he heard Cal call out then. "Come up to the house with me!"

"Frank! Norm!" someone else called out. "Hurry up!"

John walked to the edge of the steps, a sense of danger coming alive. Several of his men approached, some running, some on horseback. John felt his gut tighten when they came into better view, obvious agony on their faces. Sheriff Potter was with them, sitting on a lathered, panting horse. The man did not have to open his mouth for John to realize why he must have come.

"Tess?" he asked anxiously, every muscle tensing until he thought he might explode.

"Worse," Potter answered. "I don't even know how to tell you, John."

"Just *tell* it!" John seethed. "What's happened, Hank?"

Hank looked away for a moment. "They, uh, they took your

kids. Ken was stabbed, so many times the doc can't really count them all. He's in a real bad way. Might not make it."

A round of curses moved among the men there, and John struggled to breathe, a rage burning so great in his soul he literally felt as though flames ate at his gut. "Billy Williams?"

Potter took a piece of paper from his pocket and handed it over to John. John gripped his rifle in one hand and grabbed the note with the other, glad Tess had taught him to read years ago. The kind of life he'd led growing up, he never had the chance to learn. He opened the note and read it, then wadded it up.

"Briggs!" he growled. He turned to his men. "His real name is Lonnie Briggs! Nine years ago I blew up a cabin full of outlaws led by a *Darrell* Briggs! He and his gang of men raped a twelve-year-old Indian girl! Took turns with her! Now somehow his goddamn brother has linked up with Sam Higgins, and they have my kids. *My* kids!"

"Jesus!" one of the men muttered.

"How in hell did that kid get the better of a man like Ken?" another asked.

"Because Ken *trusted* him!" John shouted back. *"Everybody* trusted him! But I didn't! I should have trusted my gut instinct and never *hired* that lying sonofabitch!" Teeth gritted, he turned to the sheriff. "Where's Tess? Where's my wife?"

"She's okay, John. She's waiting for you at Jenny's. She said to tell you to bring her riding clothes, and her old leather, wide-brimmed hat. I'm tired as hell, but if you give me a fresh horse, I'll ride back with you yet tonight. There's a bright moon. It's pretty easy to see. I'm just damn sorry to bring you news like this. I sent a posse out to see what they could find, but too much time had passed, and there just wasn't much of anything to follow."

In all his years as a Ranger, John could not remember feeling this kind of desire to kill someone, in the slowest, most painful way he could. "Sam Higgins is going to be the sorriest sonofabitch who ever walked!" he seethed.

"What do you want us to do, John? We're all ready to help," Cal told him.

John could hardly think. Breathing hard, he paced a moment,

still gripping the rifle. "Get Sheriff Potter a fresh horse. Saddle one for me, the gelding, maybe, the one Tex calls—" The words caught in his throat. Tex! And his sweet little Honor. She must be so afraid without her daddy. "Uh . . . Jake." God, he couldn't cry in front of his men. "You know the one I mean, Cal. And, uh, Shadow. Saddle her up for Tess, and I'll take Pepper and White Sox along for spares."

"Yes, sir," Cal answered, leaving right away.

John began pacing. "Jesus, Tex picks the craziest names for the horses, doesn't he?"

A couple of the men laughed lightly, and John knew it was only to help him handle this situation. He felt like he had to keep talking or go crazy. He couldn't let this consume him . . . yet. He had to think fast.

Tex! He'd named the beautiful red gelding John prized White Sox because the only coloring on the horse other than its golden red was the bottom half of all four legs, which were white.

"You're taking Tess *with* you?" Frank asked.

John rubbed at the back of his neck, still pacing. "The note says Tess and I are to come alone. You know Tess. Even if the note *didn't* say for her to come, she'd go anyway. A mother will do just about anything for her kids."

"So will a father," Frank said.

John blinked back tears. "Somebody get Maria quick. Tell her to come help me pack Tess's riding clothes."

"I'll go," Bill Decker offered.

"You really going after them alone, John?" Marv asked. "You know they're out to kill you."

"I have no choice. They've set their rules. The only trouble is, Sam Higgins has forgotten who he's *messing* with . . . and Lonnie Briggs will damn well find out!" John went back inside the house, looking around the familiar dwelling, remembering happy times around the table. He wondered if he would ever again feel Honor's little arms around his neck. He could not think of any torture cruel enough to visit upon a man for doing what Lonnie Briggs had done. "I'll skin the bastard alive!" He seethed.

Twenty-six

Thunder rumbled overhead. Tess sat staring out the window at the rain, agonizing over wondering whether or not Tex and Honor were warm and dry. Surely Lonnie Briggs and Sam Higgins could not be evil enough to make the children suffer, to starve them or let her precious little Honor get too much sun. Surely they would not abuse them physically or . . . kill them.

No! What kind of men would kill innocent children? Who could look into those innocent eyes and—

She heard horses approaching, and her agony was made worse by the knowledge that poor John must have ridden all night to get here, and after a long day of driving cattle. He must be so tired. But so was she. How could a mother sleep when her children were taken away from her and she had no way of knowing how they were being treated?

She glanced at a clock on the nightstand—1:00 A.M. It was still dark outside, but by the light of Jenny's oil lamps outdoors, she could make out three men. One dismounted before his horse even came to a halt. That would be John.

Lightning flashed, and she saw a yellow slicker. She could not tell who the other two were, but she guessed they would be Sheriff Potter and perhaps ex-Ranger Frank Fuller.

Now she could hear John talking to Mary Sanders, who had come to help Jenny and Doc Sanders tend to Ken. Oh, how she dreaded seeing John's face! She heard heavy footsteps, then the door to the room she'd shared with the children opened. She remained looking out the window, her throat so tight it hurt, her eyes welling with new tears. Lightning flashed again and a clap of thunder literally shook the house. Tess thought how very fitting that was, a grand announcement of the entrance of a man whose anger could be as packed with power and fury as that lightning.

"I'm sorry," she said quietly. She heard the door close.

"Sorry? What the hell for?"

Tess could not help the sobs that poured forth then. "I . . . was shopping . . . shopping . . . such a . . . frivolous . . . stupid . . . thing to be . . . doing." She covered her face and wept.

In a moment strong arms lifted her from the chair and embraced her. She wrapped her arms around John's neck and sobbed bitterly, taking strength from his embrace. She always felt stronger when he held her this way . . . like that first embrace when he came to rescue her from the *Comancheros*. A flood of hope poured into her at the realization of who this man was. For eight years he had been far different from the John Hawkins who wielded his fury against the *Comancheros*. But other than this needed tender moment, she knew he would become the old John . . . the man known as Hawk . . . ruthless, determined, fearless. Just having him here gave her courage, and hope for her children.

"Don't be sorry. You couldn't have known."

Tess felt the momentary softness go out of him, felt his muscles go rigid. He pulled away, keeping a firm hold of her arms.

"It's time to be strong, Tess, like the woman you were when I first found you."

"But . . . that was just . . . me." She took a handkerchief from where it was tucked into the waist of her skirt and blew her nose and wiped at her eyes. "I can . . . handle anything . . . someone does to me. But . . . my babies—" The tears came again.

"Tess!" John said sternly.

Finally she met his eyes. Oh, the fury there! If she didn't know him, she would be afraid of him. Drops of rain still showed on his finely chiseled face, and as when she first met him, he had the look of a wild Indian about him, as vicious and cunning as any renegade Indian or outlaw.

"Do you think *I* don't want to weep?" he asked her.

For one brief moment she detected tears, sensed he could break down and cry just as openly as she did. His jaw flexed and he blinked; then he took a quick, deep breath, turning away for a moment. "There is no time for crying," he said. "I had Maria pack your things, and Frank packed some food. I brought extra horses."

Tess watched him quickly wipe at his eyes, but his back was still to her. Finally, he turned and faced her again. "We'll leave as soon as the sun is up. The note said I'd find them where most outlaws are found in Texas. That has to mean Thieves' Hollow, in the Guadalupes. I know the way there. Along the way we'll check every hangout, every cave, every abandoned cabin, in case something goes wrong for them along the way and they abandon the children . . . or worse." He walked past her and stared out the window. "We will find them, understand? And if Sam Higgins thinks he finally has my ass, he'll damn well find out different! He and Briggs picked the wrong man to do this to!" He faced her then. "And the wrong *woman!* The Tess I saw that night, the woman who shot a man and saved my life after terrible abuse by outlaws, is the Tess you're going to be now! Just like now I'm the man who sank a knife into Chino's heart as easy as breathing! The man who blew Darrell Briggs to pieces! Only his *brother* won't die that *easy!"*

Tess grasped his wrist, closing her eyes and running a hand along his powerful arm. "I am only strong when I am with you."

"Oh, no, Tess. That kind of strength comes from inside. And when your children are at stake, you find a strength you never even knew you possessed."

She reached up and touched his face. "My poor John. You must be so tired."

"It's you I'm worried about. You probably haven't slept yet either."

She kissed the palm of his hand. "No. And I couldn't now if I tried." She turned away and wiped at more tears. "I'll change. It gets light quite early this time of year. We should leave the minute we can see well enough and put in as many hours as possible today. We should try to sleep a few hours later in the day, though. When we find the children, we will have to be rested and ready, especially you." She drew a deep sigh. "John, the whole town has been wonderful. They formed a posse to go search, but they found nothing. Because of the way the note was worded, I asked Sheriff Potter to please not send men out too far, and not to notify the Rangers. Higgins said to come alone. I didn't want to make any big decisions until you got here."

Their gazes held in mutual horror, mutual agony.

"I want to talk to Ken," John told her. "Mary Sanders said he's conscious, but it will be a miracle if he lives."

"Then we will have to pray for a miracle."

John turned away. *"You'll* have to do the praying." He opened the door. "Mary will bring in your things."

"John."

He hesitated, his back still to her.

"Ken blames himself."

John stood silent for a moment. *"I'm* the one to blame, Tess. That's the hell of it. I didn't trust my instincts, and this is what I get for it. I'll never forgive myself for this one."

His voice broke on the last words, and Tess ached for him. For all his toughness, the hard life he'd lived growing up, all the fighting and killing, if anything happened to Tex and Honor, it would destroy him.

Twenty-seven

A gracious Mary Sanders led John to Ken's room, where her husband was unrolling bandages. Jenny sat on the other side of the bed, holding Ken's hand, her head bent down. John walked closer, noticing a bloody heap of clothes at the foot of the bed. His rage deepened when he saw Ken. He was covered to the waist, and from there up he was a mass of bloodstained bandages.

Jenny looked up, and John was almost shocked to see how she had aged in just these few hours. Her hair hung loose from what had been a fancy, curled coif; her eyes were baggy and puffy from crying; her whole face sagged from sorrow. "John," she said softly. She just shook her head.

John turned to the doctor. Harry Sanders had been quite young when he arrived in El Paso ten years ago, but he'd done a good job, and everyone trusted his abilities. He'd literally saved Tess's life when she delivered Honor after a long, harrowing labor. Harry had three children of his own now and was a member of the town council. He was a slender, quiet man, dedicated to his work, and John felt Ken could not be in better hands. "Will he live?" John asked him.

Sanders shook his head. "I honestly don't know. I've never taken so many stitches in my life. I tried to give him laudanum to help ease the pain, but he insisted he didn't want anything that might make him sleepy until after he saw you. The most dangerous thing to watch for now is infection." He walked closer and motioned for John to bend down a little. "I'm not sure he'll be able to walk if he does live. He says he can't feel his feet and legs."

John closed his eyes, feeling sick inside. Not only had his children been stolen away, but his best friend might die, all because he had trusted a friendly young man who called himself Billy. "Can I talk to him?"

"You can try. He slips in and out of consciousness."

John walked over to the other side of the bed from Jenny and leaned over Ken, grimacing at the sight. "Ken?"

Ken made no reply at first.

"This is all my fault," Jenny sobbed, her head still down. "All my fault. I brought Billy out to the ranch. Oh, God, I wish I was dead. I wish Billy had done this to *me,* not to Ken."

John sat down in a chair the doctor had been using. He rested his elbows on his knees and thought a moment. "Jenny, his name is not Billy. You saw the note. His name is Lonnie Briggs, and if anyone is to blame for this, it's me. I'm the one who killed his brother. I'm the one who broke up the cattle-rustling ring Sam Higgins was a part of. Worst of all, I'm the one who ignored my doubts and allowed Lonnie Briggs to work for me. If I could cut myself a hundred times and take Ken's place, I'd do it."

Jenny raised her head, wiping at her eyes. "I know you would. Oh, John, those kids, little Honor—"

"They're going to be all right," John interrupted. He could not bear the thought of his sweet little Honor, the terror she must be feeling; or Tex, how responsible he must feel for his little sister, but how helpless because of his age. "Tex is a fighter, a damn tough kid. He'll be brave about this. I know him. And he'll watch out for Honor, make sure she's protected from the sun. If he has to give up food so she can eat, he'll do it. They fight sometimes, and he teases her, but in a situation like this he'll protect her with his—" He stopped short. He could not say the word.

"Hawk," Ken groaned.

John rose and leaned close to him. "Ken?"

Ken opened his eyes, and a tear slipped out of one and trickled down the side of his face. "I . . . failed you. Never . . . did that . . . in the old days. I . . . turned my . . . back. I trusted that . . . sonofabitch."

"So did I, Ken. Don't forget that."

"Gettin' old. I ain't . . . no use to you . . . anymore."

"Damn it, Ken, I'd still trust you with my life, and you know it! You're my best friend, and when I go after Honor and Tex, I don't need the worry of you giving up because you think this is your fault! I need you, Ken Randall, and you're like a second father to those kids."

Ken's eyes started to flutter shut.

"Ken?" John said in a raised voice.

Ken looked at him again.

"You listen to me, you sonofabitch! Don't you dare die on me! It's raining out. It's not a good day to die!"

Ken studied him a moment, then began to grin. "Oh, yeah . . . I . . . forgot about that."

John felt the pain of old memories. When they used to ride together, John always lived by the Indian adage that only certain days were good days to die. He jokingly claimed that he would never die on a cloudy day. Ken's remembering the joke meant he was alert, and maybe the memory would help him recover.

"And have you forgotten how many times you saved my ass all those years ago?" John asked.

"You . . . saved mine . . . too."

"Yeah, well I might need you to save mine again someday. You just hang on. Too many people need you, including Jenny. Besides, do you want me to have to tell Tex and little Honor that you're dead? Think how that would break their hearts. They love you, and I'm bringing them back. Do you hear me? I'm bringing them back, and Lonnie Briggs is going to hurt a lot worse than you're hurting right now. I *guarantee* it!"

Ken managed to nod just slightly. "I . . . know you. If anybody . . . can find them kids . . . it's . . . Hawk." He closed his eyes. "I'm . . . so damn . . . sorry, Hawk."

"Well, so am I. You trusted Lonnie because you thought *I* trusted him. And seeing you here like this now makes me even more determined to make Lonnie Briggs and Sam Higgins pay for this! Tess and I are leaving in just a little while. You make sure that when we get back with the kids, you're walking around and doing just fine."

"I'll . . . try." Ken took a deep breath. "Everything . . . hurts so bad."

"And you're a tough man." John reached over and squeezed Jenny's hand. "Take good care of him."

"You know I will." Jenny sniffed. "John, I'm so scared for you and Tess. You know it's your life Sam Higgins wants. Lonnie, too."

"Well, they are not going to *get* what they want! But I will get what *I* want, which is *their* lives!"

"God, John, be careful. If I lose Kenny, and you and Tess—" Her body jerked in a sob. "I'd have no reason left to live."

"We'll be back. You can count on it."

"I love you, John. I always have, you know."

John straightened. "I'll make you a deal. If Tess and I come back with the kids, all in one piece and unharmed, you promise to marry Ken."

Jenny smiled through tears. "It's a deal."

"Hawk . . ."

The word was barely audible, but John caught it and leaned closer to Ken.

"When you . . . move in on . . . Lonnie . . . and Sam . . . make sure . . . it's a cloudy . . . day."

John could not help grinning a little. "It will be a *damn* cloudy day for Sam Higgins and Lonnie Briggs!"

Twenty-eight

Tess buttoned her riding skirt, wondering where she found the strength. Her body ached everywhere and longed for rest; but mentally she was alive with visions of the terrible things that could be happening to her children. She could only take relief in the fact that little Honor had her brother with her.

Tex was so protective of his sister. He was a tough little guy, like his father, and just as brave. The trouble was, he was brave enough to try something foolish in defense of his sister, and Tess feared he was with men who would hurt him for it.

She buttoned on her suede vest over a white cotton blouse, ignoring all rules of proper conduct by wearing no undergarment beneath the blouse. She and John could be in for a long journey under the hot sun. She would be miserable enough in this outfit, boots and a suede, split riding skirt. Added undergarments would only make her more miserable. Most women would be shocked to know she wore none, but they were not searching for their children in the hot Texas sun.

She studied herself in the mirror, tucking a few more pins into the bun she'd rolled at the top of her head. She would be cooler wearing it up, especially with a hat on. John walked in, and she turned to him. "Do you notice anything?"

He looked her over. "Like what?"

She reached for her floppy, wide-brimmed leather hat and put it on. "Good. If you don't notice, maybe no one else will."

John sighed, taking off the leather vest he wore and then his shirt. "You could tell me what I'm supposed to notice."

She faced him again as he tossed the shirt aside and pulled on only the leather vest. "I'm wearing nothing extra under this blouse."

He looked her over again, and for a brief moment Tess thought about what they would be doing right now if not for the awful tragedy of their children. She wondered if either of them would ever feel like making love again. If they did not find Tex and Honor, or if the children died, nothing would ever be the same.

"Why no underwear?" John asked.

"For the same reason you just took off your shirt. It won't take long for the morning sun to turn into a branding iron. Once we're out on the trail alone, I might even take off this vest."

John nodded, a hint of another kind of longing in his own eyes. He picked up his shirt. "I had Maria pack some of your creams. You'll need them. And we'll have to go easy on water."

"I know." Tess closed her carpetbag and walked closer. "How is Ken?" She could feel his rage, watched him stiffen.

"I said all the things I could think of to make him want to live. Doc Sanders is not sure he'll be able to walk."

Tess closed her eyes, wondering how much grief a person was capable of bearing.

"This is so unfair to you, Tess," John said.

"To *me?*"

"You suffered enough nine years ago. That God of yours should not have allowed this to happen."

"He isn't just my God, John Hawkins. He's yours, too, and right now he's testing our faith. He will get us through this."

"Maybe." John started for the door. "You just pray real hard that He helps me figure out what to do once we find Honor and Tex. And if they're hurt or killed, don't ever ask me to go to church with you again." He turned and faced her. "And don't ask me to think like a Christian when I get my hands on Lonnie Briggs and Sam Higgins. There won't be anything Christian about it!"

He walked out, and Tess followed, thinking how much he was

like the John Hawkins she hardly knew, the one she met that night he infiltrated the camp of *Comancheros*. The ruthless, bitter, violent John had returned. It hurt to realize that all her years of trying to teach him a different way of life might have gone to waste. Sam Higgins might have not only stolen her children but her husband, too.

She pressed her hand to her stomach. How could she tell John about her pregnancy now? If she didn't tell him, and lost the baby during this awful journey, what would that do to John?

She blinked back tears and walked out to see Jenny meet John in the hallway on his way out. "Good luck, John. God be with you."

He quickly embraced her and left. Jenny turned and hugged Tess. "Oh, Tess, if you don't come back—"

"I'm more afraid for John than anyone else," Tess answered, struggling to stay strong. "It's him they want. And if John Hawkins has to walk right up to them and let them fill him with bullets to save those children, he'll do it."

Jenny patted her back. "Don't I know it. God, the look in his eyes, Tess. All the years I've known him, I've never seen that look. It's downright scary even for his friends." She kissed Tess's cheek. "I wish there was something I could do to help."

"Just stay here and help Ken get well," Tess told her. "His friendship means so much to John." She turned to embrace Mary Sanders quickly.

"The whole town will be praying for those children," Mary told her. "You know that."

"I know," Tess said softly. "Please pray for John, too." She walked outside, where John already sat on Shadow, gun belts hanging crisscrossed over his chest. He looked every bit the renegade himself, and for the next few days or weeks, he would most likely behave like one.

Several men from town were there to offer their services, some saddled up and wearing firearms.

"Let us go with you, John," Frank Fuller argued. He stood nearby holding the reins of his horse, rifle in hand. "We can hang back. You have no idea how many other men Higgins might have talked into helping him with this. He's not your only enemy, you know."

"Nobody knows that better than I do. But I'm not taking any chances with my children. If it's me they want, it's me they will get, but I'll make sure they regret asking me to come!" He turned and watched Tess mount up on White Sox. "I don't like this one bit—you having to go along." He looked back at Frank. "Maybe there is some way we could use a decoy."

"No!" Tess told him firmly. "Those are my children out there, and if we get them back, they will need their mother, especially Honor. Do you really think I could sit here *waiting?* Not knowing what's happening? Wondering if I'll ever see any of you again? If you leave me behind, John Hawkins, I'll follow anyway. Then I *would* be out there alone!"

John sighed and shook his head. "Well, I know you well enough by now not to argue."

A round of light, nervous laughter rippled among those standing there, but it could not erase the tension and agony of the moment.

John scanned the good people who had gathered. "I appreciate your offer of help, but I have to handle this my way. Just don't expect me to bring anybody back for a trial!" He turned Shadow. "Let's go, Tess."

He rode off, leading Pepper by a rope tied to his bridle.

Tess glanced at Frank. "Thank you, Frank. If we . . . if we don't make it back, do whatever you need to do with the ranch. Give it to Ken, if he wants it, or just sell it and divide the money or the land among all the men."

"You'll be back," Frank tried to reassure her. "You're ridin' with John Hawkins."

Tess smiled sadly, then prodded White Sox into a gentle lope, following after John and leading the sturdy gelding called Jake. Jake was loaded with supplies for their journey.

From here on it was just her and John . . . and the unforgiving land, and unforgiving men.

Twenty-nine

"I want my mommy!" Honor pouted.

"Your mommy is coming," Lonnie told her. "Your daddy, too." He plopped her onto his horse.

"They can't find us if we keep riding," Tex said. He folded his arms and stood defiantly near his horse. "Me and Honor are staying right here till they come. You and Mr. Bates can go on without us."

Truby kicked dirt over their campfire. "Mount up, kid, or I'll smack that frown right off your face."

"Go ahead! I'm not going *any*place! Lonnie said yesterday that we were just going for a ride. But he didn't stop. My pa will wonder what happened to us."

"Let them wonder." Truby walked over and grabbed Tex, who kicked him hard in the shinbone with the toe of his leather boot.

"Ow!" Truby yelped. "You little Indian bastard!" He grabbed Tex by the hair and made ready to hit him.

"Truby!" Lonnie shouted. He walked over and shoved the man. "Not yet. I want these kids well and healthy when John Hawkins comes looking for them."

"Then tell the brat to quit talkin' back to me! He keeps it up, and I'll knock his brains out, whether you like it or not!"

"Go get on your horse," Lonnie ordered.

Grudgingly, Truby obeyed. Lonnie turned to Tex, who struggled not to show tears. "Go ahead and mount up, kid."

Tex glared at him. "You're *bad,* aren't you? You lied about your name."

Lonnie knelt in front of him. "Look, I promise not to hurt your sister, okay? And you won't be hurt either, if you just do what me and Truby tell you. This won't take very long. I just need to get your ma and pa out someplace where nothing can happen to me. I did some bad things, and I know your pa would try to turn me in if he knew. I want to talk to him about it, maybe see, since I worked so good for him, if he'll put in a good word for me and help me keep from getting arrested. That's why I had to give a different name when I worked for your pa. I wanted to prove to him that I'm a changed man. Now I have, and if I can get him to come out here to talk to me, maybe we can straighten it out. And I want your ma to come so's your little sister won't be scared."

Tex studied Lonnie's blue eyes, his bright smile. He remembered his father didn't really trust the man and was rude to him when he first came to the ranch. "I think my pa was right about you. He didn't trust you. I could tell. My father knows about them things."

"Well, now, I guess he *was* right. 'Cause like I told you, I *have* done some bad things. But I don't intend to do anything bad to you or your sister, I promise. And as soon as your mother and your pa come for you, you can go to them. I just want to be able to talk to your pa alone."

"You better *not* let anything happen to Honor. You don't know how mad my pa can get. And he used to be a Texas Ranger, and he was really good. He caught a lot of bad men, and he'll catch you if *you* do anything bad!"

"Where are we going?" Honor asked.

"Well, now, that's a secret. But you'll know soon enough. We'll be meeting up with a couple other men, and then we'll all wait for your mother and father."

"You won't hurt Honor?" Tex asked.

"I won't hurt her."

"You won't let her get sunburnt?"

"I won't let her get sunburnt."

"C'mon! Let's go!" Truby barked. "If the kid won't go, tie him up and *make* him go. Better yet, shoot the little bastard and leave him for Hawkins to find. That will make him even more anxious to find the girl . . . and probably make him more careless. The man is probably already on our trail, and that makes me nervous after all the things I've heard about him. The sooner we reach Higgins, the better."

Lonnie stood up. "Why don't you keep your mouth shut, Truby?" He looked down at Tex. "Get up on Maggie, Tex. Don't pay any attention to Truby. He just gets excited too easy. Do what I tell you, and I'll make sure your sister stays safe."

Honor started to cry. "I want to go home." She sobbed.

"Don't cry, Honor." Tex finally decided to get on his horse. "Pa will come for us real soon. He'll take you home."

"Sure he will." Lonnie gave Honor a reassuring hug. "Don't you worry about a thing, cutie pie. Uncle Lonnie will make sure you're okay."

"You're not her uncle," Tex reminded him.

"Let's get movin', or Hawkins will catch up to us before we want him to," Truby told Lonnie. He took hold of the reins to Tex's horse and rode off.

Tex clung to his saddle horn, his mind racing with confusion. No matter what else was true or not true, he loved Honor and had to protect her. Even if Truby hit him, he would not run away unless he could figure out a way to take Honor with him.

Thirty

Tess followed John through the gates of Fort Bliss. She felt as though she was following an outlaw. From behind, one would certainly take John for one. His straight, black hair hung nearly to his waist. He wore only his leather vest, with ammunition belts hung crisscrossed over both shoulders. Two rifles rested in cases tied to either side of his horse, and he wore a six-shooter on his hip, a large sheathed knife tied at his waist. Instead of a hat, he wore a red bandanna around his forehead.

There were moments when he actually gave her the shivers, reminding her of the very *Comancheros* who stole her away. Indeed, he was dark as any Comanche or Apache, and he had painted black circles under each eye to protect them from the sun's glare on his high cheekbones.

In contrast, she wore a brimmed, leather hat low on her forehead, to protect her face from the sun. She wore leather gloves to protect her hands, and her long blouse sleeves protected her arms. She wore no weapons, but a rifle boot was tied to her gear, a Winchester shoved into it. John insisted she have it handy in case she needed it for protection.

Some of the soldiers inside the fort stared, and she did not doubt those who did not know John thought they were watching some renegade warrior bringing in his captive. The sight of the soldiers made her long to be able to send the whole army after Lonnie Briggs. But something like that could cost the children their lives. Besides, there were times when John Hawkins alone could handle what a whole army could *not* handle. When he was a Ranger, the army had used his expertise several times in hunting down criminals.

For years in Texas there had been considerable animosity and competition between the Rangers and the US Army. Most Rangers were loyal Texans and ex-Confederates. To them the army represented the Union, and they did not belong in Texas; nor did they have any business getting involved in events involving Texas laws, and *out*laws.

Now the two factions cooperated a little better, and the Rangers had been revamped into a larger, more sophisticated unit of men who enforced Texas law, taking over more and more for any problems that once were up to the army. Most Indians were on reservations now. The railroad ran all the way to El Paso and beyond to California. Law and civilization had come to Texas, and a need for army forts was fast dwindling; but the recent kidnapping of her children was a reminder that there was still a savage element in this land.

John halted his horse under a sprawling pecan tree in the fort's courtyard. "Captain Booth is coming," he told her. "You might as well get down and sit on that bench under the tree and relax for a minute."

Tess obliged, watching Captain Booth head their way. She recognized his wiry frame and his bowlegged walk. He walked at a fast pace, accompanied by an army officer and several soldiers as well as a group of rugged-looking men sporting all sorts of weapons. She knew they would be Texas Rangers.

"John! I got a wire from Sheriff Potter in El Paso!" Booth shouted before he got close enough to talk in a normal voice.

John dismounted and reached out when Booth got closer. The two men shook hands.

"I'm damned sorry, John. My God, we were just talking about something like this three weeks ago. This has to be your worst nightmare!"

"It is."

"How's Ken?"

"He's in a bad way. I think he's tough enough to pull through, but his spirits are low. He blames himself for this."

Booth removed his floppy leather hat and shook his head. "Poor Ken." He glanced at Tess, who stood beside John. "How are you holding up, Tess?"

"I don't really know. I just feel sort of numb, still in shock, I guess."

"We all are." Booth looked back up at John. "This Lonnie, he is Darrell Briggs's brother. We checked it out. Their pa was killed in the war, and Darrell rode with Quantrill. Their mother farmed, barely got by. Lonnie helped her, but Darrell continued to run wild, a real troublemaker, drank a lot, things like that. Every once in a while he brought home money stolen from banks in the North. That helped his ma and Lonnie, who was about twelve years younger than his brother. Some say he all but worshiped Darrell, and he always planned on joining him when he got older. Then he was killed . . . and we both know how."

"He raped a twelve-year-old Indian girl," John reminded him. "I blew his ass to hell, and I'll do worse to Lonnie when I get my hands on him!"

Booth looked him over, shaking his head. "I've got no doubt about that, Hawk. I wouldn't want to be in Lonnie's shoes, or Sam Higgins's." He scratched at his beard. "Anyway, I guess after Darrell was killed his mother went into a real bad depression and stopped eatin', ended up starvin' to death. Lonnie blames all that on you, apparently. Our men out in the Houston area found people who knew him well enough to hear him talk about gettin' you someday for what you did. The young sonofabitch saved newspaper articles about you retirin' and all, and even subscribed to the El Paso paper, so he could find articles that might be about you. I guess that's how he knew about you marryin' and about the kids and all. He's smart, and determined."

John turned away for a moment, throwing back his head and sighing. "What's the news on his own past? Has he broken the law before?" He began rolling himself a cigarette.

Booth rubbed at his neck, and Tess took off her hat and put her head back against the tree. She closed her eyes, hating to have to even talk about Lonnie Briggs.

"Oh, he's had lots of skirmishes with the law, probably would have been as bad as his brother if he'd been in the war and rode with Quantrill and all. He's been in lots of fistfights, likes his whiskey, and an old girlfriend of his was found dead. He's also suspected of, uh, rape. Nothing could be proved on the death or the rape. I reckon it's because he's so charming and good-lookin', or so they say, that people just can't believe he'd do anything like that. I ain't never seen him, but I'm told he's right handsome." He glanced at Tess. "Sorry to talk about these things in front of you, Tess, what with some of the things you've been through yourself, and now this terrible thing with the kids. I'm damn sorry for all of this."

"You can talk about anything you want in front of me, Captain. If it might help my children, it doesn't matter."

John lit a cheroot and turned around. "Anything else?"

"Well, we only know he's in cahoots with Sam Higgins, and probably Truby Bates, the man Higgins shared a cell with in Yuma. We have no way of knowin' if the other man who escaped from the prison wagon is helping him. He could be in Mexico by now. His name was Ron Calhoun, guilty of all sorts of crimes, includin' shootin' a woman, bank robbery and ra— Uh, well, a no-good all around."

Tess wiped away a piece of hair stuck to her face because of perspiration. "Would Lonnie be cruel to the children?" she asked quietly.

"I don't know, Tess. I really don't know. I like to believe he wouldn't. But then they're John's kids, and he hates John. So does Sam Higgins. I can't believe either one of 'em would hurt the kids." He rested his hands on his hips. "John, I've got men ready to ride with you. The lieutenant here at the post even said you could take some of his men. We all want to help you find them kids."

John puffed on the cheroot, then took it from his mouth. "I

appreciate the offer, but they said to come alone, and that's what Tess and I are going to do."

"You don't know how many more men they might have helping them by now."

"I don't care. I can't risk them meaning exactly what they say by showing up with half an army and getting my kids killed over it. All I need from you is your thoughts on where you think they are taking Tex and Honor. All the note said was it was a place in the Guadalupes where they would be able to see us coming from a long way off. Most of the way there is damn desolate country and I hate dragging Tess through it, but we have no choice. My guess is they're talking about Thieves' Hollow and Eagle Pass. What do you think?"

Booth turned to the rest of the men. "You soldier boys can go on about your business, I reckon. You men with me, take a rest till I'm through here. If we're not ridin' with Hawk, you need to spread out and get back to normal duties."

"Sure, Capt'n," one of them answered. He looked at John. "We're all real sorry about this, Hawk. I'm kind of new and never rode with you, but I've heard plenty. I have a feelin' you'll get your kids back, and I don't doubt them men will be the sorriest creatures ever walked."

The rest voiced their concern and regrets with various comments, some of them shaking John's hand.

"Go get 'em," one man told John, squeezing his hand.

"I intend to do just that," John answered.

"We're here to help any way you need," another told him.

"I appreciate that, but there really isn't much you can do."

The others departed, and John turned his attention to Captain Booth. "What do you think?"

Booth removed his hat and fingered the brim as he spoke. "I think you're probably right. My guess is they will deliberately leave signs for you. Once in a while they will stray off the path, do what they can to stay ahead of you and maybe try to confuse you. But it sure sounds to me like they're headed for Eagle Pass. It's one of the few places where they can have a virtual fortress, able to see anyone coming from a couple miles away. They won't want any confrontation with you till they get someplace where there is no way you can sneak up on them. That's Eagle Pass. There is still a cabin up there, far as I know. I'd like to send a pack of Rangers there and shoot it out or starve them out, but with the kids involved, that changes the whole picture."

"It does for me, too. I can't just go in with guns blazing. That's the hell of it. I intend to check every possible campsite and hideaway along the way, in case they leave one of the children off for some reason."

"You might stop at Lena's place and see if her and the girls know anything." He stopped and glanced at Tess. "It ain't a very reputable place, Tess, but the ladies there will help if they can. They, uh, like John a whole lot."

The remark brought her more alert. The place was most likely a whorehouse for outlaws . . . and any lawmen like John who cared to pay them a visit. "Oh, I have no doubt they did," she answered wearily, glancing at John.

"Years ago," John told her. He puffed on the cheroot again, turning his attention back to Booth. "I agree with your theory. They want to be sure I find them, so they won't just go into hiding and wait for me to track them down. I will still have to do some tracking, make sure I follow their route in case, like I said, something happens to one of the children and they leave him or—" The word stuck in his throat for a moment. Honor. His precious, sweet, innocent Honor. "Or her off somewhere. I think I know where to pick up their trail. They took one of Jenny's horses, a black-and-white with one front hoof bigger than the other. Makes it easy to track her."

"I sure wish I could go with you, John. I could follow, hang back."

"No. It's too big of a risk. I just wanted to check with you and see if you agreed they are probably headed for Eagle Pass." He threw down the cheroot and stomped it out. "Thanks for the offer, but I have to do this alone."

"Well, Lord knows you don't need much advice from anybody. You know that country like the back of your hand. I just hate to see Tess have to ride into that hellhole and go through somethin' like this."

"Yeah. So do I." John looked down at Tess. "You ready to ride? We have a lot of hours of light left."

Tess quietly nodded. She stood up and put her hat back on. "I'm ready."

Man and wife mounted up, and Booth shook John's hand again. "The good Lord be with you, John."

John smiled sadly. "If He is, it's because of Tess, not me." He nodded to Booth and headed out, and Tess followed.

Several men along the way wished them luck. Tess found it amazing how fast the word had spread and warming to know how many cared. She followed John away from the fort and toward a horizon rimmed with barren mountains. Every mile from now on meant being farther away from friends and loved ones . . . and help. Never had the word alone held more meaning.

Thirty-one

For nearly nine years Tess had slept with John Hawkins. She bore him two children: one dead, one alive. She attended social functions with him, even got him into church once a year. Yet the man she'd been following the last two days was like a stranger. He was so tight with anger that he had barely spoken, and there had been no more embraces—just riding all day and dropping dead from exhaustion at night.

Tess knew John's mind was racing with plans for what he should do and with dread that he might make a wrong move that could cost the lives of his wife and children.

It was hot . . . so hot. Tess ached for a cool bath, for the shade of a tree. She wanted to cry at the thought of how hard this had to be on poor little Honor. John and Tex never seemed much bothered by the heat, but sometimes the heat made Honor sick. Her own head ached from it, and she worried about the life she carried in her belly . . . a life John still did not know about.

They followed a pathway that sometimes looked like a road and sometimes looked like nothing but open country with no road at all; but John seemed to know where he was going, and she never doubted him. Few men knew Texas better than he did.

She drew on her horse's reins when John held up his hand, signaling for her to stop. She waited quietly while he listened. Finally he motioned for her to come ahead. She rode up beside him. "What is it?"

"I hear buzzards," he told her. "And I smell something foul."

Tess neither heard nor smelled a thing, but her stomach went into a knot. "It couldn't be—"

"Who knows?" John interrupted abruptly. "Follow me until I tell you to stop, and after that don't you dare come one inch closer until I have a look."

Tess's heart beat so hard it hurt. They wouldn't! No man was so vengeful that he would murder a child, was he? No! She must not even think it!

John urged his horse into a gentle lope, leading his spare horse up a ridge that dropped off on the other side at a much steeper grade than the one they had just climbed. Something lay farther out in the flat area beyond the bottom of the hill, not far off the narrow road.

"John—"

He grasped the reins of her horse when she rode up beside him. "Stay here. It's probably just a dead animal."

Tess fought tears as he rode ahead. She was sure she saw a piece of cloth on whatever it was that lay below. How could it be an animal! And if it was one of the children, what a horrible thing for John to find! He would never, never be the same again. Nothing about their lives would ever be the same. And poor John would blame himself for all of it, not just for going against his instincts about Billy Williams, but because this was all happening because of enemies he'd made.

She felt so responsible herself. If only she'd never gone shopping. She closed her eyes and prayed harder than she had ever prayed. She couldn't even look, until finally John called her with a shrill whistle. He motioned for her to come forward, and she literally groaned with relief. He would not allow her to see if the body was one of the children. Tears of relief spilled down her face as she rode down to meet him, hardly aware of the heat for her joy in knowing her children were surely still alive.

When she reached John, she glanced down at the animal, a dead coyote.

"Shot through the head," John told her. He held out the little shirt Honor wore to protect her arms from the sun, and Tess gasped. "They're telling us that if we don't cooperate, we could find our children like this."

Tess bent over and, without any warning from her own body, vomited. She could not help the tears that came with it. She clung to her horse's mane, resting her head on the mare's neck when she finished, and a firm arm came around her waist, lifting her from her horse.

"I'm all right," she protested.

"Here. Drink some water and wash the taste from your mouth."

Tess could hardly see for her tears and the strain of being sick. With shaking hands she took a canteen from John, who held her close in front of him on his horse.

"You by God shouldn't have had to come," he told her. "You're thinking about what happened to you, aren't you?"

"I . . . can't help it."

"This is different, Tess. These men are bastards, but they aren't *Comancheros,* and their reasons for taking Tex and Honor aren't to sell them or—" He didn't finish. He drank some of the water himself. "You're going to get some rest. We both are. We'll be no use to the kids this way."

"She's still just a baby, John."

"Of course she is. But Tex isn't. He'll do anything he can to protect her."

"I know he will. But he's just a little boy."

"He's smart, and he's brave." He hung the canteen over a leather hook on his saddle and put his other arm around her. "Damn it, you've been through enough hell in your life."

"I'll be okay as long as I'm with you." How could she tell him about the baby? What terrible timing. And if he knew, he would send her right back in spite of Higgins's demands. There was no way she was going back. Her children needed her, especially poor, sweet little Honor. What if she or Tex were hurt when their parents found them? There was nothing more comforting than a mother's arms. She remembered when she felt that way about her own mother, before she died in a fire when she was still a young girl.

She'd vowed then that she would be the best mother she could when she was older, for as long as God allowed her to live.

John leaned over, then put something in her hands. "Here. Take the reins to your two horses. Just hang on to them until I get us to that shady spot over there. The setting sun is casting a shadow in those rocks. It should be a good place to rest." He squeezed her hands when he gave her the reins, and she rested her head against his chest as he rode to their campsite. When they reached the spot, Tess clung to his strong forearm, and he lowered her to the ground.

John dismounted. "I'm not the least bit hungry, and I'm sure you aren't either, but we'd better at least force down a piece of jerked meat and some water," he told her, "and a little bread. We won't make a fire. There's nothing here to make one with anyway. We'll have to gather anything we can tomorrow for making a fire tomorrow night, unless we find a place to stay."

"You mean there *are* places to stay on this godforsaken trail?"

"Oh, there are actually a few ranches here and there, honest people that outlaws and rustlers leave alone; and there are even some outlaws who have made homes for themselves and turned to farming or ranching." He grasped her arms. "How do you feel?"

Tess met his eyes. There he was, a wild, painted warrior, not John Hawkins. "Better." She moved her arms around his waist and rested her head against his chest again. "I hope I see you smile again, John. I miss you."

He put a big hand to the side of her face. "I'll smile again, just as soon as I put my arms around Tex and Honor." He kissed her hair and gently pushed her away. "You sit down. Don't make a move until I have your bedroll ready."

"I should help."

"Not tonight."

"You're just as tired as I am."

"There were times on the trail as a Ranger when I didn't sleep three or four nights in a row."

Tess just shook her head at his tenacity. "I promise to be more help after tonight. I just . . . I could handle anything that happens to me. I would rather be burned at the stake than have Honor hurting and lonely."

"You know I would, too." John unloaded their gear from the horses, then removed the saddles from the riding horses. "We'll ride the spare horses tomorrow, give these two a rest." He took an iron pan from their pack and poured water into it, giving each of the horses a drink. Then he spread out a bedroll, putting his own right beside it. "Lie down over here. Not very soft, but at least cooler."

Tess removed her vest and boots and lay down. John took some jerky from their supplies and handed her a piece. "Try to eat this."

"I don't think I can."

"Try. Even a couple of bites is better than nothing."

Tess sighed and bit off a piece, chewing it slowly, but the blankets John rolled up for a pillow looked too tempting, and she lay down. Almost instantly her arm fell limply down and sleep began to consume her.

"Her . . . shirt," she said, slurring the words from agonizing weariness. "What did you . . . do . . . with her . . . little shirt?"

"I threw it back," she heard him say. "It stank like that dead animal. Even on her dirtiest, sweatiest days, I never knew my Honor to ever smell bad. She always smells sweet."

His voice broke on the last words. A few minutes later Tess sensed John lying next to her, and his arm came around her. Safe. She always felt so safe with this man.

She felt a slight shaking movement then, and she came more awake. It took her a moment to realize what was happening. John Hawkins was quietly weeping. After she first met him and during their entire married life, she had never known him truly to weep when he was with her. She suspected he'd wept alone when their premature son died, but he never cried in front of her.

She remained turned away and did not say a word. He would be too embarrassed. He clung to her a little tighter, and she kissed his arm.

Thirty-two

Morning brought cloudy skies, which in turn brought slightly cooler weather. Tess went behind some rocks to relieve herself, and while there she vomited again. She forced herself not to cough and choke, hoping John was too busy saddling the horses to hear her. If this kept up, he would eventually figure out what was really wrong. By then she intended to be too far away for him to even consider sending her back home. She could only pray this sickness would be short-lived so he would never know until they were through this dreadful event.

She buttoned her riding skirt and straightened, taking a deep breath and trying to look fresh and rested. Neither fit the way she felt. She walked back to their campsite to see John standing and staring at the horizon, his face raised, a morning breeze blowing his hair away from his face. She knew without asking he was praying his own way . . . to his own god.

She sensed that somehow he was taking in the strength of the land, the very air he breathed. Just watching him now made her feel more confident, braver, more determined, more in love with him.

How strange the way they had come to be together . . . and how strange, that after nine years, she was still learning new things about him. In that one moment, that one vision, she was more sure than ever that they would find Tex and Honor. Yesterday's shocking scare was not so frightening now.

She walked down to their camp and began rolling up the

bedrolls, aching for hot coffee. She said nothing to John when he finally returned and began packing the horses. Tess began tying some of the gear onto the packhorses.

"You should rest and let me do all the packing," John told her.

"I've done my resting, and the sooner we get the horses ready, the sooner we can be on our way. There is no time to waste," Tess answered. "I don't want to slow you down. I can do my share, John Hawkins. Besides, you're the one who should get his rest when he can. You're going to need all your strength when we find Tex and Honor, and you'll need to be alert and ready for anything."

John did not reply. He threw his saddle over Shadow, then came over and picked up her saddle. "I don't want you lifting anything. That's an order."

Tess frowned. "Why not? I've hoisted a saddle plenty of times."

"Not pregnant."

Tess closed her eyes and turned away. "How did you know?"

"I have good hearing, remember? You were sick again this morning."

Tess sighed and faced him. "Is there no hiding *any*thing from you?"

"I doubt it." John threw the saddle over Sadie. "Besides, I count weeks just like you do. You haven't had your time for a couple of months now."

Her eyebrows arched in surprise, and she reddened a little at his frankness about something she was always embarrassed to discuss. She watched him cinch the saddle.

"I don't know why in hell your god picked now for you to be carrying," he added, obviously angry as he continued throwing gear onto her horse. "It's goddamn dangerous, even in the best conditions. Doc Sanders said you probably would never have another child. All I can do now is pray my own way that you don't miscarry on top of everything else I have to worry about. But you by-god better do every damn thing I tell you, understand? If you try doing too much, I'll leave you off at one of the ranches along the way and find a woman who will act as a decoy for me."

Tess blinked back tears, almost feeling guilty for being pregnant. "Who on earth would be brave enough to go with you pretending to be me?" she asked, feeling upset with him but not wanting to. After last night . . . the way he wept . . .

"I know of a few who would gladly go with me."

"Oh?" Tess felt a hint of jealousy.

"There is a ranch another day's ride from here, but we might be able to make it by nightfall. I know the people who own it. They'll let us sleep in a real bed. That's what you need. And some home cooking. It's just possible Lonnie went by there himself. Maybe they have some news about Tex and Honor."

"And is that where there is a woman who might be willing to take my place?"

"Several."

Tess put her hands on her hips. *"Several?"*

The slight grin on her husband's face dispelled some of her hurt feelings over his reaction to her pregnancy. "It's a place Ken and I visited a few times."

"Whores?"

He returned to finishing packing his own gear. "What the hell? You know by now from Jenny that they aren't all bad. Knowing you're my wife, they'll treat you like a queen."

"And how will they treat *you?"*

He turned to pick up one of his rifles and shoved it into its boot. "Real good, I expect."

"Oh, I expect so, too."

He stopped working and faced her. "Tess, it's been nine years, and most of them weren't much to look at even back then. Besides, I'm married to the most beautiful woman in Texas."

Now the tears wanted to come again. "Do you mean that?"

He rolled his eyes. "You know better than even to ask."

Why, oh why, did these damn tears come so easy? The children! Her babies in such terrible danger and now this pregnancy . . . "Beautiful . . . and pregnant," she added. She turned away. "I'm sorry you're upset that I'm carrying."

In the next moment his arms came around her from behind. "My God, Tess, it isn't you I'm angry with. It's this whole mess we're in, the fact that you could miscarry and *die* out here! And I wouldn't know what the hell to do about it. This should be a very happy time for us." He squeezed her against him and kissed her cheek. "And you should be home, where you could rest and be safer." He moved one hand over her stomach. "This is a miracle, after what happened with the son we lost. I don't want you to have to go through that again."

She moved her own arms over his and grasped his wrists. "And I don't want *you* to have to go through it, John," she said, weeping. She quickly wiped at tears with one hand then. "Oh, damn it! You need me to be strong. I'm sorry for all this crying and vomiting and . . . oh, John, I'm slowing you down. Without me along, you could probably get ahead of them and—"

"Stop it, Tess. You're doing great. For God's sake, you're just about the strongest woman I've ever known. As far as getting ahead of them, I don't want to. I don't want to risk them seeing me getting the better of them, or they *will* kill Tex and Honor. They have to believe we're trailing along, just like what we're doing. And we have to check every possible place they could have stopped along the way. I don't want to risk one of the children being left off somewhere and us missing him or her." He straightened and turned her around, hugging her close. "And you are not slowing me down. When I stop it's because I think it's necessary, not just for you, but for the horses, and even for myself. You were right to say I need to be rested and ready for whatever is coming."

She wrapped her arms about his waist. "They want to kill you! I can't live without you."

"Yes, you can, if you have to. But you won't have to, because I will find a way to get us through this, Tess. And if God chose this time to let you be with child, then maybe that's a good sign. Maybe you're damn well meant to carry this one all the way.

This baby's birth will just be a celebration of our family being back together again."

She breathed deeply to help curb her tears. "Do you really think so?" she asked, looking up at him.

"I *have* to think so, and so do you. Maybe that will help you hang on to this one."

Finally her tears subsided, and she managed a smile. "Maybe you're right."

He grasped her arms and gently pushed her away. "You know how angry I am right now, Tess. Sometimes that anger will seem directed at you, but you must know I don't mean it that way." He turned, still holding one arm. "Come on. Let's get riding." He lifted her onto Pepper. "We might be able to make it to Lena's place by nightfall."

"Lena?"

He cast her a sly smile as he mounted Shadow. "If she's even still there."

"What are whores doing running a ranch?" she asked, deciding she might feel better if she changed the subject.

He turned to cast her a wry smile. "I didn't say what kind of ranch it was. Most of the men who come through these parts haven't seen a woman in weeks or months, or they have been in prison a long time, or they're the type that most other women just will not bother even looking at, much less go to bed with. These women make a lot of money helping out men like that."

"I'll bet. Does Jenny know about this place?"

John grasped the reins of one of the packhorses and handed them to her. "She used to work there."

Tess just shook her head as John took hold of the reins to his own packhorse and headed out.

"Just remember that from here on you can't trust any of the men you meet," John told her. "Most of them are thieves and murderers, but the majority of them also live by a code, and that's that you can rob banks, even kill people doing it. You can rob trains, hit a man over the head in an alley and steal his money, cheat at cards, drink till you drop, and gamble your life away. But most of them, no matter how bad, man or woman, will stop at hurting kids. I'm hoping Lonnie won't find any extra help along the way because of that. Maybe someone will even try to get the kids away from him. It's a slim hope, but something to help you keep going."

They rode on quietly for a few minutes, but Tess felt a need to keep talking so she would not cry again. "What is this Lena like?"

She watched his back, and he shrugged. "A lot like Jenny."

Tess could not help the jealousy that kept welling up inside, but it helped keep her from thinking about the horror of her missing children. "It *will* be nice to sleep in a real bed tonight."

"Don't count on it. For all I know Lena is gone, and the place has been long vacated. If Lena and some other women *are* still there, don't be surprised about anything I do or say when we get there. The nicer we are, the more Lena will tell us, if she knows anything. And from here on, whenever we get someplace where there are people, you stay close to me."

"In a whorehouse? I wouldn't go more than two inches from your side!"

John laughed lightly. "Jealousy puts a little life back in your veins, doesn't it?"

Tess took a deep breath. "I do feel stronger."

"Good. I *need* you to be strong. It helps *me* be strong. And a good night's sleep will do us both good. We won't lose that much time, because Lonnie also has to stop to rest. I don't think we're more than a day behind them. I just hope that whoever he's with, none of them are abusive to Tex and Honor."

"How do you know Lonnie has someone with him?"

"After Ken was found and Jenny told Sheriff Potter who must have taken the kids, Potter had someone check to see if anyone else in town knew Billy. The man he sent went right to Joe Beal. You know Joe."

"Yes. The biggest gossip in town." Tess took her hat from where it hung around her neck and put it on.

"This time Joe's nosiness turned out to help. He knew Lonnie—as Billy, of course—said some man came to El Paso looking for him one day. Lonnie had left him some kind of letter. The guy told Joe he and Lonnie were good friends and meant to get together when Lonnie was done with roundup. Joe said this guy worked at the blacksmith's for a while. They say he's pretty ugly-looking, has big bags under his eyes. He fits the description of one of the men who escaped with Higgins. He used a fake name; but if he's who we think he is, his name is Truby Bates."

Tess shivered. "I hate the thought of the children being with a complete stranger. Honor must be terrified."

Now Tess felt spent of tears, and she knew John had shed all he was going to shed. From here on they had to be practical, determined, relentless. John had to be the ruthless man he once was, and she had to be the woman who survived an ordeal with *Comancheros*. She straightened her shoulders, heading into what she knew would be another long, hot day.

Thirty-three

"You sure we're goin' the right way?" Truby asked Lonnie.

"I checked this part of the country plenty good when I planned all this," Lonnie answered. "And we came through here when we left Sam and Calhoun off at the cabin, remember? Why in hell can't you remember the way better yourself?"

"Hell, everything looks the same out here—rocks and dust. I hated it when we came through here to go to El Paso, and I hate it still. I'll be glad to get out of this godforsaken hellhole. I can't believe I'm putting up with this heat and dust and two brats for Sam Higgins."

Lonnie shook his head. "I don't know how Higgins put up with you all those years in a cell together," he told the man. "You talk too damn much."

Truby sniffed hard, then spit. "You gotta talk out here or go crazy."

"Well, I have things to think about, so shut up! You might be Sam's friend, but you're not mine."

The two men rode through a deep canyon, their horses' hooves echoing against the canyon walls. Lonnie still kept Honor on his horse in front of him, and the little girl's head hung down from weariness.

"You *gotta* think because you're scared about my pa coming," Tex told Lonnie. "You're gettin' scared, aren't you?"

"You shut up, too, kid."

"Talk about *me* talkin' too much! That kid never quits," Truby complained. "I'm gettin' sick and tired of him always talkin' about his pa comin' for us," Truby said.

Tex curled his nose at Truby's smell. The man's shirt was soaked with sweat, his beard caked with dust. "You *oughta* be nervous," Tex told him. "My pa could be hiding behind a rock right now, waiting to shoot you right off your horse!"

"Shut up, Tex," Lonnie warned. "Don't make me have to tell you again."

Tex held his chin proudly. "You lied to me, didn't you? You don't want my pa to just come and talk to you. I can tell by the way Truby talks. You want to *kill* my pa, only you can't, on account of he's too *smart* for you."

"Oh, yeah?" Lonnie wiped sweat from his own brow with his shirtsleeve. "Then you will *never* be that smart, 'cause John Hawkins isn't really your pa."

"He is *too* my pa!"

"Nope. Word is he adopted you. Your real pa was a real bad man. *Real* bad. He did bad things to your mother, and that's how she got you. You're a bastard, Tex. What do you think of that?"

"I am not!"

"Yes, you are." Lonnie decided that getting the boy to think about something else might shut him up. Besides, Tex talked incessantly about John, and it irritated him as much as it irritated Truby. "A *bastard.* I bet you don't even know what that is."

"It's something bad. I can tell by how you say it."

"That's right. A bastard is a kid nobody wants. Its mother marries anybody she can to give the baby a name. Some mothers even kill their bastard kids. You've got bad blood in you, boy, and it's not John Hawkins's blood. Even if it was, it would *still* be bad, because Hawkins is a bad man, too. He killed a lot of men when he was a Ranger, a lot of them for no reason. My brother was one of them."

"My pa's not bad! He did a lot of brave things. He saved Ken's life, and he put a lot of bad men in jail."

"He also put a lot of them in their *grave*. But you shouldn't care one way or another, because he's not your pa."

Honor raised her head. "He is *too* our pa!" she chimed in with her tiny voice. "You quit saying that!" Her lips puckered with anger.

"Oh, he *is* your pa, Honor. I'm just saying he's not *Tex's* pa. All the men told me so. He doesn't even really love Tex. He just pretends he does. But he does love you, because you're his own."

There was a moment of silence, and Lonnie enjoyed figuring out a way to shut Tex up.

"You're lying again!" Tex finally said, some of the spunk gone out of his voice. "He's my real pa, on account of I look just like him."

"You look like him because you've got Indian blood from the bad man who fathered you. Probably Comanche or Apache. But your pa, he's Sioux. That's what the men told me. Heck, I bet the only reason John Hawkins comes after you two is because of Honor, not for you."

"I don't believe you."

Lonnie could see the boy was about to cry. He shrugged. "Believe what you want. It's true, though. You think about it." He wanted to laugh at the doubt and terrible hurt he saw on Tex's face. That should shut him up for a while.

Thirty-four

"Well, well, well. If it ain't the devil himself!" The voluptuous woman who opened the door to the weather-stained, two-story frame house, also opened her arms, grinning through painted lips. "Handsome as ever, and I'll bet *mean* as ever!"

The woman laughed as she threw her arms around John, patting him on the rear. Tess watched from the shadows, knowing it was silly to feel jealous, but she could not help it when she thought of how many women like this John must have been with before he married her.

"Hello, Lena. I wasn't sure you'd still be here."

Lena, her obviously dyed black hair coifed into a mass of curls, and her blue-velvet dress cut so low it was a wonder her nipples didn't show, leaned up and kissed John smack on the lips. "Of course I'm still here. Most of the other girls are gone, but there are always more to take their places. I've got four others living here now, and there are plenty of men who still ride through here often enough to keep us happy and rich. Hell, my ranch has actually grown, but I've never had to shovel a stall or rope a steer!" She laughed again, a shrill, almost wicked-sounding laugh. "I can always find men to help out. I'm doin' damn good." She grabbed John's hand. "Come on in! Lord, I can't believe how good you still look! I've seen a few other Rangers now and again, and when I heard you got married, I couldn't *believe* it! *Hawk?* God, I cried myself to sleep a lot of nights over that one!

Say, you didn't maybe get rid of the wife, did you? I'd sure like to—"

"Lena!"

Tess noticed John jerk the woman's arm a little.

"Will you let me get a word in?"

The woman sobered. "Sure." She studied him closer. "Say, you don't look so good. Something in those eyes. Something wrong?"

John let go of her hand. "Yeah. Something's very wrong." He turned and looked out at Tess. "Come on in, Tess."

Tess had never felt more awkward. She had visited Jenny once when she ran a saloon, but to actually walk into a real house of ill repute . . . "I don't know, John," she protested. "Maybe we can sleep out in the barn or something."

"It's all right."

"Who's out there?" Lena asked. By then four other women had gathered behind her, staring hungrily at John. When Lena asked who was outside, they all looked over her shoulder, trying to see.

"My wife," John answered.

"Wife? Lord in heaven, Hawk, why in hell didn't you tell me? You let me talk like that in front of your *wife?"*

"You hardly gave me a chance to let you know she was with me."

Lena looked him up and down. "Well, I guess something *is* wrong. You're outfitted like you're going to war, and here you are in the middle of Nowhere, Texas, visiting a whorehouse with your wife in tow. You have some explaining to do!" She went to the door. "Come on in, honey. We don't bite."

She glanced up at John, and Tess suspected she was thinking of adding to the comment. She took a deep breath and walked inside. John put an arm around her.

"This is Tess," he told Lena. "Tess, this is Lena." He glanced at the others. "I don't know the rest of these ladies."

"Ladies, he says!" one of them spoke up. She was huge, at least two hundred pounds or better.

Lena laughed. "To a man like Hawk, who understands us, we're damn well ladies." She looked John over again, then nodded to Tess. "Hello, Tess." She put out her hand, and Tess obliged her with a handshake.

"Hello, Lena."

Lena, a tall, thin, still-attractive woman, turned to the others. "The big one there is Tubbs. She doesn't mind being called that. She knows she's fat. Some men like them that way."

Tubbs grinned and nodded, and Tess nodded in reply, hardly knowing what to think of any of them.

"You have really pretty red hair," Tubbs told her. "I can tell it's natural. I have to dye mine to get it this red."

Tess was amazed at her honesty, and the fact that Tubbs did not seem to care that Lena called her fat.

"The washed-out blonde here is Millie," Lena continued, pointing to a plump but not fat, middle-aged woman, who looked as though she'd never been pretty, even when she was young.

"And Annette," Lena continued, nodding to a young woman with light brown hair and green eyes. She was the only one in the group who actually was pretty, but Tess did not like the way she looked at John. She wore only ruffled bloomers and a camisole, which was partially untied at the top, revealing a good deal of bosom.

"And Sondra," Lena added. "She's new." She pointed to a rather shy-looking, plain woman, who Tess could hardly believe slept with men for money. She looked like a simple housewife and wore no paint on her face. She smiled in a friendly way, also nodding to both Tess and John.

Lena put her hands on her hips. "So, Hawk, what in the world brings you here, with your wife, no less?"

John kept a firm arm around Tess. "My wife needs a good night's sleep in a real bed instead of on the ground. She's completely worn-out."

"Well, you look pretty worn-out yourself. Something bad wrong?"

"As bad as it gets," John told her. "Men like me make a lot

of enemies. One of them escaped from prison a few weeks ago, and he wants my ass. To get it, he's kidnapped my son and my daughter. Tex is only eight years old, and Honor is five."

Lena sobered, as did the other four. "Dear God," Lena said. She took Tess's arm. "You poor thing. Come sit down. Sondra, go make her some tea. Are you hungry, Tess?"

"Not really." Tess sat down on a velvet love seat. "Thank you."

"Have someone make some soup or something," John told Lena. "I want her to eat whether she likes it or not. Neither one of us has slept more than a couple hours the last three days. I'd like nothing better than to ride like hell and overtake these bastards, but I can't be my best when I'm so goddamn tired I can hardly think straight."

"Please don't use the Lord's name, John," Tess said wearily.

"Would you look at this," Lena said, folding her arms and looking John over. "I never thought I'd see the day when a woman ordered you not to cuss. By God, John Hawkins really *is* in love." She shook her head. "Sit down and tell me the whole story. This old enemy of yours, he's got friends helping him? Do I know him, or any of them?"

John sat down next to Tess, and Lena took a seat across from them. "I don't think you know them." He removed his hat, then the ammunition belts he wore over his shoulders, plunking them on the floor. "The main one is Sam Higgins, used to be sheriff in El Paso, until I proved he was involved in cattle rustling. Actually, Tess put me onto it."

"And I almost got you killed by not telling you soon enough," Tess said, holding her head in her hands. "I'll never forgive myself for you getting shot in the back."

"Say, I heard about that from Ranger Pete Newton, quite a few years ago. I told Pete you'd make it. You're the toughest sonofabitch I ever knew. Ken always said you were too mean to die. Say, how is Ken, anyway?"

John sighed. "He's in a real bad way. He was watching Tex and Honor when one of Higgins's men caught him off guard and stabbed him several times. When we left the doc wasn't sure if he would live or die."

"Oh, dear Lord." Lena sighed deeply. "You know what? I'm going to have Tubbs draw both of you a bath. You two are going to wash up, and you're going to sleep like you've never slept. You can explain all this to me in the morning. You both look too tired to talk half the night. The sun's not even set yet, but I'll bet you'll both be asleep before your heads hit the pillow. Early morning, I want to know everything, John Hawkins, how in the world you two got together in the first place, who these men are who have your kids, and why—all of it. That way the girls and me can keep a lookout, pass the word to travelers, things like that. But I do want to know why this pretty little wife of yours has come with you when you're chasing outlaws and kidnappers? I mean, I know she wants to find her children, but I know you work best alone, John."

John moved behind Tess and began massaging her neck and shoulders. "They left a note. They want Tess and me both to come—alone. What they really want is to torture us by taking the kids, and torture me by getting their hands on Tess and then killing me. It's not going to happen."

Tess felt his grip tighten a little.

"Hell, no, it won't happen," Lena answered. "I know you well enough to know that."

Sondra brought in a tray with two cups of hot tea on it. "Here you go, honey," she told Tess.

"My wife has suffered enough," John added. "That's how I met her. I managed to rescue her from *Comancheros*."

The room hung silent for a moment. "Oh, no," Tubbs finally said.

"Well, well," Lena told her. "You must be quite a woman, Tess, to survive something like that."

"She is," John answered. "She looks small and dainty." He squeezed her neck. "But she's damn tough when she has to be, and brave as any man I've known. She doesn't deserve what's happening now."

Tess glanced up at him and smiled sadly. "I'm not that tough."

"The hell you aren't. Drink your tea and go take that bath. I'll explain everything to Lena. When you're done with your bath, I'll be along."

Tess sipped some tea, then looked from Lena to John. "Just so you take your bath without any help."

Lena chuckled. "We'll fix him up right in the same room where you're sleeping. Nobody else will be in there." She sighed deeply. "I gotta say, Tess, you are one lucky woman."

Tess took another swallow of tea. "I know that better than anyone."

"Well, you two sure are a pair—this rugged, wild-looking, ornery man with a dainty, proper lady like you." She shook her head again. "I just can't get over it." She got up from her chair. "I'll help prepare a tub for Tess. We've got some new ones, John, real porcelain. And I always keep hot water on the stove for baths. You two relax for a little while, if that's possible. I know it's probably almost impossible. What a damned mean thing to do, take somebody's little kids. I'll say one thing. This Sam Higgins is one crazy man to mess with the likes of you, John."

She walked out of the room, ordering the other women to come and help her and to find a decent nightgown for Tess. Tess sipped her tea again, then set down the cup and settled into John's shoulder. In minutes she finally drifted off, sensing John picking her up in his arms and carrying her. She didn't care where, didn't even care now if she took a bath.

Thirty-five

Tess relished the cool freshness of a wet rag, smelled sweet soap. She was so tired she didn't even care that Lena was helping John bathe her.

". . . she's carrying," she heard John say.

"Oh, my God," Lena answered. "She shouldn't be doing this. Good Lord, Hawk, what if she miscarries, and you're out there alone with her!"

"It's a chance we have to take. If I tried to make her go back she would just turn right around and follow me. A mother's love can make a woman do just about anything to save her own, and it's the same for me. My little Honor is a tiny, delicate thing with skin like snow and hair as red as her mother's. It makes me sick to think how scared she must be, and to think she might be hurting, abused in some way . . ."

Tess could feel John's rage.

"All the men I've gone after, I've never wanted to make any of them suffer like I want to make these men suffer, Lena. I've killed a lot of men, but it was self-defense, or just because they damn well deserved it. The thing is, when I killed a man, I killed him quick and dead. But these men, I want them to suffer. The worst part is, I can't go in there with guns blazing, and they know it. One of my own bullets could kill my own child."

Tess felt someone toweling her off, then smelled lilac water, felt its coolness splashed over her. "Now, that should feel good," Lena told her. "Here. Let's get a gown on you, Tess."

"Thank you so much," Tess muttered, slipping her arms into the gown.

"Nothing's too good for the wife of John Hawkins. You just lie down in this bed now."

Tess gladly obeyed, welcoming clean blankets, a real mattress, a soft pillow. "Come and sleep, John," she muttered.

"I'll be back soon. I need a bath myself, and the other women have to change the bathwater first."

Tess felt him kiss her cheek, her eyes. "Poor little Honor . . . and Tex . . ."

"We will find them, Tess, and they *will* be okay."

She put out her hand and felt John hold it for a moment.

"Please sleep. After tonight we have to ride hard, Tess, and I don't know for how far."

That was the last thing Tess remembered. The next thing she knew, she heard Honor crying, but she could not find her. She began running toward the sound, but her feet just would not move fast enough. She got on her hands and knees and crawled, coming to a black hole. Far below she saw Honor, reaching toward her. Tex was trying to lift her, but he was too short to raise her high enough.

"Mommy! Mommy!" Honor cried, her blue eyes wide with fear, tears on her rosy cheeks. Tess lay down and reached into the hole, straining to touch Honor's hands. She could not quite touch her fingers. She stretched her arm as far down as she could, and just as she managed to finally touch the girl's fingertips, Billy showed up behind the children, wearing his usual bright smile, his blue eyes sparkling. Suddenly he jerked both children away, and the black hole closed up.

"Honor!" Tess screamed. "Wait! Honor!"

Suddenly Tess awoke, the words actually coming out in a loud groan. A strong arm came around her, and, confused from the nightmare, Tess fought the grip, suddenly remembering her own abduction.

"Tess! Tess, it's me. John!"

Someone shook her lightly. A lamp had been left lit in the

room, and Tess stared blankly into John's face, taking a moment to realize who it was, and that she had been dreaming. "John," she groaned. "I saw them. I saw the children. They were in a black hole calling for me. Maybe that means they've been buried alive! Maybe—"

"It was just a nightmare." John scooted up against the head of the bed and pulled her between his legs, her back to him, his arms around her. "Sit up a few minutes and talk to me. Get the dream out of your head. Sometimes if you go right back to sleep the dream continues." He gave her a squeeze. "And remember, they don't dare hurt those kids or kill them. Without Tex and Honor alive, they can't lure me to whatever they have planned. Tex and Honor are the bait, and as long as they are, they won't be harmed. They'll be all right."

Tess relished his strength. "Yes, maybe you're right." She sighed deeply, shaking the dream from her head. "What time is it?"

"I don't know. Midnight, maybe."

"How long have you been here?"

"A couple of hours."

It had still been light when she went to bed. "You talked to Lena that long?"

"There was a lot to tell her. And I figured if I stayed out of the bed, you would sleep better."

"I couldn't bear this without you. I promise that by morning I will be much better, able to stay on the trail longer. It's just . . . I've had to get over the shock of the children being taken. I think now I can stay calmer, do what I have to do, no matter what that is. I'll be all right, John . . . as long as nothing happens to you."

"Nothing will happen. I promise."

Tess turned her head and leaned back and John met her mouth in a tender kiss. He smelled good . . . bathed. Did Lena help him with his bath? Somehow she didn't even care. He loved her. He belonged to Tess Hawkins. Even Lena respected that.

"Has Lena seen Lonnie, or that Truby Bates?"

"No. Apparently they are avoiding other people. I have no doubt they're headed for Thieves' Hollow. We'll pick up their trail where we left it yesterday."

"How on earth can you tell it's their tracks? Half the time I can't see them at all, the ground is so hard. How do you follow them?"

"You just have to know what to look for. There are a lot of signs showing horses or something as heavy has been through certain areas, even where it's pure rock. As far as the tracks, that horse of Jenny's has one front hoof that is bigger than the other three. Her tracks are easy to read."

"For an ex-Ranger, maybe."

They sat there quietly a moment before John spoke up. "I've been teaching Tex how to read and follow tracks."

Tess ran her hands along his forearms. "Tex adores you, you know. He worships the ground you walk on. I'm sure he's reassuring Honor right now that their daddy will find them and rescue them. He thinks you're the bravest, strongest man who ever walked." She raised one of his hands to her lips and kissed it. "And he believes you are his father. No one who sees you two together would ever think otherwise. Hardly a day goes by that I don't thank God that you agreed to marry me and give Tex your name, John. It's so wonderful to know how close the two of you are, how much you love Tex."

"I love him the same as if he came from my seed." John scooted down again, pulling Tess with him. "We need to rise early. Let's get as much sleep as we can."

Tess settled against him, and he moved an arm around her, pulling her so close that she kissed his shoulder, and fell asleep breathing his manly scent, a wonderful, rugged smell that reminded her of things wild and free . . . even dangerous.

Thirty-six

"Where we going, Tex?" Honor whined the words as she snuggled next to her brother.

"I don't know." Tex put an arm around his sister, feeling very manly in looking out for her, the way his father cared for his mother.

"I'm hot, and mosquitoes are biting me." Honor started to cry.

"Be quiet, Honor. Truby gets mad when you cry. I don't trust him."

Brother and sister shared the same bedroll at night. And now that Tex no longer trusted Lonnie and knew Lonnie was "bad," Lonnie had begun chaining the children together at night so that it would be difficult for them to run away. The chain was wrapped around Tex's right ankle and Honor's left ankle, tight enough so they could not slip out, and locked with a padlock.

Truby slept nearby, snoring loudly. It was Lonnie's turn to keep watch, and Tex suspected he was not watching just for wolves or coyotes. He was watching for John Hawkins. He was scared.

"This chain hurts my ankle, Tex," Honor sniffed.

"I know. It hurts mine, too."

"It's all red."

"Mom will fix it better."

"When?" Honor rubbed her runny nose on her arm. In the crook of her other arm she still clung to her rag doll. "I'm all dirty," she said before he could answer. "I wanna take a bath. Mommy would never let me get this dirty. She'd make me change my clothes. And I don't like to have to keep Lonnie's shirt around me when the sun is out. Why'd he leave my shirt by that stinky ole dead animal?"

"I don't know, Honor. And you gotta stop complaining. I'm hot and dirty, too, but we just have to put up with it till Pa finds us."

"Maybe he won't *never* find us."

"Sure he will. Pa can find anything. Ken told me that." Tex heard a mosquito buzzing, and he waved his hand hard to try to chase it away. For some reason mosquitoes hardly ever bit him, but they feasted royally on his sister. He tried his best to keep them away from her.

"Do you think it's true, what Lonnie said about Daddy? That he's not your pa?"

"No. He's just making that up to get me confused." Tex decided not to voice his own doubts to her. It would only make her feel worse.

Could it be true? He did not want to believe it. He wanted to cry just thinking of it. Surely John Hawkins loved him. He wouldn't be the good father that he was if he didn't. But even if John did love him, it still hurt to think the man might not really be his father. And if his father really was the bad man Lonnie said he was, did that mean he would grow up to be bad himself? Did his mother hate him when he was a baby? Did she still secretly hate him?

"What if Daddy doesn't find us?"

"I told you, Pa can find anything. He's the best tracker in Texas."

"Where's Uncle Ken?"

"I don't know. I didn't see him anywhere when Lonnie told us to come out and go for a ride. He said Ken left for a while, but I'll bet he lied about it. Maybe he hurt him."

"Will he hurt us?"

Tex sighed. "Quit asking so many questions. I don't know the answers, Honor."

"You won't let Lonnie and Truby hurt me, will you?"

"No. I'll kill 'em if they hurt you. I don't know how, but I'll kill 'em." Tex meant every word, but again he wondered if that meant he was bad after all? Surely it wasn't bad to kill someone in defense of a little sister. "Try to go to sleep, Honor."

"I can't. My ankle hurts, and my bites itch . . . and Truby snores too loud."

"I know." Tex patted her cheek. "Maybe we can figure out a way to run away."

"Where would we go? There's no houses out here, and there's snakes and coyotes. And we would get thirsty, but there's no water."

"I know all that. But it doesn't hurt to think about it. Maybe I'll come up with an idea. You know how good I am at riding. I could ride real fast and get away. Maybe I could even steal one of their guns first."

"Mommy says we aren't supposed to touch guns," Honor reminded him.

"Be quiet. Truby might hear you," Tex whispered.

"Mommy says guns are dangerous for us to touch," she whispered in reply.

"I know, but Pa wouldn't care if I used one to help us get away. And anyway, he's gonna teach me how to shoot a rifle when I'm bigger, so I can hunt."

"That's different, Tex Hawkins," Honor chided in a loud whisper. "Mommy says holster guns are real dangerous."

"Not if you don't cock them till you're ready to shoot them. Pa showed me."

"Daddy told you never to touch one of his holster guns."

"I know. But this is different."

"I'm scared, Tex. If you get hurt, I'll be all alone with Lonnie and Truby. I think Truby is mean."

"So do I. But I won't let him ever hurt you, Honor. I promise."

"I'm glad you're with me, Tex."

Tex patted her cheek again. "We'll be okay, Honor. You'll see. Don't be scared. It might take a while, but Pa will find us. I know he will."

"Will Mommy be with him?"

"Sure she will."

"I'm hungry. Truby only gave us one plate of beans all day. I don't like beans."

"I know. But you better eat whatever he gives you so you don't get sick. You gotta eat, Honor. Promise me that tomorrow you'll eat."

"Okay."

"Now go to sleep. The mosquitoes aren't so bad now. Pa says after a certain time of night they don't bite so much."

"Maybe they go to sleep, too."

Tex smiled. "Maybe they do."

Honor giggled. "I wonder if mosquitoes have beds."

Tex felt better that she'd found something to laugh about. "Their beds sure wouldn't be very big, would they?"

Honor giggled again and snuggled even closer. "I love you, Tex."

"I love you, too."

"Even if we don't have the same father?"

"Even if we don't." The thought made Tex want to cry, but he couldn't cry in front of Honor. It would make her afraid. Whether John was his real father or not, Tex loved him, and his one goal when he grew up was to be just like him. That meant not crying in the face of danger. And it meant protecting his loved ones. He just wished he was bigger and stronger . . . as big and strong and as good with a gun as John Hawkins.

Thirty-seven

"Tess," John said softly.

His dark hair fell around her face. His warm lips searched her mouth, and his hard body moved on top of hers as he pushed up her gown.

Tess opened her eyes, waking from an exhausted sleep and realizing the sun was rising.

"This could be our last time," John told her, caressing her eyes, her lips, her throat, with gentle kisses.

"Don't say that. Don't ever say that." The thought made Tess lean up and meet his lips. Her heart screamed for her children, but she also knew John could very well be right. One last time. Desperate, they needed this one last time, in case death should rob them of ever doing it again. And somehow they both needed the intimacy, the strength they derived from being a part of each other.

Tess drew in her breath when he filled her with all that was male about him. He had a way of making a woman want to be possessed, owned, adored, ravished. But this time she could feel his fire, his anger, his intensity. His kisses were hot, desperate, as though he truly felt he must make her remember what this was like with him.

No! Men like John Hawkins did not die. In any normal confrontation, no matter how dangerous, he had no match. But if he had to walk to his death to save his children . . .

Tess arched up to him, feeling like a rag doll in his powerful presence. "I love you, John," she groaned. "I love you. I love you so."

He pushed hard, groaning in both anguish and pleasure. Tess wondered at how this coming together could be so strangely exotic and compelling at such a terrible time. Always before it was for pleasure, something they did out of desire and the deep love they shared. This time it seemed to be a way of feeding on each other's strength, helping each other cope, and maybe . . . maybe to say good-bye in the sweetest way possible.

Their union lasted several long minutes, neither wanting to let the other go, neither wanting to face the sunrise and what it might bring. Would they ever see their children again? Would John Hawkins have to die to save them? Would they both die, leaving their children to a horrible fate?

Tess breathed deeply when he finished, leaning up and kissing him, a deep kiss of love made desperate by the fear of losing him. Yet surely God meant for both of them to live, for the baby she carried.

John rested with his elbows on either side of her, twisting some of her red hair into his fingers. "This is a hell of a time to be making love to you."

Tess touched his lips. "We both needed this," she said softly. "I feel better, stronger. A good sleep helped, but we haven't really said good-bye, John. We have only taken strength from each other. Let's just get dressed and go now. We have to get the children and go home. Tex will want to see his horses, and Honor will want a hug from her daddy."

John closed his eyes and moved down slightly, resting his head on her chest. "Tess, if we get them back, and I kill every man involved in this . . . if Honor has been abused in the worst way . . ."

"Don't think that way."

"I couldn't live with myself. I wouldn't want to live at all."

Tess ran her fingers through his hair. "I can't believe there is a man walking who is that evil. She's just a tiny little girl. She's just bait for us, that's all. Stop thinking the worst."

He rolled away with a deep sigh. "I've been telling you the same thing. I guess I should take my own advice." He got up and headed for the washbowl. "We have to get going."

Someone knocked on the door. "You two up?" It was Lena.

"We're up," John told her.

Lena cracked open the door and peeked inside. "Tubbs is cooking breakfast. You told me to wake you early." She looked John over and grinned before closing the door again, and Tess sat up.

"John Hawkins, you're naked!"

John poured some water from a pitcher into the bowl. "It's nothing she hasn't seen before."

Tess tried to think of a reply, but nothing would suffice. And what did it matter? He was right. Flabbergasted, Tess lay back down while he washed and dressed.

"I'll go saddle up the horses and tie our gear back on," he told her, strapping on his six-shooter. "You wash and dress. Lena had one of the girls shake the dust out of your riding skirt. Soon as you're ready we'll eat and be on our way." He pulled his hair back into a tail and tied it with a thin strip of rawhide, then tied the red bandanna around his head. "I'll go get some ashes out of the cookstove and put the soot on my cheekbones again. It helps the sun's glare, Tess. You should try it, too."

"I'm all right as long as I wear my hat."

John quickly rolled himself a cigarette, then lit it and held it between his lips while he again hung the ammunition belts over his shoulders. Tess could see him hardening before her eyes, again becoming the ruthless man, the determined, strong, vengeful warrior.

"You sure you're strong enough?" he asked.

"I am. I want to reach them as fast as we can."

He took a long drag on the cigarette before heading for the door, then turned to her once more. "It's going to get rougher, Tess. We're headed into the salt flats before we reach the Guadalupes. Stifling heat, dry as a bone, nothing green."

"And my children are putting up with the same misery. That's all I have to know to keep going."

John nodded. "I love you," he repeated. "I just hope you can hang on to that baby."

He left, and Tess hurriedly washed and dressed. She pulled her hair into a bun over which she would set her hat. It would be far too hot to wear her hair down. She packed her things into the carpetbag John brought in for her last night, then looked out a front window to see John already bringing the horses to the front of the house. His dark skin glistened in the morning sunrise, and the way he looked now made her shake her head at realizing that not an hour ago he had made love to her.

She took a deep breath and said a prayer. "Dear Lord, keep my children and husband safe, and let me carry the life in my womb to full term. Give me strength to face whatever is to come." She picked up her carpetbag and headed out.

Thirty-eight

Sam got up from the bed he'd just shared with Bernice Carter, from Thieves' Hollow. He'd paid her to come here to Eagle Pass to help "entertain" him and Calhoun while they waited for Lonnie to show up.

"I want more, Sam," the woman told him, pouting.

"Bernie, don't you ever wear out? Get Calhoun in here if you want more. I've got a lot to think about." He dressed, and Bernice pulled a blanket over herself and rolled over with a pout.

"I ain't in the mood for no woman," Calhoun called from outside the ramshackle cabin. Built high against a rocky cliff years ago by outlaws, the cabin was in an ideal spot for seeing someone coming—high enough to make it impossible for anyone to reach them without being in plain sight, and easy to kill.

"When are we gettin' out of here, Sam? I'm gettin' bored. You sure this plan of yours is gonna work?" Calhoun complained. He stood at the torn screen door. "We've got money from robbin' them settlers way back, and you have plenty more in Mexico, or so you say. I want to spend some on women and cards and whiskey. Hell, I don't even know John Hawkins. I don't care if he lives or dies."

Sam glanced at Bernice, a young woman in age, old in experience. She wasn't the prettiest thing he'd ever seen, but she sure knew how to make a man feel good. He'd promised to take her with him to Mexico once he'd done what he came here to do, where he would help her start a saloon and brothel of her own. He had no real intention of actually taking her there. She would end up in a grave with John and Tess Hawkins. Once he left here, he was leaving a satisfied man, and free to do whatever he pleased once he reached Mexico.

He walked outside, where Calhoun sat back down in a rickety chair on the front porch. He nursed a bottle of whiskey. The hot, yellow sun of the day had settled into a large, red ball that was fast disappearing as night sneaked in on them.

"For one thing, you're not getting any of my money in Mexico unless you stay here and help me," Sam told Calhoun. "And you'd *better* care if Hawkins lives or dies, because if he lives, *you're* the one who will be dead. With a man like that, it's you or him, no escape, no forgiving. And don't forget that if it weren't for me and Lonnie, you'd be sitting in some cell at Leavenworth by now. No whore to show you some fun, no whiskey, no freedom."

"Yeah, and pretty soon no privacy and no sleep. We'll have two bratty kids here whinin' away."

"A few punches in the mouth will shut them up."

"Hell, Sam, I ain't one to go hittin' no little kids."

"These aren't normal children. They are the offspring of John Hawkins, the bastard who made me rot in prison for eight years. I owe him, big time. I owe his wife, too. The bitch will pay, and so will John Hawkins! I just wish Lonnie would get here. I hope nothing went wrong."

"How long we gonna stay here if Lonnie don't come back? And how much longer do you think it will be before he comes?"

"How in hell do I know? These things take time."

"Maybe Lonnie just shot Hawkins when he saw him and took off."

"Lonnie wants him to suffer as much or more than I do. The man blew his brother into a hundred pieces. I remember when that happened. He was in trouble with the people of El Paso all the time. They tried to get him kicked out of the Rangers because he was as lawless as the men he went after. Texans decided it was time the Rangers were more respectable. Hawkins didn't quite fit the picture. Then he married and settled, and things died down. I expect they made him a damn hero after he broke up the cattle-rustling ring."

"Well, Lonnie's been gone an awful long time."

"He's a smart kid, and charming as hell. I'll bet he had every man on Hawkins's ranch eating out of his hand. Maybe even John Hawkins himself."

"Maybe, but you gotta admit, it's gettin' boring up here away from town. Can't we at least go get a different whore? I'm tired of this one."

"She's not leaving. She might tell someone about us being up here. Just quit worrying about Lonnie showing up. He's planned this for a long time. This will all be over soon, and John Hawkins will cease to exist. So will his offspring."

"You're meanin' to *kill* them?"

"If I have to. I would rather sell them in Mexico, make some money off of them."

"Hell, one of 'em is just a tiny girl."

"Tiny girls grow into women, and they can be trained any way a man wants to train them." Sam grinned. "I don't give a damn what happens to the seed of John Hawkins. Hell, in Mexico a pretty little girl can bring pieces of gold from a good brothel owner."

Calhoun swallowed more whiskey and licked his buckteeth. "All I know is, Lonnie better show up pretty soon."

"Don't you worry. The kid has enough charm to fool even the likes of John Hawkins. He knows we're expecting him to get here pretty damn quick, and he's got enough hate in him to do whatever he has to do to make this work. He'll be here all right. I gave him till the end of June, and I've been marking the days on that calendar I got back at Thieves' Hollow. We're getting damn close." Sam rubbed his hands together. "Damn close."

Thirty-nine

A weary Jenny opened her front door, surprised to see a group of women standing outside, including some of the more prominent of El Paso; Florence Daniels, wife of the owner of a mercantile; Rachael Patterson, wife of a bank manager; Louise Jeffers, wife of the owner of a feed supply; Ruby Watson, the owner of a restaurant; Tess's friend, Bess Johndrow; and Mary Sanders, the doctor's wife. Mary was no surprise. The young, very kind woman had devotedly helped her care for Ken the last several days, and her husband came often to check on him. But the rest of these ladies had never been overly friendly to her because of her reputation.

Jenny put a hand to her hair, realizing how terrible she must look. Between crying every day and totally neglecting her own care, she must look a hundred years old, she was sure. She had quickly twisted her hair into a rather messy bun that morning and not touched it since. She wore a plain gray dress, cut as "properly" as any garment these ladies would wear. She could not wear anything good because of the constant care Ken took. She still often got blood on her clothes, and she had to diaper him like a baby.

"Hello, Jenny," Mary spoke up. "I told the Ladies Auxiliary how you have had to devote so much time to caring for Ken and that you are completely neglecting yourself, let alone how tired you must be. Your roomers have been eating elsewhere, and they all comment on missing your cooking. In that respect, we have all brought food, not for your roomers, but for you, and soup for Ken. And we are all here to clean your house, change the sheets, and clean in your guests' rooms. I know you haven't had time to do any of those things, so we came to do it for you."

Jenny just stared at them, speechless. Were her ears working right? Had she fallen asleep at Ken's bedside and was dreaming?

"We will also do your laundry," Mary continued. "I told the ladies what a lovely house you keep here, how hard you work to keep it nice. And, of course, lately you just haven't had the time. I know you have a mountain of laundry because of Ken's bedclothes, and—"

"Wait!" Jenny put up her hand. She shook her head. "I can't accept all this. You women all have your own work to do, and children to care for, and—"

"We have all made provisions, Jenny," Ruby spoke up.

"But you have a restaurant to run!"

"I have good help. They will handle it."

Jenny looked around at all of them. At least ten women were here, all holding loaves of bread, pies, kettles of soup, and the like. She could not help the tears that welled in her eyes. "Well, I . . . I don't know what to say. I'm overwhelmed." She quickly wiped at her eyes. "This is the last thing I expected." She sniffed. "Please forgive the way I look . . . the way the house looks . . ."

"That's why we're here," Mary answered. She moved inside and put an arm around Jenny, and the rest of the ladies came inside, some of them seeing the house for the first time. Mary directed them to the kitchen, and after delivering their food, they spread out, attacking the boarders' rooms with a vengeance. Jenny just sat down and watched, astounded. She looked up at Mary.

"Why are they doing this? Most of these women hate me."

Mary sighed. "They don't hate you, Jenny. They just have long memories, and they tend to be a little too judgmental. I have explained to them how much you have changed, and that you want to marry Ken. I've told them what a nice place you run here, and a little bit about how you ended up . . . doing what you once did."

Jenny frowned. "You know about my childhood?"

"Tess told me some of it. Most of these women don't understand how and why some women . . . well . . . choose a different kind of life, shall we say?"

Jenny smiled through tears. "Well, I just . . . I don't know what to say. This is wonderful, Mary. I'm sure it was all your idea."

"All I did was explain the situation and remind them of their Christian teachings." Mary leaned down and grasped Jenny's hands. "How is Ken this morning?"

Jenny wiped at more tears. "A little better. I actually got him to drink a little tea. He's just in so much pain from all the stitches. He can barely make a move without something hurting, and his heart is so broken over the children. He asks every day if I have heard anything."

"You just tell him to remember who went after them. Lord knows John Hawkins is a man no one wants for an enemy. Sam Higgins must be the dumbest man who ever walked on two feet!"

Jenny managed to laugh through her tears. "That's for sure." She rose from her chair, watching in wonder as the other women ran back and forth, Louise Jeffers, a stout, dark-haired woman with a commanding air, giving orders like an army general. She was not totally surprised to see Louise, who along with Mary, had warmed more to her after helping deliver Tess's son. Both women understood the hell Tess had been through at that time and had gained a better understanding of the unique problems some women had. "I'd better go look in on Ken again. He'll be wondering what all the commotion is about."

"And I had better get to work helping out here," Mary answered, grinning.

Jenny left her, feeling crazy with wonder at what was happening with Tess and John . . . and most of all with those poor children. She prayed constantly that they were all right, and that sweet little Honor was not being abused.

She went inside her room, where Ken lay propped up slightly. His eyes opened when she came in, and she put on a smile for him. "Well, you're still awake!"

"Can't sleep," he answered weakly. "Too much . . . pain. And I . . . can't help thinking . . . about Tex . . . and Honor. I should . . . be with John . . . helping him and Tess . . ."

Jenny leaned over to feel his forehead. So far there had been no major infections. "Ken, even if you were completely healthy, John would not have let you go along. The note said he'd better come only with Tess and no one else. He would not have taken the chance on what they might do to the children if he took anyone with him."

"I know." He closed his eyes. "What's all the . . . commotion . . . out there?"

"Believe it or not, the Ladies Auxiliary of El Paso is out there cleaning my house and doing my laundry! They even brought food over."

"The . . . Ladies Auxiliary?"

"I know. It's hard to believe. I'll explain more when you feel better. I'm just very grateful for their help."

"I'm . . . glad. You've . . . worked so hard . . . Jenny. I know . . . I'm causin' you . . . to lose customers."

"Don't worry about it. Helping you get well is more important."

"A lot of good . . . that does John. He shouldn't . . . have to be out there . . . handling this all alone. And you . . . shouldn't have to . . . be wearin' yourself out . . . takin' care of me."

Jenny shrugged. "I *love* you. Of course I'm going to help you. Besides, who else would do it, you old rascal? You and I go way back. Hell, you used to come visit me at Lena's place, remember?"

" 'Course I remember. I've always . . . had feelin's for you, Jenny. I . . . never did like . . . sharin' you . . . even with John. But I knew . . . he was . . . special to you."

"Not that much more special than you, Ken Randall. And now John Hawkins is a happily married man, and I'm a lonely old woman, in love with a lonely old man. Want to get hitched?"

Ken frowned. "You . . . serious?"

"Serious as hell. We can live here or at the ranch, or start our own ranch. Whatever you want to do. I didn't realize how much I really did love you until I thought you were going to die on me."

He studied her still-pretty green eyes. "You really . . . mean it . . . don't you?"

"I really mean it. All you have to do is get well enough to make our wedding night enjoyable. That should give you some incentive."

He grinned sadly. "I can't . . . really feel well . . . till I set eyes on Tex . . . and my little Honor again."

Jenny sat down and grasped his hand and raised it to her lips. She kissed the back of his hand. "I know." She closed her eyes. "I'm not very good at praying, Ken, but maybe you and I . . . we could try it."

Ken squeezed her hand. "Sure. Why not? If I . . . can't be there . . . to help John and Tess . . . then we'll send . . . somebody else."

Forty

"I don't remember it bein' this far to Eagle Pass," Truby complained.

"The farther from civilization, the better," Lonnie reminded him. "We'll have Hawkins right where we want him."

"How do you know he'll even find us?" Truby wiped at his nose with the back of his hand.

"Because he's John Hawkins, that's how. Whatever he wants to find, he finds, even in country this big."

"And you'll both be sorry when he *does* find you," Tex told them.

"You shut your trap," Truby barked at the boy. "I'm gettin' tired of hearin' the same thing out of your mouth every day. You keep it up, I'll gag you. That wouldn't be much fun in this heat."

"I don't care. And you better let my sister have a bath and some sleep in a real bed pretty soon. She's not strong like me. She threw up three times today already."

"I know damn well how many times she's puked," Truby answered. It was his day to take Honor with him on his horse. "Half of it is on my damn pants."

"She can rest when we reach Thieves' Hollow," Lonnie told Tex. Sweat ran down his face and neck, and his clothes were stained with it. The three of them rode slowly today, the horses feeling the effects of the heat and long miles. "We can get fresh horses there, too."

"I'm not leaving Maggie anyplace," Tex told him. "She would miss Jenny, and she would feel bad out here all alone."

"She's just a damn horse," Lonnie barked. "I'll leave her wherever I damn well please."

"She's *Jenny's* horse!"

"Not anymore."

Tex gritted his teeth, wishing so much that he was as big and strong as his father. "I *hate* you, Lonnie Briggs!"

"The feeling is mutual, you little Indian shit. And if you don't shut up I won't get help for your sister."

"You *better,* or she'll die, and then there won't be nothing you can do to stop my pa from killing you! You gotta take good care of us, or you won't have anything to make my pa come to you. I'm not stupid. You won't kill us or let us die, 'cuz then you wouldn't have anything to trade for my pa."

Lonnie drew his horse to a halt and took from his mouth a thin cigar he'd been smoking. "Well, now, aren't you the smart one?" He rode closer. "You're right. I won't kill you or let you die, but all I need to do is keep you in one piece, so if I want to beat the shit out of you, I'll do it. In fact, I think you and your sister are both spoiled little shits who probably never got a good spanking your whole lives."

Tex held his chin high. "We never needed one. But even if we did, my mom and my pa would never touch us like that. Pa don't believe in spanking."

"Well, I *do* believe in it," Lonnie warned. "And so does Truby. So you better watch your mouth, or the first one we'll spank is your sister. You want that?"

Tex was furious with himself for wanting to cry. He glanced at Honor, who sat with her head drooping from fatigue and the heat. Her little slat bonnet hid her face, but he knew that in spite of wearing the hat, her face was burned from the reflection of the sun against rocks and sand. His pa explained once that a man or woman can get burned that way, even if their face is protected from the sun above.

"No," he answered Lonnie. "And you're the baddest man I

ever knew for sayin' you would spank my little sister. You're a coward, Lonnie Briggs. A great, big yellow *coward!*"

Lonnie rode closer. "And your pa killed my *brother!* Blew him to bits!" He grasped the front of Tex's shirt and jerked him off his horse and onto his own.

Tex glared defiantly at him, bracing himself for whatever was to come, refusing to show fear. But inside his stomach was in knots, and his throat felt tight.

"I want your pa to *hurt,* kid, understand? Your ma, too! So don't get cocky and think I *won't* kill you and your sister, because I just *might,* if you get me mad enough!"

"No, you won't!" Tex spit in Lonnie's face, and the next thing he knew something slammed across his own face. He landed on the hard ground, sand and gravel biting into the other side of his face. He heard Honor scream his name. Someone picked him up and hit him again. He whirled and fell forward, his mouth landing against a rock. He felt his front teeth go through his bottom lip. Honor screamed and cried, and Tex feared someone was hurting her, too. He felt himself jerked up, then plunked on a horse.

"Now," he heard Lonnie say. The voice came from right behind him. Apparently Lonnie had set him on his own horse so he could hang on to him. "The next time you smart off, I'll do this to your sister. You want me to hit *her* this way? There's other things we could do to her, too. You understand what I'm saying, boy?"

Tex could feel blood running down his chin and neck, and he put a hand to his mouth. Seeing blood on it scared him. He couldn't let them hurt Honor like this; and he couldn't help his own tears. He simply nodded in reply to Lonnie's demand, still finding it hard to believe that the kind, smiling, friendly Billy Williams could do these things. His father had been right all along not to trust this man.

Honor sobbed his name over and over, and Truby kept telling her to shut up. Tex looked up to see the man shaking her.

"Lay off, Truby!" Lonnie warned him. "I don't want her hurt unless Tex keeps giving us trouble. Besides, she's sick." He no more got the words out of his mouth than Honor threw up again.

"Shit!" Truby cussed. "She got it on my boot. I'm gonna stink to high heaven."

"You already stink," Lonnie answered. "Where we're going, you can get yourself a bath and wash your clothes, so quit worrying about it." Lonnie hugged Tex close against him and tousled his hair. "There, see? Long as you're quiet, I won't let Truby hurt your little sister, okay? Understand?"

Tex nodded, his hands balled into fists. *Just wait till my pa finds you!* he wanted to say again. But for Honor's sake he decided to be quiet. Lonnie got his horse moving again. "Let's make tracks. By tomorrow noon we'll be at Thieves' Hollow. It's a hangout for some of Texas's finer citizens, if you know what I mean. You can have yourself a bath and a whore and the kids can sleep some. Then we'll head out. Another day's ride from there we'll reach Eagle Pass and wait for Hawkins."

"You sure it's safe to stop at this hangout you told me about?"

"I'm sure. I know one of the whores there. She's crazy about me. We'll go straight to her. She'll put the kids up for us, and she won't rat on us. It probably wouldn't matter anyway. If the men there know it's Hawkins's kids we've got, they wouldn't care. Half of them who hang out there would like to fill his gut with bullets as much as I want to. Even so, it's probably best not to say nothin' about who they are. We'll wait till night and go straight to Thelma's place."

"I ain't sure we've got all this planned out right," Truby told him. "What if Hawkins catches up with us before we reach Eagle Pass?"

"He won't. He's got his wife with him. If it was him alone, I'd be worried. Now quit your complaining. By tomorrow night you'll be in a nice soft bed with a nice, soft whore."

"Sounds damn good." Truby gave Honor a quick, hard squeeze that made her gasp. "Quit cryin', girl, else you'll get whupped, too." Honor's sobs turned to sniffles, and she kept her head down.

Tex tried to lick at his lip and could tell it was already swelling. He angrily wiped at his tears.

Forty-one

The sun shone down in a relentless white light, and at times Tess felt blinded. She resorted to smearing black ash under her eyes as John did. Sometimes she simply closed her eyes and trusted her horse to follow John's.

It was impossible to ride as fast as they would like. The horses would give out, even the riderless ones. Their only consolation was that Lonnie could go no faster than they, leaving them no more than two days behind the kidnappers.

John continued to follow Maggie's tracks with the stealth of a wolf following scent. Even though he knew where the children were being taken, he wanted to follow every step of the way, in case something went wrong. They might find one of their children sick . . . or dead . . . somewhere along the trail; and Tess knew John was haunted by the realization Honor would be the most likely one to have problems. The thought of how loving and gentle he was with his little girl made her heart ache not just for Honor, but for John. In that respect, Tess knew John loved Tex all the more, for the simple reason that their son must be doing anything he could to protect his sister. Tex, the child she once did not even want . . . the son she now loved with her very life.

The trail led to shelves of hard rock, and John had to dismount to study the tracks more closely. At least here, a high wall of red rock cast a shadow over them. Tess waited while John stood up and literally sniffed the air. A hot breeze brushed over them out of the higher wall of rocks, and John scanned the hundreds of crevices and holes that marked the wall.

"Get off your horse," he told her.

Tess did not question why. She simply obeyed.

"Take the horses down off this rock shelf," John continued. "Find a place to hide them and yourself, out of sight of the rocks above us."

"John?"

"Just do it. We're being watched."

Tess could not imagine how he knew. "What about you?" she asked, her heart pounding with fear.

"I'm going to rout them out. Most likely it's someone wanting our horses and supplies . . . and maybe you."

Tess glanced at the rocks above. "How do you know it isn't Lonnie and the children?"

"They won't make a move like this until they reach Eagle Pass." John pulled a Winchester from its boot on his horse. "Get going."

Tess swallowed. "I love you," she told him.

"Just get out of sight before—"

A shot rang out, and John whirled and fell, the rifle spilling out of his hand.

"John!" Tess screamed.

He rolled back to his knees, blood streaming from a wound in his upper left arm. "Get out of here!" he yelled at her. "Do like I said!" Grimacing with pain, he reached for his rifle and began running.

"Dear God," Tess whispered. Quickly she grabbed the horses and pulled at all four of them. Because of the gunshot, they were skittish and uncooperative. It took all of Tess's strength to urge them back down the shelf, while a barrage of shots continued to pour out of the rocks above. None came close to Tess or the horses. They were shooting at John!

"God help him!" Tess cried as she managed to bring the horses down the escarpment, then slid and fell on loose rock as she tried hurriedly to lead the horses and herself out of sight. In spite of losing her footing, she clung to the reins of the horses, knowing that if she let go, one or all of them might run off.

By the time she reached bottom, her suede riding skirt was covered with scrapes and dirt, and her hands ached from clinging so tightly to the reins. She found an overhang of rocks where she could pull the horses out of sight. Quickly she tied them to a lonely, straggly pine tree that seemed to grow right out of the rock. She yanked John's other Winchester from its boot and grabbed a pouch of ammunition that hung next to the rifle boot. John needed a diversion, something to help him do whatever it was he was going to do, something to distract the attention of whoever was up there.

Tess retracted the rifle lever and moved out from under the rock shelf, slowly raising her head to scan the rocks above. She could see John nowhere, but she caught a glint of sunlight on something, and she knew it was most likely someone else's rifle. She raised her own rifle and took aim. She knew she would not actually hit anything, but perhaps if she could draw their attention . . .

She fired, once, twice, three times. Then bullets spit into the dirt beside her and pinged off the rock shelf. Tess ducked down. *Good,* she thought. She had their attention. She waited a moment, then fired back again, inviting another barrage of bullets. She ducked down, closing her eyes and praying for John. If anything happened to him now, what in the world would she do? She could never find her way back out of this desolate place.

She ducked her head to keep from being sprayed with rocks, as more bullets whizzed past her and chipped into the red rock she used for a shield. She nervously shoved more cartridges into the Winchester.

"God, help me! Help me!" she whimpered. For all she knew, John was lying somewhere bleeding to death. All she could do was wait, virtually pinned down by however many men there were shooting at her from the rocks above.

Minutes seemed like hours. "John," she said quietly. "Where are you?"

She struggled to keep her sanity, terrified that if John could not get them out of this, she would end up in the same situation as when she was taken by the *Comancheros*. Then she reasoned that if John could take on a whole gang of such men, he could take care of whoever was up in those rocks. She had seen him in action, seen him at his most vicious.

The thought made her feel braver. She rose to fire again, and it was then she realized things had suddenly grown quiet. Echoes of men shouting rang amid the rocks, some talking in Spanish. Then she heard more shooting. This time no bullets came her way.

John was up there! Her heart pounded, and her breathing was actually painful.

One man cried out. Tess strained to see, but the only thing visible was the glint of guns, sometimes little puffs of smoke. She was actually relieved still to hear shooting. That meant John was still alive.

Another man cried out. More firing. Had John been hurt a second time? Bullets pinged and sang, the sounds echoing against rock walls. All grew quiet again, almost too quiet. Tess watched anxiously. Maybe John was dead. She heard a blood-curdling war cry then, and a man with long, dark hair suddenly appeared, jumping from one rock to another. John! Bullets flew again. John was running, letting out war cries, firing his rifle almost continuously. Another man screamed.

John disappeared again, and yet another man cried out. John reappeared on a rocky ledge above, dragging a body. The man was kicking and screaming. John kicked him over the ledge, and the man's body seemed to take forever to fall. It landed hard, bounced, fell several more feet, bounced again, then rolled down a gravelly escarpment and finally landed facedown on a rocky ledge about fifty yards away.

Tess turned away. She did not want to see the body. What she'd just witnessed reminded her of just how violent John Hawkins could be.

At least he was alive. She blinked back tears of relief, setting her own rifle aside and shaking from the traumatic confrontation. She waited in the shade of the rock until she finally heard John call for her.

"Tess! Are you all right?"

She moved from under the ledge and saw him coming toward her, leading three horses with one hand, holding his rifle in the other. That arm was caked with dirt and blood, and more blood flowed from the still-bleeding wound.

"I'm down here," she called to him. "Come here and let me do something about that wound!"

Sweaty, bloody, still breathing hard, John led the three extra horses down the rocky hill to where Tess waited.

"John! Thank God!" Tess reached out and embraced him around the middle.

"You did a good job of drawing their fire," he told her. He let go of the horses and moved away from her, grimacing as he sat down and leaned against the rocky wall of the overhang. He put his head back and closed his eyes. "A couple of Mexicans and four Apache. Hard to believe the two would hang out together, considering they've been enemies practically since the beginning of time. I guess if you're an outlaw looking for women, free horses, whatever, you run with anybody else who wants the same thing." He took a long, deep breath. "I couldn't take the chance of one of them living and somehow getting help. Before I killed the last one, I asked if they had seen anyone riding with two young children. He said he hadn't. I just hope Lonnie and the kids don't run into a bunch like this. They would be no match for them, and men like that would take Honor to Mexico and . . ."

He looked away.

"Get some whiskey and douse it on this wound, will you? You'll have to dig out the bullet." He grimaced. "I need . . . some water, too. And something . . . to bite on."

Dread filling her soul, Tess did as he asked. How she hated hurting him, but she had no choice. She dug around in their supplies for a flask of whiskey, then took down a leather case she had brought along that held cotton strips for bandages, a needle and thread, and various salves. She got a canteen of water from where it hung around John's saddle horn.

"Get something to cover your riding skirt with," John told her. "I don't want . . . to get blood all over it." He breathed deeply. "And a needle and thread. Get something . . . to stitch it with."

"I already thought of that," Tess answered, shuddering at the thought of literally sewing his skin like a piece of cloth. She untied a cotton blanket from one of the packhorses, then carried everything back to John, sitting down facing him and putting the blanket over her lap. Then she unbuckled the leather belt she wore around the waist of her riding skirt. She laid it across John's lap and uncorked the canteen, handing it to John.

John gulped some water, then gritted his teeth when Tess poured whiskey on his wound. He set the canteen aside, then yanked his hunting knife from its sheath and handed it out to her. "Trade you for the whiskey," he told her.

Tess gave him the whiskey and took the knife. John drank down two long slugs of whiskey, then leaned his head back and closed his eyes. "Pour some of the whiskey over the knife first," he told her. "Give me a couple minutes for the whiskey I just drank to get into my blood and then do what you have to do. Might as well get this over with right away."

Tess took the whiskey from his hand, looked down at the knife. How many men had he killed with this same knife? At times like this her life seemed unreal. She once lived such an ordinary life, married to an ordinary man, a man who showed what a coward he was the day the *Comancheros* attacked and Abel hid under the bed while she fought them by herself. What a contrast John Hawkins was to Abel.

"Hand me a couple of rocks to squeeze in my hands while I bite on the belt," John told her.

Tess set the whiskey aside, keeping the knife gripped tightly in her right hand as she turned to pick up a rock, one thing that was in plentiful supply here. She put it in his left fist, then put her hand over John's when he closed his fingers around the rock. "I hate hurting you, John."

He leaned up and reached over to pick up the whiskey again, taking yet another long drink, then leaned close to her. "Being a settled, married man now, it's been a long time since I got drunk, Tess Hawkins, so get this over with before I get so drunk I do something stupid, like attack my wife." He kissed her lightly, giving her a grin.

Tess could not help smiling a little herself. "You are something, John Hawkins." She put another rock in his other hand. "Please tell me you didn't just use this knife on one of those men you just killed."

"No. Didn't need it."

Tess shook her head, holding out the knife then and pouring whiskey over it. She drew a deep breath, praying that God would help her find the bullet quickly.

"Use all your strength, Tess. The worst thing you can do is be hesitant and *afraid* to hurt me. If you don't cut deep and quick, it's going to hurt me a lot more. Understand?"

Tess nodded.

"Put the belt between my teeth."

Tess did as he asked, then scooted closer and took hold of his arm. She felt him tense up and reminded herself he was right. The faster she did this, the better. She closed her eyes and swallowed, then looked at the hole in his arm, gritted her teeth, and cut deep and quick. She fought tears when John grunted and stiffened, his muscles tensing into rocks. She refused to look at John's face and see the pain there. She poured more whiskey into the wound, and he groaned.

Quickly Tess felt inside the wound with her thumb and, to her relief, found the bullet. "I've got it, John!" There was no way to get it out but to cut him again, opening the muscle where the bullet was embedded. John groaned loudly, and Tess fought tears as she literally dug the bullet out with her fingers. "It's out! It's out! Oh, I'm so sorry to hurt you like this, John!"

She threw the bullet aside and poured more whiskey into the wound.

John spit out the belt. "Jesus, give me more whiskey!" he groaned.

Tess handed it to him. "*I* am giving it to you, not Jesus," she told him, her way of scolding him for using the Lord's name in vain.

John gulped down more, then grinned. "You are something, woman."

"I still have to stitch it. Then we have to pray you don't develop infection." She threaded the needle, wondering how she managed to do so when she was so nervous. She raised the belt back to his mouth, and John again bit down on it. Tess pressed against the wound with one of the cotton strips, trying to soak up enough blood to see well enough for stitches. John's groans pained her deeply as she yanked the needle and thread through his skin, taking nine stitches in the form of a "T" to close the wound.

"I'm done now, John." She began wrapping the wound with the cotton bandages, then tied them tightly. She took another deep breath and rested back on her heels, looking down at her bloody hands. She wiped them as best she could on the blanket. "I have to wash my hands," she said absently. Finally she looked at John, only to see he'd passed out.

Forty-two

"There you go." Thelma Leeds laid out some towels for Honor. "The water is just right, and I have nice, clean towels here for you, and some clean clothes. I have a friend with a little girl just about your age. The poor little thing died, and Sarah has these clothes of hers you can wear. Now, let me undress you, and—"

"No!" Honor scowled. "You go away! I want my brother! I don't want anybody else."

Thelma straightened, frowning at her. "I'm just here to help, child."

"I don't want your help! You're a bad woman. You even *smell* bad! I want to see Tex! How come he can't be with me?"

Thelma Leeds, a tall, string bean of a woman, rolled her eyes and pushed a piece of mousy blond hair behind her ear. "Just a minute." She stomped to the door of the bedroom where Honor had been led, and opened it, calling out. "Lonnie Briggs, bring her brother in here!"

Honor heard footsteps. "What the hell is wrong?" Lonnie asked her.

"The brat wants her brother. She won't let me help her."

Lonnie pushed her aside. "What the hell do you want your brother in here for? Thelma's a *woman*. You don't want any boys in here, do you?"

"Tex is my brother, and he won't look. I want to see Tex. I'm *scared* without him." Honor folded her arms, lips pouted, her little heart pounding with fear. She had not been away from Tex's side since they were first stolen away. And she did not want this strange, bad woman seeing her naked.

Lonnie threw up his hands. "All right. But I'm going to have a man at the window and at the door, so don't you and Tex get any cute ideas, understand? You got no place to run to even if you tried. And when you're done with your bath, Tex has to clean up, too. I don't have any clean clothes for him, so Thelma will wash his shirt, socks, and underwear. He'll have to wrap himself in a blanket till his clothes are dry."

"That will take about five minutes in this damn heat," Thelma spoke up from the doorway. "God only knows why I've stayed out here for so long."

Lonnie turned. "Because you are so crazy about me, honey, and you knew I was coming back." He walked up and kissed her breasts. Honor noticed that Thelma was so tall, Lonnie's head only came to her neck. She thought they looked funny together. "Hey, Truby, send Tex down here," Lonnie called out then.

"You're getting me in deep trouble," Thelma complained. "If John Hawkins happens to come through here, Lonnie Briggs, and he knows I helped you—"

"You'll be in big, big trouble!" Honor interrupted. "I'm gonna tell my daddy that you helped, and he's gonna come here and arrest you. Maybe he'll *hang* you!"

"Shut up, you little brat!" Lonnie told her.

Honor heard Tex's footsteps, and she wanted to cry when Lonnie roughly shoved her brother inside.

"Your sister won't take a bath without you." He leaned close to Tex. "No lookee now." He laughed, and Honor hated the sound of it. He made her feel bad for taking a bath in the same room with Tex. She had never thought a thing about it before.

"Don't try anything stupid, kid," Lonnie told Tex. "I'll be right outside this door, and Truby will be standing outside the window, so you can't get away."

He closed the door, and Honor ran up to Tex and hugged him. "Are you okay, Tex? Did he hurt you some more?"

"I'm okay," Tex answered. Honor didn't believe him. She knew he wanted to cry, but he wouldn't. She studied his swollen lip, the bruises on both sides of his face. One eye was also black and swollen.

"I'm sorry, Tex. It's my fault he hit you. I should've stopped crying."

"It's okay. You take your bath like they said. You'll feel better if you take a bath and sleep," he told her. He walked around her and sat down on the edge of the bed, his back to her. "Can you unbutton your dress okay?"

"Yes. You know I always dress by myself now," she answered. "Mommy sews the buttons on the front of my dresses so I can do them myself." Honor undressed and climbed into the washtub. "I can even wash my own hair. Mommy says I'm big enough. She says I shouldn't take my bath in front of Daddy or you anymore, but I'm scared when I can't see you, Tex. How come I can't take a bath in front of you?"

Tex shrugged. "I don't know. I guess when girls get old enough, boys aren't supposed to see them anymore. I used to see you all the time when you were a baby."

Honor giggled. "Daddy sees Mommy naked. I know, 'cuz I saw them once."

"That's different. Married people can do that. That's how they get babies."

"They do?" Honor thought about it. "How?"

Tex sighed. "Never mind. That's for Mom to tell you."

"But how do *you* know?"

"I just know, that's all. I've seen horses and stuff like that. Pa says I'll understand better when I'm bigger. I don't much care right now."

Honor scrubbed her knees. "Do you think we'll get away, Tex?"

The boy shook his head. "I've tried to figure out how, but I don't know. Lonnie watches us all the time. I just wish I was bigger and stronger. I'm sorry, Honor."

"It's not your fault." Honor pouted. "Lonnie is a mean man! I *hate* him! Daddy is gonna do bad things to him. I hope he beats Lonnie up for hurting you."

Tex nodded. "He will."

"And he *is* your daddy. You look just like him, and he calls you 'son.' Lonnie is just trying to make you feel bad, saying Daddy's not your pa."

Tex nodded. "Probably."

"I can't wait till Daddy catches up with us. I'm gonna say 'ha-ha' right to Lonnie's face when Daddy makes him cry!"

"Me, too," Tex told her. "Hurry up and get done so I can take a bath, too. Lonnie says I have to wear a blanket around myself."

Honor giggled again. "That will look funny!" She finished washing, then dunked her head to rinse her hair. She climbed out of the washtub, drying herself as best she could. She pulled on the small pair of drawers Thelma gave her. "Will you comb my hair, Tex?"

"Sure I will. Can I turn around?"

"Yes." Honor pulled a plain blue cotton dress over her head. "This dress doesn't have any buttons," she said, looking down at herself. "How does it look, Tex?"

The boy shrugged. "Kind of big, but it's okay."

Honor looked around for a comb, spotting one on a dresser, where a number of jars and bottles were perched. She picked up the silver comb and studied it, deciding it was clean enough. "Here," she told Tex.

Tex came over and started combing her hair.

"Ouch!" Honor protested.

"You have a lot of rats from all the riding and the wind and stuff," Tex told her. "Mom is gonna have a fit when she sees what a sunburned mess you are. She always keeps you so pretty. I can't fix your hair like she does."

"I know. That's okay." Honor gritted her teeth and let him

comb out her hair as best he could. "Can you make a braid? It won't blow all over if you make a braid," she told her brother.

"I think I can. I've watched Mom braid your hair lots of times."

Honor studied him in the mirror. Her brother stood half again taller than she, and it seemed funny that he could be her brother at all, he was so dark. He looked just like Indian or Mexican boys, but then so did her father. "Thanks for watching out for me, Tex. I'll tell Daddy what a good job you did."

"I won't never let them hurt you, Honor. I'll shoot them if I can."

"I know you will. I love you, Tex."

"I love you, too." Tex looked around for something to finish off her braid, then noticed a small barrette lying on the dresser. He fastened it around the end of her braid.

"I'll comb your hair after your bath," Honor promised him.

"That's okay. I'll just tie it back with something like Pa does."

Honor faced him. "Where do you think they are now, Tex? Do you think they're okay?"

"Sure they are. They'll catch up to us real soon."

Honor hugged him again, resting her head on his chest. "I miss Mommy and Daddy."

Tex patted her back. "Don't worry. You'll see them again."

Forty-three

Tess sat propped against a rock wall, using a blanket behind her back for more comfort. *If there is such a thing as comfort out here,* she thought. In spite of how hot the days were, it was chilly at night because there was nothing in this part of Texas to hold the heat—no grass, no trees. She shivered under a second blanket she had draped over her shoulders. She had maneuvered herself beside John and nudged his body enough to let it slide down so that his head fell into her lap. She kept a rifle beside her in case it was needed, and she sat there praying half the night that John's wound would not become infected. No worse tragedy could befall a man like John Hawkins than to lose an arm.

For hours she gently stroked his hair away from his face, as he slept soundly. She hoped that was all it was. He did not truly seem unconscious now, as he had earlier. He stirred several times, groaned, even opened his eyes once, but he did not speak. She suspected all the whiskey he had drunk earlier was the reason he slept so hard now. She kept a blanket over him, studying him in the moonlight. Guns and knives and killing were no more foreign to him than breathing, yet now he slept so quietly, and a few nights ago he had wept for his children.

She longed to sleep, but worry kept her awake. She missed home. She missed Ken and Jenny, wondered if Ken was even still alive. Where were her babies? Would she be able to hang on to the new baby she carried? Would she ever cook in her own kitchen again? See Maria and the other women at the ranch? Hold her precious Honor in her arms? See Tex's handsome face?

The thought of embracing both the children again was the only thing that kept life in her weary body, kept her from giving in to the desire just to lie down and sleep forever.

Her thoughts were interrupted when the horses whinnied. Tess thought she heard steps against the rocky ground in the distance. All senses came alert, and she grabbed her rifle, waiting, trying to see by the light of a half-moon. Had one of the thieves John shot survived? Was he sneaking up on them to try again to kill them?

John's head still lay in her lap. She carefully raised the rifle. No one could sneak up on her from behind because of the rock wall, and she sat under the rock shelf where she'd taken cover earlier in the day. The horses whinnied again, and a coyote again yipped in the distance. It was otherwise dead silent. Then came the crunching sound of footsteps again. She raised the rifle to her shoulder, swallowing, watching, waiting. If only John were not so full of whiskey. He'd know what to do. Now it was her turn to keep watch, her turn to protect John.

Something came closer. It sounded heavy. It was certainly no small animal. And it came on so slowly, she could not imagine it could be anything else other than a man sneaking up on them. She could hear the rhythmic rush in her ears from the pulsed pounding of her heart. She saw something dark appear, coming up over the escarpment below . . . and in a panic, she fired.

The horses reared and whinnied. Something fell hard. John yelled out and sat up, ripping the rifle from Tess's hand and swinging it at her. She caught the movement just in time and ducked. The rifle butt hit the rock behind her.

"John! John, it's me! It's Tess!" she screamed.

He grabbed her by the hair of the head and shoved her against the rock wall, planting his left hand around her neck. She was astonished at his strength, considering that was his wounded arm. He began squeezing.

"John! No! It's Tess! John, wake up! Wake up before you kill me!"

He suddenly loosed his grip. "Tess?"

She rubbed at her throat and coughed. "Yes!" She walked a few steps away. "I . . . saw something . . . heard it sneaking up on us. I thought . . . it was a man. I was . . . frightened . . . so I shot at it."

"Good God," John groaned. He looked around. "I don't see anything."

Tess walked a little closer. "Over there." She pointed in the moonlight. "Over there someplace."

John ran a hand through his hair and breathed deeply. "Jesus," he muttered. He stumbled toward where she pointed and knelt.

Tess rubbed at her throat again as she walked over to the horses and did her best to calm them. She had unloaded them herself, made sure they got some water, fed them a few oats from a bag she and John had brought along for just such emergencies. It wasn't much, but maybe it would keep them going until they found some grass farther ahead.

"It's a deer," John called out to her. "You've killed your first game animal, Tess Hawkins."

Tess grimaced as she walked back to the campsite. Her back hurt where John had slammed her against the wall. "Too bad we aren't home, where we could clean it and smoke the meat. It's a shame to waste it."

"Sure is." John walked closer, then embraced her with his right arm. "My God, Tess. I heard the gun fire, and I thought someone was shooting at us again. I saw the rifle and just reacted. In my mind—"

"I know. It's all right."

"No, it isn't. My God, I could have killed you."

She pulled away slightly. "I will agree with that. Now I know why I am glad I am not your enemy." She rubbed at her throat again.

Damn it, I hurt you!"

"John, I understand. Come sit back down. You've been sleeping with your head in my lap. Maybe we can lie down together now and get at least a few hours' more sleep."

"Tell me what I hurt. Are you all right?"

"I think so." Tess spread out the blankets better. "Come lie down, John."

He walked over and sat down beside her. "Are you sure you're all right? What about the baby?"

"I'm all right. It's just my back. You threw me against the rock wall."

"Shit!"

"John, please don't swear."

"I can't help it." He grimaced as he sat down beside her, holding his arm.

"How is your arm?"

John sighed. "I don't know which is worse, my arm, or the headache that whiskey gave me, let alone how I feel about practically choking my own wife to death."

"Come lie back down, John. Lie on my left side, so I don't bump into your arm. I'm glad you're awake. Now I know for sure you weren't unconscious or getting sicker."

"It's too early to tell about infection." He knelt and picked up his rifle. "I probably broke this damn thing. My God, what if I'd managed to hit you in the head with it?"

"You didn't. Lie down, John."

With a sigh, he moved in beside her, lying on his back. "In all the manhunts I've been on, I've never felt like this—constantly ready to explode. I'm sorry, Tess, for this whole damn mess. It's my fault."

"You couldn't have known."

"I *should* have known. One of the reasons I considered not marrying you was because I knew something like this could happen, and I didn't want you or any of my children involved. Now look where we are."

"We are where we are, and it can't be helped. We can only go on from here."

He settled down a little closer beside her, leaning down and kissing her cheek. "Are you sure you're all right?"

"I think so, but I am amazed at how much strength you have in your wounded arm."

"I wasn't even aware of it at the time, but I sure can feel it now. It hurts like hell. I probably started it bleeding again."

Tess turned to face him. "I hope not. Try to rest some more, John. I'll rewrap your arm in the morning." She leaned closer and kissed his lips, putting a hand to the side of his face. "I'm sorry I shot off that gun without thinking. You were sleeping so hard. Now I've ruined everything for you."

He grasped her wrist and kissed her palm. "This whole thing will end soon. Tomorrow night we'll be at Thieves' Hollow. It's a hell of a place to take you, but someone there might have seen Tex and Honor and can tell us if they are still all right."

"How long before we actually reach Eagle Pass?"

"Only about twenty-four hours after Thieves' Hollow."

Tess sighed deeply. "So close." She settled in beside him.

John remained raised up on his right arm. He leaned down and kissed her eyes, her lips, then grimaced from the pain in his arm. "I'm so damn sorry, Tess. I know I hurt you." He kissed her again. "This will all be over soon. I promise."

She had felt his rage, had received only a small taste of what he could do. She did not doubt his last words. It would all be over soon. She only hoped that when it was, John Hawkins would still be alive, and so would Tex and Honor.

Forty-four

Lonnie offered up another round of drinks, allowing the whiskey to boost his own courage, as well as the willingness of the tavern's patrons to talk. He figured maybe some of these men would be willing to help in the downfall of John Hawkins. He had filled them with whiskey and then brought up the subject of Hawkins to get their reaction. Plenty of the men here knew of him, and some had served time because of him.

One, called Sly Baker, took a bullet in the gut ten years ago, a bullet fired from John Hawkins's gun. Baker had even pulled up his shirt to show others the deep, scarred hole in his belly, bragging that he had survived the wrath of John Hawkins.

"I'd like to fill *his* gut with lead," he'd announced.

Some men here actually seemed to respect John. Those were not the men Lonnie wanted. They had to truly hate the man.

Once he managed to rouse all of them against Hawkins, he explained that Hawkins blew up a cabin where his brother and some other men were holed up after stealing cattle.

"You don't blow a man up for that," he said rousingly. "You bring him back for proper justice. My brother might have been hanged for it, but by-God, Hawkins didn't have a right to blow him to pieces!"

Most of them loudly agreed, several taking another drink. Lonnie looked over at Thelma, who only shook her head. After making sure the children were sleeping, Lonnie had shared an hour of wild, very satisfying sex with the woman, after which he told her he intended to find more help in facing John Hawkins by seeing if some of the men in her saloon would go to Eagle Pass with him. Thelma advised him against it.

"Just keep quiet and get the hell out of here in the morning," she asked. "You'll get me in trouble telling the whole town I've helped you. I don't care to have a man like that upset with me."

"The hell with Hawkins!" Lonnie answered. "I'm tired of everybody telling me I'm supposed to be afraid of him. I have the upper hand now. He'll have to dance to every tune I play for him."

The whiskey was working its magic. He felt braver every minute. Truby was off rollicking in some whore's bed, and Thelma had a couple of women watching the children. Tonight Lonnie was the center of attention, and he enjoyed it. He won men over with his sureness. Barmaids and whores hung around him like bees buzzing around blossoms. He felt brave and victorious, and again he reveled in how easy it was to sway people to his side with his looks and charm.

He climbed up on a table then and waved his arms, yelling for everyone to quiet down. "I've got something important to tell you," he said confidently. "Sly, you'll really appreciate this. Torey, Jim, I know you two spent prison time because of Hawkins, and I know you'd like to hang him by his balls."

All three men, and several others, laughed at the remark. "How in hell do you think you can do that?" Sly asked.

Lonnie slugged down another shot of whiskey. "Well, men, it just so happens I smuggled something into your little settlement today that none of you know about. And it's going to get me John Hawkins's ass."

"What the hell are you talkin' about, Lonnie?" Jim Parker asked.

"I'm talking about revenge, Jim. Pure-all revenge. You want a taste of it? You want to share in the torture of John Hawkins?"

The room quieted. "What in God's name do you mean, Lonnie?"

Lonnie gave them all his most confident smile. "A little boy named Tex, and his little sister, Honor. Their last name is Hawkins."

Things grew even more quiet.

"What?" Sly asked.

"You heard me. I kidnapped John Hawkins's kids and I'm taking them to Eagle Pass and holding them there . . . for Hawkins. He and his wife are coming for them . . . alone."

Smiles faded.

"How in hell did you manage that?" Torey Hill asked.

Lonnie jumped down from the table "Because I'm *smart,* that's how." He enjoyed the way everyone stared at him in absolute awe, or so he thought.

"Smart?" Jim shook his head. "Man, you're the dumbest kid who ever walked."

A rather nervous laughter filled the room, and Lonnie sobered. He faced Parker, a man about his size but older and balding. He needed a shave, and some of his teeth were missing. "That's a damn shitty remark, Parker. I ought to blow you away for that."

"The man is right, kid," one of the other men spoke up. "You gotta be crazy, takin' John Hawkins's kids. I sure wouldn't want to be in your shoes. I'm not even real happy you brung them kids here. That means *Hawkins* will be comin' here."

Lonnie scowled at the man, then turned in a circle, addressing all of them. "What the hell kind of cowards *are* you all? He's one man. *One man!* If he's so darn ornery, how did I get his kids from him? Me and another man are taking them to Eagle Pass, where a couple more men are waiting for us. I've planned this for years, and now I'm going to get my chance at John Hawkins. And this is *your* chance to get a piece of him. What the hell are you afraid of? I've got his *kids!* Don't you see? He can't come at us with both guns blazing, because he'll be afraid of hurting them. We've *got* him! Don't some of you want in on the fun?"

They all seemed to relax a little.

"Maybe you're right," Sly spoke up. "I think maybe I *will* come along."

"He's scared," one of the others put in. "That's why he's askin' for your help."

"Hawkins is helpless as long as Lonnie has his kids," another said. "Heck, I don't have anything against the man, but I've heard enough about him to want to watch this one. I'll come with you, kid. I'm pretty handy with a gun. Name's Jeb Little."

Jeb stepped forward and put out his hand.

"Thank you, Jeb Little." Lonnie shook his hand firmly, then looked around at the others. "Anybody else?"

They all looked at each other, and two more stepped forward, strong-looking men who both wore guns.

"Mike Shore," one of them told Lonnie, nodding to him. "I've heard enough about that half-breed to know I'd like to see this, too."

Lonnie smiled and nodded in return.

"Dan French," the second man said. He was older and graying, but still looked capable. "Hawkins chased me clear into Oklahoma once, after a bank robbery. Hell, all I did was shoot a woman's finger off."

A few men laughed.

"Anybody else brave enough for this?" Lonnie asked, scanning all of them again.

"You mean *crazy* enough?" Torey Hill asked.

Lonnie shrugged. "If that's the way you want to think. But I guarantee, I'll be back here in a week or so, and I'll be telling the story of how I got the best of John Hawkins and took my time doing it."

Those who had agreed to go with Lonnie grinned and nodded.

"What the hell are you going to do with his kids once it's over with?" Jim Parker asked.

Lonnie slugged down one more shot of whiskey. "Who cares? Hell, one of the men waiting for me hates Hawkins's wife just as much as I hate Hawkins. She had something to do with him being put in prison. When we get hold of her, she'll die, too. At best, she'll be shared by every man there and then sold off to Mexico. The kids can be sold, too. The boy looks strong. I think he'd make a good field hand. And the girl, she's pretty as a picture, red, curly hair, fair skin, blue eyes. She's going to be a real looker someday. I think she'll bring a fair price. If she was older, I'd have a try at her myself."

"Most of us ain't into hurtin' women and kids," someone spoke up from the roomful of men. "If you're so brave, Briggs, why don't you just call John Hawkins out like a man and get it over with?"

Lonnie sneered at him. "Because I *want* the man to suffer, like my *ma* suffered, and *I* suffered, after he blew up my brother! You calling me a coward, mister?"

"Might be."

Lonnie stepped closer to him. "Maybe you'd like to back that up. Maybe you'd like to see how much of a coward I *am*. I'll have a showdown with you anytime." He spread his legs slightly, his hand poised over his six-shooter. The others backed away.

The man who had challenged him, a blond with a solid build and steady, brown eyes, backed off. "I've got no beef with you. I'm not even wearing a gun. I only carry a rifle. You want to shoot somebody, save it for Hawkins . . . if he gives you the chance. You'd best understand that John Hawkins is as sneaky as the wildest Apache, and we all know how cunning they can be. You're looking to die, mister."

Lonnie's hands moved into fists. "It's John Hawkins who's going to die, but not before seeing his wife raped and dead, his kids helpless!" He turned to the four men who had agreed to go with him to Eagle Pass. "You men meet me tomorrow, first light, over at Thelma's whorehouse. The kids are there. By tomorrow night or early the next morning we'll be at Eagle Pass. And my guess is we'll only have to wait one or two more days for John Hawkins to show up."

He cast a disparaging glance at the blond-haired man, then walked out with an arrogant strut.

Dan French turned to the blond-haired man. "What do you think, Sage?"

Sage Owen shook his head. "I think it takes a real coward to hide behind two little kids and a woman," he answered. "If you hate John Hawkins that much, go ahead and help him. But I sure as hell would not want the man on *my* ass."

He set down an empty shot glass and shoved his way past Dan, who in turn looked over at Thelma, standing on the stairway so she could see everything going on. She wrapped a shawl around her shoulders and stepped down into the main room, telling her bartender to close up without her.

"I'll be at my place, Jack," she said.

"I don't like this, Thelma," Jack said with a frown. "You shouldn't be involved."

Thelma shrugged. "What the hell? Lonnie showed up with those kids, and I had to take them in. I'll just be glad when he leaves tomorrow and takes the brats with him. I can only hope John Hawkins doesn't find out I helped."

Forty-five

"That's it. Thieves' Hollow." John pointed to a ramshackle settlement along a wide arroyo that flowed about half-full. "It's one of the lowest areas around these parts. That's why there is some grass, at least in spring, and they're able to grow a little food. By August that arroyo usually dries up. There isn't enough land and grass there to support a ranch, but it's enough to graze a few stolen horses that come through. That's how the place got started—outlaws and horse thieves holing up there. Then the prostitutes came, and kind of a town sprouted. Practically all their supplies are stolen goods that outlaws bring in."

Tess enjoyed a breeze that felt cool compared to the heat of the last few days. She realized then that she didn't even know how long they had been gone, and El Paso, Ken, home, all seemed so far away, almost unreal. "Why don't the Rangers just go in there and clean it out?" she asked.

"We've raided the place many a time, but you can't arrest men who haven't been caught in the act, or actually identified as the culprits of a robbery or rustling, whatever. All we could do was arrest those we found who were actually wanted men at the time. Not every man down there is wanted for something, but you can bet they're all hiding out for one reason or another, or just there to hang around with their own kind. Some are out of prison and don't really know where else to go."

He started rolling himself a cigarette, and Tess glanced at the bloody bandage on his arm. "I don't like the thought of you going down there. Half the men there probably know and hate you."

"Probably. But if Lonnie has already been there, they know the kind of mood I'm in. I don't think they will want to mess with me." He reached into a supply pack and pulled out a six-shooter, twirled the chamber, and loaded it from the belt around his waist. He handed it over to her. "Keep this handy, and don't hesitate to use it. Even if you misinterpret someone's intentions, you won't be shooting anyone who doesn't deserve it, even the women."

Tess raised her eyebrows in surprise as she cautiously took the gun. "The *women?* You'd shoot a woman?"

He lit the cigarette. "I'd shoot the likes of those who live down there. There aren't any Lenas or Jennys down there, Tess. The women down there would knife you in the back and rob you of your purse any chance they could."

Tess looked down at the gun. "Have you . . . been with any of them?"

"No." He took a drag on his cigarette. "I didn't care to pick up some disease that would make me less of a man, if you get my drift."

Tess just shook her head, and John glanced at her. "Bear with me, Tess. You're seeing a part of my life that I left behind when I married you, and sometimes I've had to be the man I was then. You'll get your husband back when this is over. I promise."

She met his gaze. "Just so I get him back alive."

He smiled grimly. "I'll do my best." He started down the rocky bank before them. "Take it slow. This is a pretty slippery grade."

Tess shoved the handgun into the waist of her skirt. She followed John, still worried about his arm. He had woken at sunrise claiming his head was screaming at him. There was fresh blood on his arm, but he'd refused to let her rebandage it. She knew it surely pained him immensely, but he did not want to waste any time. They were only a day or so from Eagle Pass, too close to the children to worry about pain or infection, or a raging headache. They had ridden all day to get here, and she knew he was miserable the whole time.

"How is your head, John?"

"Feels like somebody is inside it using a sledgehammer," he answered. "It's just been too long since I got drunk, that's all. This headache will be gone tomorrow."

The horses skidded off and on. Rocks tumbled and slid down the embankment, and dust rolled. John halted his horse when they reached the bottom, turning to Tess. "How about you? Any problems you haven't told me about?"

Tess touched her belly, which still showed no signs of pregnancy. "Not so far."

"You wouldn't lie to me, would you?"

She smiled sadly. "You've been through one miscarriage with me. You know I could never suffer another one without you knowing it."

"It can happen. At least that's what I'm told. You haven't been sick the last couple of days, and it would be just like you to try to hide it, Tess Hawkins, for my sake."

She studied his rough appearance and felt like laughing at his concern. Right now he would frighten the life out of any ordinary woman. "I assure you that I have not lost this baby. And thank God I haven't felt sick for the last two days."

John sighed, looking toward Thieves' Hollow again. "I don't like this one bit. Remember what I said about using that gun, man or woman."

"If it's to protect you, I can shoot anyone."

John threw down his cigarette. "Let's go."

Forty-six

Tess could hear piano music, undoubtedly coming from a saloon. Shrieking laughter accompanied the music, and she shuddered to think of the kind of people who took up residence in Thieves' Hollow.

"Let me do the talking," John told her. "Keep your eyes open and that gun in your hand."

"You mean, you want me to *carry* it, out in the open?"

"I want you to carry it and *use* it if necessary. Don't stop to think about it. When it comes to guns, you never give the other man first choice, and believe me, there isn't a man or woman down there whose life is worth sparing."

Tess took a deep breath for courage as the voices and laughter from town, if it could be called a town, grew louder. She drew her horse to a halt when John slowed his own horse. Someone was riding toward them. Tess pulled out her handgun as John had instructed, and she waited for him to make the first move.

The other man rode closer. He was quite a big man, tall and well built, with messy blond hair that sprouted in various lengths from under his hat. When he came close enough to see John's face, he stopped, his own face showing both surprise and not a little fear.

"What the hell—" He backed his horse slightly. "Is it really you, Hawkins?"

"It's me."

The two men studied each other quietly a moment, and the

man from town moved his gaze to Tess, then back to John. "It's been a long time."

"Sure has, Sage. Have you kept yourself out of prison?"

Sage shrugged. "I've spent a night or two in local jails, nothing big." He looked at Tess again, nodding and tipping his hat. "Sage Owen, ma'am."

Tess nodded in return, but held her gun steady. "Tess Hawkins."

Sage glanced at the gun she held, then glanced nervously at John again. "I heard you'd married. Congratulations."

"Cut the small talk, Sage. I need to know if there is anyplace in that hellhole of a town behind you where a man can bed for the night without getting knifed?"

"In Thieves' Hollow?" Sage grunted a laugh. "Well, I suppose the safest place would be the barn out south of town. There's a shed of a house beside it. Hugh Barnes lives there. He farms just a few beef, enough for steaks to feed the men who hang out here. He's no thief or murderer himself, just a quiet man who likes it here because nobody bothers him. He'll put you up."

"All right." John leaned on his saddle horn. "Now, how about telling me how you heard I had a wife."

Sage swallowed. "You know. Word gets around. Grapevine says you quit the Rangers and settled, with an honorable woman, no less. Some of us find that damn hard to believe." He glanced at Tess again. "But I can see just looking at her that the rumors were right." He moved his gaze back to John. "Why in hell she picked a mean, vicious, unforgiving, no-good sonofabitch like you, I'll never understand."

John grinned and shook his head. "Well, Sage, I thank you for the compliments. But I have to agree. I don't understand it either, but I sure wasn't about to argue with her decision."

Sage laughed lightly, but his nervousness was evident. His smile faded when John rode closer to him, his own smile gone. "Why do I have a feeling you know why I've brought my wife here? Want to tell me what you know?"

"Me? Hell, I can't begin to imagine why you'd come to a place like this with a respectable woman in tow."

"Is that so?"

Tess was stunned at how fast John's six-shooter was suddenly drawn and aimed, straight at Sage. "You haven't seen two small children come through here, have you?"

Sage swallowed and shook his head. "No! What the hell are you aiming that thing at me for?"

John cocked the gun. "Because I want the truth, and I want it quick. No kids?"

Sage moved his hand toward his own gun.

"Don't even think about it, Sage. You know better. I'm talking about my son and daughter, and you will either tell me what you know, or I'll blow your guts out. It's simple as that."

Tess could see Sage visibly shaking. He swallowed again before speaking. "I . . . uh . . . never really saw them."

"What does that mean?"

"It means . . . I know they were here . . . but I never saw them."

"Did you see a young, good-looking man named Lonnie Briggs?"

Sage nodded. "He was . . . in the saloon . . . last night."

John pressed the six-shooter against the man's belly. "Did he say he had a couple of kids with him? *My* kids?"

Sage rolled his eyes. "Shit, John, we all told him he was crazy! Hell, you know me. I've done just about everything wrong there is to do, but I stop at hiding behind a woman's skirts or behind little kids."

"What did Lonnie have to say?"

"He was just bragging. You know, like he was really somethin', stealing away John Hawkins's kids. He asked for help, took four men with him when he left this morning."

"And you didn't see my son or my daughter?"

"No! I swear, I didn't see them. They were kept over at Thelma's place."

"Who joined up with Lonnie? Anyone I know?"

"I . . . I don't know. Maybe. One was Sly Baker."

There was a moment of silence, and Tess could feel John's rage without even seeing his eyes. *"Baker* is with my kids?"

"You know how it is around here, Hawkins. What the hell could I have done to stop it? I'm serious. I would have, if I could. But I'm no John Hawkins."

"Who else?"

"A man by the name of Jeb Little. A Mike Shore, and, uh, Dan, uh, French, I think."

"I know French, but I don't know the other two."

"You've been out of circulation a long time, Hawkins."

John's horse whinnied and pranced slightly, as though sensing its master's tension. "Four more men," John seethed. "And I have no idea what kind of men a couple of them are, if they're capable of—" He took a deep breath. "That makes eight men, that I know of. My little girl must be terrified."

"Hey, Hawkins, you're not my favorite person, but you and me, we have a little bit of an understanding, you know? I mean, I helped you fight them Apaches while you had me under arrest, remember? I helped you save someone else's little girl from them bastards. I served my time for stealing them horses, lucky to keep my head out of a noose. You spoke up for me, and I appreciate that. I don't want any bad feelings between us now. I'm sorry about your kids, but I couldn't stop it."

John pulled the gun away but kept it aimed at Sage. "Sure you couldn't. You're too much of a *coward!"* He slowly released the hammer of his gun. "You say my kids spent the night at Thelma's?"

Sage nodded, sweat beading on his forehead.

John holstered his gun, closing his eyes and shaking his head. "My sweet, innocent little girl sleeping in that bitch's bed! God only knows what she and Tex saw and heard, let alone what they could have picked up in that place, lice, bedbugs, who knows?"

Sage removed his hat and ran a hand through his hair. "Thelma is down there in the saloon tonight, if you want to ask her about the kids. But that's a damn dangerous place for you, Hawkins.

My advice is just don't go down there at all. Just get on out to Eagle Pass. That's where Lonnie said he was taking them."

"If he even still has them."

"You think he's lying?"

"I don't know. You said you never saw them. For all I know Lonnie just wants me to *think* he still has them so I'll come to Eagle Pass. First I need a definite count of how many are there, so I make sure I kill every goddamn one of them! Miss Thelma Leeds probably has all the information I need, and I'm going to get it from her!"

Sage shook his head. "It's your ass. I sure as hell am not going back there with *you* walking into town. I'd have to dodge too many bullets. Where John Hawkins goes, trouble goes." He looked at Tess. "You'd better keep that gun handy, ma'am."

"I intend to do just that."

Sage sighed. "I'm right sorry about your children, ma'am." He looked back at John. "You're riding into trouble, Hawkins, and I'm riding *out* of here."

"I wouldn't expect any different from you. Get going, before I decide to blow you away for being such a coward."

Sage looked away, then turned his horse and galloped off. John turned to Tess. "You ready?"

"Ready as I'll ever be, I guess."

John started forward.

"John."

He stopped and turned.

"You don't *really* think the children could be dead, do you? I mean, is that what you meant when you said Lonnie might not even have them anymore?"

He turned away again. "With the likes of Lonnie Briggs and Sam Higgins in charge of them, who knows? I just need to hear from Thelma that they're okay. Besides, what I do when I go to Eagle Pass will depend on knowing for sure the kids are up there. Thelma Leeds is the only one who can tell us for sure."

He urged Shadow into motion again, and Tess followed, still holding the six-shooter.

Forty-seven

Tess gripped John's handgun tightly, keeping it at her side, her finger on the trigger. She hated guns, although considering whom she'd married, that seemed almost humorous. She told herself that whatever she had to do today, it was for the sake of Tex and Honor, and perhaps necessary to save John's life. Besides, this would not be the first time she'd shot at someone. She'd done the same thing when the *Comancheros* attacked her farm, and when John handed her a gun during her rescue.

They tied their horses in front of the saloon.

"John Hawkins?"

The words came from a young man standing outside the tavern door.

John stepped up onto the boardwalk. "Might be."

The young man looked around, as though making sure no one else watched. "I knew you were coming, and I also heard enough descriptions of you to have a pretty good idea what you look like. Never met you myself, but from what I hear, I'm glad I never had *reason* to meet you."

John stayed to the side of the swinging saloon doors so no one could see him. "Whatever you heard, it's probably true." He took a thin cigar from his shirt pocket and lit it. "What's your name?"

The young man, short and slender, had to look up to meet John's eyes, and Tess could see he was nervous. "Joe Allen."

John puffed on the cigar a moment before speaking. "Well, Joe Allen, I'll make a deal with you."

Joe looked him over with nothing but respect in his eyes. "Yes, sir?"

John took the cigar from between his teeth. "I don't know why you're in this sin hole, and I don't much care. My advice is that you leave here and never come back, but not until you help me out."

"Help you out? Why should I?"

John pulled his gun and placed it under the young man's chin, pushing up. "Because you don't want to die, right?"

The young man swallowed. "Right."

"Is Thelma Leeds inside the saloon there?"

"Y . . . yes, sir."

"Good. Now, my deal is, you watch the four horses I just tied here and make sure some piece of scum doesn't come along and steal them. If they're still here when I come back out, I won't kill you. How's that for a trade?"

Joe managed a nervous grin. "Sounds like a pretty decent offer. I'll watch the horses."

John lowered his gun. "Thanks, Joe." He moved back, and the look in his eyes made it obvious he meant business. He turned to Tess. "Come on. And make sure you stand where no one is behind you."

Their eyes held for a moment, and Tess took a deep breath. "Okay." She followed John inside the saloon, wincing at the strong smell of whiskey and smoke, dirty spittoons and even dirtier men. Nearly everyone looked up when they entered the room. Tess guessed that was common for anyone who walked into this place. Because of the kind of men who patronized such establishments, those inside could not help having an interest in newcomers. For many of these men, however, John was no stranger. She could not help being surprised at how quiet the room became. Men set down drinks and laid down cards.

"Shit!" one man swore. "He's here."

"Hawkins," another said quietly.

A tall, thin, hard-looking woman moved away from the bar. Her faded, wine-colored taffeta dress looked well worn and was frayed at the hem. It hung low on breasts that also hung low. She was not ugly, but she was far from pretty, her too-big brown eyes heavily accented with color.

"John," she said, sporting a hint of a smile. "What on earth brings you here? I . . . I thought you quit the Rangers."

"I'm not here as a Ranger, Thelma, as you *damn* well know!" Thelma shook her head. "What do you mean?"

John looked around the room. "Any of the rest of you want to tell her what I mean?"

No one answered.

"Just what I thought," John said with a sneer. He looked back at Thelma. "Come here, Thelma."

The woman stiffened. "No, you half-breed bastard! You take that pretty little whore you married and get the hell out of my saloon! You're not a Ranger anymore. You can't tell me what to do, and you can't tell these *men* what to do! You've got no authority here anymore!"

"Yeah," one of the men joined in. He stood up. "Get out of Thieves' Hollow, Hawkins, else you'll find yourself dead, and the woman there will be left to us." The man deliberately grasped his privates and jiggled them, chuckling.

Even Tess was surprised at how fast John's six-shooter was out, cocked and pointed at the man. "The *woman* happens to be my *wife,* and you, mister, are not fit to even *look* at her!"

The gun went off, and Tess gasped when the equally surprised victim flew backward, then looked down to realize where John had shot him. Blood quickly spread out at the crotch of his pants.

"Oh, my God!" the man groaned. "Oh, my God, I think he shot my balls off! My God! Oh, God!" He sank to the floor, holding his crotch.

"Bastard!" someone yelled. "Get him!" The man started forward, and John fired again. Someone moved to his right, and John's right arm flew out. He bashed a man in the head with his six-shooter, and Tess held out her own gun, waving it at the other men in the saloon.

"I'll use it!" she warned.

One man in the process of rising sat back down.

"She won't use it!" someone else yelled. *"Get* him!"

Three more men dived for John, who fired once before another jumped at him from behind the bar. Tess fired at another attacker, somewhat stunned to realize her aim was true. The man fell back with a hole in his chest.

In spite of one man clinging to his shoulders, John raised a foot and kicked the third man hard in the chest, sending him sailing halfway across the room and spilling tables, chairs, drinks, and cards in all directions. John grabbed the man who had jumped him from behind and flung him over his shoulder, landing him so hard on a table that the table split in half.

Tess noticed a movement to her right, and she turned to see Thelma and the bartender headed toward the end of the bar where she stood. Quickly she faced them, aiming her six-shooter.

"You two stay right there!" she said.

Thelma's eyebrows arched in surprise.

"I mean it!" Tess said. "I've used this gun before in defense of my husband! I'll do it again!"

One more man tried his hand at John, whose gun had gone flying in the first confrontation. John tossed him over the bar, and the man crashed into a stack of glasses and landed against a mirror. Glass shattered, showering down from the wall and shelf. Thelma screamed and ducked. The bartender bent over, and when he rose up again, he had a gun in his hand. Without hesitation, Tess fired. The bartender flew backward, a bloody hole in his forehead.

"You *bitch!"* Thelma yelled.

Tess pointed the gun at her. "Don't you move one inch!" she told the woman, struggling not to think about having just killed two men. "I'll do the same to you!" *May God forgive me,* she thought. She wished she could feel as guiltless as John about such things.

John dived for his gun and shot at yet another man who drew on him, opening a hole in his belly before he even got back to his feet. John rose then, waving his gun at those left.

"Tess!"

"I'm all right," she reassured him, keeping her eyes on Thelma.

A large, bearded man who had been sitting at the bar through the whole event, drinking and ducking, suddenly blindsided John in the right jaw. Tess gasped, and John stumbled sideways, but he never went to his knees. He turned and grabbed the wide-eyed assailant by the shirt front, and with one hand he dragged the man to a window and kicked him through it, shattering the lettered glass. John whirled then, panting, his wounded arm bleeding. He also had a cut on his right cheek. He scanned the room he had just literally destroyed. "Anybody else?" he asked.

The dead lay silent, and others groaned. The first man's screaming was now reduced to literal sobbing as he still grasped the crotch of his pants. Those left unhurt just stared. No other man made a move.

John turned his attention to Thelma as he approached the bar.

"You stay away from me, John Hawkins!" she screamed at him.

Tess moved away from the bar and kept an eye on those still watching. None of them looked ready for any kind of confrontation with John. John holstered his gun and jumped over the bar to drag a screaming Thelma out from behind it, one strong arm clamped around both of her arms, his other hand grasping her hair tightly and pulling so that her head tipped back. She kicked at him, calling him every name she could think of, bastard, half-breed, savage, murderer . . .

John slammed her across a table, clamping a hand around her throat, just tight enough that she had to stop screaming. "Now," he sneered, "I want to know about my son and my little *daughter!* I want to know if they are all right! I want every *detail,* you slut! I want to know if they were harmed, in *any* way! If they've been fed right! If they are well! I want to know if more than one man left with Lonnie Briggs! I want to know *everything* he told you about what he has planned!" He let go of her throat and jerked her to a sitting position. "Are you going to tell me, or do I have to *beat* it out of you, you filthy whore!"

Thelma spit at him. "You wouldn't beat a woman, John Hawkins!"

John backhanded her and sent her sprawling from the table to the floor.

Tess was astonished. Never had she known John Hawkins to lay a hand on a woman. Ken told her more than once that in all their dealings with "the scum of the earth," John had never used his wrath against a woman physically.

Reaching right inside and ripping one side of her dress away from her breast, John jerked Thelma back to her feet. Blood ran from her nose, more from a cut on her lower lip. "Don't make me hit you again," he said through clenched teeth. "I'll do it until your face can't be repaired if you don't tell me about my son and daughter! Has Lonnie done anything to them? Has he hurt them?"

"No!" Thelma wiped at the blood on her face with a shaking hand. "Not the girl anyway. She's okay. A little sunburned, but okay. I even let her take a bath and gave her some clean clothes. Honest!"

John shoved her into a chair, and Thelma shivered as she pulled the ripped side of her dress over her exposed breast. "What do you mean, the girl?" he asked. "Has my *son* been hurt?"

Thelma closed her eyes. "Look, John, it didn't happen while they were with me, I swear. He was already hurt when they got here."

"Oh, no!" Tess exclaimed, glancing at John.

"Keep an eye on the others," he ordered. He licked at the blood on his lip. "Hurt how?"

Thelma shrugged. "Not terrible or anything. Lonnie told me the boy kept talking about how you'd come and get them and they'd be sorry, and Lonnie got tired of hearing it. When he told the kid to shut up, he wouldn't. And the kid kept telling Lonnie they'd better not hurt his sister, or he'd find a way to kill them. He just got tired of the little bas— I mean, the kid smarting off all the time. He told Tex to be quiet, and he wouldn't, so Lonnie clobbered him. When they arrived at my place, the boy had a puffy lower lip, a black eye, and bruises on both cheeks."

John straightened. "And my daughter?"

"She's fine. I promise. She wouldn't let me or Lonnie help with her bath. She only wanted Tex with her." She folded her shaking arms. "She hasn't been touched. I know Lonnie. He wouldn't do that. She's scared, but she hasn't been harmed."

"And what about the rest of the men with him? What are *they* like?"

"I don't really know. She's just a little girl, John. They won't hurt her."

"They'll *kill* her if I don't show up!"

Thelma cried out when he jerked her back to her feet by the hair. "You could have brought those kids down here while Lonnie slept, hid them somewhere, had all these men keep them from Lonnie till I got here! You *knew* I'd come! But you let Lonnie go off with them."

He shoved her hard, and she fell against a table with a grunt, then lost her balance and fell to the floor.

"I could *kill* you!" John growled. He stood there panting, and for a moment Tess thought he really would take out his knife and slit her throat. "Were my kids fed right?"

Thelma groaned and managed to get to a sitting position. "Yes," she answered, holding her side. "I think you cracked some of my ribs."

"You'll live, for what that's worth. Was there just one other man with Lonnie?"

Thelma nodded. "Truby Bates, he called himself. Lonnie said . . . there were two more . . . waiting for him at . . . Eagle Pass. Sam something . . . and I think the other one was . . . called Calhoun. I'm not sure."

"And then Lonnie got more men from here," John offered.

"Four," Thelma answered. "They all . . . have it in for you . . . one way or another."

"And you let them all go off with my kids." John looked around the room. *"All* of you! I don't mind being dealt with directly, face-to-face! But to take out your old grudges through innocent children is different! You're all a bunch of stinking cowards!"

Thelma looked up at him. "I told Lonnie he . . . shouldn't do it. I . . . told him he was . . . crazy. I tried to talk him out of it."

"Well, you didn't try very hard, did you? And after seeing what he was up to, instead of finding a way to help those innocent, abused children, you still went to bed with Lonnie, didn't you? A good-looking young man who can poke himself into you half the night is more important!" John leaned closer and grasped her arm in a painful grip.

"Please don't hit me again," Thelma begged.

"You know, Thelma, there are whores who are still ladies, and whores who are pure sluts! You're a *slut!*" John walked around her and over to Tess. He took the six-shooter out of her hand, then looked down at Thelma again. "Did Lonnie mention any special plans for when I get there?"

Thelma shook her head. "He just said the kids were his insurance that you would come. He figures . . . he's got enough men to do you in . . . with no trouble."

"All the men in the world aren't enough to keep me from my son and *daughter!*" John answered her. "Apparently Lonnie Briggs doesn't know who he's dealing with, but he'll soon find out!" He scanned the room again. "I don't know how men like you live with yourselves!" He put a hand to Tess's waist and led her outside. Tess could still feel his rage when he lifted her to her horse.

"John, your arm—"

"The hell with my arm!" He mounted his own horse and, taking the reins to both packhorses from Joe, kicked his horse into a hard run. Tess had to do the same to keep up, until they were farther away from the settlement. It was just light enough to see an old barn up ahead, and John slowed his horse.

"This must be the place Sage told us about. Stay here. I'll talk to the owner."

He went inside, and Tess shivered at his mood. She wanted to rebandage his arm, since she noticed the bandage was soaked with blood. She also wanted to wash and dress the cuts on his face and hands. How much more would he go through before this was over? How much more would they *both* go through?

John finally returned, taking the reins of his horse and the two packhorses and leading them toward the neighboring barn.

"I just remembered you shot two men," he told her, "saved my life. You did good, Tess." He led the horses inside the weathered barn. "I'm proud of you."

Tess closed her eyes. "For killing two men?"

"For doing what you *had* to do. There could be more of the same ahead." He closed his eyes and breathed deeply. "It's going to be a bitch, Tess." He faced her then, his whole countenance exuding rage, his face badly bruised, the skin of one cheek split, his hands and knuckles scraped and bleeding. Blood trickled out from under the bandage on his arm.

"John, let me—"

"Never mind!" he snapped. "Just—" He turned away again. "I've never been short with you before, and I've never hit a woman, no matter how worthless she was. It was just the fact that Tex and Honor were here, and not one person lifted a finger to help them." He sighed deeply. "Make up a bed and get some sleep. By tomorrow night we'll reach Eagle Pass." He headed for the door.

"John, where are you going?"

"I'll be right outside. I just have to be alone for a while."

He walked out, and Tess sat down in some hay, putting her head in her hands. She hated the men back in the saloon for more than not helping her children. They had made her kill two of them, something deeply against her nature and beliefs. If only she could be as sure and unfeeling about it as John. But she could not. She wept.

Forty-eight

Sam sat on the cabin porch, leaning back in a wooden chair, his feet propped up on the railing. He puffed a cigar, watching the sun settle behind endless rock formations on the western horizon. It was then he spotted several men approaching below the cliff.

"Well, it's about time," he muttered. "Hey, Calhoun! I think Lonnie is finally here—and he's brought help!"

Calhoun shoveled down a last piece of smoked beef and shoved his plate away, picking up a bottle of whiskey. "Clean this place up a little, will you, Bernie? It's a damn mess."

"What can you expect?" Bernie answered him, retying her robe around her naked body. "The water you hauled up here from Thieves' Hollow is about gone. I can't even take a bath."

He curled his nose. "Don't I know that!"

"You don't smell any better, kid."

He ran a hand through his hair. "If that's Lonnie out there and he has those kids with him, John Hawkins won't be far behind, and before long we'll be living it up in Mexico. You can have all the baths you want."

"You're taking me with you?"

Calhoun shrugged. "Maybe, if you quit bitchin' about everything."

"I won't bitch, but first you'd better make sure I get out of here alive. You better make sure Hawkins knows I didn't have anything to do with you taking his kids."

"Hell, I *didn't* take them! Lonnie did. I'm just along for the ride, honey, and the money."

"It *is* them!" Sam yelled. "They just signaled me!"

Calhoun hurried out, standing on the porch to watch.

Sam stood up, keeping the cigar between his teeth. "I can almost taste John Hawkins," he sneered. "Maybe we'll roast him alive and eat him." He cast a wicked look toward Calhoun. "What do you think half-breed meat tastes like?" he said with a grin.

Calhoun swigged down some more whiskey and shrugged. "From what I've heard about John Hawkins, I expect it's tough," he answered.

Sam laughed. "He's still just human, kid. Don't you worry about any of this. We've got plenty of help now."

The men below began making their way up the snaking, narrow-ledge road that led to the cabin. Sam rubbed his hands together. "I've planned this for a long, long time. When Lonnie visited me in prison, and we talked about this, I gotta say, I doubted we could make this work, but, by-God, we did it!"

"Look at that. Lonnie brought extra men. I hope he didn't tell them they were gettin' *paid* for this. I'd hate to split that money up *too* many ways."

"If he's smart, he didn't say anything about money. Hell, it wouldn't be hard to find somebody who'd like to kill John Hawkins just for the fun of it." Sam took the cigar from his mouth. "Give me some of that whiskey."

Calhoun handed it over, and Sam took a long swallow. "I can see one of the kids now. See the boy on the spotted horse? That must be the bastard Tess Hawkins had by one of the *Comancheros*. Look at that dark skin and long hair. No wonder she married Hawkins. She figured the kid would look Indian, so Hawkins would look like his real father. I still can't believe a woman like that married somebody like John Hawkins, but then after being with *Comancheros*, a woman can't be too choosy."

Calhoun chuckled. "Is she pretty?"

"Tess Hawkins? Hell, yes, at least from what I remember.

Auburn hair, blue eyes, clear skin, a body that makes a man's mouth water."

"We gonna have a chance at her?"

"Of course we will. She'll be coming with Hawkins."

The riders were about halfway up the ridge, and Lonnie removed his hat and waved. "Higgins! I told you I could do it!"

Sam waved back. "He's got the girl with him. I can't believe John Hawkins has a little girl. Look at the sun on her hair. It's red, like her mother's." He shook his head. "Hawkins can't be far behind. He must be going crazy at the thought of his little girl being in my care. I've never enjoyed myself so much in my whole life."

They waited for all the horses and men to arrive, and Sam greeted Lonnie with laughter and a firm handshake. "You did it, kid! You smooth-talking sonofabitch! You have to tell us how you managed it."

"Shit, I had Hawkins's wife and kids eating out of my hand. Even Hawkins grew to trust me. I even saved a foal and its mother that belonged to Hawkins's son. Worked on his ranch. And by the way"—Lonnie dismounted, grabbing Honor down and holding her at his side with one arm like a sack of flour—"that friend of Hawkins you said you didn't like? Ken Randall? He's dead. Seems somebody stabbed him about twenty times when he wasn't looking, poor guy. And to think he was supposed to be guarding these kids."

Sam laughed, looking down at Honor. "Well, lookee here." He tousled her hair, and Lonnie moved her to his chest, holding her tightly in both arms and keeping her face out so she would be readily visible to Sam. Sam grasped her chin and looked her over.

"Don't you touch me!" Honor pouted. "You're a big, ugly bad man, I can tell! I don't like you!"

Sam laughed even louder, throwing his head back when he did so. "So, she not only looks like her ma, but she's got her ma's smart mouth on her! It sure is easy to tell she's Tess

Hawkins's daughter, all right." He leaned closer. "What's your name, kid?"

Honor answered by soundly kicking him in the chin.

Sam grunted and put a hand to his face, and the other men laughed. Finally, Sam grinned, too. "You better look out, girl, or I'll throw you right over that cliff, and your daddy will find you *dead*. That will make him cry. Do you want to make your daddy cry?"

Honor just stared back at him with her bottom lip hanging out.

"My pa doesn't cry about *nothin'!*" Tex spoke up. He still sat on his horse.

Sam looked up at him, then left Honor to walk closer. "Oh, I guarantee I'll have your pa crying in no time," he told Tex.

"You're the one who will be crying!" Tex answered.

"Oh, I doubt that, boy. What's your name, anyway?"

"Tex. And my sister's name is Honor."

"Honor?" Sam shook his head and chuckled. "Imagine that. John Hawkins with a daughter named Honor." He laughed again, shaking his head, then looked back at Lonnie. "I want these kids kept inside at all times. I don't want Hawkins to see them until I'm *ready* for him to see them. Take the girl inside and have Bernie fix her something to eat. Once the little brats are asleep, we can talk. I want to hear all about what happened. Lord knows Calhoun and I are hungry as hell for some diversion from the long, hot, quiet days out here. We need some entertainment, and it has finally arrived." He turned back to Tex. "Get down off that horse, boy, and go on into the cabin with your sister."

"What are you gonna do to my pa when he comes?"

"Oh, you don't want to know. But you'll get to watch when the time comes."

Sam grabbed Tex's arm and gave it a yank, jerking the boy off his horse. He threw him to the ground, and Tex scraped his face on the gravel.

"Don't be a pain, boy, else it's your sister who will suffer and not you. Understand? I'm not fond of kids, especially not John Hawkins's kids."

Tex brushed dirt and blood from his left cheek as he sat up, then got to his feet.

"Go on inside," Sam ordered him. "There's a woman in there who will get you something to eat." He watched Tex walk dejectedly toward the cabin, then turned to Lonnie. "You did good, boy, damn good! Who are these other men?"

"I found them in town, talked them into coming with me for a piece of John Hawkins . . . and maybe his wife."

"You can count me in on that one," Truby spoke up.

They all laughed, and Sam relit his cigar. "Twenty-four hours, boys. I give him twenty-four hours."

Forty-nine

Tess waited, never feeling more lonely. She sat in the dark barn, finding sleep impossible. She felt suddenly abandoned by her husband. The John Hawkins who abused the woman in the saloon, and who barked angrily at her earlier, was no John Hawkins she had ever known, not even the one she first met.

She'd looked around outside, but could not find him. Maybe he had gone back to the saloon and gotten himself in more trouble. For all she knew he was dead.

All she could do was pray. Only God knew what would happen tomorrow and the next day. Only God knew what she might have to endure, how they would find their children, if any of them would survive this.

"All I want is my children back," she quietly prayed. "And my husband, Lord . . . not just in the flesh, but in the heart."

She could not blame him, but she had seen the worst of John Hawkins. She always knew what he was capable of doing when necessary. She just did not know how to handle him when he became this angry, this vengeful. Ken told her once that there were times when they rode together that he simply did not dare speak to John.

You just gotta leave him be and let him get over it, Ken told her.

In their entire marriage, the problem had never presented itself to this degree.

"Please end this!" she prayed. "Don't let my children suffer. Give us strength and wisdom for what must come."

She could not help the sobs that enveloped her. It was all just too much, the tension, the not knowing, the worry, the physical strain, the pregnancy. She felt helpless, and hopeless. It actually felt good to cry. She wept so that she could barely get her breath, not even aware that John had returned. Suddenly he was just there. She gave a startled gasp when his strong arms came around her. She turned and wrapped her own arms around his neck when she realized who it was.

Now he was the John Hawkins she had come to know and love. Now she felt the embrace much like the one he gave her when he came to rescue her from the *Comancheros*. He was a man with two sides to him, each as different from the other as possible.

"God, don't cry, Tess," he said softly, stroking her hair. He sat down and pulled her onto his lap, rocking her. "I'm sorry for the way I talked to you. I'm even sorry I lit into Thelma Leeds. You have to believe I've never done that to a woman before."

"I know. I know."

"This is just different. I've never had so much at stake. To think they were here, right here, and no one tried to stop this!"

She felt him tensing up again. "I understand."

He gripped her tighter.

"Please don't leave like that again," she told him. "I was . . . afraid you went back there . . . and got yourself killed." She clung to him, breathed in the scent of him. Even when he needed to bathe, he never smelled bad. He simply smelled of the earth, the sun, the wind, leather.

He sighed deeply, kissed her hair. "I've done my share of weeping, Tess. Don't think I haven't. And what happened earlier, I was just so furious at the fact that all those people knew what was happening, and just because they hate me, they let it happen. It made me feel so damn responsible. That's the hardest part for me. It all comes down to this being *my* fault, and I can hardly stand it. It makes me feel like the times I saw my own mother being abused, and I was too little to help her. That's how I feel right now. I hate the feeling, Tess. I hate it so much that it makes me so damn furious I can't control my reactions."

He kissed her tears.

"That's when I just have to go off alone," he continued, "so I don't take the fury out on someone close to me. What makes it all worse is knowing how Tex is feeling right now. I'll never forget how it felt to be too young and small to help someone you love." He closed his eyes and pressed his forehead to hers. "I have felt a little bit that way all through this, unable to help my own children."

"I have to think God will help you, John. I have to think we're going to get through this. I just worry what the cost will be to you."

"It doesn't matter, as long as Tex and Honor are safe."

"But I know you," she wept. "You'll walk right up to them if it means making them release the children. And that's what they want, John." Her tears came anew. "That's what they want."

He gripped her face between his hands. "I know what they want, Tess, but they aren't going to get it. I've been thinking about this. I think I know what to do."

She grasped his hands. "What do you mean?"

He pulled away and leaned back against the wall of the stall where they sat. "Out there alone, I, uh, prayed . . ."

Tess sensed it was a strain for him to even say the word prayed. The confession surprised her, but knowing John, she did not press the issue. She just let him talk.

He sighed and leaned his head back, and in the soft moonlight she could see him close his eyes. "Maybe you were right."

"About what?"

He shrugged. "You know. About . . . answered prayer."

Tess weighed her words. "What makes you say that?" she asked cautiously.

He drew up his knees and rested his arms on them. "After I . . . you know . . . prayed . . . I remembered something. I can't believe I forgot about it in the first place, but someone, or something, made me remember."

Curiosity helped allay Tess's tears. "Remember what?"

He leaned forward then and pulled her between his legs, wrapping his arms around her from behind. "There is another way up to Eagle Pass, a back way."

Hope began to soothe Tess's aching heart. "Then we can sneak up—"

"No," he interrupted. "*I* can sneak up on them, but I need all their attention directed elsewhere. That's where you come in. And that's the part I don't like about the plan. If not your life, you'll be risking something worse, a hell you've already been through."

Tess knew he meant her capture by the *Comancheros* . . . and her rape at the hands of Tex's father. "It doesn't matter, John. I'll do anything I have to do to get the children out of their hands. You know that."

He kissed her hair. "You will have to go there alone, Tess. You will even have to find your way there alone for a good ways before Eagle Pass. I don't doubt they will have men watching in all directions. We can't let them see me at any time. By tomorrow afternoon we'll be close. I'll have to leave you then, take another way over. You'll have to go on by yourself, and you'll have to try to make them swallow the story that I'm dead—that I was killed back at Thieves' Hollow. They know damn well what a dangerous place that is for me, especially now that I'm just an ordinary citizen and not the law. They just might believe you. If they aren't expecting me, I have a chance to get the better of them. Surprise is always the best weapon. I doubt any of them know about the other way up to the pass. I learned about it when a man I was tracking disappeared behind some rocks in the area. When I followed him, I ended up in a cave that opens up behind the open area where the cabin is situated. It's too narrow for a horse, and in places almost too narrow for a man, and I don't think anyone else knows about it. I never told anyone, not even Ken. The man

I was after was Indian, and it's possible only the Apache know about the cave."

Tess sat up straighter and turned slightly to face him. "John, that's it! I knew God would help us find an answer!"

He rubbed at tired eyes. "The only trouble is, it's been years since I found it. Time can change a lot of things. I only hope I can still get through some of those places. If I can't, I'll have to come around the regular way, and it's all but impossible to hide yourself when you approach from the front. To make matters worse, you'll already be up there with the kids. I'll be in a hell of a fix. I might have to surrender myself to get you out of there."

"Your idea will work, John. I know it will!"

He touched her face, wiping her remaining tears away with his thumbs. "There is one thing you have to understand, Tess. If this does work, I will probably end up eliminating every man there. As long as my family is in danger from even one of them, I can't let them live, which means doing some very *un*-Christian things. I'm not a man to turn the other cheek, especially not when my family is involved."

"God understands."

He only sighed and shook his head. "Maybe." He touched her cheek with the back of his hand. "You have to get the children out of there. I don't want them to see what happens."

"I'll do what I can. It all depends on what happens when you get there, and if I'm even able to help."

"That's what I'm worried about. There will be a lot of shooting, and I will have no way of knowing your situation until I get there. I can't think of any other way to do this. I need an edge, and this might be it. I'm just worried you might end up suffering the same horrors you suffered nine years ago, and maybe lose that baby."

She leaned close, resting her head against his chest. "I won't lose the baby, John. I know it in my heart. I can do this. I've been through the worst hell a woman can suffer, and I survived. All of a sudden I'm not afraid. God made you remember that cave, and as long as I know you'll be coming for us, I can face them alone."

She turned her face up to his, and he met her lips with a gentle kiss that turned into one of possessiveness, ownership. He laid her back in the hay. "Don't forget you're mine," he whispered.

"What woman who's been with you *could* forget?" she answered. "Just hold me. Whatever happens, know that I love you, more than I have ever, or will ever love anyone."

John pulled her tight against him, and Tess rested her head on his shoulder, kissing his neck. Something dripped onto her cheek and ran toward her lips. She tasted his salt.

Fifty

A short night's rain added a miserable humidity to the day's heat. John drew his horse to a halt and reached out his hand. Tess took it, wanting to cry at the pain she saw in his eyes.

"This is where we part company," he told her.

She clung to his hand, wanting to remember its size, the feel of it. She forced a look of bravery.

"This will work, John. I have faith in this being God's will, and I have faith in *you*." She squeezed his hand before letting go of it. "God be with you."

He looked away and began rolling himself a cigarette. "I'm not so sure He will be, with what I have planned, if I can get my hands on Sam Higgins and Lonnie Briggs." He sealed the cigarette, then lit it. "Do you think you can find it alone now?"

"I'll find it."

"Be sure to take the farthest left fork when you see the trail break off about three miles ahead. And if you encounter anyone along the way that looks suspicious, shoot him. God knows there are still enough renegade Indians around and wandering outlaws in this place that no woman should be riding out here alone, but we have no choice. Don't be afraid to use that rifle or that handgun. I'm going to have you take both packhorses. If they ask where my horse is, tell them you left it back at Thieves' Hollow because you had to get out of there fast. And you will have to appear as though you are genuinely grieving."

Tess smiled sadly. "I *will* be genuinely grieving." Her voice broke momentarily. "I might be losing you."

He lit the cigarette. "Tess, look up."

She quickly wiped at tears and did what he asked.

"What do you see?"

"Clouds. It's very overcast."

"Good. If it stays this way through tonight, you don't have anything to worry about."

"What?"

He took a long drag on the cigarette. "It's not a very good day to die." He gave her a wink and turned his horse, kicking it into a hard gallop.

Tess watched until horse and man became only a small dot, and she wondered if this was her last sight of John Hawkins alive, her last touch, the last time she would hear his voice.

Pain gripped her chest as she headed toward Eagle Pass, part of her dreading what was to come, another part of her taking hope and joy in the fact that by tonight she would see her children again. Whatever happened then, at least she would be with them.

She rode alone for unending hours, the surrounding, desolate mountains eerily quiet. She took turns with the horses, sometimes riding the packhorses so Pepper would have a break from her weight. But she felt sorry for Jake and White Sox. There was no time to stop and relieve them of the gear they carried. She could only hope all three horses would survive the grueling, nonstop journey. If the packhorses gave out, Pepper should at least be able to get her there, as long as she kept relieving him of any weight for short periods of time. The poor horses needed a complete rest, but she could not bear the thought of going even one more night without seeing Tex and Honor. More important, she hoped Shadow could make the long journey with John's weight on her back. She was a good, strong horse, but the race to get to Eagle Pass in time could kill her.

The gray day turned to an even grayer dusk, and she ached from being in the saddle so long. The packhorses began to lather and pant, but she sensed now that she was close. She could understand why outlaws preferred such a place to hide out. Who would want to bother coming here to search for them?

Finally she spotted what looked like a cabin in the distance, sitting high in the rocks. Yes, Sam Higgins and Lonnie Briggs chose the perfect place to lure her and John to. From their rocky perch they could see anyone coming for miles around, and pick them off like a turkey shoot. The trail John told her to follow had been true. She knew the cabin ahead must be the one where her children were being kept.

Her heart beat so hard she could hardly breathe. She could only pray now that John had made it through from the underground cave that led to this place, and she worried that after all these years he might not even be able to find it. The entrance could be covered with brush and rocks, or the tunnel itself could be caved in. And if he did not make it through, the next few hours would be the worst of her life.

Swallowing back her terror, she rode forward, and just as always happened in country like this, the cabin was much farther away than she'd guessed. It took nearly an hour to get close enough to see it well, which meant its occupants could see someone coming long before. She was most likely already being watched.

She kept her eyes fixed on the cabin as it became more and more visible and detailed. Her heart nearly stopped then when she heard a whistle, the kind a man would use when signaling someone.

"Lord, help me through this. Help me know what to do."

She kept moving forward, and she saw a few horses grazing on sparse grass below the cliff where the cabin was perched. It looked as though there was some space behind the cabin, but not much area before another sheer wall of rock spiraled upward behind it. More rock walls surrounded the sides, and now she could see why the only way to approach was from the front . . . unless John could find that tunnel.

She told herself not to look around. She did not want the men above to suspect she was watching for someone. They must believe she had come here alone.

She rode ever closer, dreading every step. Now she could see two men standing on a porch at the front of the cabin. They would most likely be Lonnie and Sam. She held her chin high and rode forward at a slightly faster gait.

"Tex!" she screamed. "Honor!"

"Mommy," she thought she heard. It was a tiny, faint voice, muffled by distance.

"Honor! Tex!" she screamed again. "It's Mommy! I'm here!"

"Hold it right there!"

Tess gasped, startled by the voice, which came at her from much closer. A man walked out from behind a large boulder to her left, carrying a shotgun.

"Get down off that horse."

Tess obeyed, feeling numb. She determined not to show one ounce of fear, and she walked straight up to the man who spoke, able to see him well enough in what was left of the daylight to notice heavy bags under his eyes.

"You're the one called Truby Bates," she stated firmly.

He placed the end of the shotgun barrels at her throat. "Well, now, missy. How do you know that?"

"I know the description of one of the men who escaped with Sam Higgins. Ugly, with bags under your eyes. You certainly fit the description," she sneered.

Truby shoved the shotgun a little harder, so that Tess had to step back to avoid having her air cut off. "And *I* heard you was an uppity, smart-mouthed woman. You fit *your* description!" His gaze raked over her. "In a lot of other ways, too. We're gonna have a good time with you." He grunted a chuckle, then looked around. "Where in hell is your husband?"

Tess closed her eyes, feeling a very real grief. "John Hawkins is dead," she answered. Her fear at the moment made tears come easily. She could only hope they would help convince the man she told the truth. "I hope all of you are satisfied. You wanted John dead. You got your wish."

Truby looked around. "I don't believe you."

"Believe what you want, you scum! He was killed back at Thieves' Hollow. I came here alone to get my children. I was afraid to bring anyone else for fear of what you might do to Tex and Honor. And with John dead, you no longer have reason to hold them. I want my babies!"

The man looked around again, and Tess enjoyed seeing the worry in his eyes.

"From what I've heard, there ain't a man back at Thieves' Hollow capable of gettin' the better of John Hawkins."

"It doesn't take skill or guts to shoot a man in the back! Ask Sam Higgins about that. *He* can tell you! Back-shooting men and burning women and children alive are his *specialties!*"

Truby looked her over again. "You got any weapons on you?"

"Only those on my horse."

"We'll see about that." Truby walked up to her and began feeling around, taking his time at her breasts, reaching under her skirt and probing between her legs.

"Hey, Truby, save something for us!" Lonnie shouted from above.

Tess remained rigid, forcing herself not to think about this horrid man touching her. If this was what she had to endure to see her children, then so be it.

"Why didn't you bring somebody with you?" Truby asked. "Why would you come here alone?"

"I told you. Because Lonnie *told* us to come alone. If I showed up here with some other man, he might hurt my children."

"Where's Hawkins!" the words boomed from above, and Tess recognized the voice of Sam Higgins. It chilled her to hear it again.

"Dead!" Truby shouted up to him. "Killed back in Thieves' Hollow!"

Tess glanced up, saw Sam and Lonnie talking. She had no doubt they were very worried and nervous.

"Look out, Truby!" Sam called down. "She's probably lying!"

Tess met Truby's eyes. "You saw me coming, probably from

miles back. You are camped here *because* you can see anyone approaching. If John was with me, you would know it. My husband is dead, and I want my babies back."

Truby looked around again. "He ain't here!" he shouted up to Sam. "You seen as well as me that it's just the woman that came." He turned to Tess. "Let's go. Start climbin', lady."

"Why?" Tess asked. "It's John Hawkins Sam wanted. Now he's dead, thanks to all of you." It was not difficult to cry. There were still so many things to cry about. "Give me my children and let me go home."

Truby grunted a laugh. "Did you think it would be that easy? Your husband ain't the only one Sam Higgins wanted. You ain't exactly his favorite person either."

"The plan was to lure my *husband* here, was it not?"

"Look, lady, the rest of us have put up with a lot of waitin' around for this, and we ain't gonna let it end without gettin' somethin' out of it. If you saw the ugly whore we got up there stayin' with us, you'd realize how good you look right now. Fact is, I ain't never seen a better-lookin' woman, except maybe in some half-naked paintin' hangin' over a bar. Now get goin' before I knock you silly. You want to see your kids or not?"

"Hold it, Truby!" Sam shouted. "Something doesn't smell right."

"John's dead!" Tess screamed. "He was shot in the back at Thieves' Hollow! Please, let me see my children! I am alone. I've come all this way, and I want my children!" She could see Sam and Lonnie again exchanging words.

"I don't believe it," Lonnie said. "That half-breed sonofabitch is up to something!"

"He's *dead,* I tell you!" Tess screamed. "Why else would I have come here alone!"

Again Higgins and Briggs talked. They looked as though they were arguing. They were worried, as well they should be! *Good,* Tess thought. *A good argument will kill more time.*

"I say we take her up to the cabin," Truby shouted. "I don't see nobody around. Where the hell could he hide? The place I just hid is the only thing that comes close to good enough to hide a man the size of Hawkins. Besides, we would have seen him comin'. We ain't took our eyes off the horizon for two days."

Again Sam and Lonnie talked. Then Lonnie shouted down the order. "Bring her on up."

Truby grinned. "Get moving."

Tess forced her legs to move. She lifted her skirt slightly and started up the cliff.

Fifty-one

Tess felt ill at the sight of Sam Higgins. Never a good-looking man in the first place, prison and passing years had aged him more than she'd expected. His hair had receded to a near-bald stage, and what was left of it was white.

Truby Bates stood behind her, and Lonnie Briggs stood beside Sam, grinning that hideously handsome grin. Two more men stood behind Sam, and another two were perched in strategic places in the rocks just below the cabin.

Tess moved her gaze to Lonnie. "You gutless, murdering scum!" she sneered. She turned to Sam. "And I see you are still the despicable coward you were nine years ago," she said forthrightly. "No *real* man gets what he wants by cowering behind two helpless children!"

Sam's reply was to slam the back of his hand across the right side of her face. Tess heard a crack the moment he hit her, and pain shot through her right cheekbone as she whirled and landed against the outside wall of the cabin. She grunted when a strong hand gripped her upper right arm tightly and jerked her straight again.

"That was for my *first* year in prison!" Sam snarled.

"Mommy!" she heard Honor screaming. "I want to see my mommy!"

"They're hurting her! Let me go!" Tex yelled.

A woman screamed from inside the cabin. "Ow! You little bastard! He kicked me, Calhoun! Did you see that?"

"Mother!"

Tex. He sounded close. And apparently the eighth man of the group was inside the cabin. She tried to free herself from Sam's grip, but it was impossible. When her vision cleared, she saw him! Tex! He was pounding at Sam's right arm.

"You let her go! Stop hurting her!" he screamed viciously at Sam.

"Tex, no!" Tess screamed. Sam shoved Tex hard, landing the boy against a wooden chair. Tex let out a little scream, but he got right back up and came for Sam again. Lonnie quickly grabbed the boy, wrapping his arms around Tex so he could not use his own arms. "I've just about had my fill of you, boy," Lonnie said. "You're gonna get a good beating!"

"No! Wait!" Tess screamed. "Please don't hurt him!"

Sam wrapped his arms tightly around her from behind, holding her helpless as Lonnie slugged Tex, sending the boy down the steps.

"No!" she screamed again. John! Where was he?

Tex, his bleeding lips pressed together in a rage against his own tears, got up and came for Lonnie again, and Tess could see the same mean determination in his eyes as she'd seen more than once in John's eyes.

"Tex!" she pleaded. "Don't let him hurt you. Honor needs you!"

Tex stopped at the top of the steps, glaring at Lonnie, his small fists clenched tightly. Tess could see other cuts and bruises on his face, and she felt sick at the sight. Had Honor also been abused this way?

Tex glanced at her, then back at Lonnie. "My pa will *kill* you for this!" he snarled.

"Your pa is *dead!*" Lonnie answered.

Tess's heart broke at the look on Tex's face, first shock, then disbelief, and then an agonizing horror. There was nothing she could do about it. For now poor Tex had to believe what he'd just been told.

"You're a *liar,* Lonnie Briggs! You lied to me before, and you're lying now!" Tex screamed the words through tears.

"Well, boy, I wish I *wasn't* lying, because *I* wanted the honor and pleasure of killing John Hawkins myself! If I can't have that, then I'll take second best. I'll have a good time with your ma here, and then sell the three of you in Mexico." Lonnie jerked Tex up to the porch by his hair and dragged him back inside the cabin. "Calhoun, you and Bernie take the brats out back and *keep* them there!" he ordered.

"Let go of me!" Tex growled.

"Shut up, kid," a man answered.

"No! No! No!" Tess heard Honor screaming. "I want to see my mommy! What did you do to my mommy! Where's my daddy!"

"Your pa is dead," a woman answered.

Honor started crying hard, and Tess could hear a struggle, then the closing of a door. Now she could tell the screaming and crying was taking place outside, somewhere behind the cabin. It was torture to hear her children crying, to know they were being terrified and not be able to go to them. Then it hit her. Out back. The children had been taken behind the cabin, the very place where John just might be able to get his hands on them . . . if he'd found that tunnel and made it through.

Sam grabbed her by the hair then and dragged her inside the cabin, literally tossing her onto a bed, where she bumped her head against the wall.

"Mommy! Mommy!" she heard Honor scream again. The girl started to come back inside, but a dirty-looking, bedraggled woman with red lips and mousy blond hair grabbed her away and closed the door again.

"Honor," Tess tried to scream, but she remained stunned from the blow to her head and could barely speak. At least she'd seen them, she thought. She'd seen Tex and Honor, and they were alive and fighting. *If only I could touch them. Hold them.*

Sam picked up some rope and walked to the back door. He opened it and threw the rope outside. "Tie them up," he ordered.

"I don't want them getting away from you again and barging in here."

"My pa will get you for this!" Tex yelled. "You just wait and see. He's *not* dead! He's *not!*"

"He's dead, all right," Sam answered. "Your pa failed you good this time, boy. He's not coming for you or your sister or your ma. You're all going to Mexico." He closed the door. "Soon as the rest of us have some fun with your ma."

Whatever the cost, Tess knew she had to stall for time. Most important, she had to keep the attention of Sam Higgins, Lonnie Briggs, and Truby Bates on her . . . and away from the back door. Inwardly she prayed desperately that John had found his way to this place and was somewhere close.

She sat up straighter, feeling dizzy, terrified she might lose her baby. She felt an egg forming on her forehead, and for a moment the voices of the three men inside sounded far away.

". . . tied the brats up good . . ."

"They'll bring a good price in Mexico, especially the little girl."

"I feel cheated . . . wanted to get my hands on Hawkins myself."

"Damn it! All we've been through for this, and all we have is a woman and two brats."

"I could almost taste Hawkins's blood."

A barrage of horrible cursing followed, and through a daze Tess could see Lonnie thrashing about the cabin, knocking dishes off the table, overturning the table, smashing empty whiskey bottles against the wall, cursing his luck, cursing whoever it was that killed John Hawkins, robbing him of the pleasure.

"We've still got the woman," Truby Bates reminded him. "Take it out on her."

"I get her first," Sam spoke up. "I have more reason to want to see her suffer than you do, Lonnie. It was Hawkins you wanted. I'm sorry you didn't get your wish, but I've still got part of mine."

Tess's vision became more clear as he spoke. The cabin was a filthy mess, trash, clothes, old food everywhere. The two beds inside were a tumble with dirty bedclothes, and Lonnie had made an even worse mess during his fit of rage by not being able to kill John himself.

Sam reached for her then, and she felt her blouse being torn open. Think! She had to think! She had to keep their attention but also try to avoid their intentions. Sam reached inside her camisole, and she suddenly grasped hold of his hand and yanked it up to bite it as hard as she could.

Sam cried out, and when he jerked his hand away, she scooted off the other side of the bed.

"Bitch!" Sam growled.

Lonnie laughed, but his eyes glittered with hatred and a need for revenge. "Things aren't working out so well for you either, are they, Sam? You better not try sticking something else in her mouth. She'll bite it off."

"Shut up!" Sam snapped at him.

"Don't tell me to shut up, old man."

Sam faced him, and for a moment the two of them glared at each other, looking ready to clash.

"What's wrong?" Tess asked, reminding herself John was surely outside somewhere. He had never failed her. He wouldn't fail her now. "Are the two of you nervous about something?" Pain pierced her right cheekbone with every word she spoke.

Both men faced her, and Truby Bates, who was still inside, walked up beside Sam.

"What the hell should we be nervous about?" Lonnie asked.

Tess shrugged. "I have no idea. You just both seem awfully edgy with each other. Are you worried my husband will just suddenly appear? That his spirit will somehow get through to this world and rip out your hearts?" She deliberately smiled. "I knew you were a *coward*, Sam Higgins." She looked at Lonnie then. "And you're an even *worse* coward than Sam here, too afraid to stand up to Ken Randall, so you had to knife him while his back was turned! You both will surely burn in hell for abusing those children out there, and for all the other despicable crimes you have committed!"

Sam came around the end of the bed, and Lonnie also walked closer, his fists clenched.

"Something's not right," Sam told Lonnie, keeping his eyes on Tess. "I want the *truth,* Tess Hawkins, or I'll shoot that bastard of a son of yours, and you don't even want to *think* about what I'll do to that little girl!"

Horror filled Tess at the despicable comment. *"What* truth?"

Sam grasped her around the throat, his big hand nearly closing around her slender neck. "About John Hawkins! There's not a man back in Thieves' Hollow skilled enough to get the best of Hawkins, so where is he? He's *alive* isn't he?"

He shoved Tess against the wall and pinned her there. Tess faced him squarely. "You're *afraid!*" She grinned, dying inside but determined not to show it. "You're afraid John Hawkins will return from his own grave and come for you!"

"Let her go, Sam," Lonnie ordered. "Hawkins would never have let her come here alone if he was alive."

Sam loosened his grip slightly, then jerked Tess forward by the neck and slapped her again across the same side of the face, sending her sprawling across the bed. She felt faint from the awful pain.

"You don't know Tess Hawkins," Sam answered Lonnie. "The bitch *would* come here alone if that bastard half-breed told her to do it to distract our attention."

Tess screamed when she was jerked off the bed by the hair and yanked up in front of Sam. "The truth, woman. I swear to God I'll kill your son and let Calhoun out there rape your daughter. He's been wanting to do it! Is John Hawkins alive?"

John, where are you? She could not risk such horror for Honor, or the death of her son. "Yes," she answered, and in spite of her pain and terror, she could not help smiling at the look in Sam's eyes. "He took the chance of waiting until after dark," Tess added, trying to think of anything she could to keep their attention from the back of the cabin. "He knew you'd see him by day, and in spite of what might happen to me while he's coming, we agreed this was the only way."

Sam literally threw her against a wall, cursing as he did so. "Truby, get outside and warn the others! Line yourselves up along the pathway up here. That's the only way to get here. There's eight of us and only one of him, and only one way up. Even in the dark he can't make it past all of us."

"I . . . I don't know, Sam," Truby balked. "Shit, with everything I've heard—"

"Get your ass outside before I put a bullet in you myself!" Sam snapped. "It's only been dark an hour or so. If nobody saw him before that, then it's still going to take him a couple more hours to get here." He turned to Tess. "We'll be ready for him!" He stepped closer. "And by the time he gets here, we will all have had a piece of his woman!"

Tess took a deep breath, glad that at least they still thought it was the front of the cabin that had to be watched. "Go ahead," she dared Sam. She glanced at Lonnie. *"Both* of you." She needed to keep them distracted, even if it meant rape. "After being bedded by John Hawkins—" She looked them over derisively. "I won't feel a thing. You're *all* pitiful excuses for men!" She untied her camisole. "Do you really think you can satisfy any woman who has already been with John?" She smiled in a sneer. *Think about Jenny,* she told herself. *The raunchy way she talks sometimes.* "Take off your britches, and I'll see how you compare to John Hawkins."

Lonnie removed his gun belt, then his leather vest, then his suspenders. "I'll show you a comparison," he told her with that same glitter in his eyes. "How about a *younger* man?"

Tess put her hands on her hips, struggling against her own pain and dizziness, and a desperate longing to go to her children. John! If he didn't make it soon— "There isn't any younger man alive who is better with a woman than John," she answered, hoping to make them so self-conscious they would not be able to get aroused. She turned her attention back to Sam. "And you, you bald, used-up old man. After being with that pig of a woman out back, you're probably so diseased that John won't *have* to kill you. You'll die from some horrible filth *she* gave you. Did you know that a person goes insane before dying from venereal disease? Let alone the other horrible things he or she goes through first."

"She's trying to put us off, Sam," Lonnie said. "But you can bet she's terrified inside." He dropped his britches and stood there in his underwear. "And if John Hawkins is on his way here, I intend to be able to tell him I've already had at his woman. After that, the rest of the men can take turns. Then we'll bring the brats back in here so Hawkins can't come barging in shooting. I can't wait to see the look in his eyes when he finds out he got caught because his own wife told us he's still alive." He stepped closer to Tess, grinning. "Don't you worry, Sam. John Hawkins is still ours, and so is his *woman!*"

Fifty-two

Feeling his way in the dark, John squeezed toward the opening behind the sheer rock wall at the rear of the cabin at Eagle Pass. He could see the stars now. Close! So close! Pulling his six-shooters and ammunition belt along with him, he'd maneuvered through the ancient tunnel that led here, feeling like a mole digging through the earth. His hands, and the skin on his arms, belly and back were scraped to a bloody pulp in some places.

Part of the tunnel had fallen in over the years, and he'd had to use his fingers literally to dig his way through some areas, fighting the awful darkness, the threat of being buried alive. With a desperate viciousness he clawed at the last remaining rocks in his way, then threw his guns and ammunition belts out through the opening, feeling horror at the thought that this had taken too long to save Tess.

He sucked in his belly and dragged himself through an opening only a child should try to get through. He stayed there on his knees a moment to get his breath and his bearings.

"Mommy!" He heard a child cry.

"Honor!" he whispered. He slung his ammunition belts over his body, feeling his own blood dripping down his arms, back, and stomach. He picked up his gun belt and quickly strapped it on. He'd had to leave Shadow, his supplies, and his rifle behind. His six-shooters were all he had.

He closed his eyes and took a deep breath, telling himself to pretend he was rescuing someone else's family, not his own. If he thought about them being his own loved ones, he might hold his little girl in his arms a little too long. He might look at his son when he should be watching something else. His first attention had to be on getting rid of the danger, and that meant getting rid of every man at that cabin.

He made his way to a crack in the canyon wall, and through it he could see the lighted cabin. He heard crying, knew it was Honor. "Jesus," he groaned, realizing that for the first time he was not saying the name as a cussword. He was asking for help.

There was barely enough moonlight to make out someone behind the cabin. No, not just one. *Two* people. Years of tracking outlaws and Indians had taught him literally to see in the dark at times when he had to. It looked as though one of the people behind the cabin was a woman.

Now he heard her voice. ". . . hurry up and get their thrills." He could catch only part of the words. ". . . tired of waiting out here."

"I'm tired of waiting for my turn with the woman," a man answered.

No! Was he too late for Tess? His gut wrenched at the thought of what she might be suffering. He never should have let her come here alone, but how else could they do this without risking the children?

"Mother!" He heard Tex cry.

"Mommy! Mommy! Tex, why are they hurting her?"

"Shit!" John swore in a whisper. He squeezed his way through the crevasse in the canyon wall, then dropped down, listening and watching for a moment to make sure there were only two people behind the cabin.

"I don't know," Tex answered his sister in sobs. "I can't help her, Honor. I tried."

John closed his eyes against his own ugly memories.

"You two shut up, or I'll gag you," a man said.

John strained to see, and as his eyes adjusted he could see Tex and Honor lying on the ground, in a position that made it appear they were tied. A man and a woman stood on either side of them.

"I don't like this," the woman said. "If John Hawkins really is still alive, he could be anywhere."

You're damn right! John thought.

The woman started walking his way, and John slunk behind a scrubby pine tree.

"Mosquitoes are biting me," Honor cried. "I can't scratch them away."

"Too bad," the man told her.

"When are we leaving this dung heap?" the woman asked as she came closer. "I'm tired of peein' out here. I want my chamber pot, and I want a bath."

"It won't be long now," the man answered. "Hawkins is either dead already, like his wife said, or he'll *be* dead when Sam and Lonnie are through with him. I think he's already dead and his wife just made it up that he's still alive to throw us off, make us nervous. Either way, we'll be on our way tomorrow, with a woman and two kids to sell in Mexico."

The woman turned around. "I'm downright jealous, Calhoun. I've been the only woman around here for weeks. Now you're all interested in this new one."

"You know men, Bernie."

"You're a stinky, ugly lady!" Honor shouted at her. "My mommy is a whole lot prettier than you."

Bernie laughed and came under the pine tree to lift her skirts. "Yeah, well you're a smart-mouthed kid who—"

She did not finish her sentence. John rammed a knife into her back, then quietly dragged her off behind a boulder and left her there.

"Bernie? How come you didn't finish what you were saying?" the man asked. John remained crouched. If the woman didn't answer, the man was bound to come and investigate. He could hardly believe his luck, finding the children outside. If he could get rid of the man with them, they would be away from danger when he went inside the cabin. But Tess must be inside.

"Bernie?"

John heard a crashing sound from inside. "You bitch!" someone yelled. It took all his willpower to keep from running inside to help Tess, but first he had to eliminate the man outside so the children would be safe. The man started toward the tree.

"Bernie?" he called again.

Quickly John darted forward, ramming his knife into the man's belly before he had time to react. He let him fall over his arm, then half carried, half dragged him over to where the woman's body lay.

"Hawkins!" the man groaned. "You . . . must be . . ."

"John *Hawkins,*" John finished for him in a low growl. He sliced his knife across the man's throat and dropped him, then wiped his knife on the man's shirt and shoved it into its sheath. He hurried over to where the children lay, clamping a hand over Honor's mouth so she wouldn't cry out "daddy." She wiggled and kicked.

"It's *me* Honor! Daddy! You have to be very, very quiet, understand?"

"Pa!" Tex whispered. "I *knew* it! I *knew* you'd come! Mother said you were dead. She was just tricking those men, wasn't she?"

"That's right." John took his hand from Honor's mouth and began slicing through the ropes that tied the children's wrists and ankles together. He wanted nothing more than to hug them for hours and to weep at the realization that they were still alive and seemed to be all right. But there was no time now for any of that. He had to help Tess.

"Daddy," Honor sniffled. As soon as she was free of her ropes, she clamped her arms around his neck. "Daddy," she sobbed. "Daddy! Daddy! Daddy!"

"Honor, my precious baby," John whispered. He pried her away from him, but took a moment to kiss her sweet face several times over. "You have to let go of me, precious. Let me finish cutting the ropes on Tex's ankles. Daddy has to go help Mommy."

His heart ached at the way she stood there sobbing as he finished freeing Tex. He thought he could see bruises and swelling on the boy's face by the dim moonlight. "Are you hurt, Tex?"

"Lonnie beat him up bad," Honor whimpered before Tex could answer. "And now they're hurting Mommy."

"I'll be okay, Pa." Tex quickly hugged John tightly. "I knew you were alive," he wept. "Ain't nobody can hurt my pa."

"Come with me," John said, picking up Honor in one arm and Tex in the other. He hurried them over to the crack in the rock wall behind the cabin. "Both of you go through here and wait on the other side of this rock wall, understand? Don't go too far because there is a hole farther back that leads to a tunnel. I don't want you to fall into it."

"Don't leave us here, Daddy," Honor cried.

"I have to. If you want me to help Mommy, you have to do everything I tell you, understand? It's very important. I can't do what I have to do if I have to worry about you two getting hurt. If you stay behind here, nothing can happen to you. I'll go help Mommy, and then send her out here to you. She'll be with you till I'm through with Lonnie and Sam and the others."

"Are you going to kill all of them, Pa?" Tex asked. "I hope you do."

John glanced at a shivering Honor, so innocent. "I'll, uh, scare them away," he answered.

"Where are Bernie and Calhoun?" Honor asked.

"I already scared them away."

"No you didn't. You killed them, didn't you?" Tex said. "I hope you did. Calhoun touched Honor in bad places. And Lonnie and Sam let him."

John felt ready to explode. "You just stay here and do exactly what I said. I'm depending on you, Tex. You keep your sister here and wait for your mother, understand? You've taken good care of her up to now. I'm proud of you."

Tex hugged him around the waist. "Be careful, Pa. They want to kill you."

"I know that, son. Can I count on you to stay behind this wall?"

"Yeah. If that's what you want."

"Good." John leaned down and kissed both of them on the cheek. "I love both of you more than anything on earth. I won't let those men hurt either one of you again."

With great reluctance John left them, praying he would live to see them again.

Fifty-three

Tess managed to fend off Lonnie a few extra minutes by reminding him and Sam that they were fools to turn their attention to her, when John Hawkins could be sneaking his way up to the cabin this very minute, killing each of their men one at a time on his way.

"He hasn't had enough time to get here," Sam kept arguing. "Go ahead, Lonnie. I'll let you be first."

Sam drank heavily, and Tess guessed he was nervous and afraid, thinking the whiskey would give him more courage, not just for facing John, but to perform sexually.

She stood between the bed and the wall, reveling in every moment the two men argued. Lonnie kept throwing things in fits of rage, drinking, stumbling around. Sam kept going to the door to ask if anyone had seen John yet.

"I think she lied the other way," Lonnie told Sam, stepping closer to Tess again. "I think Hawkins really *is* dead, and she just told you he's alive because she figured it was the answer we wanted, figured it would keep us too nervous to have at her." He leaned close, and Tess could smell the whiskey on his breath. "Is that how it is, little lady?"

Tess faced him squarely. "That's for me to know and you to find out; but if John is alive, you will find out in a very painful way."

She watched the confusion and anger in Lonnie's eyes.

"Damn you!" he swore. "I'm tired of you playing games,

you bitch!" He yanked off his long johns and stood naked before her. He grabbed her hand and forced her to touch his hardness. "I'm gonna show you how much better it is with a younger man," he sneered.

Tess spit in his face. Lonnie drew in his breath and ripped open her camisole, throwing her onto the bed, then climbing on and straddling her. Tess clawed at his eyes.

"Sam, come hold her down!" Lonnie yelled.

Tess felt strong hands grab her wrists and push her arms down with such pressure that it hurt. She spit at Lonnie again as he began pushing up her dress. "It's time you paid, woman! I don't intend for Hawkins to get here before I shame his wife!"

Suddenly the back door burst open, and a bloody, wild-looking John Hawkins stood in the doorframe, looking as vicious as an untamed animal.

"John!" Tess cried in relief.

Sam let go of her and dived for his gun, but too late. John's guns were already blazing. Sam went down with a bullet in each knee, and Lonnie was hit in the buttocks as he tried to scramble off the bed. He screamed and crumpled to the floor. Sam tried to reach his gun, and John fired again, opening a hole in the left side of Sam's chest. The man cried out and flew backward across the other bed.

Everything happened in a matter of seconds. Tess rolled off the bed and grabbed Sam's gun from its holster while he lay there groaning. In her pain and delirium and hatred, she aimed it at Sam's head.

"No!" John ordered. "Leave him for me! Get out back! Run to the rock wall and call out for Tex and Honor!"

Tess knew there was no time to argue. She had to ignore the way John looked, standing there a shirtless, bloody mess. She headed for the door, then screamed and crouched down when the front door burst open. Instantly John fired again, and Truby Bates went down.

"Get going!" John ordered Tess. He jumped over bodies and headed outside.

Tess felt momentarily bewildered. She looked around at the bodies. Lonnie still lay on the floor, screaming and holding his rear end. Sam lay groaning on the bed.

"Bastard," he mumbled. "Dirty . . . half-breed . . . bastard."

Gasping with the growing pain in her right cheek, Tess clung to the handgun and ran out the back door. She could hear more gunfire outside.

"John," she whispered. "God, don't let him die."

More gunfire. A man screamed.

Tess stumbled into darkness. "Honor!" she cried. "Tex!"

"Mommy! Mommy!"

"We're here!" Tex called out. "Back here!"

Tess retied her camisole as best she could and ran toward their voices. She ducked under a scraggly pine tree, then felt Tex take her hand.

"Come back here behind the rock wall, Mother. Pa said for us to stay right here."

"Tex," Tess groaned. "Honor. My babies . . ." She followed Tex through the narrow crack and collapsed, pulling her children into her arms. She broke into sobs of relief that she was actually holding them close again and wept their names over and over.

"It's okay, Mom," Tex told her. "We're okay. I got beat up, but I don't care. They were hurting you."

"I'll be all right, Tex," Tess assured him. She kissed him several times over, turned to Honor and kissed her, hugging her close.

"Where's Daddy?" the girl asked, starting to cry again.

"He's coming," Tess told her. "He just . . . has to make sure . . . we're all safe."

Another man cried out, a chilling wail, as though in horrible pain. Tess closed her eyes and clung to Honor. A furious John Hawkins was meting out his own form of justice. She knew by the sound of that scream.

Fifty-four

John shot two more men on his way out the front door, recognizing one as Sly Baker, a man he'd shot years ago during an arrest.

Counting Lonnie and Sam, and the third man he'd shot inside the cabin, as well as the man out back, that left two others to find, if there were still only eight men involved. One of those lay screaming at his feet. He had tried to run, and John's guns were empty. Rather than take the time to reload and maybe lose this one, John had holstered his gun and tackled the man down. This one apparently lost his gun or never had one. He surprised John when he slammed a rock against his forehead. In spite of the dizzying injury, John managed to yank his knife from its sheath; he came down with a hard blow to the man's left shoulder, then his eye.

The man's screams stirred no pity in John's soul. All he had to do was remember what was happening to Tess when he came through the door, remember the purple bruise on the right side of her face, remember the cuts and bruises on Tex's face . . . and the fact that these men had allowed one of their own to touch Honor.

Pain seared through his head, and blood trickled down his face from the wound just inflicted on his forehead. The blood made it difficult to see, and waves of blackness surged through him. He struggled to concentrate and keep from passing out.

He was too close now to give in and allow whoever was left to kill him.

He crouched, quickly reloading one of his six-shooters. "This is John Hawkins," he shouted. "Come on out, and I'll let you live! I just want to make sure there is no one left to threaten my wife and children!"

He thought he heard a whimpering sound farther down the trail that led up the front way to the cabin.

"It's all right," he repeated. "Come out and give up your gun."

Now he heard a man literally crying like a woman. "John?" came the voice. "You tellin' the truth?"

John blinked and wiped blood away from his eyes. "Of course I am," he answered. "Who are you?"

"It's . . . me," came a shaky voice in reply. "Dan French. Do you . . . remember me? I . . . I never did . . . a whole lot of wrong things."

"Sure, Dan. I remember you. Just come out and give me your gun and you can be on your way. You're the only one left."

John could barely make out the outline of a man who rose from behind a rock, his hands in the air. "I . . . I was gonna run . . . but I knew you'd chase after me . . . and kill me. And I can't see so good in the dark, you know? And just now . . . I didn't do no shootin'. That's the God's truth, John."

John walked closer. "Hand over the gun."

Dan hesitantly handed over his weapon. John took it, then turned it on Dan and fired, exploding his kneecap. Dan screamed and fell, grasping his knee. "You bastard!" he screamed. "You promised! You promised!" He screamed again, then started to cry. "You bastard! Bastard! You . . . said once . . . Indians keep their promises!"

John knelt beside him, grasping his hair and yanking his head back. "Don't forget I'm half-*white*," he sneered, "and white men are notorious for *breaking* promises!" He pressed the gun against the man's eye. "Now, I want the *truth!* Are you the last one I have to worry about? I've shot five other men and stabbed two more. That makes seven. Are there more than eight men involved in this?"

Shivering and crying, Dan answered. "N-n-no. I'm the last one. And you . . . gotta remember, John. I . . . gave myself up. I never . . . shot at you."

John stood up and threw Dan's gun aside, then dragged the man by the hair toward the cabin.

"Wait! John! This ain't fair! It ain't fair! Oh, God, my knee!" Dan screamed all the way inside the cabin, struggling to get away but in too much pain to have any strength. "What are you doing?" he begged. "Where are we going? What are you gonna do to me, Hawkins!"

"Only what you deserve. Any man who helps kidnap innocent children *deserves* to die."

"How! Kill me right now, Hawkins! Kill me now!"

"I don't expect it will be that easy, Dan."

John shoved him inside the cabin, where he saw Sam Higgins crawling toward the door, holding a gun he'd taken from one of the other men. John walked over and kicked the gun away. Higgins looked up.

"Hawkins!" he sneered.

John shoved his own gun in its holster. "You should have given yourself up and stayed in prison, Higgins. It would have been like paradise compared to what you're going to suffer now!"

Sam's eyes widened. "Wait. Please!"

"I can't even stand the sound of your *voice!*" John growled, kicking Sam in the teeth.

Sam grunted and rolled over, making gurgling sounds. Fighting the blackness that kept trying to consume him, John managed to drag the two bodies left on the porch inside. Lonnie lay on the floor, groaning, blood pooling around him from an apparent severed artery.

"God, help me," Lonnie muttered.

John walked over and knelt close. "God doesn't have anything to do with this," he told Lonnie. "Except for helping me find you and save my wife and kids."

Lonnie looked up at him. "You . . . stinking . . . murdering Indian!"

"That's what I am," John sneered. "And your brother and his men raped a little Indian girl. That's why they died!"

"I . . . had this . . . all planned. I *fooled* you . . . Hawkins!"

John took out his knife and held it under Lonnie's nose. "Who's the fool *now,* Lonnie? Remember when I said I could be your best friend, or your worst enemy?"

Lonnie blinked back tears.

"Well, now I'm your worst enemy!" John sliced off the end of his nose.

Lonnie screamed and rolled away. His wailing was music to John's ears. He walked out, stumbling a few times and grabbing things for support, managing to get down the steps. He found the body of the man he'd stabbed in the eye. He lay unconscious but still breathing.

With his last bit of strength, John managed to drag the man inside the cabin, piling him on top of two others. The only bodies left were the man and woman he'd killed out back. They would just have to lie there and rot. He began picking up clothes and blankets and threw them over the bodies. As far as he could tell, Lonnie, Sam, and Dan French were still alive. Some of the others might be, but it didn't matter, and he was glad Sam and Lonnie were conscious. He could not make them suffer enough.

"John, no!" Dan protested, apparently suspecting what was to come next.

John paid no attention, his rage out of control. Honor! Sweet little Honor. They had let someone touch her. Maybe there had been more than one. Had they done something worse? And Tex, a little boy trying to be a man, getting beaten for trying to help his sister and mother.

He knelt close to Lonnie again. "You don't have such a pretty face anymore," he told him, "but then it doesn't much matter. You'll be dead soon."

"Please . . ." Lonnie protested. "Just . . . shoot me."

"Too easy."

John turned to Sam, rolling him over. Blood poured from the man's mouth, and he stared wide-eyed at John. "Remember what you tried to do to my wife and son a few years back, Sam?" He enjoyed the look of horror in the man's eyes. "You tried to burn them up in their own home." He rose. "An eye for an eye, Sam." He took the wick from an oil lamp and poured the oil over the bedclothes that he'd spread over the bodies. Then he took the chimney off another oil lamp that was already lit.

Again envisioning these men abusing his children, he tossed the lamp, and instantly the clothing and blankets were aflame. He stumbled outside, enjoying the screams of those who were still alive inside.

Fifty-five

Tess waited, clinging to Tex and Honor. Things had been quiet for several minutes. Then she heard men screaming.

"Stay here," she told the children. She moved to the opening in the stone wall to see the cabin windows lit up with fire.

"John. Oh, my God!"

Someone stumbled out the back door. She could see his silhouette against the flames.

"Mommy! Fire!" Honor screamed. She had sneaked over to look through the opening. "Where's Daddy?"

"I think he's coming, Honor."

"Did all those bad men go away?"

Tess closed her eyes. "Yes, darling. I think . . . they ran away."

"Pa killed them all, that's what," Tex spoke up. "I'm *glad*. I told them Pa would come, and they would be sorry."

"Killing isn't always the answer, Tex. We're getting into a time now when you have to understand that the *law* must take care of these things."

"Pa *is* the law."

"He is no longer a Ranger, Tex."

"Yeah, but he's still the best there is. And those men wanted to kill him, and you, too. I'm *glad* they're all dead," he repeated.

Tess took him aside. "We want Honor to think they ran away," she whispered to Tex. "Please don't talk about them being dead, son."

Tex shrugged. "Okay. But I know they are, and I don't care."

"Tess!" John called out.

Tess hurried back to the opening. "Over here!" She pushed herself through. "Come on out, children."

"Daddy!" Honor hurried through the opening and ran toward John, whom she could see clearly now because of the bright fire behind him. "Daddy! Daddy!" She reached up, and John picked her up, coming over and half-falling to the ground beside Tess. He dropped a couple of blankets he'd brought with him and held Honor tight. "My sweet baby girl," he groaned. "Please tell me you're not hurt."

"I'm not hurt, Daddy. You just saw me a little while ago. Remember?"

John kissed her cheek over and over. He moved an arm around Tess, and Tex tried hugging both of them together, so that the four of them sat huddled in each other's arms.

"John, you're covered with blood from head to toe!"

"I had to crawl through that tunnel and over rocks like a damn snake. Scraped half my skin off. And my head—" He wiped at more blood that dripped into his eyes. "One of them . . . hit me with a rock. And I think . . . my arm is bleeding again."

He grabbed them all close again. "It doesn't matter about me. What about you? I'm sorry I didn't get here soon enough. I never should have let you come here alone."

"I'm all right. I think my right cheekbone is cracked or broken, but you got here before they—"

"Even so, after what you've been through in the past . . ."

"John, I'm okay. The important thing is I'm still carrying. If I can get home and rest for a week or two, maybe I'll hang on to this one." Tess pulled away. "Poor Tex is bruised and cut. He tried to fight Sam because Sam hit me. He was such a brave little man, John."

John pulled Tex close. "I'm proud of you, son."

"What about me, Daddy? I didn't cry very much. Just sometimes."

John pulled Honor close again with his other arm. "Of course

I'm proud of you, too." He kissed them both again. "I brought a couple of blankets. We'll sleep here for tonight . . . start back as soon as you feel like traveling," he told Tess, his voice strained, his breathing still rapid. "We'll go try to find Shadow, then head south . . . pick up a train, and take it back to El Paso. I don't want you riding that far again all the way home, especially not through that same barren country. There are more trees and grass for the horses if we go south."

"Let's try to get below first, John," Tess suggested. "My horse and the packhorses are still down there. I need to dress your wounds, and we have bedrolls. I want to get the children away from this place. Can you make it back down?"

"I can try."

"Don't let go of me, Daddy," Honor pleaded.

John clung to his daughter, and they all walked around the side of the cabin, ducking away from the heat generated by the huge ball of flames. John was glad he had dragged all the bodies inside. The children would not have to look at them.

"They won't come back, will they?" Honor asked, keeping her arms tight around her father's neck.

"Heck no," Tex answered. "They're all—"

"Tex!" Tess grasped his shoulder.

"Oh. They ran away. Pa won't let them come back."

The fire lighted their way.

"John, are there any bodies out here?"

"No."

Tess knew that meant he'd pulled them all inside the cabin before setting fire to it. She shivered at his ruthlessness. They all hurriedly made their way down the steep pathway. Tess slipped and fell twice. When they finally reached the bottom, John set Honor down and went to his knees.

"Damn," he muttered. "Everything is going black."

"My God." Tess quickly spread out one of the blankets. "Lie down, John. I'll go through our things and try to find the bandages and whiskey."

John lay down, turning onto his back, exhausted. Honor

curled up beside him. "I like sleeping by you, Daddy. I'm not scared anymore."

John moved an arm around her and held her close. Above them the fire roared red and yellow into the night sky.

"I bet Lonnie and Sam and all those bad men ran away real fast when they saw you, didn't they, Daddy?"

John smiled sadly, almost too exhausted to talk. "Yes, pumpkin . . . they ran away . . . real fast."

Fifty-six

"Did you talk to her? Check her out?"

On their way south, Tess and John had been welcomed into the home of a kind Mexican family who sympathized with their injuries and circumstances.

"She's fine," Tess answered John, referring to Honor. "I bathed her, had a good talk with her and Tex. One of them . . . touched her . . . said he was just tickling her. But nothing else happened. I don't think Honor even realized how wrong it was, but Tex did."

They lay in bed together in the room of the Mexican family's older son. Tex and Honor slept soundly on the floor.

John stiffened. "My God."

"John, she's all right."

"You're *sure?*"

"Yes. Tex is big enough to understand what I was talking about. They never . . . well, they never took off her clothes or anything like that."

Tess knew rage still welled in his soul. He made a growling sound and sat up, putting his legs over the edge of the bed and sitting there with his head in his hands.

"John, she's all right. And she had Tex with her. That meant a lot to her. I can't believe what a little man Tex was through this whole thing. I could tell by the way Honor talked. And poor Tex is the one who suffered physically. Except for Honor's sunburn, and the fact that the heat made her sick, she was not physically abused the way Tex was. I'm worried he will have nightmares about it for a long time to come. He saw and heard things that are going to stick in his mind for a while."

Tess sat up also, moving to touch John's shoulder and kiss his back. "He knows you killed all those men, John. You have to talk to him. He has to understand that not every problem can be solved by killing the enemy. Everything is changing. If you can encourage Tex to sit down and study and learn, maybe someday he can go to college and learn to be a lawyer, learn to fight the criminals a new way."

"Instead of *my* way?"

She stroked his arm. "You grew up in a whole different world, John, a world with no family of your own, no law, no father . . . no love."

He raised his head. "Until you came along." He turned to face her, moving one leg up onto the bed. "I'll talk to Tex. I'll make him understand."

"I know you will. You're a good father, John Hawkins."

"Lord knows that's a miracle. I sure never had any example to learn from."

Tess winced as a sharp pain shot through her right cheekbone. "I think every bone and muscle in my body hurts," she said. "You must feel even worse. You're covered with cuts and scabs, and that clean bandage I put on your arm already has a spot of blood on it."

John sighed, stretching out onto his back. "You know me. I'll survive."

Tess shook her head in wonder. "Oh, I am sure you will." She lay down beside him again. "Someone must be watching over you whether you like it or not, John Hawkins."

They lay there quietly a moment, staring into the darkness.

"I can hear them breathing, John. Isn't that a nice sound?"

"It sure is."

"I can't believe this nightmare is over, and that we all survived it. I'll be so glad to get home. It seems like we've been gone for a month."

"I have cattle to get to market."

"And I have a baby to nurture. The life inside of me must be very strong to have hung on through all of this, John. It's another boy. I just feel it. And he has your strength."

He moved an arm around her. "In some ways you are much stronger than I am, Tess Hawkins."

The night was still, quiet, except for the soft singing of crickets.

"It seems so strange, lying here like this," Tess said, "so peaceful, and so unreal, after what happened three nights ago. Are you going to tell Captain Booth what happened to—" Tess could not even bring herself to say their names. "Well, what happened at Eagle Pass?"

"Sure. I'll tell him the cabin accidentally caught fire, and everyone was trapped inside. He'll know what really happened, but it won't be the first time ole Cap has doctored a report because of me."

"I have no doubt about that." Tess rubbed her hand over his solid forearm. "I thought I would lose you, or perhaps one of the children. Thank God! Thank God! We can only hope now that Ken survived."

"We'll wire El Paso as soon as we reach a town, let Jenny know we made it and that the kids are all right. We'll find out then if Ken is still alive."

Tess blinked back tears of relief. "I love you, John, more than ever. You're a good man."

He laughed lightly. "Now there's one a lot of people would argue over, including God Himself."

Tess smiled. "God Himself made you remember that cave and tunnel. So He must approve of what happened after you got there. Sometimes God uses us for his own vengeance against the wrongs Satan brings to this earthly world. God needs soldiers, men brave enough to fight the battle here on earth. He knows you're a good man."

"Leave it to you to find a way to excuse the fact that I killed eight men . . . and a woman."

Tess rose up on one elbow and leaned down to kiss him lightly. "We all have our demons, John, and we all have to settle with them and with God our own way. It's the good in you that makes a little part of you sorry for what happened, and that is why I love you. Let's just go home now and love each other and our children and try to put all the horror and the anger behind us. I want to laugh again. And I want to cook and bake and clean and do all the common things that make me weary but happy. I want to see those two new foals and watch them grow, right along with my precious son and daughter." She gently stroked his hair away from his face. "And I want to grow old with you."

John grinned, taking her hand and kissing her palm. "You sure you want to keep putting up with me?"

"I've seen the worst and the best of John Hawkins, and I love both men."

She kissed him once more. Then Honor stirred and began to whimper in her sleep. Suddenly the child sat up. "Daddy! I'm scared! Did those men come back?"

"No, darling, they did not come back," Tess told her.

"Is Daddy here?"

"Yes, he's right here."

"Can I come up there and sleep by him?"

Tess smiled and moved off the bed. "Yes, but lie still. Your daddy needs lots of rest. I'll sleep on the floor with Tex."

"Thank you, Mommy."

Tess gave the girl a hug and helped her into bed. She immediately snuggled against John. "I love you, Daddy."

"I love you, too, pumpkin."

"Nobody can get me when I'm by you, can they?"

"No one can get you when you're by me. *No* one."

Fifty-seven

Tess was surprised and touched at the size of the crowd that met them at the train station, including Mary and Doc Sanders, the Johndrows, the Pattersons, Sheriff Potter, Captain Booth, the Jefferses, many others, who apparently knew about the wire John sent telling the sheriff that they were all right and were coming home.

Ken and Jenny were also there, Ken in a wheelchair. Jenny ran up and embraced Tess.

"My God, look at you," she said, standing back and looking Tess over. "Oh, Tess, you have to tell me everything that happened. You poor soul, all bruised." She looked up at John. "And you! This is about the worst shape I've ever seen you in, except for—" She noticed the children then. "Tex!" she screamed. "Honor! How are my two favorite kids in the whole world!" She hugged and kissed both of them, and some of the men shook John's hand, telling him how glad they were to see him come back with the family in one piece. The questions began.

"What happened?"

"Where are Sam Higgins and Lonnie Briggs?"

"How did you do it?"

John did not answer any of them, except to tell Captain Booth that "there was a fire—they were all killed."

Tess saw the look in Booth's eyes. "I see," he said. "Well, an accident is an accident." He grinned. "Good to see you back, John."

John turned to Ken, who looked away. "I'm glad as hell to see you out of bed, you old buzzard," John told him, putting out his hand.

Ken finally looked up at him, tears in his eyes. He took John's hand, and John squeezed Ken's hand reassuringly.

"This is as far as I'll get for some time," Ken told him, "but I intend to stand up and walk when I marry Jenny."

"Ken!" Tess exclaimed. "She's finally agreed to marry you?"

"I sure have." Jenny came around to stand beside Ken, holding Honor in her arms. "I never knew how much I cared till I thought I'd lose him. But I'm going to keep running my boardinghouse. The things that need doing around here never end, especially in maintaining that big house, so Ken is going to live there and help me. Hope you don't mind, John."

John smiled, meeting Ken's gaze again. "I'm losing a good hand, but for this, I don't mind." He shook Ken's hand once more. "Congratulations, partner. Can I be your best man?"

"You've *always* been the best man," Ken answered. "I'm so damn sorry, John, about the kids and all."

"So am I, for not trusting my own instincts. It's over, Ken, and we're all right. You have Jenny bring you out, and we'll talk about it."

Ken nodded, quickly wiping at a tear on his cheek. "I take it Briggs and Higgins and the others are all, uh, with the Lord, shall we say?"

"Oh, they're all somewhere, but I doubt they're with the Lord," John answered, grinning.

Ken finally laughed. "Wish I could have been there."

"Well, I could have used you." John took Honor from Jenny's arms. "We're all pretty tired and anxious to get home," he told her.

"I'll bet you are," Jenny said.

Tess thought how nice the word home sounded.

"We have a four-seater buggy ready for you," Jenny told them. "Louise Jeffers loaned it so you could ride home in comfort. We figured the wife and kids have probably had their fill of horseback riding for a while. And we weren't sure how badly injured you might be."

"Thank you, Jenny." Tess held on to John's arm, and John carried Honor in his other arm as they left the train platform and headed for the buggy. Tex held his mother's other hand, and others carried their supplies and brought the horses, which were tied to the buggy. Jenny exclaimed over getting Maggie back, laughing and hugging the mare around her neck.

"I would come with you and help for a while," Jenny told Tess, "but I have to take care of Ken."

"Don't worry about it, Jenny. I have Maria and the other Mexican women at the ranch to help." She decided not to say anything yet about the baby. She would wait until Jenny came out to visit again.

John climbed into the carriage and sat down with Tex and Honor on either side of him. Tess climbed into the seat facing them, taking joy in looking at all three of them, alive and smiling. Women put baskets of food into the carriage, pies, breads, cakes. Tess felt overwhelmed at their thoughtfulness.

"You can return the baskets the next time you come to town," Mary told her.

Tess looked at John, and she knew by his eyes he was moved by the gesture. Harold Jeffers snapped the reins and got the carriage in motion, and the Hawkins family headed home. John pulled Honor onto his lap, and she rested her head against his chest.

"Tex kept saying you'd come, Daddy." She clung to the blue-calico shirt John wore. "I was scared, but Tex wasn't."

"Tex is a brave boy, brave like his father," Tess told her.

Honor sat straighter and looked at John. "I forgot to tell you, Daddy. That bad man, Lonnie, he said you're not Tex's pa. He said Tex's pa was a real bad man who did naughty things with Mommy to get Tex borned. How come he said that, Daddy?"

Tess's smile faded, and she looked at John. For the next few minutes no one spoke. Tex sat looking at his lap.

"Was Lonnie telling the truth?" he asked.

John handed Honor over to Tess, then moved an arm around Tex. "You might as well know the truth, Tex. You're old enough."

Tess's heart pounded with the ugly memory of Tex's father, and with concern that Tex might be hurt by the truth.

"Lonnie was telling the truth," John told Tex. "Your mother was stolen away once by *Comancheros*. They were very bad men, like the ones who took you and your sister. But your mother was really brave and strong. She fought them, but there were too many. She couldn't help what happened to her, but it doesn't change the fact that she is an honorable, good woman, and because you grew inside of her, she loves you like she loves Honor, and like she'll love the baby she's going to have."

"Mommy's having a *baby?*" Honor asked.

"Yes, she is," John answered, giving Tess a supportive smile. He squeezed Tex's shoulders. "What happened to your mother was a terrible thing, Tex, but in a way it was wonderful for me. I'm the one who went to help her, and if not for that, I never would have met and married your mother. I was a very mixed-up, lonely man then, but I fell in love with Tess, and with the baby she was carrying. When you were born, it was like my own son being born, and I have loved you ever since as if you came from my own seed. There is no difference between the way I love you and the way I love Honor. Do you understand that?"

Tex looked up at him with tears in his eyes. "What was my real pa's name?"

Tess hated the memory, hated the name, but it was time for the truth. "Chino," she told him. "And at one time I suppose he was just an innocent boy like you. Maybe he never had a loving family like you do, someone to teach him right from wrong. There is usually a reason why men turn out the way they do, Tex, and someday your father will explain his own background to you. He could have been just as bad a man as Chino turned out to be; but he's a good man now, and I am sure that somewhere inside, Chino also had good in him. Do you want to know how I can tell?"

Tex moved his gaze to meet his mother's eyes. "How?"

"Because of you. You are a good, good boy, brave, honest, smart, loyal. You must have gotten some of those things from your real father."

Tex thought a moment, then turned to John. "Did you kill my real pa?"

John closed his eyes. "Yes I did. I had no choice, Tex."

Tex looked at his lap. "I'm glad, if he hurt Mom. I don't want to be like him. I want to be like you."

John stroked the boy's hair. "You'll be *better* than me, Tex. You will obey the laws, and you will live according to civilized rules."

Again there came a moment of silence.

"You really love me?" Tex asked John then.

"I would die for you, Tex. You know that. I have already proved it."

Tex nodded. He looked up at John again. "I would die for you, too."

Their gazes held.

"By-God, I believe you would," John answered. He pulled Tex into his arms. "I think you would."

"I love you, Pa."

Tess could not help the lump that rose in her throat. She remembered when she was little that her mother used to say some good always came from the bad in life. John Hawkins was one hell of an example.

FROM THE AUTHOR

I hope you have enjoyed *Texas Passions*. It is a sequel to *Texas Embrace,* so you might want to find that book, too, and read more about Tess and John Hawkins. If you would like information about all the forty-plus books I have written, simply send a self-addressed stamped envelope to me at P.O. Box 1044, Coloma, Michigan 49038. Thank you for your support.

Rosanne Bittner

Please turn the page
for an exciting preview
of MYSTIC DREAMERS,
a March, 1999 hardcover release
from Forge Books.

One

By white man's terms, the year this story begins is 1832, during moon when the ponies shed . . . May.

"Take pity on me. Show me the way, and protect my people."

A naked Night Hunter trembled from four days of hunger and thirst. The red heat of the afternoon sun penetrated his skin, but he ignored the pain, celebrating his suffering. Four days ago his uncle, Runs With The Deer, warned that he must come to the Big Waters of the sacred Black Hills to seek a vision.

"A wolf spoke to me about you in a dream, my nephew. It told me you must go to the Big Waters. There the wolf will come to you and tell you of a woman you must seek, for without her you cannot become a true leader of the People. This woman has power, and she will help you become a leader of the Oglala."

As a member of *Naca Ominicia,* men who represented the entire Lakota Nation, Runs With The Deer's dreams held great significance. He commanded great respect, and so, alone on a high ledge that overlooked the Big Waters, Night Hunter waited faithfully for the wolf to come to him.

He listened to the gentle flow of the river at the bottom of the canyon, breathing deeply of the sweet, cool air that hung rich with the scent of wet pine needles. These sacred hills, nearly black with thick groves of deep green pine trees, harbored powerful spirits. Other Oglala men, and sometimes women, came to this sacred place to seek visions.

Again Night Hunter drew on his sacred pipe, letting the sweet smoke fill his lungs. He held the pipe aloft and sang to the God of the Sky.

"Take pity on me," he repeated. "Show me the way, and protect my people."

Despite his powerful build, weakness consumed him, and raising his prayer pipe took great effort. With shaking hands and arms, he offered the sacred pipe to the four corners of the earth. At each point, east, west, north, south, he again sang his prayer, his voice husky from a dry throat. He lowered the pipe toward the ground, praying to sacred Mother Earth. Here he had experienced his first vision at fourteen summers of age. In that vision the moon and the sun moved side by side, and then the moon passed over the sun, blocking its light. Moon Painter, the Oglala priest, told him then that he should be called Night Hunter.

He lived up to his name, hunting at night, his vision sharper in the night's darkness than that of others of his clan. Unafraid of the spirits of the darkness, he once killed a buffalo after dark, an accomplishment that brought him great praise and adoration from his fellow warriors, even from the wise old men of the Big Belly Society. For the next ten summers he pursued his quest to be a leader among the Oglala, a *Wicasa,* Shirt Wearer. From there he hoped to become *Wicasa Itacan,* one who ruled the Shirt Wearers.

Night Hunter swayed, then fell. The gravelly earth cut into his elbow and forearm, and he grimaced as he managed to ease himself back up. He crossed his legs and laid his pipe across his knees. Taking a deep breath for courage, he slid his hunting knife from its sheath and deftly sliced into his left arm, then stretched it out so that the blood from the wound dripped onto Mother Earth. He must show the Great Spirit his willingness to sacrifice even his own blood for the gift of a vision.

Could the woman of whom the wolf spoke be Fall Leaf Woman? He had enjoyed her slippery depths many times since the day two summers past when she caught him alone and boldly offered herself to him. She dropped her tunic, exposing her womanly mysteries, enticing him with licks and caresses that caused him to fall under her power. Since then she continued to brazenly offer herself to him without reservation.

Fall Leaf Woman truly seemed to care for him, but he did not feel deeply for her. Lately she annoyed him with her constant pestering, and it seemed that wherever he turned, she hovered nearby. Surely such a woman could not be his intended. She held no special powers. Whomever he chose to call first wife must be a woman of great honor, one who would cost many horses, and who would not offer her physical self without a great price. Fall Leaf Woman did not hold such honor; he could have her for no price at all.

As the sun lowered, the western trees and hills cast a shadow over Night Hunter. His body shook with a chill, and he nearly passed out again. Thunder boomed overhead, rousing him from his stupor. The earth began to shake, and a powerful dizziness overcame him as the thundering noise grew so loud it hurt his ears. Then he saw it, a herd of buffalo stampeding toward him. Their pounding hooves shook the ground, yet they did not touch the ground at all. They charged out of the sky, so many and so fast that he could never run fast enough to avoid being trampled.

He sucked in his breath and waited for whatever must come, and just before reaching him, the herd suddenly parted and thundered around him on either side. Wild, black eyes glared at him as shaggy heads darted past. He heard their snorting, felt the hot breath from their nostrils, yet their feet stirred no dust once they touched the canyon ledge where he sat.

The herd suddenly vanished, and silence reigned once again. Then, from where the great beasts charged out of the sky, a bright white cloud approached, swirling and eddying as it floated closer and finally came to rest on a nearby outcropping of rocks at the edge of the great chasm before him. Gradually, the cloud changed shape, forming a white buffalo.

Then a black cloud, outlined in yellow, swirled and tumbled toward the white buffalo, settling beside it. The black cloud then took the shape of a wolf with yellow eyes. The menacing beast began to prowl around the white buffalo as though stalking it. When it seemed ready to pounce, the head of the buffalo quickly transformed into a woman's face, her long hair white and shaggy like the buffalo's mane. She looked down at the wolf, and the animal backed away. Then one leg of the white buffalo turned into a slender arm that reached out and touched the wolf's head.

"One day you, Night Hunter, will be my husband," she told the wolf. "But then your name will be Stalking Wolf."

She withdrew her hand and became a buffalo again. She ambled away, and the wolf turned to Night Hunter, its yellow eyes filled with wisdom. "She is the woman you must marry," the beast told Night Hunter. "She is blessed by the white buffalo. When you find her, do not let her go."

The wolf turned and chased after the white buffalo. Night Hunter watched until both figures again became only clouds, which soon disappeared into the red sunset. Then a blinding flash of light exploded across the sky, causing Night Hunter to cup his hands over his eyes. A great warmth enveloped him, and when he dared look again he saw a man standing before him with outstretched arms and a hairy face. He wore a simple robe, his long hair and the hair on his face lighter in color than Night Hunter's hair.

The man's gentle, comforting gaze held Night Hunter in rapture for several minutes, but the vision did not speak. As Night Hunter watched, he spun around, and his robes fell away until he wore only an apron about his loins. His hair and skin turned darker, and his extended arms bulged with more muscles, until he grew into a powerful giant of a man with feathers sprouting from his arms and back. Finally, the feathers covered his entire body, and his head transformed into the head of an eagle. He opened his beak and spoke.

"The man who appeared first represents peace, as will the woman you take as a wife. I am the Feathered One, and I represent the power of the Oglala, as do you, Stalking Wolf. Go and seek the woman of peace among the people of the Burnt Thighs. Some call her the white buffalo woman."

The Being soared away, disappearing into the clouds. Night Hunter, whispering his new name of Stalking Wolf, stared after it in awe and confusion. A terrible dizziness washed over him then, and he fell, hitting his head on a rock. He breathed deeply of the sweet smell of pine before lapsing into unconsciousness.

The next morning Runs With The Deer and other Big Bellies came to check on Night Hunter. They found him lying near death, his head and left arm scabbed with blood.

"Take him, quickly," Runs With The Deer ordered. "Moon Painter must pray over him, and his mother and sister can tend to him."

The others managed to maneuver Night Hunter onto a travois tied to a horse. They hauled his limp body back to camp, but Runs With The Deer remained behind, staring out over the valley below.

"What have you seen?" he muttered, wishing his nephew could speak. He noticed a feather on the ground, and he stooped to pick it up, but a sudden wind whisked it away. It floated out over the valley below and disappeared.

Two

Star Dancer listened attentively to the Oglala messenger called Runs With The Deer. Like her own father, the visitor belonged to the Lakota Big Belly Society. More important, he belonged to *Naca Ominicia,* a man who represented the entire Oglala tribe before the *Wicasa Yatapickas,* the four great leaders of the Lakota Nation.

A mixture of burning curiosity and undeniable fear coursed through Star Dancer's veins, for upon arrival, Runs With The Deer specifically asked to speak with her father, Looking Horse. If a *naca* came so far to deliver a message, the reason must be of utmost importance, and Runs With The Deer looked at her strangely when he first entered her mother's tepee.

Star Dancer sat quietly in the shadows with her grandmother, Walks Slowly, keeping quiet while Looking Horse entertained his important guest. Star Dancer's mother, Tall Woman, seemed nervous as she served the men a meal of venison and wild onions. Star Dancer saw excitement and pride in her father's dark eyes at playing host to an esteemed visitor from the Oglala Nation.

"He must be here to talk about you," Old Grandmother whispered.

Star Dancer hoped her *uncheedah* only teased, as the old

woman often did; but somewhere deep inside she knew Walks Slowly might be right. Runs With The Deer continued to glance at her repeatedly, his dark eyes showing deep wisdom and awareness. His mostly white hair hung in long braids over his bare chest, and sweat glistened on his dark skin. Star Dancer thought how fitting it was that he belonged to the Big Bellies, for his own belly did indeed hang over his lap. Her father, however, retained a fine build in spite of his advanced years, and Tall Woman still bragged about her husband's enduring good looks.

Following their meal, Looking Horse offered Runs With The Deer a pair of beautifully quilled moccasins, for custom required a host to present his honored visitor with a gift. Runs With The Deer graciously accepted the moccasins, and he in turn offered Looking Horse a brightly quilled, wide leather banner, as a sign of friendship and goodwill.

"This is a fine gift," Looking Horse told his guest. "I will drape it over the neck of my finest war pony when I ride to the next Lakota council gathering on Medicine Mountain." He carefully laid the banner across his lap and shared a pipe with Runs With The Deer. Star Dancer waited impatiently to discover the reason for Runs With The Deer's visit, and finally her father asked the pertinent question.

"And why does a great Oglala leader such as yourself honor the Sichangu and my own dwelling with his presence?" Looking Horse asked cautiously. Star Dancer knew that even though her father held a high position among his people, Runs With The Deer enjoyed much greater importance among the entire Lakota Nation. Looking Horse must choose his words carefully, in order not to offend the Oglala man.

Runs With The Deer thought a moment, obviously weighing his words before he spoke. Then he leaned forward, resting his elbows on his knees.

"I come to the village of the Burnt Thighs to speak about my nephew," he answered, using the Siouan dialect most separate tribes understood. "He is called Stalking Wolf, because of a vision that came to him one moon past at the Big Waters of *Paha-Sapa*. He suffered many days with no food or water, and he cut his arm in an offering of blood to *Wakan Tanka*."

Runs With The Deer stopped and frowned, thinking a moment before continuing. "My nephew has suffered two vision quests, and has also twice sacrificed his blood in the Sun Dance, once at seventeen summers, and again at twenty summers. Both times he braved the pain of the skewers piercing his breasts and the calves of his legs. He did not cry out, and he danced longer than the others, dragging the leg weights and straining against the skewers at his breasts until they tore away. Even then he made no sound, for he takes honor in suffering for the prosperity of the Lakota Nation."

Looking Horse frowned with intense interest. "Your nephew must be a very brave and honored man."

"Ayee! At twenty-four summers he is already a Shirt Wearer. Crow and Pawnee scalps decorate his lance, many of their horses now in his possession. He cleanses himself in the sweat lodge often, and he prays constantly to be blessed with the powers of the sky spirits and the animal spirits. He rides against the enemy with no fear, and he has killed many buffalo with arrow and lance. I come here on his behalf."

Star Dancer glanced at her grandmother, thinking what great wisdom the hundreds of wrinkles around her eyes represented. Still sharp-minded, her mother's mother listened closely to the visitor's words, her dark eyes sparkling with curiosity. Walks Slowly loved to gossip, and a visit from a mysterious warrior of another tribe did indeed give her something new to chatter about. Her silence during this visit was unusual, for the old woman usually talked almost constantly.

"And what is it your nephew would ask of me?" Looking Horse inquired. "Why did he not come to me himself?"

"He chose not to come because he believes that here among your people is someone so special that he must not look upon her until he has your permission. He has gone to hunt buffalo. His father was killed many seasons past by the hump-backed bear. Stalking Wolf must provide for his mother and sister. When we all meet for the annual council on Medicine Mountain, he will then present his petition before you."

A refreshing rush of air swept through the dwelling, and Star Dancer could smell Runs With The Deer's perspiration. She longed to go out and wade in a nearby stream to cool herself, but she dared not leave.

"And what is Stalking Wolf's petition?" Looking Horse asked.

Runs With The Deer sat a little straighter. "It is said among the Oglala that a young Sichangu girl has seen the white buffalo, and that she carries the hairs of the buffalo in her medicine bag. Because of this, she is considered holy. It is said that this girl is your own daughter."

"It is true that at ten summers my daughter saw and touched the white buffalo," Looking Horse answered.

Star Dancer's throat constricted with a sudden rush of dread when the stranger nodded. Runs With The Deer again turned to her with a critical gaze, and she looked down, feeling embarrassed and afraid. She took pride in the fact that she'd seen and touched the sacred white buffalo, an experience that brought honor and attention to her father. She held little doubt that Looking Horse always wished for a son. Tall Woman never conceived again after giving birth to her, and that brought much grief to her mother's heart. When Star Dancer told her parents about seeing the sacred white buffalo, presenting to them a fistful of hairs she'd pulled from its mane, Looking Horse showed a new pride in his daughter, and that helped soothe Tall Woman's disappointment at not being able to give him a son. Star Dancer's value as a holy woman now made her just as important as a son to him.

After her experience with the white buffalo, the tribal priest declared Star Dancer destined for great things and high responsibilities. That destiny always seemed far away, part of a remote future that would never come to be; but now, suddenly, it visited her, in the form of old Runs With The Deer.

"Stalking Wolf believes a vision he experienced one moon past has meaning that involves your daughter," Runs With The Deer continued. "So says our holy priest, Moon Painter."

He explained the vision, and Star Dancer knew it indeed held great meaning, for no warrior shared such a personal event with utter strangers unless it was vital to the future of the Lakota Nation.

"The black wolf then spoke," Runs With The Deer finished, "telling Stalking Wolf, 'She is the woman you must marry. She is blessed by the white buffalo.' " Again Runs With The Deer paused and looked at Star Dancer. "The vision is a sign that Stalking Wolf can only marry a woman who shares the spirit of the white buffalo."

Star Dancer's cheeks began to burn, and she fought an urge to cry. Had Runs With The Deer come to take her away?

"Among the Lakota Nation," he continued, addressing Looking Horse again, "only your daughter has seen and touched the white buffalo. Stalking Wolf wishes to meet Star Dancer and ask for her hand in marriage."

Star Dancer glanced at her grandmother again, and the old woman grinned with excited delight. Her *uncheedah* surely considered this announcement a wonderful event, and the thought of making her grandmother happy helped Star Dancer handle her own dread.

"And would Stalking Wolf take my daughter away from us?" Looking Horse asked.

Runs With The Deer nodded. "His sister is not yet married, and his mother never took another husband. He will not take her away from her people. It is easier for the young ones to learn to live with a new people than for the old."

Looking Horse frowned and nodded, then turned to Star Dancer, who waited with pounding heart, trying to tell her father with her eyes she did not want this union, did not want to leave her family.

"I must give this much thought and prayer," Looking Horse informed Runs With The Deer. "As yet I have never approved of any of the young men who have come to me asking for my daughter's hand. Just as this man called Stalking Wolf feels he must marry someone very special, so do I believe my daughter must do the same. The one called Stalking Wolf seems worthy, and his vision has much importance."

"More than you know." Runs With The Deer drew a deep breath, and Star Dancer could see he was trying to pull in his belly. "Listen well, my friend, for I have not told you all of my nephew's vision."

The man's words were spoken with great reverence, a portent of yet another revelation about the warrior Stalking Wolf. Star Dancer momentarily forgot her own concerns, and her *uncheedah* leaned forward, cupping a bony hand behind her ear to be sure she heard well.

"Stalking Wolf had yet another vision," Runs With The Deer said, lowering his voice. He looked around at all of them, then back to Looking Horse. "He has seen the Feathered One."

Looking Horse straightened in shock, and Tall Woman gasped.

"My, my, my," her *uncheedah* murmured quietly, putting her hand to her mouth. The announcement even piqued Star Dancer's interest. She'd been taught since her first moment of understanding that a vision of the Feathered One constituted the most sacred vision any Lakota man or woman could experience.

"The Feathered One!" Looking Horse spoke the words reverently.

Runs With The Deer held his chin proudly. "At first he appeared as a man wearing robes. Then he became naked and grew feathers. His head became that of an eagle's. He told Stalking Wolf that he would find the white buffalo woman here, among the Burnt Thighs."

Looking Horse sighed deeply and studied the banner still draped across his knees. "In one moon I will bring my daughter to the annual council at the great circle of stones on Medicine Mountain. Until then, I will think about all you have told me.

Tell Stalking Wolf he may speak with me about this at the council."

Star Dancer felt dizzy from this sudden decision that could change her life forever. Her father knew little about Stalking Wolf. Was he handsome? Ugly? Kind? Cruel? How could her father so easily agree to consider giving her over to a complete stranger? And at Medicine Mountain! She'd gone there only once, when her father took her to a special Sichangu council meeting to talk about her experience with the white buffalo. The place seemed to hold magical powers.

"My daughter is only fifteen summers," Looking Horse continued. "From what you have told me, this man seems worthy of her hand, but Star Dancer must meet him and approve of him. She will come to the night dance. She will throw her blanket over Stalking Wolf, and they will talk."

Throw her blanket over a stranger? Such an act indicated a young maiden's preference, and in her heart, Star Dancer loved and wanted only Kicking Bear, the brother of her good friend, Little Fox. Since playful childhood, an unspoken bond existed between her and Kicking Bear, both secretly sure they would one day wed. Looking Horse, however, did not consider Kicking Bear worthy of her hand.

"Stand up, Star Dancer, and let this man look at you," Looking Horse commanded, "so that he can tell Stalking Wolf how beautiful you are."

Star Dancer breathed deeply and forced her legs to move. Her father expected her to be brave about this, to show pride and honor. She held her chin high, fighting tears as she rose and faced Runs With The Deer. He scrutinized her intensely, so that she felt self-conscious of every part of her body.

"She is indeed pleasing to the eye," Runs With The Deer said, finally turning his gaze back to Looking Horse with a grin of satisfaction. "I thank you for your hospitality," he added, rising. "Stalking Wolf also thanks you. I will tell him he is free to speak with you about Star Dancer when we meet in the mountains of many sheep with horns. The Crow dogs try to keep us out, but always they fail." The man spoke the last words with arrogance and pride.

Looking Horse also rose, folding his arms in front of him. "We, too, have many Crow scalps," he said with a slow grin.

Runs With The Deer picked up his gifts. "I have a ride of many days to return to the sacred Black Hills. There is still daylight left, so I will leave now." He looked at Star Dancer once more. "You will be pleased with my nephew. Stalking Wolf is a handsome man, one any Lakota woman would be proud to call husband."

But I do not know him, Star Dancer wanted to answer. *It matters not to me how he looks or how honorable he is.* She said nothing aloud. She wrapped her fingers around the medicine bag worn at her waist. Because of the white buffalo hairs it held, she apparently must wed a fierce Oglala warrior. She could not change what the wolf spirit and the Feathered One Himself proclaimed must be.